CW00503441

NEW YESTERDAY

by Frasier Armitage

Copyright © 2023 by Frasier Armitage

First Printing, 2023

Cover images courtesy of Shutterstock

ALSO BY FRASIER ARMITAGE

*Yestermorrow: A Prelude to New Yesterday*
*Rememory*
*Investation*

*Postcards From Another World: A Sci-Fi Audio Drama*

*To Lunarbelle and the boy*

Dianne,

You absolutely ROCK! Your stories are such an inspiration to me. Thank you for creating such awesome worlds

# NEW

and characters.

# YESTERDAY

Gareth,

Your support for the writing community is incredible. I learn so much from you, and I'm kind of in love with your books!

---

If I lived in New Yesterday, I would change history to make sure I had both of your stories in my brain from the moment they were written!

Keep being awesome,

F. Armitage

'THERE'S NO CURE for regret. Until now! How would you like to erase those troublesome past mistakes? Have you ever wondered what your life would look like if you'd done things different? Well, what are you waiting for? Pop on down to your local *Anderson Whitman* and see what's available in New Yesterday! That's right! If you're sick of the same old routine, now's the time to escape it. Explore limitless possibilities in the world's only city where time is as flexible as you want. With a wide range of lifestyle packages to choose from, changing your history has never been easier. So stop living in the past — make the past live for you. Wave goodbye to "if only." Don't delay. Start your new life today! Because, if your future's what you make it, why shouldn't your past be too?'

— Anderson Whitman Real Estate,
broadcast circa 2029

# ONE

IT WASN'T THE THREAT of a bullet through my head that forced my sweat to boil and bones to freeze. Locked in the elevator, floors ticked by like years. Cold steel dug into my vertebrae. But none of that caused the chaos hammering my brain, shredding my stomach, pumping ice through my veins.

No, my every nerve hung on one word —

Adam.

*How did he know my name?*

"Don't worry." The gunman tightened his grip on my collar. "This'll be over soon." I could only guess how.

Gears whirred, the soundtrack of my pounding head. From my pocket, the phone buzzed, blasting at my heart, jerking me into the wall.

"Don't answer it," he said.

His pistol jutted deeper into my back — a marionette's string tugging me any way he wanted. He slammed me against the mirror and emptied my pockets. The phone clattered to the floor, reverberating around the boxed walls of my descending coffin.

Celia's name lit up the screen.

Two seconds was all I'd need. Two seconds to answer and tell her where I was. She'd sort this out, retrograde the morning so I'd been nowhere near the 27th floor when this lunatic showed up. One phone call and none of this would've ever happened.

"Look," I said, my mouth dry as ash, "I don't know who you think I am, but you've got the wrong guy."

"I know exactly who you are." His eyes flashed, face twisted in the warp of the mirrored panel.

How many times had I glossed over that same face in warning bulletins and news reports? On pop-up alerts telling me to 'tap here if you've seen this man'? In black and white grains beneath the headlines. 'Linear Offender Still At Large,' 'Manhunt Continues,' 'Police Say No New Leads.' The most famous face in the city, and now it was preying on me, scolding me with its silent threat.

The lift steadied.

"Don't get any ideas."

Doors churned open to the underground parking lot. He dragged me to a battered minivan abandoned in the visitor's bay.

"Get in." As if I had a choice.

Empty packets of Doritos littered the passenger seat, a no-man's-land of leftovers reeking of booze and BO.

My abductor slid behind the wheel and dropped the gun in his lap. The engine wheezed as we pulled from the curb and filtered into traffic, melding with a parade of brake lights. The seat thrummed to the rhythm of the tires bumping over crumbs of tarmac.

"This is all your fault, Adam. You know that?"

"I don't—" I started but caught my tongue before it led me straight into a bullet. "Listen, whatever you think I did, I'm sorry."

"*You're* sorry? If you'd never found me, none of this would've happened."

Either he'd got a terrible sense of humor or he was a few records short of a jukebox. *Found him?* It wasn't me that had snatched him from *his* office. Maybe going linear really did make you as crazy as they said?

Outside the window, high-rises crammed us into narrow lanes, silver blurs pressing us in. Steam hissed out of vents to mingle with exhaust fumes. The street was a pressure cooker, boiling us in concrete. My skin prickled. Where was he taking me?

"Are . . . are you . . ." I stuttered.

"Spit it out!"

"Are you going to kill me?"

His hand hovered over the gear stick, reluctant to shift. "Only if I have to."

I clutched the seat while it jabbed against my shaking legs.

"It's nothing personal," he said. "I didn't plan for this. But it's the only way. Do you understand?"

What was there to understand about this guy? I sat stiff, the belt drilling into my chest.

"Just forget it," he huffed as the car sped faster down the boulevard.

Maybe if I closed my eyes, it'd all go away? I'd be back in my office going over the mall plans with Jeff, getting ready to dine clients at the gala ball later tonight, instead of being kidnapped by this madman. 'It was the only way,' he'd said. What did a person *need* a hostage for exactly?

*Just breathe. Don't think about it.* But the stench of stale sweat and the tap, tap, tap of his gun on the seat choked the air like two hands around my throat. There was no escape, no matter how tight I squeezed my eyes shut.

"What do you want?" I asked.

"I want my *life* back."

"Your what?"

"Are you deaf? You took it from me, Adam. And I want it back."

"But I . . . we've never—"

"Not you too?" He shook his head and tensed the wheel. "I was getting on just fine before you showed up, y'know? But then you came with your questions and your papers and your annoying little whine going on and on and on. You changed everything. And now you don't even remember it. This city's really done a number on you."

I could've said the same to him. Why was I even trying to talk to this psycho? Everyone knows better than to get involved with a nut job who's gone linear. I'd never met the guy until he'd strolled into my office and jammed a gun in my face. But then how did he know my name? "Where are we going?"

"To make things right."

We turned a corner and the car skirted the curb, screeching to a halt. Over the road, the Anderson Whitman logo decorated a steamed glass front. Screens filtered through properties on a slideshow, advertising apartments and houses across the city.

"Now when we go inside, you'll tell them this is your fault," he said. "You'll say you came to see me, and everything that followed has all been just a huge mistake. And then they're going to fix it so none of this ever happened. Okay?"

*Okay? What was okay about any of this?* "Do I have a choice?"

"There's always a choice, Adam. A right one . . ." He grabbed the gun. "And a wrong one."

Its harsh metal split the space between us like lightning. "You've got your gun. Why do you need me?" The circle of its barrel was a vortex, a black hole that swallowed my vision.

"Just do your part and nobody gets hurt," he said.

*Gets hurt?* I shook my head. "This is crazy. I can't . . . this isn't going to work."

"Of course it is," he said. "They'll listen to you."

"What if they don't?"

"They will. They *have* to."

What was he trying to do? Force Anderson Whitman to retrograde his past by feeding me the history he wanted? Blackmail them into changing his life by taking me hostage?

"Now what are you going to tell them, Adam?"

"That this is my fault."

"Good. And . . .?"

"And they need to fix it."

"Now just calm down. Everything'll be okay, as long as you stick to the script. You ready?"

Ready for what? Ready to lie for him so he could get a new past, or ready to have my head blown off?

I nodded.

He stuffed the gun inside his belt and tucked it beneath his trousers. "Come on. Let's get this over with."

## TWO

THE GUNMAN POCKETED his keys and lifted the hood of his coat to shield his face. In a flash, he was at my window, holding my door open. His cologne stalked me through a queue of cars and we entered the Anderson Whitman storefront.

Across the room, desks staggered towards a screened-off area where chairs surrounded a TV. Along the back wall, glass cubicles partitioned the offices in a row. Everything shimmered white. From her desk, a receptionist in a blue blazer and matching neck scarf waved us forwards.

"Welcome to Anderson Whitman Real Estate. How can I be of service?" She pasted an empty smile across her alabaster skin.

"We need to see someone about retrograding," my kidnapper said from behind me, close enough to be my shadow.

She squinted at him. Recognition flashed across her expression like a photographer's bulb, before it dissipated into nothing. She shrugged and swiveled to her screen. "Have you got an appointment?"

How could she not recognize his face? What were the press calling him — The City's Houdini?

"Didn't think we'd need one," Houdini said.

She tapped at her monitor. "I'm sorry, but all our agents are busy with other clients at the moment."

My eyes widened, flicking between her face and the gap in his open jacket, where the outline of the gun bulged beneath his shirt. She stared at me, masking her disinterest with a veil of courtesy. *Just follow my eyes.*

He caught me glancing at the gun. "Pssst." Our gaze met and he shook his head.

"You can take a seat in the waiting area, if you like?" She nodded to the group of chairs on the far side of the room.

He paced to the desk. "You *sure* we can't see someone now?" His hand caressed its rim, toying with the wooden edge as his fingers crept closer to his waist. "Couldn't you rearrange their appointments to make them free, or something?"

"I'm sorry, but you'll have to wait."

He reached for his belt. His muscles twitched as he untucked his shirt. I glanced at the girl behind the counter and her ceramic, doll-like eyes. Was he so desperate that he'd draw his gun on her? Or worse?

"You're not giving us many options," he said.

"That's the way things are, sir."

His face galvanized into a murderous scowl. Static charged the gulf between them. Another moment and he'd blast her all over the walls. A broken doll.

"Alright, then. If you say so." He gritted his teeth. His wrist snapped for the gun.

"I'm Adam Swann," I said, stepping forwards.

He stiffened.

"Yes?" she said.

"Premium package member. SSA. Swann Sinclair Accounts. It really is urgent that we see someone." Cold sweat dampened my shirt. My entire body coiled, taut as a runner on their marks, waiting for the starting pistol, the one he'd shoved beneath his buckle.

She sighed and tapped her screen again. Her face buffered along with the database until the monitor bleeped. "Oh. Sorry, Mr. Swann. I didn't realize who you were. Julie . . ." A girl at the neighboring desk lifted her head. "Julie, will you show these gentlemen to the waiting area?"

"Follow me, please." Julie strutted to the chairs, heels clacking.

Houdini's hands dropped to his sides. Away from the gun. He raised an eyebrow at me, motioning us towards the girl.

The desk clerks watched their computer screens without giving us a second look. Hadn't any of them seen the news? Didn't anyone recognize this guy?

Beyond the desks, Julie turned and dawdled by the waiting chairs. On the TV monitor, the Anderson Whitman advert played over and over. She clasped her hands together. "We'll amend the schedule and a salesman will be right with you. Shan't be a moment."

Her feet pattered back to her desk and she took a seat as if everything was fine. No problem. She wouldn't have been so carefree if she'd known how close she was to getting mowed down by this madman.

His eyes scoured the room and he fiddled with his belt. *Don't think about what he would've done to those women. What he might still do.*

On the TV, smiling faces filled the screen as the voiceover repeated the AW slogan. 'If your future's what you make it, why shouldn't your past be too?'

Inside the cubicles on the back wall, estate agents propped themselves behind desks, with their clients in front of them nodding along in time. At the nearest desk, a lone agent stood and straightened his cufflinks.

The salesman was a chameleon in Armani pinstripes, changing his skin from person to person. He pushed the glass door open and it shivered on its hinges, smeared with a legacy of fingerprints.

"Come on in," he said through a disingenuous, toothy smirk. "I'm sorry to keep you, but I've not had two spare minutes to rub together today. You're here about a lifestyle package, I take it?"

I glanced at the gunman. *What now?*

"After you, Adam," Houdini whispered, inching backwards to let me through.

"Don't be shy." The salesman shepherded us into his office. "Won't you sit down?" He pointed to the smooth leather tub-chairs across from his desk. I sank into the soft beige, and Houdini perched beside me, wrists in his lap.

"Can I get you anything?" The salesman lounged in his seat. His suit's navy lines crumpled in zigzags. "Coffee? Tea?"

I shook my head.

Houdini sat still and silent as a mannequin.

"So." A smile slithered across the face of our host. "What can I do for you, gentlemen?"

Houdini's eyes flashed at me. His fingers rubbed together as if he were polishing a coin. He glanced down at the concealed weapon and then back towards me. *Just do your part, and nobody gets hurt.*

"This is all my fault," I said.

"Please, Mr . . .?"

"Swann."

". . . Mr. Swann. Let's not get ahead of ourselves. Whatever's happened, I'm sure we can work it out. It says here you're a premium member, with a full lifestyle package. Is that right?"

"I'm joint CEO of Swann Sinclair Accounts."

"Congratulations, Mr. Swann. That must be nice for you. You got anything we could use to confirm that?"

"What do you mean 'confirm'?"

He removed a tablet from his top drawer, tapping the screen to life. "Well, we need some proof that you are who you say you are. You wouldn't believe how many people come in here claiming their lives have changed and asking for them back. Some of the stories we hear, you could write a book."

"Is that so?" Houdini said.

"In fact, just the other day, I had a man trying to convince me he was a Maharaja. All because he was sick of stacking shelves at Gracy's and thought we could alter things for him. These poor interlopers who come into the city without a lifestyle package, hoping their lives might change, and then not being happy when it does. Makes you feel sorry for them."

My captor's eyes burned into me. "I'll bet."

"What proof do you need?" I said. "ID? Driver's license?"

"ID?" The salesman shook his head. "I'm afraid fabrications are far too easy to come by these days. People losing themselves in retrogrades gone wrong. A list of clients we can check your details with should suffice."

"Our biggest client is actually Anderson Whitman."

"Wait. You don't mean Swann Sinclair Accounts, as in *SSA*?"

"That's it."

"Well, that makes things simple, at least. If you're in the AWG, running your details through the database shouldn't be too difficult." The salesman checked his Rolex. "Aren't you supposed to be hosting this big gala event at the Phoenix Hotel?"

"I was just getting ready to head out of the office when . . ." My voice trailed off and the gunman straightened in his seat. *What was I going to say? 'When I was forced at gunpoint into all this'?*

"When . . . what?" the salesman asked.

"When . . . when I . . . realized what a mistake I'd made."

"Ah. So you came straight here. I understand. Don't worry. You're in the right place." He set the tablet down on the desk and a ceaseless swirling circle spiraled across it.

"How long will this take?" Houdini asked.

"Once we've done the confirmations, amending a package shouldn't be too much trouble. What is it we need to clear up for you, that you've not been able to retrograde for yourselves?"

"Everything," I said.

"Can you be more specific?"

"It's hard to say. Nothing's been right since I met this man." At least that part was true.

"I see."

"Can we change the past so I never met him?"

"Of course." The salesman's fingers brushed across his tablet like oil on canvas. "When did you meet?"

My spine jolted upright. *When? Five minutes before we marched in. But I doubt that's what Captain Blackmail wants to hear.*

Houdini arched forwards, perched on the lip of his seat. "What does it matter?" he said. "Can't you go back and fix it?"

"Go back where? What do you think we do here? Time travel?"

"Isn't that how it works?"

The salesman rolled his eyes. "You think we've got a machine hidden away in a storage cupboard that takes us back in time?"

"You're supposed to change the past, aren't you? How else do you explain retrograding?" Houdini reddened, fidgeting with a frayed strand of thread dangling from a loose button.

I blushed the same shade of crimson as the salesman's tie as he straightened its knot and rubbed his hands together.

"I'm sorry to burst your bubble, gents, but time travel isn't possible. Not for human beings. We exist in the present. That's the *being* part of it. But we can change your present. And fortunately for us, here in New Yesterday, any changes we make today don't just ripple forwards, but backwards too."

"Are you saying things can't go back to how they were before?" Houdini said.

"Once we change a past, it's gone. You don't remember any of the histories you lived before the one you've got now, do you? It'd be ridiculous, wouldn't it? Carrying around all those versions of the past. All those tweaks and retrogrades. Drive you mad." The salesman's eyes rested on the gunman for a second too long.

*Wait a minute. Does he know?*

"But just because one past has vanished," the salesman said, picking up from where he left off without the hint of a seam, "doesn't mean it's hopeless. I'll bet we can get you something better than before. Think of it like a blanket. If you're unhappy with the way the fabric creases, we'll iron out the kinks. Make you more comfortable. Why would you ever want those creases back?"

"Some people might." Houdini's head shook faster and faster, like a broken metronome.

"Here, take a look at these." The salesman splayed folders from his drawers across the desk. On their fronts, photos of expensive manors or penthouse suites were all stamped with the Anderson Whitman logo. "If you want to build a house anywhere else in the world, you're stuck as far as time is concerned. But here, we don't just trade in three dimensions, we trade in four. You could build one of these houses twenty years ago. Longer even. You could have been born in an apartment that isn't even built yet. There are no limits in this city. We can give you anything."

"Anything but what's real." Houdini rocked back and forth on the fringe of his seat. He was a time-bomb, ticking down.

"Reality is so subjective, don't you think? If you're worried about keeping your past, a lifestyle package is just the ticket. It guarantees you the life you want to lead. We can always revert your history back to one of these. Why not flick through them? It's never too late to upgrade your package. We've got an excellent offer on—"

Time was up.

Houdini exploded out of his chair. His hands reached for his pocket and he slammed a sheet of paper on the desk. Its laminated folds blossomed, opening like the petals of a flower.

"This is what I want." He pointed at the paper.

The salesman sloped his spectacles down his nose and examined the document. "I see." He nodded. "Where did you come by this?"

"*He* gave it to me." Houdini pointed to where I sat.

"Is that true, Mr. Swann?"

Houdini turned to face me. His hand rested on his hips, tapping towards his weapon.

"What is it?" I asked.

The salesman tilted the page towards me. It was a planning document proposing that a shop move from one location to another. Except, the move would have happened six years before the date they'd signed it. There was no forwarding address, no alternative site for the previous business. But that can't have been right? They wouldn't have approved the old store to just vanish. Like it had never been there. Six years of profits disappeared in an instant. Retrograded into nothing.

Fever broke across my forehead. Sweat dripped into my eyes, stinging them raw and blurring my vision.

*Why do I recognize that page?*

*I know that slip of paper. I've seen it before. Pored hours over it, trying to find something.*

*But what?*

A name sprang into my head, clear as the glass walls of this office.

*Lottie.*

. . . Lottie?

I shook the memory away. The room spun, flexing in and out of focus.

"Mr. Swann?" The salesman's voice.

That single page jolted me like a defibrillator thunking two hundred volts through my brain. *How can I make this stop?*

"Look," I said. "I can't . . . do this."

"*Adam!*" the gunman yelled.

"I've . . . I've never seen this man before." My head fell into my hands.

The salesman dropped the laminated page and tapped his screen. "That's good. Very good. Excellent, in fact. Just what I'd hoped to hear."

The gunman reached into his belt and plucked his pistol. Its scuffed metal chamber seemed to fill the room. His hand quivered, aimed between the salesman's eyes.

"I want my life back! *Right. Now.*"

I pinned myself to the back of the chair, trying to push my way through it so I could run, but its leather frame forced me to remain.

The salesman's elastic grin stretched wide. "Won't you take a seat?" He didn't even blink. He looked at the man with such indifference. Just another customer. As if this was normal. *Is the gun invisible or something? Am I the only one who cares about getting shot?*

The gunman charged at the desk. "You're not *listening*," he said. "That store was my life and I want it back! D'you hear?" He cocked his pistol and the bullet snapped into the chamber, the crackle before the thunder.

Unruffled, the salesman eased back into his chair. "My dear boy, what do you expect is going to happen here? Do you think you can threaten me? Who do you think is really holding the gun?"

"What?"

He raised the tablet from his lap. "In my hand, I have all the changes to your histories ready and waiting. With a swipe of this screen, we'll retrograde all of this. In less than a second, you'll have been in custody for a week, and our friend, Mr. Swann, will be preparing for his gala, measuring out the champagne like none of this ever happened."

"No! That store is mine! It belongs to *me*."

"Be careful," the salesman warned. "With the way things stand, I've got it worked out for you to be arrested for your linear infraction. We can't have you roaming the streets with memories of two different pasts, can we? But it'd be a terrible shame if you got knocked down in traffic before the police found you."

"Are you threatening me?"

"Accidents happen. Even in the past."

The gunman's finger rattled over the trigger. Houdini turned his crazed, frightened eyes on me. "No, he's bluffing," he muttered below his breath. He lurched towards me and grabbed my collar, wrenching me to my feet. The gun scraped against my scalp. "You're in this together, aren't you? You set me up. Don't think you can bluff me out of what's mine."

"Are you okay there, Mr. Swann?" the salesman asked.

"I . . . I just want to forget all this," I said.

"That shouldn't be a problem." The salesman smiled. His tablet chimed. "Oh, good. Confirmation's just in. Congratulations, Mr. Swann. Checks have come back normal. Give it a minute and your new past will replace all this. I'm so sorry for the inconvenience."

"You can't do this to me!" the gunman shrieked. "I'll kill him! Do you understand? I'll *kill* him!"

"You know, it's such a shame you didn't look through our lifestyle packages. They really are rather good."

The gunman's fist clenched around my collar. His arms strained into rungs of steel, hardened by mania. I was in the middle of a standoff, caught between two men about to draw. One man's metal barrel clawed at my skin. The other sat poised with his finger ready to undo all this. And why? Because of a piece of paper? A laminated sheet. The memory of a past that disappeared.

*Lottie.*

Time flickered like a broken TV screen. The curtain was coming down. And all I could think was 'Lottie'? *Who is she? What does 'Lottie' even mean?*

"Pleasure doing business with you," the salesman said, his finger pressed against the tablet.

Death's whisper escaped from the barrel as the gunman squeezed the trigger.

The salesman swiped.

## THREE

CELIA'S FAMILIAR SILHOUETTE cast a shadow over my desk. Without a file to clasp hold of, her fingers jittered like butterfly wings.

"Everything alright, sir?"

The murmur of bleating telephones and ruffling papers mingled with a frenzy of footsteps. Keyboards tapped in flurries, echoing across the office, drifting into mine through the open door.

"Mr. Swann?"

Celia fidgeted with her nails, flicking the flecks of varnish from their half-chewed ends.

*How can I be in my office? Wasn't I just . . . no. I couldn't have been anywhere else.*

"Sorry, Celia. I was . . . what were you saying?"

"I just need you to sign this paperwork so I can laminate it for filing." She nodded to the pile of folders stacked neatly in front of me.

"Sorry, yeah, the paperwork. I zoned out for a minute." I glanced over the list, a jumble of fineprint that bled together into one tangled mess. My pen hovered above the signature line.

"Are you sure you're okay?" she asked.

"I just can't shake this feeling."

"What feeling?"

"I don't know. Like there's something wrong. Like I shouldn't be here."

"You've been in meetings all morning, sir. Exhaustion and stress can play tricks on the best of us."

I rubbed my eyes, soothing their dull ache. "Don't remind me. I'd sooner die than sit through one more under-prepared lackey projecting graphs they don't understand."

She smiled. "No risk of that, sir. I've cleared your schedule for the rest of the day. After you've seen Mr. Sinclair, that is." She gathered the nest of binders against her chest and her shoulders eased. "Would you like me to get you a coffee?"

"Do I look that bad?"

"No, sir. It's just — I thought it might help?"

"What did we agree to?"

She shrugged. "I know you said you didn't want me to feel like a tea-lady, but it really is no bother."

"I promised you'd never have to make me a coffee, and I meant it." A promise I'd regretted every morning since I hired her. But who wanted to be that kind of boss? The kind that treated their staff like underlings, expecting their every breath to have the impact of an earthquake? The kind whose office was an emperor's throne room, where the carpet wore out on ceremonial bows? The kind that never made their own coffee?

"Alright. If you insist. Mr. Sinclair is waiting for you in the boardroom to finish up the mall designs."

"Thanks, Celia. What would I do without you?"

Her cheeks flushed and she scurried out of the room.

My fingers raked through my hair. Profit margins and sales projections weren't usually enough to wring me out. Not like this.

My heart pumped, pneumatic pistons firing in my ribcage. A chill stubbled my skin. The clouds of some forgotten nightmare stormed inside my head. Dissipating. *Come on, Adam. Just breathe.*

A thud slammed on the window.

I flung myself to the floor.

Hidden below the desk, I crouched. My hands peeled from my ears and I raised my eyes to a smudge on the glass.

It was just a bird. A stupid bird flying into the window. So why did it feel like a gun just went off?

The room's quietness seeped into my lungs, steadying my breathing. Among the rubble of this morning's meetings, only a single word felt out of place. Like a scratch on a brand new screen.

*Just ignore it.*

Everything's fine.

Post-meeting fatigue. That's all.

I heaved myself up and dawdled into the corridor, past the circular 'welcome' desk. Behind it, two receptionists with headsets stared at computers.

"Swann Sinclair Accounts, how can I help you?" they chirped into their microphones. On the wall at their back, the letters SSA stood out too large, but Jeff had wanted it that way. 'Ostentation is the mark of success,' he'd said, and I hadn't cared enough to argue.

I pushed open the varnished double doors and found him waiting, poised by the drink cabinet.

"What time do you call this?" Gray streaks in Jeff's hair twinkled as the light hit them, with the view of the city through the windows at his back. "I've been waiting almost an hour to get myself a drink."

"Sorry, Jeff. What can I say?"

"Don't say anything. Here. There's nothing a glass of port can't fix." He handed me a small glass, filled to the lip with deep red sweetness, and raised his own. "Do you know what this is, Adam? It's the privilege of middle age."

"So you keep telling me."

He tossed his head back and gulped it down. "Ah. That's better. Hey, did you see the news? They're showing the trial of that linear guy they caught last week. Houdini, or whatever they were calling him."

A weight jarred at my temple. The stab of cold metal. But it faded. *Everything's fine.* "Trial?"

"It's all over the TV. You can't miss it."

"Is it really a week since they caught him?" I asked. "You think he'll get prison time?"

"Beats sending him to a loonie bin. I'll tell you something, I wouldn't want to go linear. Not for anything." He refilled his glass. "Now are we ready to crack on with this, or do you need another snifter to get you thinking straight?" On the oval table in the room's center, a scattering of blueprints and papers covered the polished walnut top. "Plenty of options for redevelopment. Any stand out?"

My eyes skimmed over the papers. "They all look the same to me."

"I know, but we have to pick. We can only send one of these blueprints for the planning board to approve."

29

I rubbed my chin. "When's the deadline for us to choose?"

"Last week," he said. "But the planners don't meet until tomorrow so there's still time for us to rejig the last fortnight. We could've sent the plans to them ten days ago if we get a move on."

Retrograding. How did we ever get by without it?

I leafed through the blueprints. "What do you think?"

Jeff rested the dregs of his port on the table, took one of the larger drawings and carried it to the window. He pushed it onto the glass and leaned as far back as his lank frame could manage without the blueprint slipping through his fingers or him falling over.

The sun's rays shone through the glass, backlighting the thin tracing-paper so only the precise lines of the architect's pen stood out.

"Come look at this, will you?"

I joined him at the window.

"You see that street there?" Jeff pointed beyond the glass, out to the avenues, around the buildings rising and falling in a waltz through the city. I followed his finger, where a green park stretched wide. Iron railings encircled it. On the corner of the block, behind the park, a derelict jewelry store encroached into the street, surrounded by overturned rubbish cans. Junk poured out, scattered over the road where traffic waited in both directions. From car windows, arms shook in wild gestures, relieving the tempers of stuck drivers who threw cigarette butts or half-imbibed cans of energy drink onto the grimy sidewalk. It was so close to the park where parents pushed prams and children played.

"I see it."

"That's where this column will start." His finger returned to the drooping paper, rolling off the window. I gave him an arm so he could hold it flush to the glass. The lines stretched tall into a pillar, at the top of which would be a spinning board with the name of the mall: 'Paradise Springs.' Inscribed beneath the design was the list of clients who'd take center stage in the main atrium. "Can you picture it?"

I shrugged. "It's better than nothing."

"Your enthusiasm astounds me."

"I'm sorry, Jeff. I'm useless with stuff like this."

"I know. That's why we're a team. I like it. The gold cladding on the pillars and the sweeping doors in the entrance, it's classy."

"It's expensive."

He smiled. "Same thing, isn't it?"

"Whatever you say."

"It'll be a lot better than what's there now, at any rate." His old eyes lingered on the park, as did mine. At this time tomorrow, it'll be surrounded by a luxury mall, built eight years ago. If they pass the application, that is.

"Shall we drink to it, then?" he said.

"To what?"

"A change of scenery." Another port trickled down. "Which reminds me, are you set for tonight?"

"Tonight?"

"The gala ball. Had you forgotten?"

My shoulders slumped. "Sorry."

"You're still coming?"

"Yeah, I left my tux at home."

"You'd better hurry, then. We're due there in an hour, and the limo's booked. Oh. And make sure you wear the thin tie. I've got a surprise for you and I want you to look your best."

"Surprise?"

"You'll like it." He winked. "I promise."

I left Jeff to clean up. Like always. He wrapped up the drawings and completed the portfolio for the planning commissioner to review as I rushed back to my office.

A bag from the dry cleaners hung over the back of my chair, and a note from Celia read 'Gala Ball Suit and Tie.' Trust Celia to remember and me to forget.

Changing into the ebony suit was like setting up an elaborate board game. Every piece had to fit just right. I straightened out the collar so it lay flat and fiddled with the tie until it hung straight. A white rose buttonhole bloomed on my desk. The sting of the pin pricking my finger never seemed worth the effort, but I did my duty and fixed the sweet-scented flower to my jacket.

In the floor-length mirror, my eyes ran up and down the two-thousand-dollar tux, but all I saw reflected was the image of that broken down jewelry store.

I should've left my office and joined Jeff to wait for the limo, but something held me where I stood. Trapped in my reflection. A name. A word that lodged itself in my brain, embedded like a nursery rhyme repeating over and over.

I couldn't shake it. Ever since I'd signed Celia's stack of papers, it hovered over me. A cloud that wouldn't pass, its meaning held in shadow, refusing to rain any understanding over my weary mind.

Lottie.

Where had I heard that name?

I'd not met anyone called Lottie this morning.

Zero bells rang.

Not even a face registered.

What was I missing? And why were my hands trembling? Was I so shy that a woman's name should make me this nervous?

A knock on the door startled me from my absent gaze. "Come in."

"You ready?" The creases of Jeff's tux were as sharp as the crystal cut of his decanter.

"Be with you in a minute."

Showtime. The gala ball beckoned at the Phoenix Hotel. But I couldn't just leave. Not yet.

I dialed Celia.

"Mr. Swann? Everything alright?"

"Can you do me a favor, Celia? Can you run a search on our previous clients?"

*I should just forget about it. It's only a name.*

"Anyone in particular you're looking for?"

*Why was I so caught up on this?*

"All I've got is a first name."

*What did I expect to find?*

"Might take me a while going through the vault," she said. "What's the name?"

My lips trembled as I formed the word. "Lottie."

The scrape of her pen crackled through the phone. "Lottie. Got it. Should be on your desk by tomorrow morning."

"Goodnight, Celia."

"Goodnight, sir."

Lottie.

*. . . Lottie?*

*What did it even mean?*

## FOUR

"EXCUSE ME, EVERYONE. May I have your attention?" Jeff said.

Golden flecks of light danced through the ornate twist of his champagne flute. His knife clinked on its crystal lip and a shrill soprano reverberated through the ballroom.

"We all know why we're here tonight, but I think it's appropriate that we toast the occasion. And who better to say a few words than my esteemed colleague at SSA, Mr. Adam Swann."

He gestured to me and took his seat, cushioned in a round of applause.

*I don't do speeches. Especially not to the AWG brigade. What's your problem, Jeff? Are you trying to lose our biggest clients?*

Conversations across the tables hummed in my ears like a swarm of wasps.

*I'll kill him for making me do this.*

Every face turned my way, a cavalry of smiles charging straight for me.

I reached into my pocket and swiped at the screen of my phone.

Message to Celia.

SPEECH. JACKET POCKET. <Send.>

I cleared my throat. "Thank you for coming to this gala evening and making tonight such a success. I'm sure you're all wondering what I'm about to say. Funnily enough, I'm thinking the same thing."

A polite sigh accompanied a ripple of dentured grins. The sheen of their false teeth matched the white silk cloth on every table. *Come on, Celia. How long does it take to write me a speech?* My legs shivered, knocking against the chair.

Just breathe, Adam.

"Tonight, as I stand here looking around the room . . ." *Don't look.* My eyes disregarded the instructions of my brain and toured the buffet of aged millionaires, all accompanied by their human money-pits. Spouses young enough to be their grandkids clung to withered arms — a pick'n'mix of bingo wings plated alongside strips of tender meat. Ancient gemstones mounted on thin strands of tacky chains and cheap necklaces.

". . . All I see are . . ." My voice cracked, fading like the ghost of feedback from a broken amp. Jeff handed me a glass of water. The first time in his life he'd offered me a drink that wasn't port. I sucked in a deep breath and smiled through the pins pricking my chest.

*All I see are . . . a host of greedy people who'd sooner die rich than live poor. What do I have in common with these Botox junkies and bloated fatcats?*

"All I see are . . ." A cough cleared my throat and the glass dug into my fingers, wrapping tighter around its stem.

My mind blanked, withered beneath the pressure of those staring eyes. Couldn't they look somewhere else? Anywhere else?

Sweat beaded under my collar as my throat tightened.

*Somebody help me.*

"All you see," a voice shouted from across the room, interrupting the awkward, expectant silence, "are a bevy of thieves and crooks."

A rustle of gowns swept the ballroom. Necks snapped one after another to where a waiter stood in the middle of the fray, unbuttoning his shirt. The ambience frosted over as his presence stained the air.

"You all know it," the waiter continued. "You're even proud of it, aren't you?"

I'd wanted someone to interrupt, but not like this.

A chorus of unease grumbled from the waiter's audience. Scowls cemented on their faces. Chairs twitched as muscles flexed and onlookers poised ready to tackle the interloper.

The man ignored the changing atmosphere and paced through the tables, stripping off his white shirt. His vest was printed with a slogan. GREED IS NO EXCUSE.

"You know how many lives you ruin every day?" He reached for his pocket. In his palm, he cradled a device.

As he crept closer, those nearest him leapt from their cushions and clamored for the doors. Chairs squealed as fading eyes caught sight of what he gripped in his hand. Discontent descended into panic. "Security!" they called.

At the room's edges, figures emerged from shadows, hampered by the narrow gaps between chairs. They rushed against the fleeing mob, searching for a way through.

"And now you're patting yourselves on the back for it," the man yelled, undeterred. "Making deals in the shadows and celebrating your lies by launching this awful, soulless arcade."

Suits and gowns battled for an exit, blocking the path of security guards trapped behind gasps and wails. Elbows shunted, locking together. Abandoned chair-backs barricaded the crowded thoroughfares.

The man inched closer.

Closer.

From the top of his fingers poked the blunt grooves of a tortoiseshell casing. A metal pin rolled across his thumb.

*This isn't happening.*

"You're scrambling people's brains."

*How did he get a grenade past security?*

"Taking people's lives."

The guards pushed against a wave of entropy. One step closer and two steps back. Whereas, unimpeded, the man drew closer with every step he took.

"How does it feel when it's *your* life that's on the line?" the waiter snarled as he unhooked the pin from his thumb and pulled it free of its casing.

A guard burst through the chairs and grabbed at the man's arm, wrestling him to the ground, but his hand launched the cylinder of death towards us.

*Run. Scramble. Now.* But my legs stuck, glued to the floor.

The shell thunked on the tablecloth before it rattled to rest.

*This is it.*

The other guards converged around the waiter, piling on top of him. One broke from the huddle to lunge for the grenade, but he was too late.

A sound erupted through its brittle casing. I closed my eyes and braced for the fire. But all that drifted towards me was a pop, like passing wind, followed by a churlish laugh.

*Was that . . . was that a fart?*

The security guard scooped it up and shook it to his ear. Another noise escaped, like a half-inflated-whoopie-cushion and a recorded giggle.

Whoever thought up the idea of a toy grenade that makes fart noises needed their head removed and examined. What sort of parent buys plastic grenades for their kids anyway?

"Open your eyes," the waiter yelled at the gaggle of shocked faces as a scrum of suits ushered him through the frenzy. A stampede of people screamed and pushed to get away, deaf to his words. "Look at what you're doing. It's unconscionable. How long until you give us all some transparency?"

Through a rip of the waiter's vest, a thick tattoo across his shoulder blades emblazoned the symbol #*TNY*.

Transparent New Yesterday.

All this carnage for an online petition? Spam emails and picket lines were one thing, but this was a whole new level of stupid. Anarchy at the click of a mouse.

Once the protest was over and they'd escorted the man out, a murmur of confusion yawned over the ballroom.

Jeff stood, waving his arms. "Settle down, everyone. Please, let's not lose our heads. Give me a minute to make some calls and I'll have this rewritten." He scurried into the crowd, towards the exit.

The phone buzzed in my hand. It shuddered through my arm like the shockwave of an explosion.

Message from Celia. *CHECK YOUR INSIDE POCKET.*

My fingers brushed against a slip of laminated paper. I removed it and glanced over Celia's handwriting.

As the urgency in the room subsided, a haze of can you believe it's and well I never's mingled like mismatching perfume to stink the air.

And then there was nothing. Stopped. Empty as a steep drop, the silence drew me, pulling me towards its edge and urging me to peer over. It was as if the room had reset.

My head lifted to a glut of smiling faces. Eyes fixed on me like spotlights, drilling through the room.

In one hand, my speech quivered. In the other, I clung to a glass of champagne.

Across from me, Jeff sat at the table staring, puzzled. His wrist wound in circles. *Get on with it.*

Panic heaved my chest. My eyes scoured the page, but the words fused into a slogan. *Transparent New Yesterday.* Then it faded, and the letters merged back into their proper form.

*Get a grip, Adam. Just read. You remember how to read, right?*

"Sorry. Where was I? Oh yes. Tonight as I stand here looking around the room, all I see are . . . opportunities. We live in a city of boundless potential. When others say the sky's the limit, New-Yesterdites don't stop there, we brush away the clouds and climb higher."

*Way to go, Celia. This is just the kind of slop our clients devour.*

"And I'm pleased to announce that tomorrow, we'll all share in the realization of a fantastic opportunity."

Jeff reclined in his chair, nodding his approval, a gentle breeze on my sail, pushing me on.

"You'll all be excited to know that tomorrow, the city planning board will consider an application for the new 'Paradise Springs' mall. It'll have opened eight years ago, if they approve it. So tonight, let's use this opportunity to celebrate, before tomorrow rolls around and we all remember differently." I lifted my glass. "To the new mall, and new opportunities."

Every arm went up in unison as champagne marched down their gullets. A wave of applause slapped at the raised hairs of my skin. The singer's husky tones once again tantalized our ears.

"Very good, Mr. Swann," Mrs. Campbell said. The old woman's wig slid as she turned her head to where I collapsed in the chair.

I peeled off my jacket and folded it across the empty seat to my left, letting the air dry the patches of sweat that seeped into its pits. Opposite, Jeff raised his glass and winked.

"I didn't realize you were so capable," Mrs. Campbell continued. *What was that supposed to mean?*

"I've heard Jeff give enough speeches," I said. "Must be rubbing off on me."

"All for the better. Waiter," she called, snapping her fingers. "Would you fetch us another bottle of champagne? We're supposed to be celebrating."

The server returned with a fresh offering to pour on the altar of inebriation. He untwisted the cork and its pop slammed through my temples like a bullet through my head, the sound bringing a memory with it.

*Where am I? Surrounded by Anderson Whitman suits. Lottie.*

*What has she got to do with this? Whoever she is.*

*The barrel of a pistol swamped into my periphery, blurring the man who pressed it against my head.*

"Adam . . . Adam?" Jeff's voice pulled me back to the ballroom — back from the precipice of memory. Every face around the table gaped at me.

*What happened? What did I miss?*

"Aren't you going to say hello?" Jeff said.

A woman stood hovering above the empty chair at my side, offering me her hand. Chestnut brown eyes beckoned my own. Her rose colored cheeks radiated brighter than the candlelight flickering from the table's centerpiece. The color of her dress complimented her curls, kissed golden by the sun.

"Enchante." Her French lilt added to the soft jazz played by the band, the perfect harmony to their clarinets. She curtsied. Finesse in human form.

I grasped her hand and shook. "It's a . . . er . . . I'm . . . er . . . I—"

"Won't you sit down?" Jeff said.

I bumbled to my feet and removed my jacket from the chair, sliding it backwards for her.

"Merci."

She smiled and took the seat beside me. Her sweet perfume traced her movements as she placed a velvet purse on the table and wrapped her fingers around an empty champagne flute.

"Would you . . . er . . . would you care for some . . . er . . .?" I offered.

"Some champagne would be lovely, Monsieur . . .?"

"Adam. Adam Swann."

"It's a pleasure to meet you, Monsieur Swann."

"Pleasure. Yes. Very much."

I drew an anxious breath, desperate not to spill the bottle of fizz over our new table-guest, much to Jeff's amusement.

"Don't mind Adam, Miss Laurent," he said. "He's quite harmless."

Liquid foam bubbled in the glass I handed her. "Merci, Monsieur."

"Everyone, may I introduce Miss Gabrielle Laurent." Jeff locked eyes with me and he mouthed the word 'surprise.'

"Forgive me for being so late. Have I missed the dancing?" she asked. We shook our heads in unison. "Do you dance, Monsieur Swann?"

"I leave the dancing to those who can."

"You don't believe there is a dancer in each of us?"

"If there's a dancer in me, they're definitely sleeping."

"That's why we have champagne. To wake them up, non?"

Her playful expression dared me to look away, but I couldn't.

"How do you do, Miss Laurel?" Mrs. Campbell interrupted, arching her elbow across my chest to shake the hand of the new arrival.

"It's Laur*ent*," Gabrielle said.

"If you say so. To what do we owe the pleasure?"

Gabrielle shrugged and swilled the champagne in her glass. "Pleasure is not to be owed, Madame. The only debtors to pleasure are those who deny it for themselves."

"How very . . ." Mrs. Campbell flapped her sagging arms as she grasped for the word.

"Precisely, Madame. For some things there are no words."

"Oh, there are words for it, my dear. Just not any I'd care to indulge in."

"You shouldn't shy away from indulgence, Madame." Gabrielle's eyes flashed towards me, brimming with silent promise.

I gulped.

"Jeff, wherever did you find her?" Mrs. Campbell cut across the table, raising her voice above the others.

"Would you believe that Miss Laurent found me?"

Gabrielle shuffled in her seat. Next to me. So close. Her sweet fragrance caressed my skin as my shirt sleeve brushed her slender arm.

"All this talk of pleasure," Jeff said, "and you still haven't shown Adam the pictures of your new yacht, Mrs. Campbell."

"You're right." The old bat swiped at John — her child of a husband. He'd taken her surname, and she'd named her last boat after him. Fair's fair, I guess. "John, darling, fetch me my phone, will you? I want Adam to see the latest addition to the family."

He scoured her handbag and handed it to her, along with her spectacles.

The low notes of the double bass struck an upbeat melody, and Gabrielle's shoulders swayed.

My neck stretched to Mrs. Campbell's tiny screen as she swiped through blurred pictures. "Here we are, Adam. This is the galley. We had it stained in the most beautiful varnish. Can you see it?"

"Yes, Mrs. Campbell." *Unfortunately.*

"This is no good," Gabrielle said, intruding on my guided tour. "I can't keep still. Isn't someone going to join me on the dance floor?" I felt the heat of her eyes welded to the back of my head.

"John, you take Miss Laurings for a turn on the floor. I want to show Adam the jib."

John stood, and Gabrielle paused. My chance to extricate myself. *Just do it. Leave this snooze fest and escape with the goddess in gold. What are you waiting for, Adam? Get up and ask her to dance.*

John passed behind me and pulled Miss Laurent out of her seat. The suave magpie guided her across the room while I filled another glass for his gold-mine of a wife.

"Can you see, Adam? Here's the mast being hoisted," the old crow cawed.

After every dozen or so pictures, my eyes lifted from the screen to glance at Gabrielle. Her presence on the floor dragged men to their feet in droves. The rhythmic swaying of her hips whispered a siren's song. Even Jeff put on his boogie-boots.

This was supposed to be my surprise. Wasn't it, Jeff?

*Forget it. You're not here to have fun. This is work. And you're with a client. So stop whining and focus.*

Resolve screwed me to my seat. I sipped at the bubbles of a missed opportunity, enduring the endless barrage of snapshots. Lost at sea, I stared mindlessly at the trumped up dinghy. Was I ever getting off this boat?

Melodies droned into one another, fusing in a medley as the evening sailed by. An ocean of excesses filled the ballroom. The clients gloated, boasting how much better off we'd made them, outdoing each other in a sparring match of decadence. I should've revelled with the braggarts, basked in every congratulatory tip of the glass, but the whole thing suffocated me. It cut off my air. I didn't belong here, with them. The ocean wasn't my domain. But I kept smiling, all the same.

I checked my watch. Could that really be the time?

"They'll be locking up soon enough," John said, as he and Gabrielle rejoined us, interrupting the seven hundredth photo of Mrs. Campbell's floating pride.

Everybody's eyes fell on Jeff, who set down his drink on the table like a judge's gavel. "But the night is young," he declared. "How does Adam's place sound?"

The youngsters chipped in at once, squawking altogether, birds begging for breadcrumbs. All I could decipher from the noise was their insistence on taking the limo straight away, and that they were sure my neighbors wouldn't mind.

"Listen," I said, "it's late and I'm not sure we'd all fit in the—"

"Let's settle it before he can say no," Jeff spoke over me, tapping his phone.

"Jeff, I—"

"Done. The limo's waiting outside. It's an upgrade, but we're still two seats short. Adam, would you care to drive Miss Laurent back to your place and we'll see you there?"

"I don't think—"

"You don't want to spoil the party, do you?" His eyes hardened into a commanding stare.

Anything for the clients. Anything as long as it's *me* who does it. "My house is your house," I said, hand on heart.

"Wonderful. Well, shall we, ladies and gents?"

They disappeared from the ballroom en masse, leaving me alone with Gabrielle. I hurried to stand, and she extended her hand, placing it in mine, letting it linger in my trembling fingers.

"My car isn't too far away," I said. "Couple of blocks. Back at the office. Do you want to take a cab? Or I can retrograde the car so it's here?"

"Or we could just walk?" she suggested with a sultry smile.

"Are you sure? After all the dancing, aren't you tired?"

"Absolut non. I could go all night." She raised her eyebrow.

I pulled at my shirt collar. *Is there a hammer pounding inside my ribcage?*

"Excuse me, sir," a waiter said, balancing the empties on a tray as he tried to pass. The sight of him coming towards us jerked me away from Gabrielle.

*What's he carrying? A grenade?*

No. A silver platter.

*#TNY.*

"Did you . . . did you see him?" I asked.

"See who?" Gabrielle said, scanning the room.

My phone rattled against my chest like the buzz of a dentist's drill. Celia's number. "Hello?"

"Mr. Swann? I didn't expect you to answer, sir. I'm sorry, I thought I'd get your voicemail."

"What is it, Celia?"

"I just wanted to let you know I've finished in the vault and the list you asked for is on your desk."

"List?"

"Of clients with the name Lottie."

Just when I'd gotten that name out of my head, its tendrils rooted deeper into my mind, slicing through me like the shards of a fractured mirror. A reflection that didn't belong there.

"Sir?" Celia's voice pulled me back to the ballroom.

"Thanks for letting me know."

"No problem, sir."

"See you tomorrow." I hung up.

"Is everything okay, Monsieur?" Gabrielle's face was a puzzle of genuine concern.

"Fine, Miss Laurent. Just work. Something waiting for me at the office."

"Where your car's parked?"

"That's right."

"Why let it wait?"

My brow crumpled in waves. "What do you mean?"

"We're heading there now, aren't we? Can't you — what's the expression — kill two birds with one rifle?"

"One stone."

"Is that what they use to kill birds these days?"

I smiled. "You'd find the office terribly dull."

"Oh, I'm sure we could liven it up." Her eyes searched mine, heat surging from their chestnut brown. "Lead the way, Monsieur Swann."

"Adam. Please, call me Adam."

"And please, call me Gabrielle."

There was only one woman's name bursting through my head. It wasn't Gabrielle.

She placed my hand in the fold of her arm as we left the ballroom of the Phoenix Hotel and headed for the lifts.

What was I doing? Walking back to the office with a woman I'd only just met to go chasing after another perfect stranger? It wasn't like I could ditch Gabrielle and go chasing after Lottie by myself. Not when Jeff expected me to keep her entertained. But I had to see that list. Something innate forced me towards it, pulling me on its leash. The same feeling that had flashed 'Transparent New Yesterday' across my mind.

On my arm dangled a stunning French woman, offering to liven up my office. What man wouldn't give their fortune for that kind of retrograde? So what was wrong with me? Why this ache in the pit of my stomach? The kind that screamed something wasn't right.

## FIVE

I WRAPPED MY JACKET around Gabrielle's bare shoulders to stifle the cold of the streets. She raised her eyes heavenward, engrossed in the soft glow of lamps and dazzle of buildings towering around us. While the skyline distracted her, I adjusted the settings in my 'home app' to heat the pool.

*Mustn't forget booze.* I ordered a few crates of champagne to be delivered last week. They'd be chilled and waiting. Better safe than sober.

"They're like Christmas trees, aren't they?" she said.

"What are?"

"The buildings. The way they light up."

I smiled. "First time in the city?"

"Is it that obvious?"

"Give it a few weeks, you'll get used to it."

"I hope not, Monsieur. How long have you lived here?"

"Me? I moved about, maybe, seven years ago?"

"And before that?"

*Before?* "How am I supposed to know?"

"You don't remember?" she asked, puzzled.

"I remember fine. It's just . . . how can I be sure? How do I know it hasn't changed?"

She nodded. "I hadn't thought about that."

"That's the thing about this place, everything changes so fast."

She pulled the jacket tighter around herself. "Doesn't it bother you?"

"What?"

"The changes."

I shrugged. "Life's about the here and now. And right now, here I am."

We rounded the corner, our feet scuffing the curbstones in time. Was she matching my footsteps, or was I matching hers?

"Still," she said, "it must feel empty. Not knowing what your life was like before."

"Maybe."

"But I suppose it's worth it, if it means you get to have everything you ever wanted, non?"

"I guess."

She toyed with her velvet purse. "And have you?"

I slowed my pace, lagging a fraction behind her. "Have I what?"

"Got everything you ever wanted?"

"Well, let's just say, I've no complaints."

"Is that the same thing?"

I stopped and she turned to face me. "We're here," I said. "After you."

She swept through the circling doors. Warm air gushed across the main lobby, replacing the evening's chill. I nodded at the security guard manning the desk and walked her to the elevator.

I should take her back to the house. Forget about the list.

My thumb hovered over the well-worn button for the 27th floor. Her reflection bounced off the mirrors on each wall, coaxing me with unspoken appeal.

"Have you forgotten which floor it's on?" she asked.

"No. It's just . . . ."

"Let me." Her hand pressed over mine, and she plunged my thumb into the button. The lift drew us up like water in its pail. "There. That wasn't so hard, was it?"

"Thanks, Miss Laurent."

"Gabrielle, remember?"

"Gabrielle, sorry."

The doors interrupted with a ping, opening onto the huge SSA symbol behind an empty reception desk. Darkness masked the corners, the desks, the recycled air. Dim bulbs shrouded the room in hints and traces, alluding to the office rather than revealing it.

"I'll just be a sec," I said.

"Am I not coming with you?"

"It'll only take a minute."

"I think we can make it last longer than that." She took my hand and led us down a corridor, moving from one door to another, trying to decipher the names on each plaque. "Which is yours?"

My collar tightened around my throat. "This way."

I felt my way through the hallway and opened the office door. She strutted over the plush carpet to my desk while I stood in the doorway. Twinkling fluorescents from the next building streamed through the window to mingle with silver moonlight.

The list taunted me from across the room. A single white page. More like a specter haunting me.

"No picture of a Mrs. Swann?" Gabrielle nodded to the sparse desk.

"What makes you think there's a Mrs. Swann?"

"I just wondered."

"Whether I was single?"

"Whether being single is what you always wanted?"

I tugged at my shirt collar to free myself from its strangling hold. "I never thought about it."

"It seems a shame," she said, "to be living in a place where you could get anything you ever dreamed of, and you don't have anyone to share it with. Doesn't it make you lonely?"

"Isn't everybody lonely, one way or another?"

She shrugged. "That'd be the first thing I'd fix."

"You think I need fixing?" I said.

"Isn't that the point of this place?" Her eyes swept an arc around the city lights beyond the window.

"I suppose. For some people. Depends on what led you to the city."

"Why did you come to New Yesterday, Adam? What hole did you want filling in?"

"I could ask you the same thing. What brings you here, Miss Lau . . . Gabrielle?"

"Oh, shall we say, opportunities?"

I raised an eyebrow. "What kind of opportunities?"

"The kind that are too good to miss."

"Sounds exciting."

"Excitement is everything, don't you think?" She was so alive, so vibrant.

I blushed. "It's definitely something. I'll give you that."

Her fingers caressed the top of the desk, teasing at the files spread across it. Inches from that single slip of paper. The answer I craved.

She cocked her head and crossed her ankles, leaning back on the wood. "Are you coming in?"

Her predatory stare forced my legs to carry me into the room. Magnetized, she pulled me closer, shortening the gap between us. Beside her, Celia's single folded sheet waited for me. Drawn to it like a black dot on a whiteboard, my eyes could focus on nothing else. Bait I couldn't resist. How was I supposed to think while Lottie's name played over and over? That never-ending nursery rhyme.

I stopped in front of Gabrielle while I still could, before her body was so close that there'd be no stemming the tide of her lips. I stretched past her golden gown and reached for the page.

The paper was coarse. *Why wasn't it laminated?*

Gabrielle clasped my hand and pushed it down. Her fingers ran up my tie. I could taste her perfume as it filled my nostrils with sweet intoxication.

"You didn't come all the way over here for just a piece of paper, did you?" she whispered.

The sheet crumpled in my palm, cloying at my skin.

*Lottie. Get out of my head.*

"Well, kinda."

Gabrielle smiled. "You're a tease, Adam. You know that?"

Sure, *I'm* the tease.

We stared at each other. She brushed her hair behind her ear. Her lips simmered with silent promises, but each new second quenched their heat.

Specks of dust floated through silver strands of moonlight and an awkward hush settled with them. The moment collapsed, as did my chest.

She dropped my tie and pulled away, stepping back like a photographer to capture me in her invisible lens. "Well, if that's all you wanted," she nodded at the paper in my hand, "then I guess we should be going."

A beautiful woman just offered me the chance to turn my desk into a mattress, and all I could think about was what's written on a slip of paper. *Pathetic.*

"It's probably for the best." I motioned Gabrielle towards the door. "After you."

"I didn't realize you were such a gentleman, Adam."

Gentleman? More like a schmuck.

As she crossed the room, I slipped Celia's list into my trouser pocket. The moonlight was too faint to try reading it now.

Why hadn't Celia laminated it? I couldn't fix it here. I'd need to get it home. And fast. The sooner I preserved it, the less chance anything she'd written might change.

"Is it true what they say about the city?" Gabrielle stumbled through the dark, back to the elevator.

"What is it they say?"

"That you can rearrange things to have anything you want?"

"It's called retrograding." The lift shut and thrummed down the levels. "You can tweak how things happened if there's something you wish you'd done different."

"I must try it sometime," she said.

"What would you change?"

She bit her lip as we slowed to a stop. "You might find out one of these days. If you're lucky."

We walked between the few cars dotted through the dreary underground lot. I searched for my keys.

"Looking for these?" Gabrielle jangled them from my jacket. She pressed the alarm on the key-ring until the lights of my green Porsche bleeped on and off. Her eyes widened. "Is that your car?"

"It is."

"I've always wanted to drive something like this. I don't suppose . . .? Oh, Adam, you don't mind, do you?"

"Well, I guess—"

"*Merci*, Monsieur," she said, rushing to the driver's door and climbing in.

With a flash of her wrist, the exhaust drew breath before it roared. She reached down her long legs, removed her glistening open-toed heels and stamped the pedals barefoot, careening us out of the lot.

"Just go steady until we're out of the city," I said.

"How can you take it slow in a beast like this?" She hurtled the gap between traffic lights, revving the engine at the white line.

"You sure you've never driven something like this before?"

A tapestry of lights speckled through the windshield as she joined an off-ramp that connected to the bypass. The buildings receded until they were just a memory on the landscape and she cracked her window.

"Are you ready?" she asked.

"For what?"

Her foot pressed to the floor. Acceleration pinned me to the back of my seat.

"*That*," she said. Wind whipped in sharp gusts, releasing the tight curls of her hair. Beyond the engine's thunder, crashing waves on the distant shore whispered along the highway.

The lights of the city behind us and starlight above glazed the dusty tarmac. Was it the speed that exhilarated and terrified me, or the fact her hand caressed the gear stick only an inch from my leg? Being this close to a woman like Gabrielle was no different to being a passenger in a speeding car. Without my hands on the wheel, what else could I do but force a smile and try not to gulp too hard?

"You must have done something right to make it in a place like this," she said.

"I'm just lucky."

"Don't be so modest."

"It's true. I don't think any of us would be here unless we had luck on our side."

"So you blame luck for sticking you with me tonight, Monsieur?"

"Whoever's to blame, remind me to thank them."

She glanced across at me and smiled.

"Eyes on the road!" I squirmed in my seat.

She laughed. "Don't be so nervous. You're in safe hands."

"If you say so. I mean, I still don't know a thing about you, Gabrielle."

"Ask away."

"Okay. So you're here for the excitement, I got that much."

"Tres bien."

"What do you . . . do for work?"

She shook her head. "Nothing that would interest you."

"Go on. Try me."

"Non, it's boring. Trust me. You don't want to know."

"Alright. I can take a hint."

"Anything else?" Her eyes flitted over me, running me up and down.

"Erm . . ." my brain riled like a horse trying to throw its rider. "Do you like . . . fondue?"

She laughed. "Of all the questions you could ask, that's the one you want an answer to?"

"Sorry. Let me think of a better one."

"Non. It's perfect. I don't mind fondue."

"Good. I'm glad we've straightened that out."

"Me too. Anything else you want to know? What's my favorite cheese, perhaps?"

I blushed. "You see that driveway coming up? That's us."

She slowed, pulled through the courtyard and up the drive. The mouth of the basement garage swallowed the headlights. She turned the keys and put the engine to sleep.

"Exciting enough for you?" I asked.

Her eyes were a cocktail of ecstasy and gratitude. Breathless, she reached out to grab my hand. "It was wonderful. There aren't many who would indulge a silly girl like me."

"Don't mention it."

She pulled my hand to her lips. The warmth of her breath and tenderness of her kiss remained until she finally released my fingers. "Merci, Adam."

She hurried to open the car door. I pulled the keys from the ignition and gathered my jacket from where it lay wrinkled on the seat.

Up the stairs at the end of the garage, the door pushed open and she followed me to survey the scene of the party.

Even at the speed she'd driven, they'd still beaten us back.

Dozens of champagne glasses fizzed away on the central marble bar in the open kitchen. In the living room, the three older clients reclined in chairs around the hearth's orange flames, their feet nestled in a cozy rug. Beyond the glass wall on my left, their younger counterparts dove into the terrace pool, wearing the spare swimsuits I kept hanging in the chalet. Jeff busied himself nurturing the firepit outside. The music blared on the patio, banished to a faint echo in the living room — the background of an otherwise amiable conversation.

John stumbled in, sopping wet, trailing the stench of chlorine across the carpet. His ill-fitting trunks slipped down his hips as he snatched a bottle of bubbly from the fridge. The cork clattered off the ceiling and bounced on the cupboards.

"Oops!" He ran with the bottle in hand and launched himself into the pool.

Mrs. Campbell watched from the sofa. Her eyes rolled before her glare frosted like the chilled champagne she swilled in her narrow cheeks. "I'll have to replace *that* soon, if it doesn't learn how to be civil."

"I don't know why you keep him around," another old millionaire said, from where he lazed beside her.

"It has its moments. Occasionally."

"Take my advice, dear. We're not getting any younger. You don't want to have wasted years with an overgrown frat boy when you could've been savoring them with someone who really floats your boat."

"I do have quite the penchant for boats." Mrs. Campbell smiled.

"I say swap him the first chance you get. Have those years back with someone worthwhile."

"I'll think about it. After all the stress of this mall, I could do with something new to go at."

"I've never known so many objections over one tiny arcade. Have you?"

"Never."

"Is it me, or do the dimwits in the city spout more nonsense these days? I preferred them when they were strong and silent. You remember those days? When everyone was more concerned about the size of their abs than business ethics?"

"One thing's for sure, I wouldn't object to exchanging John for a model with a bronzer chest and thicker shoulders." Mrs. Campbell licked her lips. "To scrub the deck, if you catch my drift."

Gabrielle stormed across the room. "You realize it's your *husband* you're talking about."

"Oh, I'm sorry, dear. Have we offended you?" Mrs. Campbell glowered over her glass.

"I would've expected a businesswoman to honor her contracts. Marriage being one of them. Or are you always on the lookout to swindle others for a better deal?"

"Now, now. Steady on. I've no problem with you speaking your mind, Miss Lawlong or whatever your name is. But I draw the line at being lectured on how to conduct business."

"I suppose you draw the line for everyone?"

"My dear, it's a good investment to change a product line from time to time. Spice things up."

Jeff appeared through the patio doors. "What did I miss?" He perched himself beside the clients.

"Oh, nothing much. We were just talking about whether it's time for an upgrade." Mrs. Campbell's eyes flashed through the glass to where John splashed around.

I handed a glass of bubbles to Gabrielle. "Here."

"How can you stomach this?" she whispered.

"The champagne? Don't you like it?"

"I mean the company."

"I'd prefer the company if it had a registered trademark."

She rolled her eyes.

"Oh, come on," I said. "My jokes aren't that bad."

"Whatever you say."

"I'll be back soon. Make yourself comfortable."

"You're not leaving me alone with these people, are you?"

"I won't be long." I nudged her to the sofas. She resisted, but conceded a seat next to Jeff.

I climbed the stairs, flicked the bedroom light, and unfolded the list from my pocket. Celia's handwriting. Everything she'd tracked boiled down to three names.

*Lingerie by Lottie.*

*Lottie's Ladle (Cafe).*

*Lottie's Labs Dog Breeding.*

Three clients. Three businesses that meant nothing to me.

Lingerie by Lottie? *Why would I need lingerie?* And as far as dog breeders go, I didn't remember owning a dog since I was a kid, and we lost Penny to a slipped disk. *What about the cafe? Did I forget to tip a waitress?*

Lottie's name crystallized so clear in my head. Shouldn't one of these stores have meant something?

I had to preserve this before some alteration in the city wiped the list clean.

Scrambling around the closet, I rummaged through old shoeboxes until I unearthed the laminator. I glanced over my shoulder and loaded the paper. The acrid bitterness of hot plastic charred the room as the machine sealed clear film over the page.

Light from the hallway spread across the carpet, along with a shadow.

My hands shook as I fumbled to cover the laminator.

A cough from the door.

I spun to face them.

Their shadow crept over the floor, up the bed, the wall.

"You don't know where the bathroom is, do you?" John stood dripping from his trunks.

*Relax. It's only John. He's probably too drunk to notice the smell.*

"Second door to the left," I said.

"Thanks." He turned to leave and stopped. *Don't stop. Just keep walking.* "Say, shouldn't you be downstairs?" He staggered deeper into the bedroom. "What are you doing?"

"Oh, nothing. Just paperwork." I raised myself tall, blocking the gap between him and the machine.

Around my shoulder, his bleary eyes glimpsed the half-covered corner of it, sharpening at the sight. "Is that what I think it is?" He pointed, stumbling as his stretched neck careened him off-kilter.

"It's nothing."

His head shifted left and right and he tried to hush his voice, but it only came out louder. "What are you doing with a *laminator*? You know it's illegal to have one of those for personal use."

*Shut up, John. Shut up right now.* "It's for work."

"Oh yeah? If it's for work, then why isn't it at the office?"

"It's . . . complicated." I gripped his arm and shepherded him to the door.

"What are you trying to keep from being retrograded, huh? Is it to do with that French fancy you brought back tonight?"

I shut us in and grasped him by the shoulders. "Listen. Nobody can know about this."

"If one of the higher-ups at Anderson Whitman found out—"

"Didn't you hear me?"

He flashed me the smile of a sycophant, the booze slurring condescension across his face. "Don't worry, Adam. I can keep a secret. For the right price." His attempt at a wink turned into a flurry of blinks. If I didn't know him better, I'd have thought he was having some kind of fit.

"What do you want, John?"

"The old bird's been a bit stiff lately. Says I need to learn some decorum."

"You want your behavior tonight to have been perfect. Is that what you're saying?"

"Everything that happened tonight, it'll be our little secret."

"Why don't you retrograde it yourself?"

"Do you have any idea how close she keeps tabs on me? It's not my name on the lifestyle package, is it? If she thought I'd changed things without her permission, I'd be a goner. Come on. One secret for another. It's not a bad trade when you think about it."

"I'll talk to Jeff and see what I can manage." I opened the door and he patted me on the shoulder.

"Second door to the left, you said?"

I showed him the bathroom and hurried back to the laminator, removing the page and stuffing the machine back in its hiding place.

*You're either stupid or careless, Adam.* I hadn't used the laminator in years. Why risk it? And for what? A piece of paper that means absolutely nothing? *Stupid. Definitely stupid.*

Hiding the list would be as dumb as making it. Not with the smell in the room. If anybody found their way up here and got a whiff of what happened, they'd be looking for a slip of paper.

My mind unraveled a thousand ways it was possible for this to go wrong, and those loose threads jumbled my muscles into knots. Legs hardened. Back tightened. My eyes faltered and the room's shadows blackened my vision.

*Get a grip. John needs you. He won't blab. Go down to your guests, put the paper on the fridge door, and nobody will know the difference. Act normal, put on a smile, and it'll all work out.*

I descended the stairs. Laughter trickled from the sofas interspersed with splashes from the pool. Through the window, the firepit blazed while the hearth's warmth percolated the living room.

I tiptoed straight to the kitchen and hung Celia's list on the fridge between invoices and old holiday photos. Incognito.

"Here you go." Gabrielle appeared at my side with a full glass of champagne. "You look like you need one."

I took the glass in my unsteady hands. "Thanks. Did you survive?"

"I can hold my own against these wrinklies."

"I don't doubt it."

"How about you? Did you get sorted?"

"Just about."

"Good. Is this what you left me at the mercy of those people for?" She glanced at the list.

I blocked her from seeing it. "It's . . . it was like that when I . . . it's nothing."

"Let me look."

"Really. It's just something for work."

"I see." She stepped past me and ran her eyes over it. Her easy manner dispelled and her shoulders fixed rigid. "Who's Lottie?"

"No one, as far as I know. It's just a list of old clients we're trying to track down."

"Well, your clients are very lucky to have someone so committed to them. Someone who's always working."

"Gabrielle—"

"I've got business of my own to attend to." She rested her half-empty glass on the marble bar.

"Do you have to go?"

"I've already stayed too long."

"Let me order you a taxi." She made her goodbyes to the others while I phoned the best cabbie in town and arranged for him to have arrived a minute ago. Less than two seconds passed before he knocked on the door.

"Au revoir, Monsieur."

Her lips glanced off my cheek and she pulled away. As quick as she'd come, she disappeared.

The rest followed suit before long, bidding their farewells in turn. John did his best to mask a knowing look as Mrs. Campbell dragged him to the limo.

Jeff loitered after the last of them.

"I'm worried about the Campbells," I said.

"You think she'll give John the boot?" He draped his jacket over his arm.

"I think we'd better rewrite tonight so he didn't make such an idiot of himself."

"Is this because of what he did to your bathroom?"

I groaned. "Do I even want to know?"

"Some free advice — use the downstairs loo until I've had a chance to fix all this tomorrow."

"Thanks, Jeff."

"Anything for you, Adam."

"You'd best get out of here before you turn all soppy on me."

"I can take a hint. Goodnight, my friend." He drained his final glass. "Oh. One last thing. Did you like your surprise?"

"Go to bed, old man."

"With pleasure. See you tomorrow." He sloped towards the door, paused and turned back to me, placing his hand on my shoulder. "By the way, I saw you when you and Miss Laurent got home tonight. It was good to see you smiling again, Adam." He grinned and tumbled to where his taxi waited in the courtyard, and, with a swipe and a tap, I brought the music to an end.

*Finally.*

I picked up the empty glasses and stacked them on the counter. Clamped beneath a magnet, the laminated list leaped out at me, berating me, demanding answers. It wasn't like I could call any of them up at this unearthly hour.

'Hi, I'm Adam Swann from SSA and I just wondered, who exactly are you, Lottie? And why are you tearing through my brain?'

*I'll visit the cafe tomorrow. See where it takes me, and hope I don't need to go to the dog breeders and lingerie shop. That's if they're still in business.*

As I pulled the French-door to the patio, a thud boomed from upstairs. I stopped. My ears tingled as they tensed, alert to every noise. There was nothing but the crackle of fading embers. Body stiff, I waited. Still nothing.

I pulled again on the French-door. Another noise from above. A patting of footsteps. One, then another. And then, nothing.

I slipped the metal poker beside the fireplace from its holder. Without so much as a sound, I climbed the stairs. The narrow hallway closed in on me. Another bang ruffled through the walls, a grating of wood, then it ceased. I inched through the dark corridor, the only light shimmering below my office door.

My fingers trembled on the handle. *Just breathe.* I squeezed hold of the poker.

*You can do this.*

*Count to three.*

One . . . someone moved inside . . . Two . . . a rustle of papers . . . Three . . . I turned the handle and swung it open.

Before me, stacks of scattered folders lined my desk, spilling onto the carpet. Open drawers spewed their contents, strewn about the room. Poised over the papers with a phone in her hand, taking pictures of every leaf in every file, stood Gabrielle Laurent.

"Gabrielle, what are you doing?"

Her cheeks flushed. Her eyes glanced away. By saying nothing, she told me everything, and yet, I had no answers. Only questions. Shots of adrenaline fired through my veins. I drew a deep breath and through grated teeth, forced the words out of my throat. "Who *are* you?"

# SIX

GABRIELLE'S EYES FLICKED to the open window before she pounced for the gap. I hurled myself to meet her spring and threw my hands around her torso, tugging her backwards. She retreated behind the desk, balling her hands into fists.

"This close. I was this close," she said below her breath.

I latched the window and stationed myself between her and the door. "You didn't answer my question. Who are you?"

She bit her lip. "I'm sorry, Adam. Really, I am. I didn't mean any trouble."

"Stop trying to change the subject."

"I'm not. It's just—"

"Don't give me excuses. All I want is a straight answer."

"I wish it were that simple."

*And I wish there wasn't a random woman trashing my study.* "Well, let me make it simple for you. Get out of my house."

"Adam. I—"

"I said *get out.*"

"I can't just leave. Not like this."

"Would you rather I call the police?"

68

"Non. Please!"

"Then start talking."

She shook her head. "It's not what it looks like."

"Oh, really? Because it looks like you broke into my house and started raiding my stuff."

"That's not—"

"*Don't.*"

Her lips quivered. "Don't what?"

"*Don't* tell me I'm wrong. Or that this is all some misunderstanding."

"But . . ."

"You think I'm an idiot?"

"Adam, please . . ."

"That's enough, Gabrielle. What are you *doing* here?"

She drew a deep breath and glanced at her toes. "You won't believe me, even if I told you."

My grip tightened around the poker. "I don't get it. One minute, we're sipping champagne together, the next, I catch you rifling through my desk. I don't even know why I'm asking you. What difference will another lie make?" I unlocked my phone.

"Wait." She threw her arms up. "Don't do this. Don't call the police."

"Give me one good reason why I shouldn't."

"I'm trying to help you." The sincerity of her eyes stilled my thumb over the call button.

"*Help* me? By turning my office upside down? What part of *this* is helping me, exactly?" I gestured at the discarded files littered across the floor, the shrapnel of an explosion.

"I'm sorry, Adam. I'm sorry for all of this."

"Sorry doesn't explain *anything*, Gabrielle. If that's even your real name." I hit *call* and lifted the phone to my ear.

"Please. Don't."

"It's too late." The line rang.

"You don't understand. They'll kill me."

"What?"

"Do you want to pull the trigger on me, Adam?"

The icy steel of a gun echoed across my temple. Invading my memory. *Again.*

A muffled voice chimed into my ear. "What's your emergency?"

I buried the phone into my shoulder, covering the microphone. "What do you mean, pull the trigger?"

"It's all on this." Gabrielle held her phone aloft. "I brought enough information so I wouldn't wake up with a different past and no clue what I was here for. But if they arrest me, they'll confiscate it. And if anything happens to this phone, then . . ." She snapped her fingers. ". . . My whole life could disappear. Changed. Along with everything I know."

"So you wake up with a different past. That's not so bad, is it?"

"If they let me wake up at all."

"Sir," the tiny voice at my shoulder barked. "What's your emergency?"

"Adam. Please."

It'd be insane to feel guilty about handing her in. *She broke into your house. Went through your stuff. She deserves to be arrested. So take that guilt swelling in your chest and bury it. Like a normal person.*

"Sir?" The insistent voice of the operator blared through the speaker.

Gabrielle's eyes misted as she stepped towards me. "Please," she whispered. "Don't erase me, Adam. I can explain. Please just give me a chance!"

*Don't hang up. Just tell them there's a burglar in your house. That's what she is. A burglar.*

My throat scratched as a conflict of words clamored to my lips. "No more games. Understand?" *What are you doing, you idiot? Repeat after me. 'There's a burglar in my house.'*

Gabrielle nodded. "I'll tell you what you want to know, and if you still want me to leave, then I'll go."

"Sir, what's the emergen—"

"I'm sorry," I said. "I thought there was a problem, but I was mistaken."

"Are you sure, sir? It doesn't sound that way."

"Everything's fine. Really."

"I can send out an officer. It might help if someone's in distress?"

"There's no need. Just a little retrophobia. No reason for alarm. We've got it all under control."

"I see."

"Can you make it so this call never happened?" I asked.

"If that's what you want. Look. As long as you're sure everyone is safe?"

"Perfectly. Just a misunderstanding. But we're getting it cleared up. Sorry about the mixup."

"Alright, sir. If you say so. Have a good evening."

"Thanks." I cut the line and pocketed the phone. "Alright, Gabrielle. Talk."

She gulped down heavy breaths and closed her eyes, steeling herself. "You ever heard of the Daily Post?"

"The newspaper?"

"Everyone remembers the headlines, but ask them who wrote the story and they always come up short."

"You're a reporter?"

"Oui."

A reporter? That's it? No spy? Secret agent? Ninja assassin? "What are you doing here?"

"Working on a story."

"Chasing a lead?"

She shrugged. "Something like that."

I glanced at the strewn papers. "What story?"

Her face hardened and her eyes darted across the room. "Can I trust you, Adam?"

"Are you kidding me? You break into my house and now you're asking if *you* can trust *me*?"

"Have you any idea what my editor would do if he knew I was talking to you about this?"

"He'd be pleased. You haven't told me anything so far. What's the story? What exactly are you looking for?"

She nodded, as if giving herself permission to talk. "Look. If this were any other city, any other place on Earth, I wouldn't be here. I wouldn't even try anything like this. Some intern at the Daily Post would contact your office and ask you for an interview, and that'd be it."

"So what's different about New Yesterday?"

"The longer I'm here, the more chance a retrograde will kill the truth, and me with it. The city's changing every minute. It's not like I've got a package with Anderson Whitman to fall back on. I need answers and I need them fast."

"If that's true, why waste your time tonight at the gala? With me?"

"It wasn't a waste." Her cheeks bloomed red.

"No. I suppose it got you into my study."

"That's not what I meant. And you know it."

"Stop pretending, Gabrielle."

"I'm not pretending. I never was. Not once."

"You almost sound like you believe that."

"Is it really so hard to believe?" Her eyes searched mine as the room's low lamplight bathed her in amber. Her dress shimmered, her rose-gilded lips forlorn and helpless now she'd blown her cover. She couldn't have looked less like a reporter if she'd tried. *A reporter. In my office. My private office.* Calm down and think.

*What would Jeff do?*

I dropped the poker. "Why didn't you just ask me for an interview?"

"I'm not the first person to come to New Yesterday looking for the truth. They sent Patrick to do the same. He woke up as a different person. I couldn't take the risk."

"But as long as you've got your phone, you'll be alright?"

"So far, so good." She cradled it to her chest.

"Alright. You said you were trying to help me. What did you mean?"

"It's . . . complicated. Without an interview, it's—"

"It's what?"

"I don't want to put you in any trouble."

"So give me an interview."

She cocked her head. "Are you serious?"

"Give me five minutes and meet me by the pool."

"You'll let me interview you? Even after all this?"

"We both want answers. If that's what it takes."

"Okay. Five minutes. By the pool. I'll be waiting." She hesitated before ambling past me. "Merci." Her shadow shrank down the corridor.

The door clattered behind her and my legs crumpled like punctured tires. Knees crashed to the floor. My head became an anchor, sinking into my hands, scuffing my fingers as they dredged the trenches of my scalp.

*Think, Adam. Think.*

I fumbled about in my pocket, mechanically dialing Jeff. Straight to voicemail. He was probably asleep in the back of the taxi. *Why bother leaving a message? She's a reporter, Jeff. A reporter!* Talking with clients, especially the press, was his department, not mine. Why had I agreed to this?

Celia.

Celia would know what to do. But no, I couldn't bother her at this time of night.

*Think.*

Through unsteady breaths, hailstones of adrenaline pounded my chest. Veins pulsed over my forehead and blood flowed in my ears, until it all slowed to a regular, gentle hum. I flicked the lamp off. My footsteps followed me in echoes down the stairs.

On the terrace, Gabrielle stared into the warm reflection of the fire, rubbing her hands over her bare arms. She scarcely noticed me join her in the firepit's glow. I placed my tux over her shoulders. The jacket draped from her neck while her perfume tinted the still night air with sweetness.

"Merci."

She'd scraped together a bottle of bubbly and two glasses. I handed her a flute, popped the cork, and poured. The foam rose in a flourish and trickled over the side. It fell onto her lap, staining her dress and dousing the phone. She tapped the screen rapidly, checking it still worked, and breathed a sigh of relief, rubbing the spilled bubbles on the arm of my jacket to soak the sleeve. With the screen alive, she positioned it in the outer-breast pocket, in place of the folded handkerchief which she used to dab herself.

"I'm not usually so clumsy," I said.

"It's alright. I bought the dress with the paper's funds. They won't mind, as long as I get a story."

I sat opposite her while the fire danced beside us, scattering beams across the surface of the pool. Countless stars reflected in the water, glistening in moonlight. "Ready when you are."

She lifted the glass to her lips. "Just so you know, we're recording." She pointed to the breast pocket where the top of her phone peeked out. I nodded and gulped my drink, bringing a flush to my cheeks as cool air soothed the bite of burning embers. She leaned forwards and drilled her long fingers on the stem of her glass. "So, I'm here with Adam Swann of 'Swann Sinclair Accounts.' Monsieur Swann, how long have you been a partner at the firm?"

"Ever since we founded it seven years ago."

She eased back in her chair, and I did the same. "Tell me how, in seven years, you made SSA the biggest firm of accountants in New Yesterday."

"It's simple. We service the clients that belong to the AWG."

"The AWG?"

"Anderson Whitman Group," I said. "Whenever a new business purchases their store through Anderson Whitman, they can opt in, and if they do, they're referred to us, and we take them on as clients."

"And you manage their accounts?"

"Let me give you an example. Take Mrs. Campbell and Mr. Hemmingway, and everyone else you met tonight. They run Gracy's. They're in the AWG, which makes them one of our clients. You've heard of Gracy's, right?"

"Of course."

"Okay, so Gracy's has been operating out of New Yesterday since 1908. There are dozens of them throughout the city. What happens in New Yesterday will have a massive impact on their business. So a company like that would want to opt in and be a part of the Anderson Whitman Group. It gives them a say on the eligibility of anyone who wants to come into New Yesterday when that person's screened."

"Because of the impact one person entering the city might have on their business?"

"You don't want someone coming in and interfering with a company's history, otherwise it'd mess with their profits, and that's where we come in. We preserve their interests, and it's the same with any other business in the group."

Lines creased her forehead. "Hang on. You said Gracy's has been in the city since 1908? But it's not even been a decade since Dr. Weiss made his discovery and they laid the first bricks in New Yesterday. How can Gracy's have been here since 1908?"

"You're not going linear on me, are you?"

She opened her lips, but checked herself before uttering a sound, sipping champagne as she framed her next question. "So to have a business in the city, you need to be in the Anderson Whitman Group?"

"Not always. Thousands of independent retailers broker their own deals with Anderson Whitman and operate small businesses. Not everyone wants to feel like they're becoming part of the machine, I guess."

"But I suppose there's only so much space for businesses in the city?"

"I'm not sure. That's a question for Anderson Whitman."

She crossed her legs and nodded. "The new mall that's being proposed by your company, to open a store inside it must come at quite a premium?"

"That's why it falls on us to make the plans. The finances are the biggest part of any planning application. We've spent weeks going over the figures. They're public record."

"How far back will the mall go, if it's approved?"

"We'll be asking for them to have built it eight years ago."

"So, if it's passed, your clients in the Anderson Whitman Group will wake up some time in the afternoon tomorrow with over eight years worth of profits in their pockets?"

"Some of them will."

"Doesn't that give them a pretty big incentive to . . ." She tailed off, waiting for me to finish her question.

"To what?"

"To . . . let's say, arrange things for a price?"

"Are you talking about bribery?"

"Your words, Mr. Swann. Not mine." She drained her glass and clasped it in her fidgeting hands.

"What are you implying? What exactly is the story you're working on?"

"What happens to the businesses already there?" she said. "On the streets where the mall will be? Will they wake up tomorrow with their livelihood disappeared? Vanished without a trace? And who would even know the difference?"

"What are you talking about? We've allocated a slot for every one of those stores inside the mall. That's what we do at SSA."

"Then how do you explain the objections?"

"What objections?"

"The ones in your office. All those papers across your floor. What do you think they are?"

"I—"

"You want to see the photographs? I took plenty."

"There must be some mistake."

"Mistake? Is that what you're calling it?"

"What else could it be? If you're accusing me of something, just come out and say it."

She remained silent, staring at me. Was that guilt on her face, or just a trick of the flames?

"Listen, Gabrielle. Whatever you think is going on, we've checked and double checked those spaces. No store owner has any reason to worry. Businesses can't just disappear. That kind of thing — it doesn't happen in New Yesterday. There are too many safeguards."

"Can you prove that?"

I sat forwards and rested my glass on the terrace tiles. "Why are you here?"

"The paper's received reports of businesses in New Yesterday disappearing overnight. Just small, independent places. But nobody seems to have any clue how it's happening, or why."

"Are you suggesting that we . . . that I . . . have something to do with it?"

"I'm just trying to figure out why someone would want to change history to make a business vanish."

Vanishing businesses? This isn't Penn and Teller. She wasn't going to fool me with a story so absurd. When had there ever been a case of a business disappearing in New Yesterday before? None that I could recall.

So why the flash of panic striking my spine and the sudden lurch of my stomach?

I stared at the fire. Smoke rose from the flickering flame into a cloud, concealing shapes that pushed themselves from the shadows. Memories that forced themselves into my vision. *A room. Glass walls. A man with a gun. The lines of a planning application.*

*"I want my life back."*

*That face. From the TV.*

*Houdini.*

*The salesman's sneer. His tablet on his knee.*

*Lottie.*

"Adam?" Gabrielle's voice broke through the haze.

I picked up the poker and stoked the dying embers in the firepit. The ghosts of a half-forgotten past collapsed. Billows of smoke emptied, taking the shape of another past with them, blown by the breeze into nothing but a wisp.

"Are you alright?" Gabrielle asked. "You seemed lost for a moment?"

"I'm fine. What was your question?"

"I was just thinking about why anyone would want to make a business disappear?"

"I don't know."

"Take a guess. What would make *you* do it?"

I shook my head. "You don't expect me to answer that, do you?"

"Why not?"

"Because . . ."

"Go on," she urged.

"Look. There could be a hundred different reasons for a person to want something retrograded."

"Including money?"

A faint breeze whistled cool air across my neck. "Do you know what the penalty is for being caught with a bribe?" I said.

"Non. What is it? A fine? A slap on the wrist?"

"You disappear. Your whole past, everything you've built here — gone."

"That's a bit extreme, isn't it?"

"It's serious. Even if you could get around the safeguards, why take the risk?"

"You don't think there are people greedy enough to try?"

"Not in the AWG."

She tilted an eyebrow at me. "You've got a lot of faith in your clients."

"We're already bringing them legitimate profits day in, day out. How stupid would you have to be to risk all that? You've met some of our clients. Did Mrs. Campbell strike you as the criminal type?"

"I suppose not."

"She's too busy on her yachts to ever get round to petty crime. And we're too busy keeping her afloat. We wouldn't allow it, even if she suggested it."

"I'm glad to hear that. But can you *prove* any of this? How am I supposed to believe what you're telling me?"

"You calling me a liar?"

"Non. Of course not."

"It sounds that way to me."

"I'm sorry, Adam. I don't mean to pry. I was sent to chase a hunch. Whoever's making these businesses disappear is powerful enough to cover it up."

"And you think they'd get rid of you if they found out what you know?"

"Silence requires sacrifices. I don't want to be one of them. But I can't stop until I track them down." She laid her empty glass on the table, sweeping her hair behind her ear.

"Listen," I said, "you want proof? Why don't you come with me tomorrow and I'll show you in person that none of our clients are responsible for whatever you think has been going on?"

"You'll show me the plans?"

"If that's what it'll take to convince you. More champagne?"

"Non. I'd better not. It's gone straight to my head."

I finished my glass and rested it next to hers. "Have you any more questions to ask me, Miss Laurent?"

She straightened the slit of her dress across her thigh, exposing the sweep of her legs. "Only one. But I'm afraid of your answer."

"Ask away."

Her lips curled. "There is so much to be said, and so little time to say it, non?"

"Time is precious."

"Oui. So, I guess my question is . . . do you like fondue?"

The tension in my shoulders eased as I laughed at hearing my stupid question from earlier repeated back. "Honestly, I think it tastes like feet."

She laughed, too. The kind of laughter that was impossible to fake. "Feet? Yum."

"I always see it at these big parties, and I wonder why," I said. "I mean, maybe you just have to be a certain kind of person to enjoy it?"

"And you're not that kind of person?"

"I guess not."

"I can believe it." She said it with such gentleness that it robbed me of any clue of how to respond. How was I supposed to argue with that? But maybe the time for us to be adversaries was over. Maybe she was tired of the game she'd been sent to play.

"You never did tell me your favorite cheese." I lifted an eyebrow.

"Oh, that's easy. Camembert."

"Of course it is. How could it be anything else?"

"Precisely, Monsieur."

As we sat by the fireside, the friction of her accusations melted into another kind of energy. Something else. Something warmer.

"We never had the chance to dance earlier," she said.

"That's true."

"Would you like to give it a try?"

What could I say beneath the pressure of those hopeful, innocent eyes? She'd broken into my house, trashed my study, and tried to steal company information. I should have been furious with her. But how could I be angry when she looked at me like that? Maybe it was the champagne dulling my wits. Maybe it was those gentle brown eyes, warm enough to soothe the sting of her intrusion.

Her disarming smile drew my hand towards her. Our fingers slipped together and she rose to her feet, tottering to her left.

I caught her, keeping her steady. "That drink really has gone to your head, hasn't it?"

"Oui. Where's the music?"

"Can't you hear it?"

Her warm body pressed against mine, more intense than the fire burning beside us. There was no sound, except the crackle of flame and our breathing, which quickened as my hand fell to her waist. "What music?" she whispered.

"Listen." I hummed an old tune, mixing the notes together, and she laughed. We swayed across the terrace tiles. A few unsteady steps edged us further from the fire. Her laughter became the music I staggered to. In a flurry, I spun us around. The sky above blurred into a thousand shooting stars. Tiles disappeared from beneath my feet, and the chill of water rushed over me, before the sound of a splash met my ears. Water stung my chest as I gulped it down. I burst to the surface in a fit of coughs, wiping at red eyes.

Across the pool, her face rose above the water, her hair sodden and her makeup running. But her laugh was still melodious, and she swam the few strokes across to me, putting herself back in my arms. The pool was our dancehall, our steps fumbled and slow. Her giggling faded, the music stopped and her lips quivered.

"Come on," I said. "Let's get you warm and dry."

I lifted her out of the water and walked her to the downstairs bathroom, running the shower hot and fast. With a loose gray hoodie and some sporty shorts piled on top of a fresh towel, I offered her the bundle.

"Merci." She leaned towards me and warmed my cheek with a kiss.

Our eyes met as she pulled away and I turned to leave.

"Adam."

"Miss Laurent?"

"I just wanted to say thank you. For the dance."

"Anytime."

"You should do it more often. You make a good partner."

"I'll bear that in mind. Do you need anything else?"

She paused, glanced away, and shook her head. "Non, Monsieur. Not at the moment. But I'll let you know as soon as I do."

Her cheeks blushed. Must be the heat of the shower. She closed the door, shutting herself in with the steam.

I collapsed on the sofa, my aching joints sprawled like a salamander in shade. The distant patter of running water trickled through the room. I couldn't turf her out. Not after I'd been the one to soak her dress.

My eyes closed and I drifted between the daze of sleep and the malaise of unconscious thought. Slumber would carry me to dawn. It didn't matter if she tried anything else with the files. She couldn't have made any more of a mess of them. What was the worst she could do? Tidy them up? Besides, she didn't seem stupid enough to jeopardize her tour of the office tomorrow when we'd straighten everything out and she'd get her story.

It was so easy to forget she was a reporter. Where did a newspaper journalist learn to dance like that? My mind replayed the steps of our slow waltz. The warmth of her body pressed against mine. Her laugh. The softness of her skin beneath my jacket.

Wait a minute.

Was she wearing my tux when she climbed out of the swimming pool? Hadn't it fallen from her shoulders after we'd tumbled in? Wasn't it still floating in the pool? *Along with her phone.*

I pictured the phone slipping out of the breast pocket, sinking deeper as it slowly filled with water, until light faded from the screen and it was no more than a dead plastic shell. I should've opened my eyes to check, but it was too late. Lulled too far along the slope between wakefulness and sleep, my body was beyond stirring. Champagne weighed my limbs, the lightness of its bubbles turned to lead, impossible to lift.

The only tangible record of Gabrielle Laurent lay drowned on the bottom of the pool while she bathed in the shower's steam.

Change swirled around me, tinting the air with new memories. What would she be when I opened my eyes? Would I have ever met her? Not just her. What kind of life was *I* going to wake up to?

*Wake up Adam. Before it's too late.* But I strayed into sleep, not knowing what I would forget, powerless to do anything about it.

And still, despite all that, as consciousness abandoned me, the last word to flash across my mind was the name I knew nothing about. Like an anchor strapped around my neck. *What am I missing?*

*Tomorrow, you're going to visit that cafe.* I forced the words to the front of my mind. *You're going to find Lottie. You're going to find . . .*

## SEVEN

A BEAM OF SUNLIGHT STREAMED through the glass wall, warming my face, impossible to ignore. The lingering haze of a champagne mist clung to my eyes.

The watch's hands blinked into shape. 2:48. *That can't be right.* I held it to my ear. No tick whispered from its gears. As I shook it, a slush murmured from inside.

My head pounded, a sweltering mess. Images of the gala ball broke through the fog in fits and spurts. Dancing. Mrs. Campbell's yacht. The after-party at our place. Champagne. And Gabby. *She must have left me sleeping on the couch and gone to bed.*

I staggered on auto-pilot into the kitchen, and laid out two plates while the bacon sizzled and the toaster clunked. Black coffee steamed in two mugs.

Up the stairs, I balanced the breakfast tray around a narrow turn of the hallway to the door of her writing room. Gabby scrunched up in the swivel seat, her bare legs tucked into the folds of my misshapen, oversized gray hoodie. Her spectacles wobbled on the rim of her nose as she pounded the keys of her grandfather's old typewriter.

"Bonjour chérie," I said, placing the tray of food on the desk next to a neat pile of papers.

She grabbed my hand and pulled it around her waist, tugging me downwards until she kissed my cheek.

"Bonjour. Merci, Adam. What time is it?"

"I've no idea. My watch is broken."

She yanked my wrist, stealing a look for herself. 2:48. "You've not been swimming in it again?"

"Not that I remember, darling."

Releasing my hand, she removed her reading glasses and rubbed her eyes. Her tired fingers bunched blonde curls into a ponytail then wrapped around the hot mug of coffee. She reveled in its bitter aroma. "Perfect."

"How's your writing this morning?" She'd been tweaking her latest book for the past six months. 'Remembering Guinevere', the fourth in her series of historical fantasy novels, and the publisher's deadline was less than a week away.

"I've almost finished this scene. What would you say sounds better? *'She lingered languidly'* or, *'She lingered listlessly'*?"

"Why don't you just leave it as *'She lingered'*?"

"Don't be so lazy . . . Wait, that's it! *'She lingered lazily.'* Adam, you're a genius!" She leaped upright, bashing at the keys and spilling coffee over the desk.

"I'll let you work, darling."

"Mm-hmm."

The door clicked behind me. She wouldn't even notice I'd left the room.

But what did I expect? For the past two years, I'd lost Gabby to her own little world until some time after breakfast. It was when she did her best writing, so she said. Always in her office, the room where she wrote her stories. Why did it used to bother me so much — being invisible until halfway through the morning?

I shook my wrist, hoping the hands might rattle enough to tell me the time, but they remained stuck at 2:48. Only one thing for it. The receipt for my watch must be knocking around here somewhere. My fingers scoured the mound of shoeboxes in the closet. Disarray disguised heaps of discarded papers, in transit towards being filed.

Beneath the pile, I brushed over the sharp edges of the laminator. Fractured remnants of last night triggered at its touch, pulsing through my temples. *The list on the fridge. Something about John and Mrs. Campbell.* I pushed the memories to the back of the closet, along with the laminator.

I groped through a jumbled mess like an archeologist digging the earth, coughing through thick layers of dust to uncover a box of receipts. A rummage through scraps of paper gave me all I needed, and I slipped the faded proof of purchase into my wallet.

Breakfast was cold by the time my dig was over. Gabby traipsed downstairs, the empty contents of her tray tottering in one hand. Her long, bronze legs gracefully carried her to the marble-topped bar in the middle of the kitchen, along with her dirty dishes.

"Have you seen my phone, mon amour?" she asked.

"Not that I've noticed. Have you lost it?"

"I checked all over the office, but it's not there."

Odd. She never went anywhere without her phone. "You want me to pick another one up for you on my way home? I can put in a call and retrograde you a new one?"

"Non. I'll keep looking."

"It's no bother. I need to stop at a jeweler's anyway."

She approached the counter where I stood. The gray hoodie covered her shapely body just enough to hint at the curves beneath. My tie straightened in her hands as she fixed the knot into place.

"That's better." She leaned towards me. Her soft lips parted. From my chest, the vibrating buzz of an incoming call gave her reason to pause. She rolled her eyes. Her hand slipped to my cheek and she stepped away, through the glass wall into the yellow sunshine on the terrace.

"Hello?" I answered.

"Good morning, Mr. Swann."

"Morning, Celia."

"News on the mall. The planners pushed back the application until this afternoon, so there's no need for you to be in the office anytime soon."

"Thanks. I've got some errands to run this morning anyway." My eyes flashed to the fridge door where I unclasped Celia's list of clients. "You couldn't look up an address for me, could you?"

"Sure."

"Lottie's Ladle. It's a cafe." The line deadened. Silent. Not even her shallow breathing bristled through the earpiece. "You still there, Celia?"

"Just bringing the details up now, sir. How's Miss Laurent this morning?"

"Same as usual, thanks."

"Here we are. Lottie's Ladle. It's in Weiss Plaza. Do you need me to drop you a pin?"

"The plaza? I should be able to find it. It'll probably be after lunch by the time I make it in."

"Alright. I'll hold off the search party until then."

"Thanks, Celia."

"No problem, sir. See you this afternoon."

I pocketed my keys and lugged a fresh coffee to Gabby. She sat staring at the view from the terrace. Along the coast, the distant outline of New Yesterday shimmered, its silver buildings reflected in the lapping ocean tide, stretching for miles beyond the bay. The sun shone across the pool in a blinding beam of white light.

"Merci, mon amour."

I kissed her forehead and left her to bask on the reclined chair. It was her favourite spot when the sun bloomed, saturating her in gold, drawing her like a bee to pollen. Why she'd ever decided to take that ski holiday where we'd met, I'll never understand. Tiny wooden chalets. Hot chocolates and an open fire. Bumping skis on snow-capped mountains. *Has it really been two years?* It seemed like only yesterday.

"Oh. Adam. Send my best to Mrs. Campbell if you speak to her today. She's expecting us for an evening on that new yacht of hers next week."

"I will, darling."

As if the pictures weren't enough, Gabby had roped us into going to see the thing in person. Perfect. Just perfect.

I scurried down steps to the garage. The automatic door cranked open onto a bright courtyard as I climbed into Gabby's Porsche. It rumbled along the highway on its familiar route down the coast.

New Yesterday's tall towers loomed ahead. The ocean glittered on my right. Sunlight danced across the scrapers of the sky, glistening on glass. An exit ramp carried me towards a maze of high-rises, away from crashing waves and white beaches. Queued behind red lights, the engine calmed to a steady purr and I switched on the radio.

"What do you reckon? You think they gonna find him guilty or not?" DJ Delicia on Drivetime 107.

"I can't believe they adjourned the case yesterday."

"Mm-hmmm. It took them how many months to catch him?"

"What are we even paying the police for if it's gonna take them that long to track down some linear freak?"

"You gotta be some kind of crazy to want things back the way they used to be. That Houdini guy. Whatever the judge decides, he's—"

I flicked through the stations. *Is it too much to ask for a little music on the radio?*

The car growled in the gloom of the underground parking lot, reverberating between concrete pillars as I pulled into my usual space. Two beeps of the alarm faded and the elevator doors clanked shut. With the car stowed in the office garage, I left through the lobby. It was pointless driving through the one-way loop to Lottie's Ladle when I could walk the few blocks in half the time.

Strolling through New Yesterday during the day was like plugging myself into the socket.

It wasn't the movement of passing crowds that gave the city its frenetic energy — it was the sound. The hiss of steam from a vent. Fierce horns of cars in the grunt of traffic. A carousel of voices laughing, crying, shouting, whispering, anxious, and at ease. Music drifted from shop radios through the squeak of automatic doors. Footsteps and signals and whistles and hums and crashes and echoes and screams. Noise was the beating drum which gave the city its pace, its verve, and it was impossible to resist being swept up in it, even on the quietest street.

From the mass of people, a pale, wiry man bumped into me. "Watch where you're going."

"Sorry." *Wait. Why am I apologizing?*

The man pushed past me and carried on against the crowd. His bald head darted everywhere at once as he barged through the swarm. The crest of a tattoo crept above the collar of his sweatshirt, showing the top half of a word — a hashtag and three letters.

*#TNY.*

My eyes followed him, but he disappeared into the tide. I tried to stop and turn but a stream of bodies pulled me, keeping me in step with their frantic march.

*Forget about it. The further away from those Transparent New Yesterday punks you can get, the better.*

On the fringe of my jacket, the faintest streak of red remained where the bald man had made contact. A splash of paint.

Ahead, a commotion split the crowd.

"Just keep moving, folks. There's nothing to see here." Police barred access to the square.

Cramped shoulders squeezed me along with the thoroughfare where the line of officers waved us around. Over their shoulders, the square was empty. News drones hovered overhead.

*Don't make eye contact. Just keep your head down and walk. Whatever's happened, you don't need to know. You don't want to know.*

A sidestreet rushed me away from the jumble of people. Fancy restaurants and high-end stores splurged around Weiss Plaza. It was a playground for the pretentious. A bonfire for those with money to burn.

On the upper balcony, overlooking the stage of intricate cobbles that threatened to split the heels of designer shoes, a sign for Lottie's Ladle hung from a wrought-iron balustrade. It stood out too large and too proud, puffing its chest like all the others around it. It definitely looked like one of our clients.

Through the automatic sweep of double doors, the interior resembled an old kitchen with a hundred dining tables. A homely stove and solid wood counters stood pride of place behind the till, with tiled flooring that belonged in a black-and-white commercial from the 1950s. Boutique chic at its most upmarket.

"Welcome to Lottie's Ladle. Do you have a reservation?" The maître d' smiled, brushing off her apron.

"No. I'm not here for food."

"That's okay. I'll get you the drinks menu. Is it just you?"

"Well, yeah. But—"

"Great. Follow me."

Before I could object, she was guiding me to a single booth along the back wall where a checkered cloth covered the small table. She laid down the menu alongside a ladle with a number etched onto the handle.

"Someone will be right with you," she said.

"Actually, I just came to—" I began, but she'd already gone.

I slid into the booth and opened the menu. For the same amount they charged for a single shot of black filter coffee, I could've had a three course meal. *This has to be a typo. What are they using to make the coffee? Golden beans?*

At the end of the table, a fifties style box-TV with knobs on the front and two aerial prongs on its top played the channel 6 news. A bald man was being arrested. The guy who'd bumped into me earlier.

"Police have caught those responsible for the protest in New Yesterday's square," the anchor said.

An overhead shot showed buildings defaced in red spray paint. Across the floor, graffiti read, 'Do you really know what happened here? Truth is not something we can make for ourselves. #TNY.'

"The group responsible are imploring the authorities not to retrograde the area. They claim it's important that people see the damage and consider the message, but the disruption to the square makes that unlikely. From what we understand, retrograding is due to take place any minute now."

I checked my jacket. The red stain on its lapel. I brushed at the spray paint, but it clung to the fabric.

The apron of a waitress blocked the TV as she hovered over the table. "What can I get you?" the girl asked, pen and paper in hand.

"I want to speak to whoever's in charge."

She started writing on the pad before she'd realized what I'd said. *What was she ordering? One 'whoever's in charge' with no ice?* "Is there anything I can help you with?"

"This place is Lottie's Ladle, right?"

"That's right, sir."

"So I'm looking for whoever Lottie is."

She raised her eyebrow, her pen rushing over the paper. *What's she scribbling now? Loonie at table nine?*

"I'm from SSA," I said. "An accountant firm. Looking to speak to an old client."

"I see." The way she said it made me doubt it.

"If you can just get me a manager or the owner, I'm sure they'll understand."

"I'll see what I can do. Would you like anything while you wait?"

*At these prices?* "I'll take an americano." *There. See. I'm not a complete lunatic.*

"Right away." She disappeared to the kitchen and spoke in hushed whispers to the barista by the stove. His eyes shot towards me as he grabbed a mug and got to work bankrupting me with the hot sludge.

Onscreen, the news anchor touched their earpiece. "And we've just had word that retrograding will go ahead and the square is reopening."

The red mark on my jacket faded. Gone.

"And now, it's over to you, Denise, for a quick look at the weather."

The waitress clunked the mug down on the table. "One americano."

"Thanks."

"I've checked with the manager, but nobody remembers anyone called Lottie ever working here."

"What about the owner? Is she available to speak with me?"

"*He* is an old man who lives in Cleveland."

*He?* "But I thought . . . why call it Lottie's Ladle?"

"I think I remember hearing that he named it after his grandmother. Sold most of the business to shareholders a couple of years ago. Is there anything else I can get you?"

*How about a refund?* "No. I'm fine. Thanks."

She left me alone to wallow over the steaming mug.

There was no Lottie. Not here anyway. And if the cafe was no good, that only left a lingerie shop and a dog breeder on Celia's list. Not exactly my usual crowd. So why did I have this name in my head? Who was she?

The maître d' approached and left the bill. For everything there comes a time to pay.

I checked my watch on instinct, forgetting it was still broken.

One job down. One to go.

I left Weiss Plaza and skimmed the fringes of a few blocks, heading towards a park. Iron railings surrounded scruffy grass, littered with empty crisp packets and crumpled tins of lager.

On the corner, a rundown jewelers with cracked windows and a ripped fabric awning hunched into the street. The door skewed off its hinges, its panels boarded up by cheap plywood. Soon, the store would relocate inside the new 'Paradise Springs' mall, but not soon enough, by the looks of it.

The rickety door moaned as I pushed it open. A bell screeched to welcome me. Grime stained the mauve carpet in patches. Behind a glass counter, covered in metal bars, the owner flicked through a catalog. His greasy hair fell over his bearded face, onto the open collar of a putrid green patterned shirt.

"Morning." I ruffled up the collar of my jacket.

"Hey," he answered in a melancholic droll.

"I've got a problem with my watch."

"Yeah? That's too bad, man." He turned the page of his brochure as if I wasn't even in the room.

*Talk about customer service.* "I was wondering if you could do something about it?"

He looked up from the page. His vacant eyes peered through two slabs of thick glass encased in gold-rimmed spectacles. "Oh man, I don't know. I mean, it takes, like, a day to make repairs, and, you know, I don't know if we'll be here or not tomorrow, because of the new mall and everything. So, yeah. I don't know, man." His dim eyes returned to his catalog, his expression never changing from unalterable, open-mouthed disinterest.

"I have a receipt for my watch that says it's from here. It's under warranty."

"Look, if you wanna exchange it, that's fine by me, man."

From the thin page of his book, he reached up and thrust his open palm towards me. I loosened the strap and placed the watch in his sticky hand. He cast his eyes across its face and turned it over. Stamped on the back, a code of serial numbers and letters engraved the metal plate.

"Cool. Yeah, it's one of ours. Let me get the file." He glided from behind the counter through the curtain to his left, clattering as he raided piles of stock.

I stared around the dirty room to the half-empty cabinets and shuddered. Why would I have ever bought a watch from a decrepit cesspit like this?

After a few minutes, he returned with a piece of paper and two plastic cases, one of them bigger than the other. "Here you go, man. I found it." He dropped the two boxes on the counter and spread the paper next to them. "Sign here, please."

"Have you got a pen?" I asked.

"A pen?"

I nodded.

"We don't sell pens," he said.

"I don't want to buy one."

"Well, why are you asking for one?"

"You got any other ideas how I'm supposed to sign this for you?"

"Oh, right, yeah. A pen. I get it, man. Sure thing."

He disappeared again and I scanned the paper he'd left. It listed the watch as being an 'exchange,' and then on another line it said, 'Return of deposit in goods.' He reappeared brandishing a cheap plastic ballpoint without a lid.

"What's this, where it says about goods deposited?" I scrawled my name across the paper.

He tapped the smaller of the two boxes. "You traded this to cover the deposit, but, like, seeing as though you're swapping the watch, you might as well have your deposit back. I mean, I can't exactly keep it when the thing we sold you broke, can I? Wait a minute. Can I?"

"No, I see what you mean." Deposit? When did I make a deposit? "Are you sure you've got the right serial number? This is definitely *my* deposit?" I asked.

"Oh yeah, man. Totally."

*I should tell him there's been some mistake.* He sniffed and wiped his nose on the back of his hand, his dull eyes fixed somewhere between me and the counter. His blank face never moved, stuck like a wax mold. *Arguing with this guy is like swimming in glue. It won't get me anywhere.*

I shrugged. "As long as you're sure?"

"Okay, man. You can set the time and then we'll see how this new watch fits."

He opened the larger of the two boxes. I fastened the strap around my wrist, where it hung loose. He stood idly while I set the time on my wrist with the TV on the wall behind him. Its cracked screen filtered endless commercials, but displayed the time in block numbers over the picture. The commercial ended and a face filled the screen.

I staggered backwards.

"Hold up, man. I think it needs some links removed," he said.

"Can you . . . can you turn that up?" I pointed to the TV.

"Sure thing. Do you wanna fill in your address and stuff where you've signed? Just for the records." He fiddled with a remote and the volume increased.

". . . can rest easy, as a sentence has finally been passed today on the man known as The City's Houdini. Judges found him guilty on five counts of linear infraction. He'll be held in New Yesterday's penitentiary for retrotherapy until he can be transferred to a maximum security facility out of the city."

"You remember that guy, huh?" the jeweler said.

Houdini's features enveloped the monitor. *That face.* It rippled across my mind. *Warped in the panel of an elevator's mirror. His sneer as he held a gun to my head. The foul odor of his breath.*

*He wanted something. A piece of paper.*

Lottie.

*Is that how I knew her name? Was it connected to Houdini?*

The jeweler tinkered with the strap while I scribbled the address on the invoice. 238 Ocean Boulevard, New Yesterday.

*No. It wasn't possible. They couldn't be connected. I'd never seen the guy before, except in bulletins.*

"There. How's that fit?"

"Much better." I turned to walk away.

"What about your other stuff, man?" He pushed the smaller jewelry box towards me. *If taking it meant I could get out of this fecal-infested slime pit without another conversation, what else was I to do?* I scooped it into my pocket.

"Thanks," I said.

"Hey. You look like you saw a ghost, man. Are you okay?"

*My mind is coming apart at the seams, and he asks me if I'm okay?* "I'm fine."

His head drooped and he returned to his catalog. I pushed the door and ran into the street.

*These flashes. They can't be real. Why can't I shake them?*

I had to know who she was.

Maybe *he* knew. Houdini.

The city penitentiary. It wasn't too much of a detour on my way home. *Am I seriously considering going to see a convicted felon all because of a few mismatched memories of something that might never have happened in the first place?*

*You need help, Adam.*

I dialed Gabrielle's number. Straight to voicemail. Same with the landline.

Who could I talk to? Not Jeff. What would he think of me?

Celia.

*Celia will know what to do.*

I headed back through the square towards the office.

A quick glance at my watch.

*I'll talk to Celia. Perhaps she can get this straightened out?*

# EIGHT

CELIA SHUFFLED INTO the office. "You asked to see me, Mr. Swann?"

"Close the door behind you, Celia."

She pushed it shut, carrying her usual assortment of clipboards and folders. "Everything's arranged with the planning committee."

"Good. I'll be glad when this is over."

"Sir?"

"The mall."

Her fingers twitched at the edge of her files. "Is that why you asked to see me?"

"Not exactly. Take a seat." I pointed to the chair across from me.

She didn't move. "Did I do something wrong?"

"What?"

"Summoning me in here. Asking me to sit down. I'm getting fired, aren't I?"

"Fired? Don't be ridiculous! I need your . . ." My mouth dried out, desolate as a desert. I cleared my throat and glanced over my shoulder. ". . . I need your help."

She shuffled on her heels. "Is it to do with the errands you ran this morning?"

"I guess."

"Something you need me to sort?"

"No. I just went to replace my watch. That's all."

"I could've done that for you."

"Don't be daft. I wouldn't ask you to do something so menial. It's a waste of your talents."

Her cheeks flushed ruby. "Thank you."

"Besides, it wasn't too far out of my way. A foul store downtown. Why I'd ever buy anything from a disgusting place like that, I've no idea."

"You don't remember buying it?"

"Come to think of it, no."

"If the shop was so horrible, perhaps it's best you don't remember?"

"You're probably right. There's a lot I seem to be forgetting lately."

Her skittish eyes ran over the room. "Like what?"

"Like . . ." *Enough small talk. Just spit it out. Focus on what you came here to do.* ". . . Do you know anyone called Lottie?"

She shook her head. "Is this about that client you were tracking down?"

"I'm not sure they're a client. I'm not sure about anything right now."

"Are you okay, sir? You don't look so good."

I perched forwards. "Do you remember that Houdini guy the police caught the other week?"

"Why'd you ask?"

"It's hard to explain." *Why is this so difficult?* "Don't you ever feel like . . . like there's something missing?"

She stiffened. "What do you mean?"

I swallowed. *Tell her. Let her talk some sense into you, before you do something stupid.* "Have you—"

My monitor chimed. Her phone buzzed, cutting through the room like a rotary-saw.

"The planners," I said.

"I've just received the email too."

"Let's have the approval documents. We'd better get this signed off."

She pushed the relevant paperwork in front of me and I scrawled my signature on the dotted line. She slipped the papers into a thin transparent film, which she sealed and bound inside the folder. It'd be the only record with the real date when 'Paradise Springs' opened, protected in a laminate sleeve from external alterations.

I pushed my chair back for a view out the window. There it was. *The mall.* The familiar spinning board with the 'Paradise Springs' logo towered high above the park. Ever since I'd started here seven years ago, it had been spinning like that.

"Where were we?" I asked.

"You were saying about a woman. And the Houdini guy?"

"Right."

Celia stared at her shoes. "Can I ask you a question, sir?"

"Anything."

She scooped up the binders. "This Lottie you keep asking about. Why's she so important to you?"

*Simple. Because I can't stop thinking about her and it's driving me out of my mind.* "It's complicated."

"Does Miss Laurent know about her?"

"I haven't mentioned it."

"It's just—" She picked at her nails. "I hope you don't take this the wrong way, but it's not like you to go chasing after women."

"Celia!"

"I'm sorry, but you don't seem like yourself." She froze, rooted to the carpet. Naturally timid, Celia shuffled constantly. But not now.

*What was going on with her?* "Anything else you want to get off your chest?"

She bit her lip. "It's alright, sir. I shouldn't hold you up from getting back to Miss Laurent."

"I'm always here if you need to talk."

"I did want to talk to you about something," she said.

"Go on."

"It's . . . I wanted to tell you . . . well, the thing is . . ."

"It's alright. You can tell me."

She drew her breath.

The door swept open, startling her into silence. The office's symphony of tapping keys and muffled voices flooded the room.

Jeff stood in the doorway, decanter in hand. "Fancy a drink before you shove off?" he said.

Celia glanced at me. "Will that be all, sir?"

"Not interrupting anything, am I?" Jeff bumbled into the office.

Celia shook her head. "It's nothing, Mr. Sinclair." She turned to me and muttered beneath her breath, "It can wait. I'd best get this arranged for filing." Her heels padded on the carpet as she shrunk away, carrying the documents with her.

"Strange one, that girl of yours," Jeff said. "If I were you, I'd be on the lookout for a prettier secretary."

"What did you want, Jeff?"

"I need a drinking buddy, if you think you can manage it?"

"I've got stuff to do."

"Like what?"

*Visit a felon in prison? Succumb to madness? Make the absolute worst decision possible because of half-baked fragments of a forgotten life?* "I want to get back to Gabby."

"I see. Did she enjoy the gala last night?"

"As much as she always does. I think after two years, she's used to them by now."

"Yeah, I know what you mean. The clients seemed to have a good time though, thanks to you."

"What did I do?"

"You let us invade your house."

"Let's just say, you owe me one." I walked him out.

"Deal. Are you sure you can't even manage a snifter? Drinking alone is so depressing."

"I'll take a rain check. Thanks all the same."

"Your loss. Send my best to the old ball and chain."

He disappeared into the boardroom. The elevator conveyed me to the parking lot, and I sat behind the wheel of the Porsche.

*Just go home, Adam. Go back to Gabby and forget all this.*

The engine stirred and I pulled away, joining the queue of one-way traffic.

*You don't need to do anything rash.*

The buildings passed in a silver haze.

*Just don't think about it. Lottie. Houdini. What does it matter?*

Shadows shifted beneath the skyline.

*Get home and pour yourself a drink and you can figure this out later.*

My hands worked the gears on instinct, merging with the inner ring road.

*What would you even expect to find by talking to him, anyway?*

Over speed bumps and backstreets, the alloys pulled me until they finally rolled to a stop. I switched off the engine and looked up at the sign. New Yesterday Penitentiary Visitors Parking.

*Don't do it, Adam. Don't get out of the car.*

Houdini's face taunted my memory. I had to see him. How else was I going to get rid of this gnawing agony?

*Maybe I should try retrograding Lottie out of my head? Uproot whatever this feeling is. Erase the woman's name from my mind.* But why should I? Why should I get rid of something just because I didn't like it?

Was this how life was supposed to feel? Like a jigsaw with only three corner pieces and no matter how nice the picture I built, there'd always be something missing?

I crunched across the gravel to a huge entrance. Dirty gray concrete rose like the wave of a tsunami. Gigantic panels swept open. The biggest door I'd ever walked through.

Beyond the entrance, a guard blocked the way. A pistol hung from his belt, the same color as his bulky Kevlar pads. Even his mustache grimaced as I approached the metal detectors, arching over the lobby like airport security on steroids.

"Put your loose items in the tray and step through." His jaw clamped on a stump of gum.

I emptied my pockets into a silver bowl and placed it on the conveyor. The guard pulled a screen from his pocket and watched the scan of my valuables pass through the box.

He waved me through the detector. "You got an appointment?"

"No."

"Name?"

"Adam Swann."

"ID?"

"It's in my wallet."

"Who you here to see?"

"I don't know his name. The papers call him Houdini."

"The linear guy?" He scowled behind his aviator sunglasses as he clicked the walkie-talkie strapped to his chest. "We've got an unscheduled visitor. Wants to see our newest arrival. Over."

He waited for a reply, nodding to the tray as it appeared at my side. The only sound was the iron of his jaw grinding on gum. I scooped my things into my pockets. The walkie crackled, followed by an indistinct mumble.

"Roger that," the guard said. "Out." He stared at me. "Let me see that ID."

I offered him my license and his head bobbed from the plastic card to my face and back again. Reflected in his shades, my body cowered.

He swiped his keycard on a pad and unlocked the door behind him. "Just keep walking. You can't get lost."

I hurried past him, beyond the partition, through the bends of a spacious corridor. Grubby tiles peeled from the walls. At its far end, bars caged off the next hallway.

Another guard waited, clanging his keys on the latch as he wrestled with the leash of a German Shepherd. The door creaked as it swung open. The dog's teeth flashed and its snarling bark reverberated from the bars. I edged towards the guard as the animal lurched, threatening to snap its chain.

"Don't worry. He won't bite unless provoked."

*Is that supposed to be reassuring?*

Its nose toured my crotch and shoes before it returned to the guard's side, panting, tongue out, tail thrashing back and forth.

"You're fine," he said. "Keep moving."

I passed into a different corridor. Smaller than the first. Shrinking. Closing in. Thick slabs of concrete constricted around me. *I shouldn't be here. I'm not a criminal. So why does being here make me feel like one?*

A cage of metal bars blocked the end of the narrow hallway. The uniformed officer beyond holstered a pistol on each hip.

Guns everywhere. More guns than people.

"Name?" the officer said.

"Adam Swann."

"Who you here for?"

"I only know him as Houdini."

"Oh. Him. Why d'ya wanna see him?"

Wasn't interrogation supposed to be reserved for the prisoners? "I've got some questions I need answering."

"What questions?"

My chest erupted. There were no windows. No light. Just the squalid glare of dim bulbs stretched along the ceiling. Who knew I was here? Nobody. "It's personal," I said.

He nodded and brandished a chain of keys, tumbling through the dozen that jangled on the metal loop before settling on one.

I stepped inside and he locked the door, trapping me in his cage.

My world had narrowed to this. This box. This cell. Chasing down Lottie had put me here. Sealed in by the intimidating clang of metal on metal.

The guard took my elbow and escorted me around the corner. Four chairs rested on this side of the glass, partitioned off from one another. A cord ran to a handset.

"You pick up the phone when you want to speak," the guard said.

"Thanks."

He left me in the booth, staring through glass to the murky room beyond. The taste of sweat laced the air. Minutes ticked by in silence. *Is it too late to leave?*

A light flashed and a figure slumped into the chair opposite. They'd bound his hands in cuffs, and he wore a torn orange overall. His bruised arms flexed and his lip bled from an open wound. That face. I'd seen it so many times on TV. But never like this.

A jagged stab wrenched my back as I felt the chamber of his pistol bruising my spine. But I'd never met him until this moment. Had I?

I yanked at the telephone and he did the same, pressing it to his ear.

"Who are you?" he said.

"You don't remember me?"

He shrugged. "Should I?"

The glass shielded him from me, like the clear walls of Anderson Whitman's office. *The salesman. A tablet on his knee. The swipe of his screen.*

"Do you know why you're locked up?"

"Retrotherapy. They tell me it does wonders." His face twitched as he peered closer. "So what do you want?"

Did he seriously not remember? "Where were you yesterday?"

"Is that supposed to be a joke?"

"No. It's just — can you remember where you were?"

"You saw the trial, didn't you?"

"Yeah, but is that the *only* place you were?"

He scowled at me and shook his head, yet his eyelid flickered in a strange spasm. "Is this another test? I'm not playing these games anymore." He moved the phone away from his ear.

"Wait!" I reached for the glass. "Please. This isn't a game. I swear."

He paused, his eyes searching mine like a predator scanning for weaknesses. "Alright. Talk."

"You ever heard of SSA?"

His head shook.

"It's a firm of accountants."

He laughed. "What do I need an accountant for?"

How could he not remember? These flashes. They were real, weren't they? "We manage businesses in the city."

At the sound of *businesses*, he shuffled in his seat. "Go on."

"I help run the firm. Got my office on the 27th floor."

He squinted hard. "What does any of this have to do with me?"

Maybe we'd really never met. Maybe these flashes were the onset of some brain disease and what I needed was an MRI. "You've never been there?"

"Why would I have—" He jerked forwards, dropping the phone. He clutched his head as though someone jabbed a knife through it. His fist slammed on the glass. He mouthed something over and over, but the phone was too far for me to hear. It looked like he was saying 'get out of my head.'

Then he stiffened straight in his chair. The wave had passed. He picked up the phone as calm as anything. "Sorry, what were you saying?"

"Are you alright?"

He shrugged. "Why wouldn't I be?"

"You just had a . . . what happened?"

"Retrotherapy. Part of my treatment. Happens when I remember something I shouldn't."

"And what did you remember?"

"I don't know. What were we talking about?"

"My office. SSA."

"Sorry. I don't have a clue what you mean. What's SSA?"

"It's my firm of accountants."

He laughed. "What do I need an accountant for?"

Open-mouthed, I stared at him, unable to speak. This was going nowhere.

"Look," he said, "it's not like I've got anything better to do. But if that's all, then are we done here?"

"Listen. I . . . the reason I came here . . . came to see you—"

"Spit it out."

I drew a deep breath. "Have you ever had flashes of something you don't remember happening, but it feels real?"

He looked over his shoulder. "What are you trying to pull? I'm going straight. You hear? I don't want to end up a gibbering mess. I've seen what happens to these linear guys. I'm not crazy. Do you understand?"

"I don't think you're crazy."

"Then what do you want?"

"I just want to know what you remember about a name."

"What name?"

"Lottie."

He bit his lip, shaking his head. "You came to see me just so you could ask me about a girl?"

"Do you know her?"

"Sorry. I got nothing. Who is she?"

"I wish I knew."

"Look, if I knew a Lottie, I'd tell you. But I don't. What's the last thing you remember about her?"

"That's the thing. I can't be sure. One minute I'm in an Anderson Whitman office with a gun pressed to my head, and the next—"

His eyes widened. A storm broke across his face as the handset clattered on the glass, swinging from its cord. He threw himself from his chair. Writhing on the floor, his body convulsed. His features twisted into a picture of seething hate. He lifted himself to his knees, clawing at the barrier between us. "It's *YOU*!" he screamed, though all I heard was the faintest whisper through the earpiece. His muscles snapped, the shackles of his memory torn apart. "You took everything, Adam. I'm coming for you. You hear me?"

"You remember!" *I wasn't crazy.* "Who's Lottie? Tell me."

"You won't get away with this!" He spat the words like venom. He couldn't hear a thing through the glass that separated us as he shook in a frenzy.

"*Lottie.* Who. Is. Lottie?"

"What?"

I pointed to the handset but his body thrashed so hard, it stopped him from reaching.

"Who is she?" I yelled. "I *know* you know something."

"Lottie?"

"Yes. Tell me!"

"I already did. I never heard of her."

"No. That can't be." I fell back into my chair and the phone dropped into my lap.

"You're pathetic, Adam. You took my life. You took it from me and you'll pay for it. I swear. I'll make you p—"

Two guards rushed in and dragged him away. His face disappeared, and my own reflection stared back at me from the glass.

\*\*\*

The drive home passed me by like a dream that fades into nothing. I stumbled up the stairs into the empty kitchen, still trying to process what had happened.

"Honey? Gabby? Are you there?"

No answer.

On the fridge, a yellow note hung.

*Taken the Mercedes into town. Found my phone in the bottom of the pool. Ruined my afternoon swim. Gone to pick up a new one. Home soon, mon amour, G xxx*

My jacket slithered off my arm and I tossed it on the kitchen bar. I twisted the cap on a bottle of wine, letting its heady perfume percolate my nostrils. Its rich fragrance cleared my busy head as I filled two glasses, ready for Gabby's return.

*I never heard of her,* Houdini had said. I could try to visit him again. Find out what made him snap. But with his retrotherapy, by the time I got through to him, he'd probably have no idea who I was. It'd be the same all over again.

*Who is this woman? Am I ever going to be free of this cage?*

*Deep breaths, Adam.*

I closed my eyes and waited alone. The quietness dulled everything.

*Lottie. Whoever you are, whatever it meant, I wasn't crazy.*

I wasn't crazy.

The shrill chirp of the landline shot a tremor across my skin. Hung on the wall beside the oven, it flashed with an unknown number. "Hello?"

"May I speak to Gabrielle Laurent?" It was a man's voice, blunt and throaty. He sounded like the stub of a cigar.

"Who's calling?"

"Never mind that. Is she there or not?"

"Tell me who's asking and I'll tell you if she's here."

"Listen pal. I've been trying to get hold of her all day. Her phone's not working and I've finally tracked her down to this number. I've got no patience left for chit chat. Understand? So you tell me — is she there or is she not?"

*What could I say to that?* "I . . . er . . . I can take a message for her."

An exasperated sigh stifled the beginnings of an outburst as the gruff voice muttered unintelligible threats beneath his shallow breath.

"Are you still there?" I asked.

"You'll give her a message, will you, kid?"

"Sure."

"Fine. You tell her the editor of the Daily Post is calling about her story. She knows the number."

"I will."

The line cut out. What on earth would a newspaper reporter want with Gabrielle?

## NINE

I ALMOST FORGOT to tell you, there was a message for you today." I rested the empty noodle-box on the carpet.

"Really?" Gabrielle shifted her feet, nestled by the fire.

"Yeah, it was so weird — some guy from a newspaper. Said he was the editor of the Daily Post, I think."

Red wine slipped down her throat. She scooped up a deep tub of half-melted ice cream. "What did he want?"

"He was calling about your story, apparently, and said you knew the number."

She licked her spoon indulgently and held a fresh dollop of ice cream in front of my face, pushing white chunks of frozen sweetness into my mouth. "How good is this? Non?"

"With Chinese food? It's gross."

"More for me."

"Do you know what it's about?"

"The editor?" She shook her head. "He'll just want an advance copy of 'Remembering Guinevere' so they can be the first to print a review, or an exclusive excerpt or interview or something."

"You don't think it's anything to worry about?"

She tapped at her phone and showed me the screen. "No missed calls. See. If he wants me, he'll ring back."

Her eyes rolled as she took another mouthful of desert and drained the last of her wine. We watched the fire fade together. Her warm body nuzzled into mine. The flames dimmed to crackling ash and the ice cream melted into a liquid slop. Her eyes closed and her breathing steadied, shallow and constant.

I carried her up the stairs. She stirred only enough to tighten her hands around my neck, and I laid her on our bed, pulling the duvet over us. I closed my eyes, swallowed by a pit of uncertainty. Trapped with this niggling feeling that I was missing something. And sleep refused to pull me from the hole I'd tumbled into.

Retrograding was supposed to fill the void, not open one. There had to be a way of pinpointing the precise moment things had changed — the exact alteration that robbed me of whatever peace of mind I used to have. But that's the problem with forgetting the past, replacing it with each new history the city throws out — how do I know what's stayed the same and what's different? What's stuck and what's gone?

Lottie. She was stuck. There'd be no getting rid of her. No bumping her off to the back of my head to fade into the night. In the theater of my mind, her name was up in lights. And every time she took center stage, my stomach wrenched as though someone had rammed a crowbar through my insides. It was a pang that only fear can induce.

I wish I knew what I was so scared of.

Before dawn peeped through the curtains, Gabby slipped out from the covers to her study. When I finally clambered out of bed to start on breakfast, the clunking of her typewriter drifted through the glow behind her office door.

Downstairs, I piled the sticky tub of ice cream on top of the leftover boxes and cartons, knocking my jacket from where it had been resting on the counter. A thud reverberated across the tiles as it hit the floor.

From the pocket, I pulled out a black, plastic box.

Rolling it in my fingers sparked a memory. *A rundown jewelers and an absentminded man in gold-rimmed spectacles. A broken watch. Signing my name. Returning my deposit.*

Was that really yesterday? *No. It couldn't have been.* There was nothing on that street except the corner of 'Paradise Springs', and it had been that way for years. *Maybe I'd just misremembered? Or dreamt it?*

While the kettle bubbled and the grill heated, I perched on the barstool and yawned, examining the hard case.

The clasp popped open. Inside, silken folds held a silver band. It was plain enough, and thick, with scratches of wear the only distinct mark on the ring itself. I plucked it from its slot. Engraved within the band were the letters 'A&C xoxo' in an elaborate and decorative style.

Instinctively, I slid it on my left hand. It slipped into place, fitting perfectly in grooves I'd never noticed before. With my thumb, I twiddled the ring around and around in a familiar motion.

The sensation.

I remembered it.

*I used to rub my thumb across this ring. Fumble with it when I was nervous, when I was in the doghouse for something, or when I had a surprise I wanted to keep from her.*

*It felt so weird when she'd slipped it onto my finger for the first time. Her face, those blue eyes and her pale skin, her brown hair held up in bejeweled clasps shaped like petals. I was so conscious of it those first few weeks — a weight on my hand, catching me out when I forgot I was wearing it.*

*How long did it take before I stopped noticing the ring on my finger altogether? Every so often, I tinkered with it. The scratch on its polished surface, where I'd caught the cupboard door in our tiny flat.*

*Her face was as clear as day, those high cheeks, soft skin, and lips as gentle as a summer breeze.*

*We'd engraved it with our names.*

*Mine, Adam.*

*And hers, Charlotte.*

*A&C xoxo.*

*My Lottie.*

The kettle clicked, snapping me out of my reminiscence. Steam shot from its spout, and the oven grill glowed red.

*Lottie.*

Of course.

How could I have forgotten?

Her face blazed across my mind. I stood at the counter, my hands still, for how long?

Blinking the memory away, I spread the bacon on foil and placed it under the grill, pouring water into the cafetiere. The bitter smell of beans spurted up as I plunged the handle down.

I rubbed at the ring.

*My wedding ring.*

The aftertaste of recollection soured my mind. It was like a layer of glue had peeled off and I could scrape the pages of my past just far enough to peek at what lay hidden beneath. But I couldn't read the words.

From behind me, the faint patter of Gabby's footsteps echoed.

"Bonjour chérie," I said.

She didn't respond. Her wide eyes fixed on where I stood as she crept around me, keeping her distance. In a flash, she pulled open a drawer and grabbed hold of a knife.

"Okay, don't move," she said.

"Gabby, what's wrong?"

"How do you know my name?" She backed away from me, the knife trembling in her hands.

"Gabby. It's me. What's got into you, dear?"

She shook her head. "Don't call me Gabby. Nobody calls me that."

"I've made you some coffee." I reached for the cafetière.

"I said, don't move!"

"Alright. I won't move if you don't want me to."

Her whole body was on edge. "Who are you?"

"Don't you know? It's me. It's Adam."

She looked at me as though I was a stranger. "How do you know me?"

"Are you kidding? We've been living together for two years. We woke up in the same bed ten minutes ago."

"You're lying!"

"You want me to prove it to you? Alright. You like the taste of noodles and ice cream. You do your writing on a typewriter rather than a laptop because you say your fingers feel like they're doing a Fred and Ginger tap dance. Your newest book is called 'Remembering Guinevere.' Shall I go on?"

"How do you — have you been stalking me?"

"Sure. Ever since we met. On that mountainside in the Alps. Our skis collided and you sent me tumbling. You remember? The snow? The chalet?"

"Now I know you're lying. I've never been to Switzerland."

*Is this a candid camera thing?* "Never been to Switzerland? Don't be ridiculous. What kind of game is this, Gabby?"

"You heard what I said." The knife quivered in her hands.

"Okay. Alright. You've never been to Switzerland. But what about the night I asked you to move in with me? Or those two weeks we spent in the Canaries? All the gala balls I've dragged you to over the years? Come on, Gabby. Joke's over. Whatever I've done, I'm sorry, okay? The coffee's getting cold."

Her head kept shaking. Her unblinking eyes darted everywhere at once. "Are you alone?"

*This isn't funny anymore.* "Do you feel unwell, darling?"

"Answer my question!"

"Yes, we're alone."

"How did you get in the house?"

"I came in from work through the garage last night."

"Through the garage?"

"Like always."

"Don't speak," she said.

"But—"

"*Don't speak!*"

From the garage below, footsteps tapped one and then another. Her tremble grew as each step croaked louder and louder. The handle twisted. Tears filled her eyes as the door swung open.

"Gabrielle, it's only me. I've got spectacular news." Jeff stepped in, facing the two of us, startled at the sight.

The knife clattered on the floor. Gabrielle's feet slapped the tiles as long strides took her to where he stood. She threw her arms around his neck and sobbed into his jacket.

"What's going on? Who's this?" He patted her blonde hair with his skinny, olive hands.

"I don't know. I came downstairs and he was making breakfast."

The tray of bacon beneath the grill churned out smoke and the searing vapor of burning flesh filled the room.

"Listen, Jeff," I said, "I don't—"

"How do you know my name?" He staggered back, stunned, like I'd just walloped him with a sledgehammer.

"Jeff, it's me. Adam."

"Am I supposed to know you?" he said.

"Shall we call the police?" Gabrielle whispered.

Jeff held her tight to his body. "You're safe now. I won't let him hurt you."

"Hurt her?" My eyes bulged. "The police? Okay. Okay, you got me. Very funny, guys. Can we please give it a rest?"

Jeff tightened his grip on the brown paper bag he carried, shaped like a bottle.

I nodded at the bag. "I think you'd better pour me some of that port, old friend. I need it more than you this morning."

"Port?" He stared at the concealed bottle. "How did you know this was port?" Round two with the sledgehammer.

"You came here for a drink, didn't you? It's not too early is it? What is it you always say? 'The privilege of middle age.' Remember?"

His eyes scrutinized me as he pushed Gabby from him, still shaking from head to toe. "You go upstairs. I'll call the police and look after this gentleman until they arrive."

Apprehensive, she drew away, bounded up the stairs and disappeared. I switched the grill off and left the bacon to char, took two glasses out of the cupboard and placed them between us. He unscrewed the bottle and distilled his red intoxication into them.

"You can start by telling me who you are," he said.

"Now that she's gone, you can drop the act, Jeff."

He sat silent.

I stared back. "You really don't know?"

He slid a full glass in front of me. "You got a name?"

"Adam."

"Adam who?"

"Are you serious?"

He put on his sternest boardroom poker face. "You've got one chance to give me a straight answer. You blow it, I call the cops. Understand?"

I nodded.

"The only reason I haven't called them already is because of *this*." He raised his glass towards me. "The privilege of middle age. It bought you one shot. Don't waste it, kid."

"My name's Adam Swann."

"And who exactly is Adam Swann supposed to be?"

"Your business partner."

"Business *what*?"

"Swann Sinclair Accounts ring any bells? We've been partners for seven years."

He drilled his fingers on the side of his glass. "And what about Gabrielle? How did you get into her house?"

"She moved in with me two years ago. This is *my* house, Jeff. So will somebody please tell me what's going on?"

He downed the port and shook his head. "Listen, friend, as far as I'm concerned, we've never met. Gabrielle's a client who's just signed a major book deal. I came here to celebrate with her, and that's all."

"Nice try," I said. "Do you know any other funny ones?"

His grimace hardened. *There's no punchline. This is real.*

As my gut churned, it was my turn to knock the port back. Liquid fire scorched my throat and seared the jitters rushing through my stomach. "Listen. I don't know what's happened, Jeff, but you've got to help me."

He spun the glass in his hands. "How about another drink?"

"Is that all you can think of? Jeff, you've got to think of something. Gabby could've killed me just now. I'm an intruder in my own house. What's happening?"

"Your guess is as good as mine."

"How can you not know me, after everything we've been through?"

"Hand on heart. Never seen you in my life."

"But . . . how is that possible?"

"You think I've got answers? I'm as confused as you are by all this." He gripped the bottle in his fist and refilled his glass.

"My life can't have just disappeared," I said. "It just *can't*. I woke up this morning next to Gabby. Business was great. I can't have just woken up and lost all that."

He shrugged his shoulders. "This is New Yesterday. It can happen."

"Things change. Sure. But nobody *disappears*. Not without a reason."

"So what did you do?"

I shook my head. "What did I do? I put the grill on and made coffee, just like every morning."

He polished off his second glass. "You said your name's Adam?"

"Yeah."

"Okay. Adam. If what you're saying about me and Gabrielle and all the rest of it is true, then Anderson Whitman might be able to clear this up."

"Go on."

"All you need to do is prove that you are who you *say* you are, and this'll all get straightened out. 'Your past is what you make it.' Isn't that their tagline? So I'm sure they can make it what it was before, maybe even better."

"Yeah. Yeah, that's good, Jeff."

"But you'll need something solid. I mean, you can't just walk into Anderson Whitman and demand they give you your life back, unless you can show them it was yours to begin with."

"Proof. You're right. I can get proof, enough for them to take me seriously."

He dipped his head. "Look. I don't know you, but it's obvious you know me. If we really are — were — partners, friends, then here, you'd better take this." He opened his wallet and plucked all the cash he had.

I shook my head, but he insisted, pressing it into my hands.

"I'll pay you back when I sort this out," I said.

"If I had a dime for every time I heard that." He smiled. "You'd better go. I'll give you a minute before I go upstairs to Gabby and make the call to the police."

"She hates being called Gabby."

"Don't I know it."

I grasped his arm and squeezed. "Thanks, old friend." I picked up the jacket from the table, threw it over the clothes I'd slept in last night and turned back to him. "Are you gonna tell the cops about what I said?"

"About what?"

"My different past."

"About you going linear, you mean?"

"Going linear? Come on, it's not as bad as all that."

"How else would you describe it?"

I chewed on my lip. "Are you gonna tell them?"

He looked at the floor and sighed. "I have to."

"Can't you . . .?"

"I'm sorry. I don't have a choice."

There wasn't time to argue with him, or plead. If the cops thought I was guilty of a linear offense, I needed every second I could get.

From my inside pocket I grabbed the keys, bounded down the garage stairs, jumped into Gabby's Porsche and sped towards New Yesterday.

On the other side of the road, rushing towards the house, the blue and red flashes of police sirens wailed. Jeff was making the call. By the time he hung up, they'd already be at the door, chasing me down.

My foot pressed on the accelerator, my thumb grazed over the silver ring on my finger. I kept tight hold of the steering wheel. The city loomed larger as I drew closer.

*All I needed was proof.* That's what he said. But what proof?

## TEN

THE FIRST STREAKS OF RAIN FELL on the windshield, brushed away by squeaking wipers. I was no different. Wiped away. A raindrop on glass.

Traffic lights halted me at every junction as the car inched through the busy suburb, each delay increasing the danger. The police would've taken my description from Jeff by now. They'd start arranging for CCTV to be retrofitted, installed in the house a few months ago. At any moment, my picture could have been on the news for the past week, making my face the most famous in New Yesterday.

I had no choice but to hurry while there was still time. While I still remembered who Gabrielle was and Jeff hadn't turned into some random port-wielding mystery man. They might've lost the last seven years — but not me. Not yet. There had to be a trace of it hiding somewhere that I could bring to Anderson Whitman.

Into the parking lot, the screech of tires cascaded between concrete pillars.

SSA. If some clue, some proof of my life still existed, it'd be lurking here. Besides, Celia would know what to do, whether she remembered me or not.

The elevator doors thrummed to floor twenty-seven and opened onto the usual melee.

A swarm of bodies rushed past me in all directions conveying papers through the office. On the wall behind the circular reception desk, the stylised letters SSA had been replaced by the word SINCLAIR'S and the girls who sat in front of it mouthed "Sinclair's Accounts. How can I help?" into their headsets as if it were as natural as breathing.

With the receptionists engrossed in their calls, no one looked up from what they were doing to pay me any attention. In the hive, I was invisible. Through a claustrophobic jumble of activity, I scurried through corridors unseen. A few paces separated me from my office, the third door on the right. But the door was gone.

In its place, a felt-covered partition screened off desks belonging to private secretaries, unoccupied for the most part. I entered with my head down. Plaques on the front of rosewood desks displayed unfamiliar names until I found the one I was looking for. Celia Burnett. But her chair was empty.

Reams of paper piled on the desk, alongside her keyboard and computer screen. That was everything. No token to clear my name, nothing leftover from my past.

In the secretary's den, the constant murmur of fingers clacked over keys, deleting mistypes on their screens without a second thought. Every punch of their keyboard jarred at my ribs. What was I, but a deleted mistype? Nothing more than a spelling error, a stray letter auto-corrected out of existence. Any vestige of me left in the company I'd built was long gone.

The secretaries never uttered a sound, but their silence was louder than sirens. Their discomfort stifled the air, turning it heavy and thick. The hairs on my neck quivered.

I hunched over, trying to make myself innocuous enough not to warrant their attention. But the more I shriveled, the sharper the pangs of my nerves tormented me, until a whisper brought the words I dreaded across the quietness of the room.

"Excuse me. Can I help you?"

A stocky man in a shirt and tie barred the aisle between desks. Aiden, but some of the underlings called him Bulldog.

"I've got everything I need, thank you." I slipped the top piece of paper from one of the piles on Celia's desk, making it look like I'd come in for something.

Bulldog's steely gray eyes searched every detail of my features, sniffing me out. From the confusion on his face, I was still a stranger. For now. "Can I ask what you intend to do with that document?" The chill in his voice matched the climate of the room, turned cold by his scrupulous stare.

"Sorry, I don't think we've met. I'm the new errand boy. Mr. Sinclair wanted me to fetch him the . . . er . . ." I glanced down at the title running along the top of the page. ". . . Schedule for planning applications. He's been delayed and sent me ahead to make a copy for him." My hand extended to shake Bulldog's in introduction.

He didn't budge. "Nobody told me about a new errand boy." His broad arms folded across his chest. What I'd described was classic Jeff. But that didn't change the fact I was a random man poking around the office.

"Look, if you want to explain to Mr. Sinclair why I got held up, be my guest," I said. "I'm sure he'd love to go through it with you bit-by-bit, in every detail, so he knows exactly who to blame." I shrugged, hoping he'd not noticed the sweat beading on my forehead.

Bulldog clenched for a moment, before unfolding his arms. "Alright," he said. "We wouldn't want to hold up Mr. Sinclair, would we? You know where the copy machine is?"

"I'm sure I'll find it."

"Kirsty," he barked, through gritted teeth. One of the secretaries shot up from her papers. "Will you show this gentleman to the copying machine?" He moved aside and she took his place.

"Follow me." She looked me over and waddled towards the boisterous reception, flicking her short red hair imperiously over her shoulder. A few feet from the elevator, she stopped and opened a door.

A dizzying haze of fluorescence escaped the tiny space, more like a cupboard than a room. A giant copier stood guard. She beckoned me inside while she remained in the corridor, pretending not to watch me.

I lifted the hood. The page I'd taken from Celia's desk pressed face-down on the glass screen. My fingers tapped at buttons until the thing breathed life, flashed white beams, and spat out ten copies all at once. It would have spewed out more, but my guardian barged past me. She mashed at the keypad and hushed the machine.

"Thanks. I'd best be off." I folded the pile of copies as I eased out of the room towards the elevator.

Lights shone behind the buttons as the lift descended. I pocketed the papers in my jacket.

27.

26.

SSA . . . Sinclair's — whatever it was called, it was the last dead end I could afford.

15.

14.

Bulldog would be sure to report me the moment my description made the news. My thumb fumbled at the silver band on my finger, while my chest pounded.

3.

2.

The ring. *That's it.* The jeweler had given me his pen so I could fill in my details. My address was on the invoice. If he still had it. Who was to say it hadn't disappeared along with everything else? But it was worth a shot. If I could get hold of that invoice, Anderson Whitman might sort this mess.

G.

B.

A ping from the elevator doors echoed through the parking lot as they opened, accompanied by the sirens of an armored police van pulling down the ramp.

I crouched behind the nearest car. The van's brakes whined and burnt rubber scorched the breeze. Four officers in full body gear slammed their doors, armed to the teeth. They huddled together. Their shadows cast long in the headlights. Through the brightness of the beams, steam hung in the air. Flashing reds and blues scattered on the walls above where I knelt. The crackle of a radio bounced in echoes through the concrete pillars and I moved with my back to the wall, cowering behind the bumper of a hatchback.

"He's in the building. Over." Then the haze of static.

A line of cars parked between me and the exit. No empty spaces. Gabby's Porsche waited across the other side of the parking lot. Too far to reach. My movements were light, their sound masked by the police radio. I crawled behind one car and the next, hidden between the bumper and the wall.

"Suspect last spotted on floor 27. Over." More static.

A ping echoed from the elevator. Two officers darted at full sprint to the opening doors, alert, their rifles pointed at the startled face of an old man who occupied the lift. He threw his feeble arms up, and they lowered their guns.

"What's the meaning of this?" the old man hollered. All the while, I crept towards the shaft of daylight flooding down the ramp, the pattering rainfall outside droning louder.

"Sorry, sir. We thought you were someone else."

"In all my years, I've never been so—"

"Sir, this facility is on lockdown. I'm afraid you won't be able to leave until we give the all clear."

The old man muttered beneath his breath. He stomped towards a car at the far end of the garage, opened the door and clambered in, huffing to himself.

The officers returned to their sweep of the area, combing the corners. A metal bumper bristled cold as I brushed against it, squeezing myself in the gap. One of the policemen stood directly across from me. Two more cars until I reached daylight.

Dusty concrete, stale to the touch, rubbed my hands and knees. With my head dipped, I peeked around the car's wheel. The outline of a pistol bulged on the hem of gun-metal-gray trousers, strapped to one of their ankles. Its handle poked out of the ridge of heavy boots.

"Floor 27 is clear. All units, keep a sharp lookout. Over." The radio's hiss mingled with the rain outside. If I'd closed my eyes, I might've thought I was near a waterfall, heading closer to the precipice. I held my breath and crawled through the shadows until I hid behind the cover of the last car.

"Clear in the lobby. How's it looking in the basement? Over."

I reached inside my jacket pocket and grabbed my keys, my palm deadening their jangle.

"All clear in this corner," one of the officers said.

Now or never. I pressed the button on the key and set off the alarm. A scream of orange lights flashed in high-pitched wails. The cops spun on their heels, kicking up dust behind them. Two sprinted towards the commotion, while the others approached slower. With their guns and voices raised, they growled commands in the direction of the noise. As they swamped the Porsche, I stood and walked around the last car, onto the ramp and out to the street. The faint blare of an alarm faded below ground while the hammering in my chest grew louder.

My footsteps slammed through puddles, soaking my pants as I fought against the downpour. The whole city knew my face now, but I had to get to the mall. To the jeweler. To the paperwork that would clear my name.

An alleyway diverted me onto Main Street. Any other sidewalk might have been empty, save for the odd pedestrian running for the shelter of the nearest doorway. But not Main Street. A brigade of business suits marched the concrete. Every face was rooted to the ground, refusing to let the cloudburst streak mascara or frizz their hair. Sodden newspapers or loose jackets became makeshift umbrellas. A constant thoroughfare, the only place in the city that rain couldn't silence.

I joined the heaving mass, blending with the hive, wading through puddles to the square. The avenues split, the park on one side leading to the mall, and a procession of businesses on the other.

On the corner, a newspaper vendor gave shelter to passing suits. In front of the stall, men stood in line. A boy hid from the rain beneath his Dad's umbrella. One careless glance in his direction was all it took for him to steal a look at me. With his mouth gaped open and his finger aloft, the recognition in his eyes was unmistakable. I pulled my coarse jacket over my face and scampered back into the crowd.

In the time it'd take for him to tell his Dad and for them to make the call, the police would have cornered off this area. *Where to hide?* The square had four main exits, but three of them funneled into the city. My only escape led towards the mall, but there'd be no reaching it now.

As I held my jacket collar to cover me, the papers I'd photocopied poked out of my pocket. My eyes caught the bold title on the page. 'Schedule for Planning Applications.' I grabbed the paper, scoured the list, and checked my watch. There was a Gracy's across the square due for redevelopment. It would be about ten minutes before the application was assessed. Against the tide of people, I blundered my way, nearing the building on the corner. A stream of bodies pressed against me, but I forced myself through.

Distant sirens approached, dispersing the crowds. I stepped into the doorway as officers flooded the square, surrounding the boy. Their key witness.

There was no back door out of Gracy's.

I was trapped.

It had only been a handful of months since Mrs. Campbell had opened this store. Jeff and I had sorted the plans, and she'd toured us around like it was the Taj Mahal. On the top floor, storage rooms and offices for the admin staff led to the roof.

My collar hid the lower half of my face. Shoppers stood idly perusing shelf after shelf at their leisure, soaking up the bland appeal of easy-listening hits through the store's speakers as if they had nothing better to do. But the eyes of the idle were the most prone to wander, more dangerous than a thousand hurried glances.

I climbed the marble staircase, twisting upwards in the center of the open space. On the first floor, the men's section was laid out in blocks. I snatched a few things from the rails and scrambled into a changing room. It took only a few seconds for the sweaty, mirrored closet to become my cocoon, and I emerged from it transformed.

In place of my designer jacket, shirt and tie, I wore joggers and sneakers, with the planning schedule tucked into my back pocket. The hood of my sweater covered my head and a pair of sunglasses disguised my eyes.

Back on the stairs, I peered over the rail. Two officers entered the building by the main entrance.

Up I scurried, through the home department, to the door at the end of the store, with 'staff only' emblazoned in green letters across its front. My watch still showed three minutes before the planning board at City Hall would review the application and make their assessment. If it passed, I had a chance, as long as I could get to the roof.

On the far side of a 'staff only' partition, a splintering wooden staircase on a rotten scaffold replaced the shining displays. All glitz for the customers, but behind closed doors, there was no sheen.

I climbed the stairs to the top floor. A doorway led to a dingy labyrinth of dark rooms, each decked out with a random assortment of spare goods. Dim lights shone at the far end, betraying the presence of two clerks. Their shadows flickered against the glass panel on the door.

I dashed into one of the storage rooms.

The hands of my watch ticked closer to the time when the planners would assess the application. Their rubber stamp would hit the page and change everything. 90 seconds more. If the clerks spotted me, how long for them to phone it in? About twenty seconds, give or take? The corridor outside their office led to the roof. Another five seconds from there, which meant I had about a minute before I should make myself discovered.

I rummaged through boxes of kettles and cookware, overcoats and lingerie, stacked like a block of jenga, and I packed out my sweater with clumps of clothing. The bras and panties were both soft and itchy against my skin. I pushed my arms into as many overcoats as I could manage, all the while keeping careful note of the tick, tick, tick.

22.

21.

Now.

My feet blustered to the office door. I barged it open. The two clerks turned, gawked at my face. I closed the door and ran through the corridor, pressed the bar across the emergency door. Out on the roof, I threw the steel clamp shut behind me, keeping an ear to the door, and an eye on my watch.

9.

8.

Alarms blared from below, through the rain that drenched my layers of overcoats.

5.

4.

Voices shouted through the corridor. The officers would be charging for the door. Sirens softened until they disappeared. They had me now. There was no need for them to have ever cornered off the street. Police flooded the building. All of them.

I ran. My feet pounded the gravel roof.

3.

2.

Pieces of soft lingerie fell out from beneath my sweater, leaving a trail where I charged. Rain hit my face, beating my skin as I reached the last concrete slab of roof and placed one foot on its edge, before . . .

1.

. . . I leapt, falling with the rain to the ground below.

Wind whipped at my face. My arms flailed wildly. Time stood still as I hung there, waiting to meet the concrete. Beneath me, the gray street suddenly changed, and in its place, green grass appeared. The building's windows vanished. Replacing them, trees reached tall and majestic.

I collided with a nearby branch and grabbed hold, caught in the twine of its bark as my three-story flight came to a sudden stop.

The planners had passed the application, moving Gracy's to a new development across town, and the officers inside with it. The park had been extended to the square all the way from the mall, these trees having stood for years.

I unzipped the topmost coat, leaving it in the branches, and clambered down onto wet grass. I wrapped the lingerie I'd stuffed to protect myself from the fall in a layer of coats and dumped it in the nearest bin. One overcoat remained to shield me from the rain, and I buried my face in its high neck. Along the empty path, I jogged towards the looming board which read 'Paradise Springs' spinning in the distance, leaving my pursuers six blocks away, with no recollection of ever having been near the square.

## ELEVEN

PILLARS DOMINATED the mall's entrance, stretching tall and swallowing me whole. I'd entered a decadent gold and marble cage. Trapped. Automatic doors barricaded me inside.

Shoppers swarmed between advertising boards. The eyes of women on giant posters stalked me as I hurried into the main atrium where information panels stood out of the floor like sentinels.

I tapped the surface of the nearest screen. The lavish image of bronze-skinned models faded, and in its place a message appeared.

HI. HOW MAY I HELP YOU?

I searched the kiosk for a list of stores. While it buffered, I glanced around. A shoal of buyers skulked nearby, each of them consumed by the lure of displays in gleaming storefronts. *Thankfully.* But one of them caught my attention. A hooded man in sunglasses stared from the window pane.

I peered closer and the hooded man peered straight back.

It was me.

I was the hooded man.

I snatched the hood and sunglasses off.

*Think invisible. Getting spotted here is suicide. The end of Adam Swann. Or what's left of me.*

A store map appeared on the screen and I scoured the list for jewelers. Goldsmiths. Ferrymans. Two high-end chains. Two clients I'd managed at SSA. Two dead ends. They couldn't be further from the small independent store I needed to find.

I rechecked the list. It wasn't like a business could just disappear. But where else could it have gone?

An ache in my stomach wrenched me double and I gasped for breath.

*Get a grip, Adam. It's not very invisible of you to be bent over hyperventilating in the middle of a main walkway, is it?*

I moved from the screen and stood by the balcony, looking down on the atrium. The fountain murmured, white noise masking the screams of children and the arsenal of footsteps. Coins lined the basin of the mall's centerpiece. Even the decorations turned a profit.

There was no way a rundown independent place would've been allocated a space here, alongside these outlets, an array of the AWG's finest.

My lungs collapsed. A throb burst to blow a hole through my chest. This had to be a mistake. The jeweler had to be here.

What if it closed in the eight years the mall was open? Moved somewhere in the city. To track it down, I'd need a computer. I thumbed through the money Jeff gave me. Plenty for a meal, but nowhere near enough for anything with a WiFi connection.

*Think.*

My eyes tracked the stores for inspiration. Every one of them looked the same. Even the stalls in the food court surrounding me had that peculiar, artificial varnish. Until I reached the counter of the 'Royal Burger Co.'

Then I saw him.

The man behind the counter.

It wasn't possible.

Half-dazed, I stumbled into the queue. Pictures of burgers tantalized from the board above the open countertop, but my eyes couldn't move from the greasy black hair, gold-rimmed spectacles and empty expression of the man at the till.

"Next please," he said absently.

I stepped forwards to face him.

"Welcome to the Royal Burger Company. What would you like, man?"

My jaw slackened, mouth gaped open. I recognized his same slow monotone. There was no doubt. I pulled back my sleeve to show him my watch and the ring on my finger. "Do you remember these?"

"Nice watch," he said.

"Don't you recognize it?"

"Er . . . I don't think so. Is that the time?" He scratched underneath his eye and yawned.

"Never mind about the time." I pointed at the watch's face. "Do you know where this came from?"

His expression never changed, no matter how confused he might have been. "Do you want a burger, or not? My supervisor's gonna kill me."

"What do you mean, 'Supervisor'? You can't work here."

"I'm not just here for the fun of it, man. Between us," he peered over his shoulder to make sure nobody overheard, "he's a real slave driver."

"What about the jewelry shop?"

"No, dude. We do burgers here."

"It was only yesterday. You've got to remember," I pleaded. "Think. The watch. You swapped it for me."

"I don't know what you're talking about, man. I've worked here ever since this place opened." He sniffed, staring through docile eyes.

My head screamed, but I couldn't make out the words. My stomach ached but not from hunger. The faces of the others waiting in line bore into me. From the open kitchen, a couple craned their necks to see what held up the orders.

"You gonna order something?" he said. "If not, I'll have to serve someone else."

"I'm sorry." I backed away, knocking into the man behind me.

"Hey. Watch it, buddy."

"Excuse me."

The man pointed at me, his brow creased in recognition. "Aren't you the . . .?"

*Run, Adam. While you still can.*

# TWELVE

RAIN POUNDED AGAINST parked cars, falling like machine-gun fire. I had to put as much distance between me and 'Paradise Springs' as possible. But my feet dragged, anchors trawling me back, forcing me to stop.

My lungs pleaded for air. Beads of water mixed with sweat, drenching my brow and stinging my eyes, blurring everything but the hammer of raindrops.

*Where can I go? Where's safe? Have to find a place to hide. But where?*

Distant sirens wailed from behind as officers streamed into the mall. Insects entering the nest.

*It doesn't matter where I go, so long as it isn't into a set of handcuffs.*

*Move, feet. Now.*

I trudged one step at a time. Aching legs hauled me beneath an underpass. Towards the ocean.

*Out of the city. It's my only chance.*

Concrete pillars. Graffiti symbols. The mark of #TNY was plastered everywhere in green and pink neon. Cars rumbled above. One more corner and it'd be a straight shot for the beach.

I rounded the edge of the last pillar and ran into a wall.

The impact jarred my leg, and I stifled a scream. I slammed my palm against the rough brick. "There was never a wall beneath the . . . Where did this . . . no, *when* did this happen?"

My eyes widened. *The list of building applications.*

I pulled the pages from my pocket and absorbed the proposed alterations. The city was changing, a constantly shifting maze. And I was lost inside it.

I doubled back, hood over my face. No time to retrace lost ground. Every moment counted, and I'd wasted too many in dead ends, bleeding seconds like an open wound.

My shadow melded with the stain of water darkening the streets. The further I ran, the tighter everything constricted. Long and sweeping terraces shrunk — elaborate frontages reduced to single windows webbed in iron.

There.

Fog seeped through a gap in the buildings ahead, spreading its breath, marking a path to the seafront where mist rolled in on the waves. Salty fret clung to my skin. And then . . .

A shadow sliced through the fog. The air cleared. Bricks and concrete emerged from the dark bulk. Instead of a path to the sea, I faced the side of a building. Another row of houses appeared from nowhere, cutting across the road, sealing me in. Another exit barred.

New twists in the maze blocked every route. If I couldn't leave by foot, perhaps there was another way?

I snaked back through an alley that flowed deeper into the city. Sirens snickered, echoing in the rhythm of the rain. Gaining on me.

Buildings tapered off as I entered an open courtyard. Busses parked in a line, standing guard in military formation. Automated ticket booths occupied the shelters of the bus station.

I made a beeline for the Retrograded Ticket Machine — an orange kiosk, stood apart from the rest. 'Never Miss A Journey Again' blazed across its front.

*I don't intend to . . .*

On its screen, I scrolled through a list of the journeys that had already taken place through the day. A sight-seeing bus tour left about half-an-hour ago. I clicked on the picture of the open-topped double decker.

'Visit the sites of New Yesterday. Taking you on a guided tour of the entire city, you'll see everything. From unparalleled architecture to beautiful beaches. Not to be missed. Duration 60 minutes.'

I paid for a ticket. My heartbeat droned louder than the machine's whirring as it printed out a stub. Until a voice from behind silenced everything.

"Don't move!"

Flashing lights tinted raindrops red and blue.

"Freeze!"

Pistols surrounded me. Their chambers loaded, snapping like crocodile jaws.

"Hands where we can see them."

Police officers encircled me, shuffling closer. A tightening net.

"This is a mistake," I said. "What have I done?"

"We've got you surrounded. There's no way out of this."

My fingers clutched the bus ticket. "I've got a lifestyle package through Anderson Whitman. You can't do this."

"All officers, move in," the cop barked into his walkie. "Now!"

Boots thundered. The unit charged. A dozen outstretched hands closed in.

I ripped the ticket.

Their hands dissolved as the retrograde changed everything around me.

Vibrations knocked me off-balance and I stumbled into a metal frame.

"Sorry about this weather, folks," a man's voice crackled through a speaker. "You'd get a beautiful view of the bay if it wasn't for the fog."

Dense mist saturated the air, shrouding the top deck of the open bus. Beyond the railings, waves crashed onto the sand, surging like the static of a broken radio.

Retrograded tickets. Worth every cent.

It'd only be a matter of seconds before the police caught on to what had happened. There were only so many busses I could've taken. Only so many tickets I could've bought to convey me out of the city.

The brakes squealed as the driver jerked to a stop.

"Seems there's some trouble ahead, folks."

Through the inky haze of fog, sirens flashed. A roadblock. Traffic forced to a standstill.

*Move.*

I gripped the rail, climbed over, and dropped to the ground, knees buckling on the asphalt.

Heavy mist invaded my breath, swallowing me just as my lungs were forced to swallow it. Its tendrils spread thicker and thicker, constricting around me as I ran for the beach.

Behind me, shadows crept through the veil. Cops posted themselves around the bus.

I skirted through the traffic and collided with the sand, my footsteps silenced by the mighty waves and pounding rain.

Deeper into the haze, I bounded over the shore. Beyond the flashing police lights. Lines of rain sliced through the mist, turning the sand to sludge. My feet sank as I waded up the coast.

I moved on automatic. Direction lost all meaning in the shroud. I had to trust my legs knew where they were going, even if my mind was blank.

Rock took the place of sand. Sharp crags forced me inland.

A solitary shadow loomed ahead, creeping through the gloom. A single turret clad in white. The lighthouse. Haven for lost ships. It guided souls to safety and shelter from the storm. Alone it stood, guardian of the desolate and adrift.

Alone.

My refuge. A place to hide.

I threw my fists against the door.

"Hello?" I called. "Hello?"

The main shaft connected to an alcove. A small room built on the side. I peered through the windows and the gaps in lace curtains, but it was empty.

A single plant pot lurked by the entrance. I tipped it, spilling muddy water.

A key.

It slotted into the lock and the door creaked open. I latched it from inside and closed out the storm. Stillness defeated chaos. The thud of rain dulled to a whisper. No fog cluttered the air.

"Hello?" I called again.

I checked the corners of the room and stepped through the gap that bridged the building to the turret. A circular shaft ascended upwards and a metal rail escorted the spiraling stairs.

My footsteps echoed as I climbed the uneven stones. Until I lost my footing.

Falling.

I reached out and caught the rail. My ring collided with the rusted banister, reverberating a shrill clink through the chamber.

I knew that sound.

I'd heard it before.

The memory crept into focus, revealing itself like an image hidden in a painting.

*It was noontime. Sunny. Warm. The clouds clumped across the sky in pockets.*

*I held a box. Inside was a ring. Not mine. Made of platinum. A thin band with a single princess-cut diamond adorning its setting. My heart raced, pulse throbbed. Sweat dripped down my brow.*

*"It's hot in here, isn't it?" Lottie. She wore her hair down, curling in waves as it fell to her shoulder. I always liked it when she let it dry natural.*

*I nodded. "You can say that again."*

*"Good, I'm glad it's not just me."*

*The sun filtered through the glass around us on all sides. I picked a spot at the curved windows. The sea stretched out far below. Behind me, a wrought-iron scaffold dominated the center of the room, covered by a worn brown sheet.*

*She took her place next to me and wove her fingers through mine, staring at the waves. Her sweet perfume mingled with the fragrance of meadow flowers we'd picked that morning.*

*"It's not just you. It's the two of us. Always will be."*
*I squeezed her fingers, trying hard not to tremble.*

*Her head rested on my shoulder. "Always?"*

*Breathe. "Always, darling."*

*"I love it here," she said. "You can see for miles."*

*"Yeah. It's a good spot."*

*"How did you convince them to open it up for us?"*

*The lighthouse keeper owed me a favor and I knew we'd be out this way today, but that wasn't important. The climb had made me dizzy. I didn't like heights at the best of times, and I'd gripped the rail as I'd neared the top. Lottie had laughed at me. Now I was here, still dizzy, but for a different reason. I turned towards her and dropped to one knee, producing the ring from my pocket.*

*"Lottie," I started, but I didn't need to say anymore. She knelt and kissed me. Her lips were so gentle, and her tears fell down my cheeks as they pressed against hers. "Lottie, I never want to leave your side."*

*"You don't have to."*

*"Forever, Lottie. What do you say? Will you stay with me forever? As my wife?"*

*"As if you had to ask."*

*"Is that a yes?"*

*Her lips pressed firm, answering for her.*

*When it came time to leave, her hand found the railing and the shrill clang of the ring cracked on metal, whining through the open shaft.*

*That sound.*

I stopped climbing, let go of the railing and stumbled back into the alcove. My legs gave way, palms brushed the tiled floor as they reached out to steady my tired frame. I was alone. Alone with the memory of a life that never happened. Hidden from me. The fog of my past.

Pushed against the splinters of cracked tiles, the cold wedding band nipped at my finger. On the wall, a pattern took shape. A silvery speckle. The same design laced the holes of the net-curtains. The shapes stretched wide, becoming sharper. Shadows grew taut. A light outside grew brighter, searing the outline on the wall.

I forced my legs to harden beneath me. The shimmer beyond the window plunged the room into a pale daze. I reached out to block my eyes from the garish beam, exposing all within.

A car door slammed. Two feet clattered on stone. Then a fist pounded on the door. A hollow bang repeated over and over.

I turned to run. But where?

Harder. Faster. Fists bashed the wood, battering my last nerves. I threw my hands over my ears, closed my eyes and rocked in place.

No way out. They'd found me.

A voice crept between the gaps in my fingers. I couldn't block it out. It pierced the shell of my solitude and forced itself through. A woman's voice. What was she saying? I peeled back my palms. "Are you in there? Come on. Open up."

Thuds bellowed from the door.

"Adam, answer me. Adam! Are you there?"

*That voice. It couldn't be?* I rushed across the room, unlatched the chain and swung the door open.

There she stood. Her shadow scattered up the wall. She stooped to shield herself from the downpour. Her timid frame shivered beneath the coat she held above her head. The headlights revealed her face as the engine grumbled in fog.

"Celia? Is that you?"

"Come on, Adam. Let's get you out of here."

## THIRTEEN

CELIA'S EYES FIXED on the road as she pulled into a suburb.

"How did you find me?" I asked.

She chewed her lip. "Instinct."

"But you know me, don't you?"

"Everyone knows you."

"I'm not talking about the news. You didn't forget like everyone else. You called me Adam. You *know* me. How?"

Her grip tightened on the steering wheel. "The same way I knew you'd be at the lighthouse."

"What's that supposed to mean?"

She shook her head. "Let me ask you a question. Do you know *me*?"

"Of course I do."

"So who am I?"

"You're Celia. My secretary at SSA. Although I guess you'd call it Sinclair's."

Wrinkles plowed across her brow in ever deeper troughs. "Your secretary? That's all you remember?"

"What are you trying to tell me, Celia?"

"What brought you to the lighthouse?"

"I was running from the police."

"And . . .?"

"And that's it. I woke up next to Gabrielle. Put on this wedding ring. And then I'm having these flashes of a woman called Lottie. The woman you were helping me find. Remember?"

"You're married?"

"Apparently. And then you showed up. The only person to know who I really am."

"Who you really are? Or who you *think* you are?"

"What's the difference?"

She pulled off the road and into a driveway. The engine's purr subsided and the rhythmic thrum of the wipers came to a stop. We sat in the stillness of the suburb.

"Is this your place?" I asked.

"You don't remember it?"

The house sagged through the smear of rain collected on the glass. Pale shutters in the windows. Forget-me-nots in plant pots on the porch. *Am I supposed to recognize it from the dozen others chained together by white picket fences?*

I shook my head. "I'm sorry."

Her chest rose and collapsed in heavy breaths. She closed her eyes.

"Are you okay, Celia?"

"Let's get you inside."

Chilled air steamed through the open door. Our coats dripped from hooks along the wall. Down a narrow hallway, I followed her.

Shallow light swathed the den in comfort. She cleared a coffee table, surrounded by an armchair and two-seater sofa.

"Do you want a drink?" She pressed a stack of magazines and papers to her chest, carrying them nowhere.

"I'd love one," I said.

"Coffee? Milk and half a sugar. Right?"

"Yeah. How did you—"

"I'll be right back."

She shuffled out of the room and I fell onto the sofa. Photographs littered the mantelpiece. The fire burned warm and inviting. Its light glanced across the photo frames, adorning the shadowy figures they contained in the same appeal.

I stood by the fireside and its heat nipped at my soaked joggers, itching my legs. The glare on the picture frame cleared. The figures in the photograph were no longer shadows. They were clear. Unmistakable. At catching sight of them, drips of sweat on my forehead fused with damp spots of leftover rain. Despite the heat pumping from the fire, a chill ran down my spine.

I grabbed the frame, smudging the glass, pulling it closer. *How? And when?* Replacing it on the mantelpiece, I picked up the next photo, and the next. All of them, the same.

A shuffle from the door.

Celia ambled into the room. In her hands, a tray wobbled with two mugs. She glanced at where I stood. A sharp breath escaped her lips as she breezed past me to the coffee table, laying out the tray as if it was nothing.

"Celia?" I didn't know what to say. What to ask.

"It's okay, Adam. Really."

"But . . ."

"Won't you sit down? Here's your coffee, just how you like it."

I propped the frame back on the shelf, unable to look away, my eyes fixed halfway between mania and disbelief. Wrapped in a glossy film, the photo showed a cloudless blue sky meeting the dark horizon of the sea. The white tower of a lighthouse beamed in sunlight. A golden beach at the cliff's foot shimmered. Faces of two figures crowded the foreground. One man. One woman. The woman's lips reached for the cheek of the man's face, her hair blowing in the breeze. His sunglasses reflected the phone's camera, his arm stretched to take the shot. Celia looked so happy in that picture. As did I.

"You don't remember any of it, do you?" She handed me my coffee and picked up her own. With both her hands around the hot mug, she seated herself in the chair.

I perched on the sofa's lip, my back straight as an arrow. "What's going on, Celia? What is all this?"

Her lips curled into a smile, but her eyes never rose from the inside of her cup. "You're not the only one who's been having flashes."

"*What!* You've had them too?"

She nodded.

"So you know what's happening? I'm not the only one?"

"When did yours start?" she asked.

"Today."

"And you're already being chased. They found you fast."

"What about you?"

"Mine started a few months ago."

"*Months?* And you never said anything?"

She blushed. "They were so intense. Just little things at first. The smell of an aftershave. Or the way someone laughed, or how they pronounced a certain word. I'd be reliving these moments, daydreams, whatever you call them, as if they were real."

"They're like glimpses."

"Snapshots."

I glanced at the pictures. "Yeah."

"And then the next instant, I'd snap back to reality not knowing where I was or what had just happened. It sounds crazy, doesn't it?"

"Not as crazy as you'd think."

"I thought I was losing my mind. Having a brain tumor or hallucinating. But it was more than that. They were tangible. More real. Like . . . I don't know. Like I was remembering them."

"Memories of a different life?"

"Something like that." Her voice trembled.

"So you remember Lottie? You must know her, right? Why didn't you tell me?"

She blew steam from the top of her mug and gulped a long sip of coffee. "A couple of months ago, we were in the conference room, and you poured us a drink from Mr. Sinclair's cabinet. We were celebrating. A big merger or deal. And you leaned in. And it was just — it was so familiar. All those flashes made sense. It *was* real. I wasn't crazy. And when you kissed me, I felt this strange relief. It's probably not what you're meant to feel when someone kisses you. Maybe it is? I didn't care. It was like I was free."

"What are you talking about? What merger? We never . . ."

"How would you know?" She arched forwards in her chair and reached for the floor. A muffled grating hissed across the carpet as she slid a beaten-up shoebox tied in elastic bands from underneath the armchair, and propped it with a thud on the coffee table.

"I think I'd know, Celia."

"Sure you would. And if it got retrograded, you still think you'd remember?"

"I—"

"We skipped work that afternoon. You drove us to the lighthouse and the beach. We took selfies and laughed and ended up back here. When you fell asleep on the couch, pretty much where you are now, you looked so peaceful. I stared at you and I had this moment of clarity. We'd done this before. This wasn't the first time. Those flashes. I hadn't dreamt them. They'd happened."

"But how is that possible? You can't tell me something like that could happen and we wouldn't know?"

"We'd been to that beach and come back here and laughed at the same jokes and fallen asleep together. Who knows how many times? But when we woke up, it was all gone. Changed. Retrograded out of our lives. And then a week later you'd wear that same tie, and I'd have one of my flashes and drive myself up the wall." Her fingers rasped the mug, her long nails tapping it with a chink, chink, chink.

"I'm sorry, Celia. I don't . . . I'm just . . ." I groped for something to say. Anything. But my brain tied my tongue in knots.

"I thought about waking you while you laid out on the couch. Telling you all this. But what would you have said? What would anyone have said? I know how crazy it sounds, to tell someone their life isn't what they remember. You can't accept it even now, can you?"

"How come you remember it, and I don't?"

"Perhaps there are some things that touch you so deeply that, even if they never happened, you still can't forget them?"

"And this was one of those things?"

"It was for me."

"Celia, I—"

"It's okay, Adam. You don't have to say it."

"I'm sorry."

"I was going crazy, just staring at you as you slept. I couldn't stand the thought of waking up again without knowing it had happened. So I left you sleeping and drove to the office, printed out a few photos from my phone, and wrapped them in the laminate we use for archiving. The preservative stuff. By the time I got back, you'd disappeared."

"And that's them?" I nodded at the photo frames.

"When I thought back over that afternoon at the beach, I remembered business meetings. I'd got tied up working late. My box of Chinese noodles had spilt all over the desk. We'd never even been in the conference room. On any other day, I'd have told myself I'd been imagining things at the lighthouse. Just another daydream. But this time, I knew better. I had the pictures to prove it."

The elastic twanged as her nimble fingers untwisted the first few bands that bound the shoebox.

"I did the same thing the next time we went for one of our drives," she continued. "And the next. Until I brought a laminator back to the house. I was sure it'd only be so long before I got busted. But they never even realized it was missing. As soon as the machine left the building, it was like it had never been there."

As she wrestled with the tighter bands, I sipped my first taste of her coffee. The perfect balance of bitter and sweet. Exactly right. But in all the years she'd been my secretary, she'd never made me coffee before.

All those frames. Those pictures lined up on the mantelpiece, watching me from the windowsill. Were they all from the past few months? *They couldn't be. I'd been with Gabby all that time.* At least, that's what I remembered.

"You mean all these are . . .?" I swept my hand around the room, towards the photographs. "Were we . . .?"

Her eyes glanced up from the box. She nodded her head and yanked at the last band, snapping it in two. "Those aren't the only pictures."

She lifted the lid and dropped the shoebox on the table, scuffing it along the polished grain and pushing it towards me. A jumble of glossy stills overflowed from its brittle edges. The box brimmed with shot after shot of the two of us. I rifled through stacks of them.

"Go on," she said. "Open one." Her legs crossed, and she eased back into the seat, swallowing another gulp of her drink. All the while, her pupils never lifted from the rim of hot ceramic.

I flicked through dozens of photographs, drawing one from the mound. Celia was laughing in the rain. My teeth were on show, and the shadow of the lighthouse hung in the cloud above us. I ripped at the film that covered the picture until I'd torn a hole. I mangled the corners and lifted out the smooth photograph, no longer protected by the laminate.

Instead of me and Celia, it showed a seagull standing on the bonnet of a car. We'd disappeared. Retrograded, once the picture was removed from its protective coating.

I threw the photograph into the pile and scraped my nails through my hair.

"And then a week ago, your face showed up on the news," she said. "You've got no idea what that was like. To know every contour of a stranger's face. Seeing the stubble sketched by some police artist and remembering the feeling of it scratching my lips. When I looked at that black-and-white drawing on the TV screen, all I saw was my reflection in your eyes. You could've done anything, Adam. A 'Linear Infraction,' they said. It was scary. To know you and never have met you before. It was like waking from a dream to find the man I'd been dreaming of still sleeping beside me."

I shook my head. "You think I don't know what it's like? Trust me. Having two different memories of the same thing. That's what got me into this mess."

"I thought about calling them and confessing what I knew, but I couldn't. They might have accused me of going linear for just knowing who you are. I had the pictures. The lighthouse. So I drove there every night. I didn't know where else to look. What else to do. And then, tonight, you showed up."

"Celia, the last time I saw you was yesterday. You were standing in my office at SSA. You were going to tell me something, and then Jeff interrupted us. Don't you remember?"

"Of course I remember. That's what frightens me. All this should have been retrograded. I shouldn't recall any of it. But when I look at that photo, it's like I was there.

When I see you now, it seems only a couple of weeks since I pretended to be asleep, watching you sneak out of here to go to work while I could still taste you. And then there's the office and SSA and the mall. I remember all of it, Adam. All of it and none of it. Maybe some of what I remember are just flashes of what could have been. But it doesn't feel that way. It feels real. All of it. And none of it."

Lottie's face flashed across my mind. I rubbed the ring on my finger. "And what about Lottie?"

"What about her?"

"Where was she in all of this?"

"You tell me."

"Don't you remember her?"

"Why should I? She's not *my* memory."

"But . . . you have to know something? You can't have all these memories of us, and not know her."

"I've never heard of the woman. Don't you get it? She's *your* life, Adam. Not mine."

My fists balled as I released a sigh. "What were you wanting to tell me yesterday?"

"I'd wanted to tell you for days but I didn't have the nerve." Her eyes glazed over with a steely glint and she stared straight at me, hard and cold, as though she was looking down the barrel of a gun. "I'm leaving, Adam."

"Leaving? When?"

"Right away. I'm getting on the next train out of here."

"But you can't. You're the only one who knows who I am."

"Do I? Do *you* even know who you are? I mean, all of this, these pictures, is that you or isn't it? You don't remember it, do you? You don't have a clue. None of us do. Not here. Not in New Yesterday. The past, our lives, they're just toys. You play with it until it's broken. And then you go and find another one to play with. I've loved you for so long, Adam. But you've forgotten me. Every time."

"I'm so sorry. Really. Whatever happened between us, I would never have wanted to hurt you." I reached over to grasp her trembling hands, but she withdrew into the cushions of her chair, twisting away from me, towards the fire.

"When I heard you'd gone linear, I thought — I hoped — you might have remembered about us. I honestly fooled myself into thinking there was a chance. For us. After all this time. But you don't remember any of it. And you never will."

"Just because I can't remember, doesn't mean you have to leave."

"When I saw you at that lighthouse, you looked surprised to see me. I knew then that nothing could keep us together. I'd already decided I had to go. To get away from this place. Move on. From you. From everything. And now I'm sure. Leaving is the only thing I can do."

"I could go with you. We could try again, away from New Yesterday?"

"You don't want me, Adam. You just want my help. What's the point of us even trying? Here, somewhere else, what difference does it make? This only ends one way. If you don't want to hurt me, then let me go."

"But the pictures. We look so happy."

"We were. It just wasn't enough for you. For either of us. It's time we both got on with our lives."

"If that's what you want."

"Don't kid yourself. It's what *you* want. I'm over here telling you about our life together and all you can ask me about is this Lottie. *That's* the life you want. The life you had before everything changed. *That's* who you went linear for. Not me. It was never me."

"This is all — it's all so much to take in."

She turned back to me and smiled, her round cheeks softening the somber of her eyes. "I suppose I should thank you. Without you, I might have been stuck here for good, living out the same first date over and over."

"I wish I could remember."

"And I wish I could forget."

I gripped the sides of the shoebox and tried to let go. But I couldn't. "You're really going to walk away from all this?"

"You can keep the photographs," she said. "If they'll help you clear your name, you're welcome to them. Just promise me you won't use them until after I'm gone. I don't want to get dragged back into whatever's between us."

"Thanks all the same. But I doubt Anderson Whitman will fix everything just because I show them a few old photos."

"It can't hurt."

My eyes rested on the laminate preserving the photographs. Their surface glinted in the low light of the room. I picked one up and ran my fingers across its front. The film clung to my skin. Bunched with the others, the image of a seagull on a car's bonnet stared at me through rips of thin plastic. "Celia. Do you ever use this kind of laminate for other things?"

"What do you mean?"

"If it preserves things the way they were and keeps them from being altered, do you ever laminate things around the office?"

"We use it all the time. Reports, documents, minutes of meetings, you name it."

"And where do you keep the copies?"

"They're in a vault at Sinclair's. Why?"

*The vault. Not that stuffy cave Bulldog kept under lock and key?* "Do you think there could be a laminated copy of something I signed just sitting in the vault, from before things changed and I disappeared?"

She closed her eyes and shook her head. "Don't ask me to do that. I told you. I'm leaving."

"Celia. Only you can help me get my life back."

The box clattered to the floor as my hands reached for hers. She tugged them back, but I took her fingers and clasped them in mine. I tipped my face towards her until our foreheads pressed together.

Her lips parted. "Please don't ask me," she whispered.

"I need you." I squeezed her hand tighter. "Will you help me?"

"It isn't fair of you to ask. You know how hard it is for me to refuse you anything. You're a criminal, Adam. Don't force me into this."

"What other choice have I got? Please, Celia. Help me."

Her rigid body thawed and she melted into the chair. The fire's glow warmed our hands together until she shrugged me away. "This is the last time, Adam. I'll check the vault. But that's it. If I don't find anything, it's over."

"Thank you."

FRASIER ARMITAGE

Her eyes misted with tears. "I really thought I'd walk out that door and be rid of this place."

"I'm sorry, Celia. Really, I am."

She peeled away, pushed past me and left the room. The front door crashed shut and a car's engine slipped into the distance.

I tumbled onto the sofa. My hand clutched at my heart. Photographs of Celia spilled from the box into my arms, berating me. I stared at her smiling face. She deserved better than to be dragged into this. What had I done?

# FOURTEEN

I KNELT TO SCOOP up the pictures littering the carpet and scraped a sharp edge poking beneath the chair.

The corner of . . .

A laminator.

From my pocket, I pulled the photocopies. The planning list, or what was left of it. A few damp pages where most of the ink had rubbed into smears. If I combined parts of each, there was still enough to make one complete copy.

The pieces clumped together as I arranged them in the machine, wrapping the bundle in clear preservative. A familiar char haunted the room.

*Who's to say Celia was even coming back?*

I toyed with the edges of photographs. The pictures were dead to me. Empty. They didn't spur the screech of gulls or the tang of salt on my tongue. No recollection of sand cloying at my toes. These stills, trapped inside the laminate, weren't memories. Not mine, at least. They were echoes fading into nothing.

Staring at Celia and trying to remember our time on the beach was like placing a shell to my ear and hearing the ocean — even if it was real, I'd only be imagining it. What else about my life did I not remember?

*What was stopping her from changing her mind and leaving the city? I wouldn't blame her.*

I flicked on the TV. Anything to distract myself.

The screen filled with the inside of a kitchen. *My* kitchen. A fuzzy figure stood in front of a woman. The figure turned and froze as their face sharpened into view.

It was me.

"New footage has been taken from CCTV inside the victim's home, giving us our first look at the fugitive, still on the loose after an eighteen-day manhunt. Police are appealing for people to come forward with any information regarding the whereabouts of this man."

Onscreen, my image stuck, held on a freeze-frame. I stiffened, open-mouthed. Eighteen days? That footage was from this morning! *How? Why? What?* The beginnings of questions rushed through my head. *Just slow down and breathe.*

I dashed to the windows to tighten the shutters, ensuring no cracks could betray me. Seconds crashed around me. My watch ticked louder and louder, every spin of the hand bringing my pursuers closer.

Closer.

*Block it out.* They must've retrofitted the camera. I turned up the volume.

"With me in the studio is an expert in Linear Infraction, Dr. Cromwell Avery, and a reformed Linear Offender, Daisy Davis. Thanks for joining us, both of you."

"My pleasure."

"Great to be here."

"Daisy, perhaps I can start with you. What prompted you to go linear?"

Beneath the girl, text scrolled across a red panel with the number for a *linear hotline* in case anyone was affected by the issues and needed to talk.

"It didn't really feel like a choice for me, Janet. I had everything I wanted when I came to the city. I was in a job I loved and then suddenly the company disappeared, like it had never existed, and I was left with nothing!"

"But you still remembered it?"

"That's right."

"Remembering it all must have made things difficult for you to accept."

"I don't know why I still remembered it," the girl said. "After the changes, my job had never existed. I'd never worked there. But I just couldn't adapt. It was like my brain insisted there was something wrong."

"And that's what led you to set fire to the building downtown?" The presenter cocked a skeptical eyebrow.

"Looking back, I've no idea what I was thinking. It was the same building I used to work in before the changes. I just thought if I could reset things, my old life might come back. I can't explain it. I was desperate."

"Well, thanks to Anderson Whitman, the building had been emptied so no lives were lost in the blaze. Dr. Avery, is this kind of behavior unusual with a Linear Infraction?"

The doctor filled the screen with a smugness that screamed 'I know it all,' whether that was true or not. "Sadly, Janet, this is typical in a linear case. It's like a seed. It starts small, but soon that seed spirals and grows, and the consequences can be devastating."

"Why is that?"

"Well, imagine spending all your days dwelling on a life that's gone. The more time that passes, the further you withdraw from that life and the more different everything becomes. Reality eventually breaks apart, creating a fracture in the mind."

On a split-screen beside the doctor, pictures of my sketch and other stills taken from the CCTV filtered in a loop.

"And that's what led Daisy to act so irrationally?"

"Precisely, Janet. The longer you spend pining for the past, the more serious the risk you'll jeopardize your safety, or the safety of others, attempting to get it back. If you can't adapt to your new circumstances, you go linear."

"And what triggers it? Going linear?"

"It all depends on the individual. Take one scenario. Let's say something prompts you to recall a tragedy that has been erased from your past. You might be so caught up in grief that it stops you from moving on with your life, which could have serious consequences. You could end up depressed, suicidal, or worse."

"All because of these multiple histories?"

"Multiple of anything isn't good psychologically, whether that's voices, personalities, or timelines. Doctor Weiss was very clear when New Yesterday got its start that the memory of multiple lives would be the end of a person's sanity. And I'm sure we all appreciate the work those good folks at Anderson Whitman Real Estate do to keep our histories singular."

"Are you saying, doctor, that anyone who's gone linear will become dangerous?"

"If they're left for long enough. They may not be a threat to society yet, but give it time. The longer they go without treatment, the greater the risk. Maybe all they need right now is some rehabilitation therapy, like Daisy here. Retrotherapy is standard in most correctional facilities. Which is why I'd appeal to this man to give himself up. Before it's too late."

"What do you mean, 'too late'?" the presenter asked.

"Who knows what this man is capable of! I'm afraid, Janet, that we have to acknowledge the fact that while he's at large, this man is a danger. He must be caught, and swiftly, for all our sakes."

"Thank you, Dr. Avery. What was your rehabilitation like, Daisy?"

"Oh, it was—"

I thumbed the remote and changed the channel, hopping from station to station — the shopping channel, *Wheel of Fortune*, endless talk shows — fleeing from the interview, desperate to shift the doctor's words from my mind.

*Dangerous.* What was so dangerous about memories?

Finally, I rested on an old episode of *Killjoy.*

*This is the one where a woman approaches Detective Killjoy and asks him to find her missing husband. Turns out she's got short-term memory loss and she's the one who killed her husband — but she doesn't remember it.*

"Hey, darling, this is the one where . . ." I raised my eyes to the chair where I expected to see Lottie crocheting while the mystery played. But the chair was empty. How many times had I made predictions before the first advert break about who the killer was?

*"You've ruined it now," Lottie would say.*

*"I might be wrong," I'd tell her, half-heartedly.*

*"If you're wrong, your twist will probably end up being better than the one in the show."*

*"Well, I might be right."*

*"If you're right, then you've just spoiled the surprise."*
*"So I've ruined it?"*
*"Exactly."*
*"Do you want me to stop guessing?"*
*She'd look up from her wool and needle. "I didn't say that, did I?"* How often we'd shared that look.

My eyes blinked and the episode was ending. Killjoy and Albright were outside the woman's apartment door, about to make the arrest.

Sergeant Albright puffed out an earnest sigh. "Do we really have to see it through, sir? I mean . . . all we've got to go on is what's in front of us, a woman who doesn't remember any of it, who isn't capable of killing."

Killjoy rubbed his head. "What we've got is murder, Ray."

"Listen, sir, that woman—"

"No, you listen, and listen hard. We're not here to investigate what people remember. We find out the truth of what happened, and that's all."

"Sir, with all due respect, the past is a secret you know and she doesn't. She can't remember anything beyond five minutes. Her life is like hide and seek, except when she starts searching, she's already forgotten what she's looking for. There's no way that woman was ever capable of murder."

"Maybe not," Killjoy shrugged. "But that's not up to us. It's not our job to rewrite the past. We type it out the way we see it, dotting the i's and crossing the t's, and that's final. I might not like the way it reads sometimes, but that doesn't change the facts."

"So what? You're just going to arrest her?"

"What else can I do? I may not remember what I ate for breakfast last week, but that doesn't mean I went hungry. We've all got to face the truth sometime — no matter how ugly it is."

The credits rolled. I pressed a button and the screen went black.

Sweat beaded on my neck, clamming my armpits. I stared at the empty screen.

*It's not about what I remembered. It's about what's real.* The photographs of Celia and me. That's real. So what was my life with Gabrielle?

Memories stabbed at me like a knife. Gabby lounging by the pool. Celia and the beach. Jeff and his bottles of port. I rubbed at my wedding ring, the pain eclipsed by the soothing warmth of Lottie's face, my only balm.

*Shouldn't Celia have been back by now? Why doesn't she call to tell me what's going on? She knows I'm here waiting.*

I paced the carpet, biting my lip, before I finally succumbed to the TV again. Radio stations played over different channels, and I scrolled through the intros of songs until I landed on one I recognized.

The opening bars flooded the room, transporting my mind to a rooftop. *Beneath a gazebo, Lottie's hips filled my hands as we swayed together. The stitches of her white dress, soft. Her cheek rubbed mine, and our lips scintillated so close together.*

The singer's voice cut into the music and I found myself somewhere else. *In a car, behind the wheel. With Lottie at my side. We belted out the lyrics, neither of us in tune. I drummed on the dash and she threw her hair back as if she was entertaining a stadium of fans.*

The chorus kicked in. *I laid in bed, the covers hiding me. A ping faded into the sheets as a text arrived from Lottie with the words of the chorus typed out. It was our song.*

Catapulted back into Celia's living room. The tune seemed empty without Lottie here. When did I ever laugh that hard with Gabby? Or sing that loud? Did we even have a song together? When did Gabrielle ever look at me that way?

The music vanished into the air, and I was stuck, trapped by memories I couldn't even say were real. But it wasn't about what I remembered. It was about what was true. I wore a wedding ring. That had to be real. As real as these photographs. As real as my memories — maybe even more so?

The door slammed.

Footsteps in the hall brought me to my senses.

Celia.

*Finally.*

She entered the living room where I stood motionless by the TV as the radio channel blared.

"Are you alright?" she asked.

I rubbed my hands over rough stubble blooming on my chin, and massaged my jaw closed. "Did you find it?"

"Your picture's everywhere. The police were crawling the building. They stopped me. Asked if I knew anything about you."

"And what did you say?"

"I told them no. It's a good thing I wasn't carrying these when they asked." From her handbag, she pulled out a sheet of laminated paper and a business card.

I snatched the A4 page. Sheen glimmered on the front of the sparse, simple document with two signatures — confirmation of the planning outcome for the 'Paradise Springs' mall. Dated yesterday and co-signed by none other than the Director of SSA, Mr. Adam Swann.

"Celia. This is it. This is how I get my life back." I wrapped my arms around her and she stiffened as I squeezed.

"There was this too," she said. "Found it in my drawer."

A business card preserved in laminate. 'Gilligan Kennedy — Collector of History. 2487 Foundry Way.'

What was Celia doing with a calling card for a seedy, backstreet collector?

I spun it over. On the reverse, clumsy handwriting was scrawled, as though she'd been in a hurry.

'FOR ADAM — IN CASE OF EMERGENCY.'

"It was hidden away under a stack of paperwork," she said. "I'd forgotten about it until I came across the card."

"What does it mean, in case of emergency?"

"You don't remember? You gave me a box to look after. Seems like a long time ago."

*A box? What box?* "So you took it to a collector?"

"I must have."

"What was inside?"

"I never looked. But I think it had a name written on it. A woman's name. Lorraine, Lucy, something like that."

My mind flashed to the office. *The rough cover of a brown file bobbled through shiny laminate. There were letters printed on it, and an image. A black blotch. I placed the file inside the box — a thick box — clunking around with a single word etched on cardboard in permanent marker.*

*'Lottie.'*

*I slid the box to Celia and she scooped it up. She said she knew somewhere it would be safe. In case anything happened. And then . . .*

And then I was back in the living room, holding the business card in one hand, and the slip of paper with my name in the other. "How can I ever thank you enough, Celia?"

"You can let me go."

"Anything you want. You've saved my life."

She pulled away. "I'm not so sure."

"What's that supposed to mean?"

"Honestly, how can you even know what your life was like to begin with?"

"I know enough."

"I hope that's true." Her shoulders slumped and posture softened. "My train leaves at two o'clock."

"You'd better hurry, or you'll miss it."

"It's okay. I've got a retrograded ticket."

"I don't know what to say, Celia."

"Here." She rooted around her pockets and handed me her car keys and phone. "Take these. But be careful with that. It's a company phone."

"Why are you giving me them?"

She shrugged. "Let's just say you could use them more than me right now. What's your next move?"

"Probably head to Anderson Whitman. See if they can help."

"You trust them?"

"Why wouldn't I?"

"I don't know. It's just . . . can I ask you a question?"

"Anything."

"Do you even remember why you came to New Yesterday in the first place?"

I glanced at the business card resting on top of the planning application. The memory of a cardboard box and Lottie's name in marker pen. "Does it matter?"

"If you don't know what you're running from, you'll never get away. Something sent you linear. There's got to be a reason."

"You think I should find out?"

"I don't know what you should do. Just don't get lost, Adam." She leaned in and kissed my cheek, then stepped back and headed for the door.

"Thanks, Celia. For everything."

She disappeared, leaving me alone with a shoebox full of memories that weren't mine. I swept the prints into the hollow box, laid the document over them and the business card on top.

With the planning certificate, I had proof of a life. The life I remembered. SSA. Gabrielle. But what about the business card? Could I just ignore it?

Did I really want to march into Anderson Whitman and settle for a life I remembered, but might never have lived? What did I want more — my memories or the truth?

## FIFTEEN

"THE SUSPECT WAS last seen exiting the 'Paradise Springs' mall," a woman's voice blasted from Celia's TV. "Security camera footage shows him leaving on foot. We interviewed an employee of The Royal Burger Company who'd interacted with him."

I tried not to hyperventilate as the news showed the net tightening around me, and I collected my laminated notes together. Into the box with the planning certificate and the photographs they went, the secrets of a life long forgotten.

My stomach groaned.

*Should've bought a burger when I had the chance.*

On the coffee table, cookies filled the plate where Celia left them. I snatched a handful.

"News just in. Police have traced the linear suspect's retrograded ticket to a tour bus. Officers are still combing the area."

I switched off the set and ran to the car. Kerr-unk slid the locks as I slithered into the driver's seat, resting the shoebox of photographs beside me. My hand remained on its top. *It's okay to let go. It's not going anywhere.*

I backed out of the drive and parked below the lamppost in front of the white picket fence.

From the moment I left the drive, a child appeared in Celia's garden, playing. The kid looked about five or six.

A young woman emerged from inside Celia's house, cradling a baby on the red-lacquered porch. She called out to the little girl.

"Come inside, sweetie. Time for lunch."

"Coming, Mummy." The daughter bounced over the grass to the front door. The woman frowned at the car and marshaled the girl inside, slamming the door.

I checked my watch. 2:18. Celia was gone. A new family had taken her place — had lived in her house for years — as if Celia had never been here.

The city had shuffled the deck again before dealing a hand to someone new. And I was sitting across from them, looking down at my last few chips.

I had enough proof to take to Anderson Whitman. Enough to get my old life back. Probably. If that *was* my old life.

From the crack of the shoebox — between the lid and the sides — photographs of Celia spilled out, staring up at me. We looked so happy together. The business card poked out of a corner. I yanked it from the bunch.

'Gilligan Kennedy — Collector of History. 2487 Foundry Way,' shimmered in tiny print.

A flash registered across my mind.

*Lottie.*

*That old file. I keep it safe in a thick box. Carry it everywhere.* I reached across for the box on instinct, and grabbed at thin air. My eyes followed, and the shoebox on the seat beside me was half its size.

What had Celia said? 'Do you even know who you are? These pictures, is that you, or isn't it?' *I wish I knew.*

My fingertips rubbed at the business card's slippery coat until the sheen faded. I crunched on a cookie and its sweetness melted on my tongue, but the chocolate in my mouth couldn't stave off the metallic taste of bile grinding at the back of my throat. No matter how many cookies I ate, there would always be that bitterness lurking underneath, waiting for me.

*Is that you, or isn't it?* I needed Killjoy and Albright, digging up the truth despite the memories. The business card was in case of emergency. I'd say this was an emergency. Whatever life Anderson Whitman would end up landing me with, that card might be my only chance to find out what was real and what was false. Wasn't that worth something?

I pictured Gabrielle, but couldn't keep hold of her. In her place, Lottie's face crowded out everything else. I hummed the melody of our song. Whatever I'd forgotten, whatever this place had scrubbed over and robbed from me, whatever temporary sweetness it had wrought, my past was in that cardboard box, safe in the care of Gilligan Kennedy. Could I really cash in my chips with Anderson Whitman without turning over those cards? What other choice did I have?

I slung the car into gear and pulled away from the curb. The motor grunted towards the highway and the city.

Fumes blew through the air-con. A line of traffic queued dormant by the underpass. Ahead, gleaming buildings reached tall. Polished glass skyscrapers glittered in pale sunlight. Three clear lanes stretched into New Yesterday, but not this crowded thoroughfare. This single road skirted the suburbs, away from the beach, away from the bustle, away from the beating drum.

The tires stumbled over a parade of potholes. The squalid pallor of the shade kept every shop-front cold, and every passing face gaunt. The rhythm of the city's core pounded, alive and vibrant, but the only notes to trickle down here were the shaky rattle of symbols hissing in the steam, and the whine of alarms floating from distant corners. A sign hung crooked from chipped bricks on the wall.

FOUNDRY WAY.

I pulled the shoebox from the empty seat into my lap as my other hand tightened around the wheel.

There. A space.

I squeezed into a cramped spot between two dented cars. My reflection waned in the blacked-out windows. With the shoebox clenched under my arm, I sidled along the cracks, over a collage of trampled rubbish and faded gang signs.

Over the street.

2487.

A torn awning stained with pigeon droppings tilted to one side above a derelict plaque — GIL GAN ENN DY'S — carved in green on a battered brown board. Caged in iron rungs, dusty windows coated the harsh exterior in a forbidding gloom. The callous rail grated on my skin as the bell chimed and the door shunted open.

"Close that door," the man behind the counter barked. It rattled shut, trapping the fusty air inside the room.

All around me, odds and ends were vacuum-packed in clear cellophane. Dust settled on the plastic gloss. A lamp. A globe. Ceramic ornaments. Pictures in frames. Memory cards. Books. DVDs and VHS tapes. All kinds of junk, littered on dark mahogany tables, wrapped in a tacky coating, dotted around the dim room.

"You buying or selling?" croaked the bulbous man perched behind the glass counter. Inside the display, a stack of jewelry and heirlooms lit by amber bulbs sparkled in their laminated casings. His serpentine fingers tapped the glass top. The smell of stale plastic mixed with intense cologne. This must be Gilligan Kennedy. The collector of history.

"I've got this card." I approached the counter and offered him the business card which he snatched. His slimy smirk showed flecks of food rotting in his yellowed teeth.

"Let's have a look, shall we?"

He produced a UV torch and ran the bluish beam across the surface of the card. An invisible note shone under the ultraviolet haze.

3.63.162/POL.

"Wait here," he said, rising from his stool like dough in an oven. "And don't touch anything!"

He turned around and waddled to the varnished cabinets built into the back wall. Drawers of different sizes formed a mosaic of lacquered wood, filling every inch from floor to ceiling. He groped at the drawer labeled 3.63, yanking it open, running the UV over the contents and licking his lips.

"Here we are." A cardboard box.

*The* box.

Beneath the clear plastic wrapping, on its side, 'Lottie' was scrawled in black sharpie.

He lugged it to the counter and blew away the dust covering it in thick clouds.

"Thanks," I said, reaching for the counter.

He resumed his keen perch. "What are you thanking me for?"

"For keeping hold of it for me." His palm spread across the top of the lid, sliding the box back towards him.

"You think you can just walk in and take it? No, no, no, no, no."

"But I have the card? It's my stuff, isn't it?"

"A business card is a receipt for goods. A proof of transaction. That's all. If you want this item, I'll gladly make you another receipt. For another transaction." His thin lips broadened into an unnatural smile. He didn't hide his greed behind false modesty, but showed it off, placing it on display like the rest of his excesses.

"Okay. How much?" I rifled through the leftover notes in my pocket and he threw his head back, his many chins stretching flat as his stomach gyrated ripples.

"Money? That's a laugh. What good is money? Here today and gone tomorrow. There's no value in it. None. But the past. That's here forever, provided it's preserved. No. The best I can offer you is an exchange, I'm afraid."

"But I've nothing to give you."

"Oh, really? Nothing at all?" His eyes rolled to the shoebox, then flashed back at me.

"Now wait just a minute—"

"I'm afraid these offers only last so long. A minute might stretch the limits of my generosity too far."

"Let me get this straight. You want to trade boxes?"

"Well, that very much depends on what's inside this tiny parcel. Shall we take a little look and see?" His mouth snarled as he sat rubbing his paunch.

"You want us to open both boxes?"

"Outrageous!" He shook his head. "This box is sealed."

"But my shoebox isn't."

"Yes. Quite a pickle, isn't it?"

I stared at the two boxes, one beside the other. Celia in the first. Lottie in the second. I had nothing but fleeting glimpses to remember each of them by. Both of my lives up for grabs, and the choice was mine. Or was it his?

"Fine. Let's open it," I said.

He lifted the shoebox's lid as though it was a sacred talisman. A stack of photographs spilled onto the counter.

"Well, well, well, what have we here?" he whispered, drawing the photographs to his face, passing a scrupulous eye over each one. "Do you remember any of this?"

I shook my head. He quivered, ecstatic as he emptied the box until he reached the bottom. His nimble fingers nipped at the two pages — the planning application for the mall in his left hand, and what remained of the tattered list of building changes from Sinclair's which I'd laminated in his right.

"No value in this." He slipped my list over the counter. But his lips curled as he read the mall application. He hugged the sheet with the signature closer to his chest, tightening his grip. I pushed the list I'd taken from Sinclair's office into my coat pocket.

"So how much of this stuff would cover what's in the box?" I asked.

"You say you don't remember these?" He glanced at the photos.

"That's right."

"And what about the girl in the pictures?"

I frowned. "What about her?"

"Does she know about them?"

"She's the one who gave them to me."

"And there aren't any other copies?"

"Not that I'm aware of."

He stroked his chin. "Where is she now?"

"Gone."

"She's left New Yesterday?"

I nodded.

The white of his eyes protruded like his stomach. His breathing quickened as he sucked up the saliva soaking his mouth.

"Well then, I think we may have a deal," he said at last.

"How much?"

"I'll need all of it to make the swap."

"The whole lot? Every picture. You can't be serious?"

"Without the complete set, it's not worth much. But taken together, it's a fair trade."

"Fair?"

"These things happened. They're part of history, and their preservation is of the utmost significance among our little group of collectors. Genuine history in New Yesterday is rare. So a find like this . . . well, it could be the only record that still exists of this girl. The two of you. It's precious. But if these photographs were separated, it would halve their value. And then who's to say more records couldn't be floating around, rather than just this set? Instead of a commodity, you'd be presenting me with a commonality. Do you comprehend my meaning?"

"What about the planning application?"

"It's a job lot, I'm afraid. Insurance. In case anyone copied these photographs. One box for another. You can take it or leave it."

"And if I take it, you'll write me another receipt?"

"If you take it, the trade's non-refundable. We're a preservation society, not a pawnbroker."

This charlatan was scamming me out of everything. All my proof for Anderson Whitman. There'd be no bartering. He was taking a life, one way or another. But which one?

My thumb toyed with the wedding ring. The dusty box in front of me clad in cellophane screamed her name. Lottie. Celia's question pounded over and over. *Do you even know who you are?*

"Well, what'll it be?" he said.

*Truth or memories?*

I slid the large cardboard box towards me, and scooped it in my arms.

"Don't you want a receipt?" he asked.

"What's the use?" The glossy corners dug into my wrist as I huffed towards the door.

"Pleasure doing business with you," he called over the tinkling bell, and I carried the box into the gray street. "Close the door behind you," his voice yammered, drifting from his vacuum-wrapped hovel. *Collectors. Bunch of crooks.*

I stepped away from Gilligan Kennedy's having literally left my old life behind, and traipsed the sidewalk back to the car. The box I now carried rattled as I hurried over the cracks. I fumbled at the keys and climbed into the car. The lock flipped shut, and I nestled the large cardboard box in its once familiar place on the seat next to me. I ran my fingertips across where *Lottie* was written across its side.

My chest expanded, blood beat in laps through pulsing veins jutting out of my temples. I inched closer to the box. To her. To the memory trapped inside that cardboard cage.

Trembling, I scraped the car key's jagged edge along the lip of the box's lid, and threw it off. It clattered on the floor. I leaned over the open top, peering in, waiting to see what secrets it harbored.

The first thing my eyes fell on was a clear bag which held the blunt, black, unmistakable contours of a handgun.

## SIXTEEN

THE APARTMENT WAS a gallery of people wearing black, all in latex gloves. Flashes of cameras dazzled everything in white. Bodies crouched, their fingers combing every surface. The inquisitions of the neighbors crowded the hallway as officers shepherded them back into their homes.

"Mr. Swann, I'm Detective Lopez. We spoke on the phone." The cop was short, her straight, jet-black hair melding with the overcoat that fell to her knees. Her hand reached to shake mine, but ended up grasping my elbow and dragging me to the kitchen counter where two mugs with fresh tea bags nestled.

My mouth gaped open. "What is all this? What's going on?"

"I can understand how disorientating this must seem. To come home to all this."

"Why are there so many of you in my house? Where's Lottie?"

The detective flipped open a notebook. "Can you tell me your whereabouts over the past two hours, sir?"

"What are you talking about? Where is she? Will somebody please tell me what's happened?" I paced the tiles, craning my neck beyond the door.

"Sir, if you'd please answer the question and I'll explain everything."

I forced myself to remain still, resisting the urges of my restlessness. "Sorry. I'm just . . . I was driving. On the road to New Yesterday. Last minute business meeting. I was about an hour into the trip when you rang, so I turned around and it's taken me this long to get back."

"Can anyone confirm that?"

"My office, I guess. Can't you track my phone or something? Why do you need to know all this?"

"I have to ask, sir. I hope you understand."

"I don't understand any of this. It sounded pretty urgent when you called. I couldn't really make out what you were saying. The signal kept cutting in and out. But it seemed like an emergency. I've been worried sick all the way home. And then I walk into this. So can you please, please just tell me what's going on?"

Her shoulders dropped. "I'm sorry to have to call you back from your business trip, but I'm afraid there's been an incident."

"A what? Where's my wife? I want to see her."

"Settle down, sir."

"Why aren't you telling me where she is?" Take a breath. No need to get worked up. My chest flattened, breathing steadied. "Is this about that meeting?"

"What meeting?" The detective's pen flashed across her notebook.

"The one Lottie was having. With those people. Tonight."

"Who?"

"Something to do with that thing online."

"Can you be more specific?"

*My whole body shook. "What's with the interrogation? You said you'd give me answers. So tell me where she is. No more questions. You tell me. Right now!"*

*"This won't be easy, sir." Detective Lopez spoke without inflection, like she was reading from a menu. "Your wife, Mrs. Charlotte Swann . . ."*

*"What's happened?" In the second between my asking and her answer, a chasm engulfed me. The inconceivable was suddenly apparent, forced into my brain, and I toppled into a pit of worst-case scenarios. A world existed in that brief interlude, and the tumult of not knowing finally broke, crashing down on me as the detective spoke the words.*

*"I hate to be the one to tell you this, Mr. Swann. But your wife is d—" I didn't hear anymore. There was no sound. No feeling. No thought. No words. No air. Just the darkness. The numbing emptiness. The interior of the apartment became a desert, and I was alone, left destitute to wander its sands. The officers swarming the place were a mirage. For an eternity, I stood alone. Then time resumed, and a voice broke through the mist, bringing me back to my senses. "Mr. Swann? Are you alright, Mr. Swann?"*

*"I . . . I can't believe this."*

*"You're registered as her next of kin and we need someone to identify the body."*

*"It isn't happening. This can't be real."*

*"I'm so sorry."*

*"Where is she?" I peered through the doorway to the living room. The main exhibit was lying on the polished*

wood floor. The detective's hand squeezed my arm tighter as I tried to shake her off.

"Mr. Swann, this is a crime scene."

"Crime scene! This is my home! Let me go. I want to see her." Two burly officers barred the way as my arms flailed. All the while, Detective Lopez never released her hold.

"Mr. Swann. You can see her. Okay? I just need you to be calm." I glanced at Lopez and drew strength from her soothing, empathetic eyes. "I can't let you disturb anything. Do you understand?"

I nodded. My lips quivered. Hands shook. The officers parted ways, and I was guided past the sofa to where her body slumped in a heap. Her jade green top was stained red from the pool she'd been left in. Hair covered her face. Her skin was so pale. So white. She lay so still. Like she was sleeping.

"Lottie. Lottie, wake up darling. It's me. It's Adam." I stooped down and reached towards her, but Lopez grabbed my hand. I tried shrugging her off, but my strength had evaporated. "Darling. It's okay. It's all going to be. . ." Salty tears drowned my eyes, streaming down my cheeks, and falling into the detective's coat as she pulled me back.

"Come on, Mr. Swann. I've got some questions I need to ask you."

"Just give me one more minute."

Lopez nodded, handing me a tissue. Through a blur of tears, I shook my head, staring at Lottie. Her legs splayed out. One of her arms flopped over her chest. The other extended away from her body, her elbow bent in the shape of a V. Her hair, wet with dark blood, fell over her ear.

Her neck twisted. A long fringe swept across her face, masking her profile. She looked empty somehow. Unreal.

"Can we give Mr. Swann a moment of privacy?" It was an order, not a question. The officers filtered out of the room. One by one. Until the last of them stooped across the far side of the lounge, his eyes fixed on a grimy, black pistol. He gathered the gun, wrapped it inside a clear bag, and sealed it tight.

It was the same bag I held in my hands as I sat on Foundry Way, the memory of Lottie's slain corpse vivid as I ran my fingers along the barrel of the heavy handgun. It looked like a toy.

Another small plastic bag lay inside the cardboard box. A flattened shard of metal, no bigger than a button. The bullet that killed my wife.

\*\*\*

"Good news and bad news, Mr. Swann." Detective Lopez slouched on the sofa they'd ransacked, scouring it for DNA. A hair. A fiber of clothing. Anything to give them some clue. "Ballistics have come back with news on the bullet."

"And?"

"It was like we thought. Fired from the gun we traced to New Yesterday."

"So you know who did it. I mean, that's the good news, right?"

"The good news is that this puts you in the clear." Lopez slurped her coffee. Her butch colleague propped next to her with his notepad open, his pen poised over the empty page.

"What's the bad news?"

"The bad news is there's still no record of who purchased the gun. We spoke to the owner of the shop it came from, after we found the registration document online. He couldn't remember owning a gun shop. Ever. Said we must've got our wires crossed. There are countless people in New Yesterday. Without a positive way of tracing down the person who met with your wife on the night of her attack, we're still without a suspect, and no real way forward."

"So what are you saying?"

"Are you sure there's nothing else you remember about the person who was supposed to meet with Charlotte?"

My frantic eyes darted around as I forced my mind back over all those things I should have asked her when I'd had the chance. I shook my head. "I've told you everything. It was something about her petition. She'd posted it online. Then a few days later, she got this phone call. She didn't even tell me if it was a man or a woman. Can't you trace the call?"

The heavy-fisted cop scribbled down everything I said. Lopez sipped at the bitter sludge steaming in her mug. "According to the records in New Yesterday, the phone they used to make the call never existed."

"There's got to be a way to trace it back to someone."

"If there is, we'll find it." She smiled at me. "Try not to think about it, Adam. We're doing everything we can. This bullet — it's progress."

Sitting with the gun in my lap, I pinched the corner of the bag containing the bullet. Even through the plastic, grains of its metal casing grated on my skin. The force of the smooth shell hitting her chest had squashed its shape until it was no more than a flat splodge. I squeezed it and the metal dug into my palm. Sharp. I closed my eyes. Pain shot into my arm, the muscles contracting around the dull projectile. How could I have forgotten this rage?

I unclenched my fist. White skin turned pink, and I slipped the bullet into the box, along with the handgun, sealed in evidence pouches. In the bottom of the box was a brown paper file with dark blotches stamped on the front, encased in laminate.

The rough lining bound a pile of papers, preserved in clear film. A sticky label showed letters written in felt-tip.

CASE FILE: CHARLOTTE SWANN.

\*\*\*

*"I'm so sorry, Adam." Detective Lopez sat, legs crossed. She'd come alone. Rain pounded on the window outside, lashing from the gray shroud blanketing the sky. "We've tried everything."*

*"Is that supposed to make it easier?"*

*"I know how hard this must be to hear."*

*"Do you? Do you really?"*

*"You're hurting right now. I get it. I can see it. I could've done this over the phone, y'know? Or sent in one of the rookies to tell you. But I didn't. I came here because I wanted you to hear it from me."*

*"Hear what? That you're sorry?"*

*"Yeah. That's right. I'm sorry. I truly am. But it's out of my hands. We've got no leads. No way of tracing the gun. Or the call. Did you expect we'd keep the case open forever?"*

*"I expected you to find them."*

*"So did I, but it doesn't always work like that."*

*"So you run into a few brick walls and you just give up?"*

*"We went over the evidence dozens of times before it got to this. But there comes a time when you have to accept that whoever did this, they're gone, Adam."*

*"So's she."*

*Lopez bit her lip. Her hazelnut eyes ran over me, alert to the haggard lines drawn on my thin face. "How much sleep have you been getting?"*

*"Why does it matter?"*

*"Do you think you'd sleep any better if we'd caught them?"*

*"Probably not."*

*"You'll never get justice, Adam. Whether we find them or not. That's not how this works. There's no way to make the situation fair or right. So you've got to find a way to live with the pain, because it's always going to be there." She brushed down her black trouser-suit and reached for her handbag. "If it helps, I brought this for you." She pulled a brown file from her bag. "If anybody knew you got this from me, they'd have my badge. But I thought it might help you find a way, y'know? It's everything we've got." Lopez stood to leave. "Get some sleep, Adam."*

I opened the file, bound in laminate where Gilligan Kennedy had spliced the official report with the notes and post-it's I'd scribbled on various pages. A black-and-white picture of Lottie's body. The ballistics report of the bullet. The autopsy and cause of death. Phone records showed the number used to make the call — a cellphone that didn't exist. And reams of notes where I'd studied the police's findings, cannibalizing it before I'd made the call to Anderson Whitman.

On the back page was a faded note written below the estate agent's headed paper.

\*\*\*

*The salesman invited me into his office, forking a dense slice of cake before he swilled it down with a long gulp of coffee. "Sorry. You caught me on my break."*

*"Thanks for meeting me."*

*"My pleasure, Mr. Swann. Now, I take it you're interested in New Yesterday?"*

*"I saw your advert on TV."*

*"Looking through your records, I can see you came to us once before, didn't you? To discuss a lifestyle package for two people? But you decided against it. Is that right?"*

*"Pretty much."*

*"I'm sorry it didn't work out."*

*"I know it's been a while since you offered me that deal for a place in New Yesterday. But I wondered if that was still on the table?"*

*"You mean you're still interested in moving to the city?"*

*"I am."*

*His face radiated through a sickly smile, half-chewed crumbs littering the enamel of his teeth. "What made you change your mind?"*

*The image of the police file flashed across my brain. "Let's just say, I've got a good reason to want to be there."*

*"Well, this is excellent news. I'd be happy to make the arrangements. Shall we look through the packages and see what's on offer? Is it still for two?"* He glanced at the silver band on my finger.

*"Just me."*

*"I see. Well, congratulations, Mr. Swann. You've made a terrific decision. It shouldn't be too much trouble to get you everything you'd like. In fact, it'll be a . . ."* he lifted the fork up to his mouth, *". . . a piece of cake."*

Some of the crumbs still clung to the headed paper, stuck to the underside of the laminate. I flicked back through the pages to the ballistics details. The gun store's address was on the other side of town.

105 North Parkway.

I reached for the keys. Then both hands dropped to my lap. My chest heaved and fingers shook. A volcano raged inside, ready to erupt and burn me to ash. I fought back the scream carried in my veins. Slamming the steering wheel, I pounded the plastic circle over and over. With fingertips pressed against my scalp, the aching bent me double. My feet stomped the floor, mouth open though no sound came out. Steam misted the window and I pushed my face against the glass, my cheeks painting Rorschach shaped blotches on the pane.

*Lottie. I'm so sorry. It was you. It was always for you. How could I have forgotten?*

I still remembered my life with Gabby. The past two years. The way her giggle echoed across the patio. The tang of her perfume. The rhythm of her breathing as she lay next to me sleeping. But it was all so distant. And Lottie — the thought of her was so raw, so visceral. Like the difference between seeing a photograph of a mountaintop and actually climbing it. Every high and low with Gabby was just a postcard marking time, but with Lottie, I stood on the peak. The sensation of her touch, her smile, it elevated me to a different level.

Even looking back at this so-called life I'd made with my European-writer-girlfriend, how could I separate the guilt from the happiness? The stab of knowing I'd forgotten Lottie diluted every smile, every laugh, every pleasure. Remembering her now, I realized the extent of my betrayal. The grief of losing her, not just once, but losing even the memory of her, burned through me. She'd been erased. Someone had taken her from me. Someone in this city had pulled the trigger and doomed her to oblivion. But I'd *allowed* myself to forget. Never again. I had to hold on to this pain. I couldn't let it go. Let her go.

*Lottie, can you ever forgive me?*

Weary from tears, I wiped my eyes on the back of my hands and forced them to the steering wheel. My ring dug into tender flesh. The gun store. 105 North Parkway.

The ticking indicator signaled as I pulled away from Gilligan Kennedy's, down the pothole-laden tarmac, back towards the underpass and the freeway. I knew where I was going. But more than that, I knew why I was here.

## SEVENTEEN

THE GUN STORE was gone. But it was still a lead. And what was I supposed to do with a lead, however hopeless, except follow it?

I needed to see the place where the gun came from. *I have to lay my eyes on it.* For my peace of mind. If any still existed amid the chaos of memory.

Even without the store, the gun remained. Sealed in an evidence bag. If I removed it from the bag, would it continue to exist? Or would it too disappear into the realm of the forgotten? The person who'd fired this gun was out there, somewhere. Perhaps there are some things that don't change. Can't change. Even here. *Who knows what traces still linger from a past long buried?*

105 North Parkway. I had to see it, to take that step, even if it led me nowhere.

Looming towers dwarfed the meandering cavalcade of traffic — a high valley of buildings and a bubbling stream of exhausts. Roads branched off like arteries toward the coast. Away from the purview of skyscrapers, the smog of fumes cleared and waves crashed crystal on the shore.

Cobbles cut through the promenade's one-way loop, running wide and straight. Pedestrians dawdled in the shadows of old-fashioned brick terraces.

I counted the numbers. 83 . . . 85 . . .

An elderly couple shook their heads at me, refusing to make way.

"It's not for cars. It's for pedestrians." The cantankerous old man raised his fist. I hid behind my sunglasses and weaved around him.

97 . . . 99 . . .

Dark exteriors of dilapidated shop fronts encroached deep onto the cobbles. The signage drooped above broken awnings.

105.

There it was — what used to be the gun store.

105 North Parkway.

A brand new building. No dreary bricks. No murky sign. No grubby doors or windows. No clues hidden in the fabric of the building. A shining glass front and bright lights showed racks of clothes and shelves of makeup on display. 'Gracy's' read the sign.

If I stared hard enough, maybe it'd change? Revert to the rundown weapon outlet? But it didn't change. That same bright, open window never so much as blinked.

A dead end. Just like I knew it would be.

I reached for the gun. It was here that someone set my wife's death in motion. Here where they'd planted the seed. And yet, it was never here. I wanted to step out and rend the building brick by brick, smash the glass panels, and tear it down until it was nothing but rubble. But what good would that do? I couldn't unleash this hurt on a place that had never existed.

This was supposed to bring me closure. *It's a dead end. What better place to get closure than a dead end?* But all it brought was an itch to my skin that I couldn't reach to scratch.

I pulled up and scoured the police report. A post-it note stuck beneath the laminate on the same page as the shop's address. 'Just like Tammy's,' it read.

How many times had I been up this road before? *Just like Tammy's.* It was my handwriting. I flipped through the file, my eyes scanning each page, every scrap of paper, and then I found it.

'Tammy's Florist — Promenade, North Beach.'

Not far. At the end of the cobbled stretch, I rejoined the one-way loop, and followed the blue parking signs to the nearest short-stay.

My feet crunched over sand-swept sidewalks. Ocean spray softened the bite in the air. The lure of sweet doughnuts and bags of cotton-candy drifted in the breeze, and the chimes of amusements on the seafront jingled in the distance. Shades of gray muted everything in melancholy. I could have been traipsing through an old black-and-white photograph.

I passed nautical gift shops and confectioneries, fishing tackle suppliers, seafood delicatessens, shoe shops, barbers and kebab houses, and there it was.

TAMMY'S FLORIST.

The sign was painted white against a soft-blue board. Displayed in the window, a vibrant array of petals adorned a wicker basket. A label poked out from the bouquet. 70% OFF. EVERYTHING MUST GO!

The door was propped ajar. I stepped from the monochrome promenade into the striking rainbow-colors of flowers lining the walls, spilling over the aisles. Their sweet aroma lingered, a fragrant musk fermenting the air between a cacophony of seeds and bulbs.

A woman busied herself behind the counter, binding up another wicker basket advertising discounts. She dried her palms on her apron before stepping from the messy countertop and joining me in the aisle where I dallied by the lilies.

"Are you here for something specific, or just browsing?" Her deep voice resonated in low tones, like a double bass.

"Browsing, thanks."

Her broad shoulders sagged. "Well, if you see anything you like, I'm here. You can fetch me whenever you're ready."

"I saw your offer in the window." I turned my face away from her. To the flowers. There was only one exit out of here and if she recognized me, I didn't stand a chance.

"Oh yes. 70% off," she said.

"Is that on everything?"

"That's right?"

"How come? Is it a closing down sale?"

She shrugged. "Could be."

"You don't know?"

"It's not up to me." Her lips pursed, and I chanced a brief glimpse. Her brown eyes rolled and her cheeks jiggled as she shook her head.

There was something familiar about the pose she struck, the way she crossed her arms, the way those stern eyes contradicted the softness of her round face. It was like I'd seen her before. I knew this woman. *But from where?*

"It's this new marina they're planning," she said. "The Anderson Whitman Group. We got the plans through last week. They'll redevelop the entire front."

"Are you sure?" There weren't any plans for the promenade. But that was SSA, and it's Sinclair's now. Who could say what changes were in the works since the business altered?

"It's already been through consultation," she said. "Could get the summons any day."

"You'll be alright, though. Don't they look after the local businesses when something like this happens?"

"You don't know much about the Anderson Whitman Group, do you?"

*I only managed the group for seven years, so no. I know absolutely nothing about it. Obviously.* I turned back to the lilies, staring across the gleaming white of their spouting petals.

"Bunch of corporate fat cats," she continued. "They only look after each other. I came to this city to run a small, independent florist. That's all. Is that too much to ask?"

"You didn't pay to be in the AWG when you set up shop?"

"I couldn't afford it. Not with the rates they charge. If I was part of their group, I'd have no trouble turning a profit. But as it is, I've got no chance. None of us independents do."

"You mean there are others in the same boat as you?"

"Look at the stores on this promenade. Every one of them's got some kind of sale, trying to shift their goods before they disappear. I don't even know why I bother sometimes. Even if I sell the lot, who's to say I'll see the money tomorrow?"

"What do you mean?"

"Ever since I got here, it's been one problem after another. If you looked back through our books, you'd see we've never had a boom in sales. Never sold our quota, not for a single day. Doesn't that seem odd to you?"

*Not as odd as the fact you're telling me all this. Strangest sales tactics I've ever seen.*

She rubbed her forehead. "Nobody's that unlucky. Not even me. And get this. I got a card in the post today from my Mom thanking me for that parcel I sent her. So I phoned her up. Apparently, I'd bought her a handbag which cost the best part of two hundred bucks. When I checked the figures, I hadn't turned a single cent of profit. So where'd the handbag come from? Can you explain that?"

"Maybe you forgot buying it?"

"Yeah. And what else did I forget?" We stood in silence staring at the shelf before she burst out laughing. "I'm sorry. You only came in here to look at some flowers and here I am, blabbering away. You must think I sound like a crazy person."

"No, it's okay. Are you saying you think the AWG are controlling your profits to force you out?"

"Ask any of the independents. How many of us can compete with them? They'd retrograde anything to keep us in our place. Now, with this new marina, do you really think they'll compensate us? You must be having a laugh."

I shook my head.

"You don't believe me, do you?" she said.

"It's not that. It's just . . . why take the risk? It's not like they need the profits. They already make enough, I reckon."

"There's only so much soil and so many flowers. This city's all they've got. And they want as much of the room as they can to grow."

"You really think so?"

She nodded. "It's the plants with the deepest roots that grow the tallest. The AWG are a weed and they're taking over, but I don't plan on just sitting back and letting that happen."

"What can you do?"

"I've got a few tricks up my sleeve. Don't you worry. If I can find a way of staying, I'll stay. These plans might fall through yet. Why fret about tomorrow when you've got today to think about?"

"And if you can't stay?" I asked.

"I'll go back home. Save a bit, and try again."

"Open another florist?"

"It's my dream. What's the point of having a dream if you don't chase it?"

I shrugged, reached out and fumbled at a white flower and damp stalk.

She wiped her apron. "Listen. I didn't want to say anything, but have we met? Your face is so familiar." Her eyes squinted and I faced forwards, confining her to the periphery.

"I'll take these," I said.

"The lilies? How many?"

"A dozen."

She scooped the flowers out of the bucket they rested in. "Shall I arrange them for you?"

"Is it extra?"

"Not today, it isn't. Who're they for?"

"My wife."

"What's her name?"

"Lottie." White lilies were always her favorite.

"Lucky girl. What's the occasion?"

"No occasion."

"You're not in the doghouse are you?" She bundled the flowers in her arms and waddled back to the counter where she filled a wicker basket with them, spreading the blooms among the wild array of leafy fronds. "I used to know a Charlotte who sometimes went by Lottie. From back home. Lovely girl."

"Is that right?"

"Yeah. Tragic, what happened to her." She wrapped the basket in translucent plastic, tying a ribbon into a bow around the gathered top.

"How so?" I asked.

"Long story. Anyway, here you are, love. That'll be Eleven-Ninety-Five."

I threw the money onto the counter. "Thanks. What was she like?"

"Who?"

"This Lottie you knew?"

"Oh, she was lovely. We went to school together. Kept in touch over the years. One of those friends who's just always there."

"Except, she isn't now."

"No. She . . . died."

"I'm so sorry."

The florist shrugged. "Don't be. It wasn't your fault, was it?"

"How did it happen?"

Her fingers toyed with a pair of scissors on the counter. "She was killed."

"Did they ever find out who?"

She shook her head.

*I shouldn't press it. Leave, while you still can.* "Who do you think could've done it?" I asked.

*Idiot. Just get out of there.*

She chewed her lip. "That's the thing. Nobody in their right mind would have wanted to harm Lottie. She just wasn't like that. She was the kind of person who only had friends."

"Could it have been an accident?"

"No. It wasn't a robbery. She was — it was cruel, what happened to her."

"If it wasn't anyone she knew, maybe it was someone she dealt with? You don't know of anyone she might have been meeting with, or anything?"

She scowled at me. *Too far, Adam.* Her grip tightened around the scissors. "What's with all the questions?"

*Get out. Now.* "No reason. Just curious."

"Is that all? You didn't answer my question before. Who are you?"

I smiled and picked up the basket. "Thanks for the flowers. I hope it works out for you, with the marina and everything."

I rushed out the door. My feet yearned to run across the promenade. If she twigged who I was, police would crawl the seafront, their sirens washing the monochrome gray with flashing red and blue. *Calm down. If you run, someone's bound to realize something's off. What kind of demented lunatic runs while carrying flowers?*

The bouquet distracted from my face, a perfect disguise as my footsteps clattered over unsteady cobbles. Concrete dampened the hollow click of my shoes as I rounded the corner where the car stood waiting. I slammed the door, blocking out the hiss of wind. My chest boiled, shoulders stretched as I lifted the flowers through to the back seat. A twang across my neck forced me to drop them. I grabbed at where the pain throbbed and massaged the muscle while my eyes glanced back over the file, still open on the passenger's seat.

'Just like Tammy's,' the note read. That was the clue I'd left myself. Now all I had to do was figure out what it meant.

## EIGHTEEN

THE SUBURB LOOKED identical to any other as I drove through a mosaic of houses surrounded by a nest of stores. Some of the bigger estates boasted a small supermarket. Others kept a quarter for local grocers, outlets and the odd charity shop. But without exception, every suburb had its own Royal Burger Co.

Inside the restaurant, white ceiling lights bathed self-service terminals in a flat, sterile uniform, as plain as the ill-fitting t-shirts worn by the employees.

"Order number 825."

I stepped to the till and collected the XL Max from the puss-ridden concierge, selecting a table as far away from a window as possible. The steaming burger wrapped in flimsy cardboard tasted bland as ever. But I hadn't come for the food.

On the table, a plastic triangle advertised free unlimited public WiFi. It hadn't connected from the car park, but Celia's phone linked from here just fine.

I spread the police file out and a slop of sauce from the bun spurted onto the laminated page. It dabbed clean with a napkin and I slurped at a straw to dilute the salty aftertaste with ice-cold sugar water. *It's supposed to taste of cherries, not the onset of diabetes.*

I flicked through the file. *'Just like Tammy's.'* There had to be an answer in here somewhere.

Black-and-whites of Lottie's body filled the page, and my stomach threatened to evacuate the mush of burger I'd swallowed. *Don't look at them.* I turned over the autopsy report and stopped at the witness statements. Detective Lopez had interviewed the neighbors in my building.

'Janice Rhys. Apartment 2309. Claimed she heard shouting earlier in the evening. Otherwise, nothing unusual.'

'Howard Jones. Apartment 2312. Heard some raised voices, but said the spouse couldn't have been the guy that did it because he's an absolute wimp.'

'Adam Swann. Husband. 'Yes, we fought that night . . .'' My eyes glossed over the words, but they didn't see letters on a page. My vision was overcome, transported back to our bedroom. Purple curtains half-closed over the window blinds reflected the light of the bedside lamp in a soft shimmer.

*"You're leaving now?" The angst in Lottie's voice grated the nerves on my neck.*

*"I told you. They want me there right away." I flung baggy shirts and hole-ridden socks into the suitcase open on the bed, second guessing every garment landing in its deep mouth.*

*"But . . . you? They want you? How did they . . .?"*

*"I'm as surprised as you. I don't know how it happened." Shadow filled the gaping drawer as I folded and refolded my towel.*

*"What I still don't understand is what you thought you were doing, going there in the first place." Her hands rooted to her hips, knuckles stiff, elbows pointed sharp.*

*Her cheeks flared redder than the wine she'd abandoned in the living room. An imposing frown etched exasperation on her steely expression.*

"It's like I said. I saw their advert on TV and I thought, you know, it looked good."

"Anderson Whitman? 'Get the life you always wanted.' Is our life not good enough for you anymore?"

"It isn't like that, honey. I just—"

"You just what? Thought it was about time for a change? Do I really make you that unhappy?"

"No, I was just curious."

"Curious? I'll bet. Curious to see what you're missing out on. Whether it was time to upgrade to a new model. Go on. You can tell me."

"Of course not." *I shook my head.*

"Is this not what you want anymore?" *The glaze on her swollen eyes glimmered, fighting back tears of rage and sorrow.*

*I stood with a pair of trousers stretched between my hands, their crisp crease draped in a languid arch as my shoulders sagged.* "Lottie. The whole reason I went to Anderson Whitman and looked into a trial package was . . . it was for you. For us."

"For me? So it's my life you want to change, is it?"

"I just want to give you what you deserve. What you want."

"And you think I can get that in New Yesterday? Don't you know me at all?"

"I thought—"

"You know how I feel about that place." *Her jaw clenched solid as her eyes squinted hatefully.*

213

"Is this because of your petition?" I dropped the cotton-print pajamas in the suitcase.

"What if it is?"

"Darling, that petition—"

"You don't think we deserve some answers? You know what they did to Tammy."

"No." My whole body soured. "We don't. That's the point, isn't it? Nobody knows." I plodded to the en-suite and grabbed my toothbrush. The tap of her foot from the bedroom hammered on polished floorboards.

"If there wasn't something wrong with what happened to Tammy, then why has someone from the city agreed to come and meet with me? Huh?" She pouted, her eyebrows raised, the same as her voice. "I need you here. To help me. You know I'm rubbish at the face-to-face stuff. How nervous I get. If I'm going to get answers, then you need to stay. Do you understand?" Her arms folded across her chest, creasing the front of her jade green blouse.

"I would, if I could get out of this work trip. But I can't."

"You won't."

"My hands are tied. I don't want to lose this job. Not after everything else. I didn't expect that going to Anderson Whitman today would end up in an invite to a sales conference."

"I don't know what you were expecting from those charlatans."

"I was expecting to find out our options. Not get a lecture from you because I now have an appointment in the city. The firm needs this. My boss specifically asked for me, darling. I can't tell him no just because you've got a bad feeling about it. Besides, whoever's coming to meet with you, they're not coming because something's wrong. It's the opposite. They're coming to prove nothing's wrong. Can't you see? Do you really want me around for that?"

"You never believed I might actually be right. Did you?"

"Honey, there are millions of people in New Yesterday. All of them living good lives. Better lives. If it was such a terrible place to be, then why hasn't Tammy left yet?"

Her face scrunched and she threw her arms up, stomping over the squeaks in the pine floor. "You don't want to be here when they arrive. That's it, isn't it? That's why you went to that estate agent today. Of all days. You're trying to run away. Run away, like you always do."

"I just want things to go back to the way they were. Before all this. Before you posted that thing online. Transparent New Yesterday. I honestly don't know what you were thinking."

"At least one of us is thinking."

I rubbed my forehead. "Have you even considered the consequences?"

"What consequences?"

"Let's say your petition takes off, and people get behind this #TNY thing. What next?"

"What's that supposed to mean?" She asked it as if it were an accusation.

"How far are you willing to go for it? Where does this rabbit-hole end?"

"See! I knew it! You don't want this. You want me to change. Just say it."

"I want you, darling. I want us. Not some fight that isn't even yours to begin with."

She crossed her arms, resolute. "Someone has to make a stand."

I stood over the half-empty suitcase, shaking my head. "Look. I get it. You've known Tammy from way back, and you keep in touch over your phone and everything. But whatever's going on with her isn't your battle. I want to be here for you. Really, I do. I want you to realize what we could have if you just . . . let this go. That it's nothing to be afraid of."

"And what if you're wrong?"

"Maybe if you could see New Yesterday for yourself, you'd be able to drop this business with Tammy, and we can go back. We could even—"

"We could what?"

I bit my lip. "We could . . . try again?"

"Try again? You're one to talk. When did you ever try? I mean really try. You give up the minute things get difficult. Even now, you think I should quit, don't you? You think this petition is a waste of time and I should step away."

"I don't want to see you get hurt. You deserve to be happy. Remember what that was like? Being happy? Carefree?"

"It's not wrong to care, Adam."

"That's not what I mean."

"What about the others?" she said. "People are getting hurt. Every day. Tammy lost everything, and she doesn't even remember it. And now she wants to do it all over again. Open another florist. She's already found a place on the promenade. And by the time she does, who knows *if she'll remember how it all went wrong? There needs to be transparency. Don't you see?"*

*"And where do you factor in all this? Who made you responsible?"*

*"I did. Me." She thumped her fist against her chest. "How many people have to suffer in silence while that place scrambles their brains? It's theft, what they did to her. Can't you see that? Unless someone draws the line, how's it ever going to change? You think they should be allowed to rob people blind and get away with it?"*

*"I—"*

*"This is bigger than me. Thousands have responded online. Thousands. I owe it to them. This could seriously turn into something, and you think I should give that up? Forget all about it and come play happy families? I'm already down the rabbit-hole, Adam. You just don't want to come with me. You should be standing by my side, instead of running off because some Anderson Whitman creep set up a business meeting."*

*"It's my work. I have to go. Mr. Strickland is sending me to New Yesterday to meet with this client. It's all sorted. There's no getting out of it."*

*"Yeah, and when did they sort out this business deal? On the exact day you went to inquire about a lifestyle package. You think that's a coincidence?"*

*"I think it's about time something went our way. Don't you?"*

*"You're really going to leave, aren't you?"*

*I closed the lid of the suitcase. The zip squealed shut. "Look. Lottie. You should come with me."*

*"Go with you? To New Yesterday? Can you hear yourself right now?"*

*"Come on. Let's go together. Forget all this. And we can—"*

*"We can what?"*

*It was useless saying more. She wasn't budging. The suitcase's wheels bounced over the uneven floor of the apartment, dragged past where she stood, her hand on her forehead, her body about to burst.*

*"Are you going to abandon me when I need you the most? I never took you for a coward, Adam. I stood up for you when people called you names. But you're just like the rest of those worms. Just go. Leave. Get out of here and don't come back!"*

*The bedroom door slammed. I turned to face the door. My skin crawled with the urge to open it. To whisper through the thick frame that I loved her. To break down this barrier between us. To tell her I'd be back tomorrow. Wasn't she more important than a job? Than a life? Of course she was. That's why I had to go. I was doing this for her. She'd see that in time. Maybe I could explain it? Help her see how precious she was. That she's the one I was fighting for. But the sound of her sobs trickling below the gap cut me short. How could I face her? How could I make her understand?*

*I said nothing. My hand fell to the cold metal handle of the suitcase and I made for the door.*

'. . . and I left and started driving, and that's when I got the call from you, Detective Lopez.' Beside my statement, there was a note. 'Phone tracked. Whereabouts at time of death confirmed.'

I closed the file. My eyes swelled with tears I refused to cry. My fists clenched beneath the table, scrunching napkins until they tore apart, frayed into pieces in the whites of my palms. I wanted to scream, but I couldn't. Not here.

'Get out of here and don't come back.' Those were the last words she'd ever say to me. I didn't want to hear them, but my ears held onto them like an echo, forcing me to listen again and again. Anger relented to a wave of anguish. *Lottie, I'm so sorry.*

I sniffed back the pain and glanced around. Nobody made eye contact. Nobody ever did in a Royal Burger Co.

*Keep it together Adam. Think. What do you actually know?* I turned the pages back to that post-it-note. 'Just like Tammy's.' Ever since Tammy had gone to New Yesterday, she'd been having problems. Her savings were being swallowed. The profits she turned just disappeared. Lottie had tried to do something about it. Started a petition for greater transparency, and then she was gone.

The image of Tammy on the petition's front-page flooded back to me. *Of course I'd seen her before. I must've scrolled across her picture a hundred times.* Today, in the flesh, she'd been so sure about the Anderson Whitman Group. But she was wrong. I knew those accounts inside out and backwards. It wasn't possible for the group to monopolize small businesses. That's what the planning office was there to ensure. A few clicks on their register and I'd have proof.

I swiped the screen. The table rattled as my leg shook. I gripped hold of the file in case I had to run, and typed the address for the planning office's online database. A circle loaded, buffering, and my eyes raised to the queue of people waiting for their meals. Two teenage girls argued with the server, holding up the line. One of them had pink cotton-candy hair. The other was wearing a leopard-print onesie.

"Yeah, I know it's vegan, but is it gluten-free?" the cotton-candy girl asked.

"If you want it gluten-free, then it'll have to come without the bun."

"But how is she supposed to eat it without the bun?" Leopard-print looked outraged.

The server shrugged. "You can have a bun, if you want."

"But then it'll have gluten in it."

"It's your choice."

"But it's not a choice though, is it?" Leopard-print folded her arms.

"You can have the veggie supreme with or without the bun. Those are your options."

"I don't even know why we came here."

The server sighed. "You took the words right out of my mouth."

The webpage flashed on my phone. I clicked on the magnifying glass to search all planning queries in New Yesterday due to be made within the next thirty days. More buffering.

Leopard-print slammed her tray on the table next to mine. "What a gonk."

"I know, right?" Cotton-candy replied, taking the plastic bucket-seat opposite.

"You'd think in this day and age they'd give you options, at least."

"Mm-hmm." Cotton-candy leaned forward. "I went to an SFC the other day and asked them if they had any vegetarian options, and you know what they said to me?"

"What?"

"They said, 'You do know this is Southern Fried *Chicken*, right?'"

Leopard-print's jaw dropped as she flung her hair over her shoulder. "Seriously?"

"For reals."

"That's outrageous. You should have posted it."

Cotton-candy took her phone from seemingly nowhere. "I'll post it now."

A box on my screen popped up telling me that my 'search retrieved no results.' Tammy said they'd sent her the letters already. But according to this, nothing was in the works. No plans. Nothing.

From the folds of my jacket, I withdrew the list of proposed planning changes I'd grabbed from Celia's desk. Half-washed away by rain, smudged words blurred across the laminate, made sticky by the residue of whatever they'd covered the XL Max with. Was it cheese?

Maybe I was looking in the wrong place? I changed the filter to show plans passed within the last thirty days, and typed in the Gracy's store address from the planning list, then hit 'search.'

"Have you seen this?" Cotton-candy showed Leopard-print her phone, chewing with an open mouth.

"Jason is such a weirdo."

"You think so?"

"He's a meat eating, loud-mouthed couch junkie."

"Yeah, but that video he made was pretty funny."

"So?"

Another box appeared. Still no results. But . . ? I was in that Gracy's today a few seconds before it moved. The address was spelled correct. What was the problem? I searched again, but the results came up with the same message, instantaneous, like it was punishing me for questioning it.

Where were the plans? What about the gun store? 105 North Parkway, now a shiny new Gracy's. There had to be a record of the changes somewhere.

"Did you get that pop-up, too?" Leopard-print glanced up from her straw.

"Yeah. I can't believe they still haven't caught that guy."

"Linear violations. Do you think he's even in the city?"

The same generic pop-up alert flashed across my screen. I tapped it, and staring back at me was a picture of my face. PRESS HERE IF YOU'VE SEEN THIS MAN.

"I doubt it. I mean, it's been three weeks, hasn't it?"

"Yeah, but if he wasn't in the city, then why are they still sending the alerts?"

"I dunno. Police are dumb."

"You think they'll ever catch the freak?"

"Who knows?"

Leopard-print nudged Cotton-candy with her foot. "Hey," she whispered. "You see that guy? Don't you think he seems a bit—"

"You mean?"

"Sshhh. Why not?"

*Are they talking about me? If I look at them, they'll know for certain it's me. Just keep your head down. Don't look up.*

"He looks just like him."

"Yeah, it's scary."

"You don't think he could be the real . . ?"

I scrambled the phone into my pocket and swept up the paperwork, bunching it together and closing the front cover tight.

"Of all the places to eat in the city, would he really come to a Royal Burger Company?"

"Not when they can't even serve gluten-free."

"Come on." The girls giggled.

I stood to leave, but so did they. We smashed into each other.

"Watch it!"

"Sorry," I said, my head down.

"How's my hair? Has he messed it up?"

"It's lush, girl."

They ignored me, sidled past and skipped to a table further down the aisle with manufactured carelessness. A young man sat alone with his phone out, recording himself.

"Excuse me. Are you Johnboy21?" Leopard-print asked coyly.

"I love your vlog," Cotton-candy gushed, pressing her chest towards him.

The man looked up from his phone. "You ladies want to be in an episode?"

I left them squealing as I hurried for the door. Relief surged through every pore. Almost enough to forget how my face was on every phone in the city.

"Ready, ladies? And . . . action."

*Hurry, Adam. Before he films more than just his duckface.*

## NINETEEN

I COLLAPSED INTO the car and heaved a deep breath. The scent of lilies drifted from the back seat, filling the cabin with their humid, overwhelming sweetness.

*"We are gathered here today, to celebrate the union of Adam Swann and Charlotte Dwyer."*

I was alone inside the car, but that didn't stop the voice from speaking, or the black of night from dissolving into pink sunlight filtered through the mottled crinkles of a canvas awning.

*My legs jellified. My stomach made to leap out of my mouth, but some slow, steady breathing kept it from abandoning me and taking off down the aisle.*

*In through the nose. Out through the mouth.*

*Lottie's hand reached across and squeezed mine. Was she as nervous as I was? All these months of planning. How had it come round so fast? Every moment until this one belonged in a vacuum. This was the start of life. Our life. The two of us. She'd been my girlfriend and fiancé, but once she'd stood in front of this elderly man with a forest of nasal hair and repeated a few words, she'd be my wife. My wife! The waiting would be over and our journey can finally begin. Was this real? Did I get so lucky as to actually be marrying this woman for real?*

*"Love is patient. Love is kind . . ."* His voice droned on, trying to replicate the effect of an echo in an amphitheater, except we were beneath a gazebo on the rooftop of our apartment block. I wished he'd get to the end already and let me say 'I do'! Behind him, lights in the city twinkled against the rich warmth of a fading sun, reddening as it dipped below the horizon.

*"Look at that,"* Lottie whispered.

*"Look at what?"*

*"The color of the sun. It's turned red just for us."*

Our guests shuffled, repositioning themselves on the few rows of seats behind us while the old man conducted the ceremony like he was performing a Shakespeare monolog. *". . . It bears all things. . . believes all things . . ."*

*"Are you happy?"* I whispered. Another squeeze of the hand. It filled me with the warmth of summer. Made me whole.

*". . . hopes all things, endures all things . . ."*

Her dress fell from her shoulders, and she extricated her hand from mine to reposition the silk strap, stopping it from slipping down her arm. As she reached for her shoulder, I caught the scent of the bouquet she gripped, waiting for the ring exchange before she'd hand it off.

*". . . Love never fails."*

The sweet aroma of her white lilies masked her perfume, drifting in the breeze, carried by the glow of the setting sun. Her lips curled as her hand returned to mine.

My chest fluttered at her touch.

Just breathe.

In through the nose. Out through the mouth.

*Those lilies filled my nostrils with each new inhalation, painting the air sweet. The aroma dimmed with the light. The corona of the sun vanished behind a building, and the memory faded.*

But my mind didn't return to the car. Another flash of memory reached out and grabbed hold of me, pulling me inside it, and I was powerless to resist.

*Before me stood the same old man. Same robes. Same hairs creeping out of his nose like the roots of a plant. The gazebo was gone, the rooftop balcony replaced by walls stained by melancholy. Rain hammered at the windows. On the front row, shuffling skirts soaked up the muffled coughs and crumples of tissues. A hand reached across to squeeze mine. But it wasn't hers. It would never be hers again.*

*"We are gathered here today to remember the life of Mrs. Charlotte Swann." The same voice labored each syllable so the vowels settled in the claustrophobic air. The pressure in my chest swelled until it choked. My eyes rooted to the mud prints on the tiled floor. Four feet away, the polished coffin reflected the funeral parlor's glare. She was right there. What remained of her. I felt it. But I couldn't lift my eyes to face her.*

*The man's voice carried on, his words an indistinct haze. How could you put a person's life into words? A jumble of letters and sounds seemed so empty. How could they ever do her justice? All those subtleties. All those moments, impossible to express.*

*I'd once caught her combing her hair, peering at herself in the mirror when she thought nobody was watching. Her face in the dim morning light as it filtered through the window. The glint on her hair as she toyed*

226

*with it. The look she made when she noticed me watching. Her shy smile, eyes cast downwards in the moment before she'd pretend to be upset with me for stealing a glimpse of her. It was the slightest moment, one of billions beyond the capacity of words. Life can't be translated into language, no matter how beautiful the sentiment. And she was so full of life.*

*The old man finished his eulogy. All that was left to do was say goodbye. What words could be uttered that I hadn't said already? That I hadn't screamed into my pillow in the twilight hours when sleep eluded me?*

*I approached where she lay, and tried to lift my head. It wasn't real. It couldn't be. White lilies adorned the casket, arranged by Tammy and couriered from New Yesterday. My shaking hand steadied on the coffin's lid. I stooped, my stomach lurched forwards, and my forehead pushed against the solid wood. I wanted to rip it open and cradle her in my arms. But that was something I could never do again. I gulped the air, swallowing it in bursts. A hand pressed on my shoulder as I forced back the pain.*

*Settle down. You can do this. She wouldn't have wanted you to sob like a freak. Not in public, at least.*

*In through the nose. Out through the mouth.*

*I held onto the lilies' scent like it was a piece of her I could take with me, inhaling it until the aroma clung to the inside of my nostrils.*

And then I was back in the car with the bunch of lilies pouring the same fragrance through a split in the plastic wrapping. I cracked a window. The scent seeped out and the floral perfume dwindled.

The memories of losing her tossed me about like a ship in a storm. One moment, I had Lottie at my side, and the next, she was gone. From high speed, I'd been stopped dead. The shift was too sudden. Too much, as though I'd driven straight into a wall.

The words of that doctor on TV flooded through me. What had he said about going linear? The longer it goes on, the more dangerous it becomes.

How much of this could I take? None of it seemed real. What even *was* real? At the same time I was burying my wife, I was serving breakfast to Gabby and taking Celia to the beach. The only thing I knew for sure was the pain of losing my wife. That was the only reality I could latch onto.

Blood pulsed around my head, throbbing in my ears, the glands on my neck bulging raw. *Maybe this is just too much. I escaped from these memories once before. Is this why I'd given Celia the file? What I'd tried to forget?*

From my pocket, I drew the phone. Its screen displayed the webpage from before, though I'd lost connection to the WiFi. 'No results,' it said. The planning register was a bust. Why hadn't it worked? I scrolled back up and reviewed the search parameters. All plans approved within the past 30 days.

I opened it to the list of planning applications I'd snatched from the office.

30 days. Of course there were no results. These plans weren't passed yesterday, they were passed years ago. Maybe the cops were right, and I'd gone linear. Is that why I still remembered Gabby? Celia? Why I'd lost everything? Because I remembered? Because no matter what the city altered, what new events replaced the old, there were some things I just couldn't change.

*Perhaps I should turn myself in. Let Anderson Whitman erase all this. Replace it. Start fresh. No one would have to know. Not even me.*

The file slipped onto my lap. I tipped the box towards me and the silhouette of the gun darkened the bottom. What was I thinking? *Get a grip. You can't do that to Lottie. Not until you know whose finger squeezed the trigger. Get a hold of yourself and breathe.*

*In through the nose, and out through the mouth.*

Whoever came from the city to meet Lottie had something to do with that petition. And the petition started with Tammy. I'd seen Tammy, and she was sure the AWG were involved. But that couldn't be true. And the way to prove it was in those planning records.

Access to any planning records older than 30 days would have to be by hard copy. Concealed in the archive of the main planning office. I scrolled down the open webpage and checked the address. City Hall. It hadn't moved. Still in the center — the beating heart with a million eyes.

*Perfect. Just perfect. They couldn't have moved it to a quiet suburb?*

Twilight masked everything. Its beaming headlights pierced the cover of darkness. Now that night had come, I was invisible once more.

My mind was anywhere but the road. I had to get those hard copies. But how? How was I supposed to get into the city, through the reception of the planning office and into that archive without being caught?

## TWENTY

THE JAWS OF A PLAN kept gnawing me awake. I needed WiFi. *Can't do a thing without WiFi.*

The train station. They were always advertising how 'free' it was, and unlike the Royal Burger Co., I wouldn't have to go inside, or be on a train to use it.

I pulled around the furthest corner of the station. The engine settled for the night, as did I.

*Where to start? A disguise? Diversion? How was I going to . . .*

The roar of train carriages startled me awake. They thundered on the track towards the station.

Why was everything so loud in the morning?

7:55.

The planning office wouldn't open for another hour.

I stretched the stiffness out of my joints. As I hid the cardboard box in the footwell, the glovebox knocked open, and Celia's junk tumbled out. Makeup. Chewing gum. Reading glasses.

I picked up the black frames and tried them on. They blurred everything, but combined with the stubble, they did a pretty good job of making me look slightly less like the guy in the news.

*Hey, why not? It worked for Clark Kent. And he didn't even have the stubble.*

No. It wasn't enough. Not by itself.

*Think, Adam. You've got nobody in the city. No favors to call in. It's just you out here, sleeping rough in the . . .*

Wait.

Sleeping rough.

That's it.

I reached for the remaining cash Jeff had given me. Aside from a handful of singles, I wedged the rest into the phone's case and connected to the WiFi. 'Retrostorage available at this station.' I ordered a locker, selected the items I wanted to leave there, and confirmed the order.

The phone and cash disappeared from my hand, replaced by a locker key, stubbed with a number. According to the retrograde, the stuff had been locked up an hour ago.

Everything was in place. Now all I needed was an accomplice. I pocketed the frames, and with my shades on and hood up, I headed for the city.

The clamor of traffic played like a soundtrack, getting louder as the buildings grew taller. Curtains and blinds flickered in high-rise windows, as though the skyscrapers themselves were waking up, opening their eyes to watch the chaos below.

Sleeping bags gathered in mounds in front of empty storefronts. The torrent of passers-by looked anywhere else. Did people know what these beggars were asking for when they pleaded for change? And here, even in New Yesterday where change was the fabric of the city, there were those who needed it, who asked every day for it, but never found any.

Lucky for me, I guess.

A bearded man sat in his blue-green sleeping bag, his tattered gloves wrapped around a polyfoam cup of cold coffee. In his lap, he cradled a plastic bag with nothing inside. But the bag was his, at least.

I knelt beside him, my nostrils clenched at the stale sweat clouding the air around him, seeping into his clothes. I deposited the pile of singles in front of him. A smile wrinkled his face, revealing his gums and what was left of his teeth. He snatched at the notes and flung them into his bag.

"There's more where that came from," I said. He stopped and stared at me with a look of desperation and hopefulness that might have been one and the same. "Are you interested?"

"More?"

"That's right. But I'll need you to do something for me. Are you up for it?"

"Anything. I'll do anything."

"You know the train station on East Parade in the Thrift District?"

"I think so."

"How quick can you get there?"

"It'd take a while. Twenty minutes, maybe more?"

"You could be there by 9 o'clock?"

"What time is it now?"

I checked my watch. "Just turned eight-thirty."

"Sure."

I produced a key from my pocket and held it in an outstretched palm. "Inside a locker, you'll find a phone and more cash. It could buy you some new clothes, get you on the start to a new life. And if you're careful about how you use the phone, you could become whoever you wanted. Change all of this." I nodded at his shelter, if you could call it that.

"What's in it for you?" He winced at the bitter coffee.

"At nine o'clock, I need you to ring the police and tell them you saw the linear guy from the news catching a train towards the West Side. You got that?"

He licked his lips, transfixed by the key. His gloved fingers reached out to clutch hold of it.

I drew my hand back and his eyes flashed at me.

"Do we have a deal?"

"Thank you," he nodded.

I let him take the key, and he slipped it under his cap. He rolled up his sleeping bag, packed it into his plastic carrier, tied the worn-out laces on his trainers, and set off limping in the direction I'd just come from. There was no guarantee he'd do what we'd agreed. I couldn't force him to make the call. Once he had the phone and the rest of Jeff's cash from inside the locker, there was every chance he'd forget. But who else could I ask to do it? This was my only chance. I had to trust that gratitude would be enough.

Now all I had to do was get to City Hall and talk my way into a Planning Archive without being recognized.

I merged with the crowd, disappearing along with everyone else, a drop of water in the great river rushing towards oblivion.

City Hall was more monument than office. Huge pillars decorated its façade. They weren't needed to keep the building upright, but they looked important.

8:48.

Loitering in front of the entrance might attract attention, so I rounded the corner. Hotels lined the street.

On ground level, each entrance had its own individual appeal. No two were alike. Yet, when I raised my eyes to the towering structures, everything past the second floor looked the same — windows spaced evenly across a concrete frame.

I stopped outside one hotel. Gold-plated spinning doors opened onto a marble interior where an ancient Greek-esque statue stood on a spouting fountain. But I wasn't drawn to the lavish museum lobby or the sun glinting off the old-fashioned ticket booth reception desk. It was the poster hung in the window that beckoned me.

PHOENIX HOTEL

MIDNIGHT TONIGHT – BOOK RELEASE

'REMEMBERING GUINEVERE'

SPECIAL APPEARANCE BY

GABRIELLE LAURENT

DOORS OPEN 10:00PM

A mockup of the book dominated the poster, and beside it, Gabby's face. Her luscious red lips curled into the smile she used to reserve for me, and only me. My own lips tickled with the memory of her kiss, those brown eyes closing and the scent of her perfume filling me with mindless passion. And beneath her, at the bottom of the poster, a tiny postscript read 'Sponsored by Sinclair's Accounts.'

Jeff was launching the book. She was his client now, and the rest. I stood staring, not at a poster, but at another life. At a life that could've been. I remembered how we celebrated the last book she released, and a piece of me yearned to be there for her now. But that piece was broken. It would never be whole. She was never mine, because Lottie was my life. My only real life. *Just look away from the window and forget.*

8:56. *Pull yourself together. You only get one shot at this.*

My feet carried me over the cracked sidewalk back to City Hall. I climbed the few steps beneath the pillars to the ornamental oak-stained doors. One of them was propped open and I skulked inside. The lifts waited down the hall, but I slipped past the few skirt-suit and white-blouse workers, opting for the stairs.

Up three flights. So far, so good. My breath heaved and sweat beaded behind my sunglasses, cloying at my eyes.

9:00. *Here goes nothing.*

The door creaked onto the third floor where the planning office was concealed. Offices ran along one straight corridor, spanning the length of the floor. Nameplates showed letters and titles that were almost as long as the names themselves.

I passed along the corridor until I reached the one marked 'planning—reception.' The door was ajar. Inside, a steady babble of chatter floated through the office.

"He's heading towards West Side."

"You don't say?"

"That's what the alert says. 'Train delays on the West Side — police in pursuit of suspect'."

"And you think it's the linear guy?"

"I know it is. It says so right here."

*Thank you, my homeless friend. You've earned that money.* With people believing I was on a train across town, even if they recognized me, they'd be more inclined to dismiss me as a dodgy lookalike. I replaced the shades with Celia's reading glasses and peeled back the hood from my hair. The door swung on its hinge.

Showtime.

"Hello, ladies. Is this where I come to get the key?"

Two clerks glanced over their glasses in unison, and stared at one another. Their faces shifted from one expression to the next, telepathically arguing about which of them would draw the short straw and have to deal with me. The loser of their silent bickering turned abruptly. "And who are you?" she said.

"I'm here to check your archive. Didn't you get the memo? From the builders? Annual inspection for building maintenance."

"Annual inspection? I don't remember us having an inspection before?"

"It's new. We're checking all the offices. Making sure there's no work that needs doing."

"Well, if you're checking the building, you should start here. You see that crack? Whenever it rains, water drips down the wall. And the windows don't open. And—"

"We'll get round to it, don't worry. But for now, I've just been asked to check your archive. For security. Data protection and all that. The rest of the building has a lower security level, but your archive needs a priority inspection. It's to keep us regulated, so we don't have to pay for a vault across town or some other nonsense. The legal team insisted. I don't get it myself, but I'm sure you both do."

Her eyebrows raised. At least, it looked that way through the blur of these lenses. "It's odd we didn't get notified."

"You should've got an email. I don't like it any more than you. They had me up at the crack of dawn for this. But the sooner I see it, the sooner I'm out of your hair."

Again, she consulted with the other girl using only the flicker of expressions and flash of eyes. Her eyebrows knitted together as she repositioned her glasses. "Alright. What's your name?"

"Jeff."

"Last name?"

"Sinclair."

"Okay. Just fill this out." She slipped the 'sign-in sheet' towards me and I scrawled an illegible squiggle as she opened a drawer and pulled out the key.

"Great. Which door is it?"

"I'll show you." She stood and shuffled past me, leading me down the hall to the last door, labeled 'Planning Records.'

The click of the latch snapped back, and the door groaned open. She switched the light, and bulbs overhead flickered across the myriad filing cabinets lining the walls.

"This is it."

"Thanks." I stepped into the room's center, studying the corners as though I had the first clue how to perform an inspection.

She tapped her foot. "Will you be long?"

"I hope not. Depends what I find." Dust tickled my throat, forcing a cough. Labels marked the cabinets alphabetically by district, followed by street. It would've been easy enough to find the records if I didn't have to squint through Celia's corrective lenses and there wasn't another pair of eyes scrutinizing my every move.

"Well, don't rush on my account." The clerk folded her arms.

"Have you got things you need to be getting on with?"

"Let's just say," she huffed, "this isn't the best start to the day."

"I know the feeling. You know what would make this go quicker?"

She raised an eyebrow.

I paced the floor, pretending to count my footsteps. "If you could find out when the last inspection was done."

"And where do you expect me to find that?"

"You keep records, don't you?"

She flapped her arms around the room. "What does this look like to you?"

"I mean digitally."

"Oh, well. Yes. Probably. But where the files will be, I have no idea."

"Well, the quicker you get me the date, the faster I'm gone."

She clicked her tongue on the roof of her mouth and sighed. "Alright. I'll check the computer. But I'll be back in a minute."

"That should be all I need."

She left a crack in the door as her footsteps faded down the hall.

I removed the spectacles and scoured the cabinets. Three of them stored planning approvals for the street where Gracy's had been moved to, each rammed full of folders. I tugged at the drawers. The metal screeched, my arms straining as I pried them open. The dim bulb was less than ideal for deciphering the system of folders, but I found Gracy's in the second cabinet along and tucked the file in my belt.

*One down.* She could return any minute. There were other buildings I wanted to check. Other approvals I needed to find. 105 North Parkway. The gun store.

On the opposite wall, there was only one drawer for North Parkway. There. I yanked the folder out, grasping it in my fingers when the clerk's voice trilled at my back, "Just what do you think you're doing?"

*Don't turn around.* "Just a random spot check." My voice cracked.

"You didn't mention a spot check before?"

*If she sees the file, it's over.* "Well, I need to check if the equipment is up to code." Slowly, I moved the folder towards the other, stuffed inside the front of my trousers. "I wouldn't want to have to come back and do this again just because I didn't do a thorough enough job this time round."

"I checked the files, but there's nothing about a previous inspection. Which team did you say you were from?"

I could feel the skepticism of her eyes buried in the back of my head. "Building Maintenance." The file pressed against my skin and I gathered my coat over it.

"So is Karen your manager, or Helen?"

I closed the drawer and turned to face her. "I think I've seen everything I need to. You've got some cracks forming, patches of damp. But it should be okay for another year."

She tilted her neck. The daggers she stared at me were sharp enough to cut me to shreds. "What happened to your glasses?"

I gulped. The frames jabbed at my leg, still in my pocket. *Stupid. Way to go, Adam.*

"Varifocals. It's easier to see without them sometimes." My heart thumped. *Just keep calm.*

"Say . . ." Lines on her face crumpled as she peered at me. " . . Has anyone ever told you how much you look like that man who's gone linear?" And then her eyes shot wide. Her wrinkles vanished as recognition swept her face with shock.

My joints tightened as though my body was gripped in a vice. "Yeah, I get it all the time." I forced a shrug. "He's gonna get caught soon, though. Weren't they chasing him on the West Side?"

"Call was a hoax, apparently." Accusation laced her tone.

"I, for one, will be much happier when they catch him."

"Tell me about it. Going linear. He's a psycho on the loose." Her eyes didn't change, pinned wide, like a hunted animal. She knew.

"Well, I'll let the boys know I've given you a clean bill of health."

She flinched as I paced towards her.

"Shall we?" I gestured to the door and she nodded, extinguishing the light before she locked the archive and rushed us back to reception.

She disappeared into her office and in my periphery, I caught her reaching for a phone.

My legs charged through the corridor. Another door opened, and I slammed into it, knocking it back against a white-haired man emerging from his office, spilling his blueprints all over the floor.

"Do you mind?" he blustered, gripping his chest.

I scurried past him, bounded to the stairs. From below, footsteps rattled on metal railings. Crackles of walkie-talkies echoed upwards.

She'd made the call. The police were already here.

I spun back into the corridor. It was empty. The old man carrying papers was gone. It didn't matter. What mattered was that my only way out of City Hall was this windowless corridor. And I had about ten seconds at most before even this hallway would be out of bounds.

I raced to the office the old man had just left, and closed myself in. The small room faced the rear of the building. Three floors up. An open window blew a draft, fluttering papers on his cluttered desk.

From the hallway behind me, rapid footsteps thumped.

I slid the window open and clambered on the sill.

"This is the police!" A megaphone blared from beyond the door.

The drainpipe was out of reach. The gray concrete of the alleyway behind City Hall concealed large vats of industrial rubbish tied up in black bags.

"We're performing a search of these offices. Please remain calm."

I held my breath and let my sneakers slip from the ledge. Wind whistled through the air, whipping up to meet me, but it did nothing to slow my fall. I stretched my legs, preparing to bend and cushion the blow as I aimed straight for the inside of the open dumpster.

My body crumpled on impact, colliding with reams of shredded paper and broken equipment. Every sinew roared. Fire ripped through my joints. A stabbing wet seeped from my side, and my teeth grit together so hard, I trembled from head to toe. Yet, somehow, I silenced the scream and pulled the bags to cover me.

Rotting garbage festered in a stench that went beyond my nostrils and penetrated my insides, seizing my stomach. It took every ounce of strength to force back the wretch. I held it, fighting against the seconds as they stalked silently by. *How long should I wait inside this putrid can? Would they have checked the window by now?*

My head poked around the bag clinging to my cheek. The window had been closed. Safe to move.

I threw the bags off, and my throat could prevent the wretch no more. My stomach lurched and a stream of vomit added to the contents of the rubbish. But with every expulsion, a raw pang screamed from my left side. I reached beneath my jacket and met with a damp patch that stained my fingers red.

A jagged shard of metal pierced a garbage bag, speckled with blood.

I forced my body upright, climbed on top of the vat and scaled the wire fence partitioning the alley. I gripped my hip. Stumbled through back streets. After a few paces, I'd found some footing and could just about pull off a walk that wouldn't attract attention.

The alley exited onto a street one block down from City Hall. I looped the way I'd come. Back to the city.

Sweat boiled on my forehead, dousing the rim of my sunglasses. My spine shivered. Pain blocked the white sun's heat, but its sharpness stabbed my eyes. Every building, every window, every car, every person was a tremor. They all shook, blurred by the intensity of morning light as it blistered the tarmac.

"Three for two!"

"Fresh fish!"

"New and improved!"

"Two for a dollar!"

Voices raged, one and then another. The sheer swell of sound disoriented me. *Where am I? A market? Have I reached the Thrift District already?*

Direction was a haze, a mire — guzzling my feet until they dragged in wades between stalls.

A tussle broke out as two hagglers bartered too hard with a seller. Bodies surrounded the fight, pushing past me.

In the confusion, I grabbed a jacket and sweater from a nearby stall, traded one jacket for another and pushed the blood-soaked overcoat into a trash can. I cradled the files to my stomach, yanked a scarf from the next stall, and plunged it into my side.

The commotion diffused and the crowds parted, filtering back to mill about the stalls. I scuffled through the fray, the vendor's shouts churning my head so I couldn't think. And then they all stopped. Their phones chimed in unison and they checked the alert.

"Anyone match that description?" a voice yelled.

"Do you see someone wearing that?" another voice blared.

"Nobody."

"Forget it then. Two for a dollar. A dollar for two."

Their phones returned to their pockets, and the usual proceedings recommenced. From the market, I swam through the city's stream, invisible even to myself. Blotches of darkness narrowed my vision. My head pounded, but the drum of the city kept me in time until the masses dissolved and the buildings shrank. I skirted the sidewalks back to the train station where my homeless friend had brought the police in droves, but was now as quiet as a cemetery.

The car waited, parked beside the tracks. I slammed the door and released a wail that shook the cabin. My new jacket peeled off and I tore at the scarf beneath my hoodie, lifting it from my skin where dark, sticky blood oozed from the puncture.

I needed treatment. Fast.

*But they'll recognize me, and all of this will be for nothing.*

And if I don't get this treated, what then?

*I have to stay awake. Snap out of it.*

A hospital. *I need a hospital.*

What other choice did I have?

The bloodied files slipped into the cardboard box and I flung the car into gear. The nearest ER wasn't too far away. *Not too far. Please don't let it be too far.*

## TWENTY-ONE

WHY WAS THERE NEVER a free parking space at a hospital? I abandoned the car. Automatic doors roared, opening their jaws like an attacking lion.

*I can't just walk in.*

Past the entrance, my feet dragged. Staggered.

"Are you okay?" A voice from the ambulance bay. Blue scrubs rushed towards me.

I waved the figure away.

They stopped. "I'll grab a gurney. Wait there!"

*Hurry.*

Around the corner, I hobbled along the back wall. Bricks baked beneath a melting sun, taking my weight, keeping me upright. My arm slid between the gap of an open window. The frame flung outwards and I hoisted myself into a deserted hallway.

Trembling, I blinked the corridor into focus. Signs overhead pointed the way to a bathroom. I followed them through the empty warren.

There.

My feet scuffed against bathroom tiles, the clatter bouncing everywhere at once, battering my ears. I slumped to the ground and fumbled at the door's lock, discoloring the latch with the black-red streaks I left on everything I touched.

Sweat soaked my side, mingling with sticky blood. I'd re-packed the wound with the scarf. The fabric clumped together, jabbing my skin like red-hot branding irons.

*Water. Need.*

The faucet ran cold, gushing down my throat, soaking my face when I could drink no more. I propped against the basin, gasping for air.

With the scarf rinsed, I dowsed the wound, wiping away the blotches of blood already crusting over my torso. Every dab was a grenade exploding on my skin, its smoke fogging my brain. Trapping the air. Can't breathe. Another explosion.

*Blind. Can't see.*

Pressure. Got to stop the bleeding. I pressed against the cut, but my hand was like a knife. The stabbing pain plunged deeper and deeper. My jaw clamped shut with the wound.

Teeth grit on one knot of the scarf. I tugged at the fabric. The rip hissed around the room as frays dropped into the sink, clogging the plughole. Torn apart. *Same as me.* I washed the material from end to end, wrapped it around the cut, and tied it in a makeshift tourniquet girded tight enough to stem the bleeding. The taps shut off, and I collapsed on the seat of the toilet. Light from the window passed across my face. My eyes closed, hands slipped from where they pushed against my side.

Drowning.

Darkness.

Black enveloped the white tiles and dazzling light and the raging sting above my hip.

***

In sharp blinks, I escaped from the blackout. Legs numb. Limbs popped as I moved. My neck ached from how I'd sat. For how long? My watch read 1:42. Then a jolt of agony struck my side and the reason I was here came crashing back. My legs gave way and I went crashing with it. Below the tourniquet, the cut roared.

Treatment. I needed treatment.

*At least I'm in the right place.*

Once I was on my feet, I could stand without too much trouble. Bending was a different story. Now I was up, I checked myself in the mirror. *As long as I don't wince too much, I might be able to pass for a normal person.*

I rubbed at the stain on my hoodie, spreading the leftover blood around until it tinged the whole thing pink. With my new jacket around me, I opened the door.

*How to get treatment?*

Beneath flickering bulbs that ran in long strips across ceiling tiles, the shuffling corridor ebbed and flowed in an estuary of footsteps. From a nearby hand-station, antibac released from the dispenser in a thick slop of goo, splurging onto my palms. My fingers slipped through the buttons of my jacket and I rubbed gel over the tourniquet, the cold liquid shooting pangs into my side.

*Can't ask a doctor.*

The smell that cloyed at the gel pervaded the ward. A simulated cleanliness. The artificial blend of chemical sterilization was a mask, covering the death and sweat and disease beneath it, veiling the ward with a hint of safety, of protection, the impression that I could roam freely and come to no harm in this germ-infested torture-center. That scent was a disguise, and though I saw through it, I couldn't help but be reassured by it.

*Maybe there's a storage closet where they keep the medicines?*

From the rooms along the ward, a symphony of voices played different parts, and never in time. Chaos pulsed through the hallway. Yet, the patients were as statues, every one of them the same. They didn't move. They just lay there, not bothering to hide the exhaustion from another night without sleep. They even wore the same gowns. I glanced inside each room to a carbon copy of the last. The only difference between them was the number of visitors around the beds.

*Medicine everywhere, hanging in bags, carried by nurses. Where are they getting it?*

In one of the ward's rooms, a nurse wheeled a cart from one patient to the next.

I stopped.

Above the whispers and hushed conversations between relatives, the booming voice of the nurse swelled like thunder. "Come on, Bill. Time for your cream." She tugged at the blue plastic screen to shield Bill from prying eyes and give him what little privacy the ward could afford. Before she'd drawn the curtain, another nurse ran in.

"Karen, we need you. It's Mr. Jones."

"I'll be right with you, Sal. I'm already behind. I just need to turn Bill and do his cream."

"There's no time, Karen. We need all the hands we can get."

"Coming."

The nurse abandoned Bill, the only man without a visitor, along with the medicine cart. I walked through the ward, up to his bed and pulled the curtain shut around us.

We were alone — as alone as someone can ever be in a hospital.

"You don't look like a doctor," he said.

"I don't want any trouble." I checked the cart. Padlocked. There'd be no raiding it. On its top, there was only what the nurse had left ready for the old man. A wad of dressing and a tube of cream.

His weak fingers pressed on a pad and the bed's motors lifted him. His eyes squinted alert, running over me a few times, multiplying the lines on his haggard face by a factor of ten. "You know I could call a nurse."

"I know."

"But I don't get many visitors. You hungry?" On the tray in front of him, his midday meal remained untouched. "You might benefit from the food more than me. You don't look so good."

"I'm not the one laid up in a hospital bed."

"Perhaps you should be?"

I gripped my side. "No thanks."

"You're injured."

"So?"

"I used to be a doctor. Not here. Before I retired to the city. Out in the big wide world."

"You used to be a doctor? Will you take a look at my side?"

"Of course, young man." He repositioned his glasses on the bridge of his nose.

I peeled back the jacket and lifted the hoodie to show him my botched tourniquet.

He peered at the scarf. His face crumpled as if he'd just eaten a rancid prune. "Hmm. Not bad. Not bad. It's a little scruffy, but not bad."

"Do you think it'll be alright?"

"The cut? I don't know. I was talking about the way you tied the bandage. Let me see. You'll need something to clean the wound. Make sure it doesn't get infected."

"I used hand gel."

"My boy, you need something more suited to the job. I know they put a lot of alcohol in that gel. But you might as well drink it for all the good it'd do. You need a cream or a balm or some antiseptic. *That* should do the trick." His eyes flashed to the tube on the top of the cart.

I picked it up.

"Seems like you need that cream more than I do," he said.

'Dermafix — Antiseptic Balm,' read the label on the half-empty squeeze-tube.

"You think that'll help?" I asked.

"That cream's not just for old fogeys. It'll sterilize whatever gash is under there. And it's from the retro-kit, so it should work fast."

"You sure you don't mind?"

"Be my guest. They only give it to me because they don't think I can get out of this cage, and want to keep me lathered up so I don't go too crinkly. But I've got a few surprises left in me. I'll be fine."

I smiled at the old man and peeled back the scarf, applying the balm to the raw skin.

"No, spread it thin and even," he said, keeping a careful eye on the procedure. "A little more each time. Thin and even."

"Thanks, Doc." After layering it over the worst of the cut, I wrapped the bandage around my torso, tearing it from the wad and knotting it through a fold.

"There. Just let that settle for a few minutes. You're a dab hand, if ever I saw one. Where did you learn to change a dressing like that?"

"No idea."

"Well, color me impressed. I've watched nurses struggle for years before they learned those kinds of skills."

"You must be sick of hospitals."

"Just so. We used to say that the best medicine is preventative. It's the only medicine they give here. 'Restrospective prevention.' Have you ever heard of anything so ludicrous?"

*He said the tube was from the retro-kit.*

"These so-called doctors," he continued, "drip-feed their medicines to stop you from ever contracting the diseases that brought you in here. But you know the crazy thing about 'retro-prevention?' Sometimes it works."

"Is that what all this is?" My eyes ran along the saline bags hovering above his head.

"It's my liver. Shot from too much booze. So they pump me full of drugs to fix it, and the more it improves, the less I'll have drunk, until there's no reason for me being here. When Dr. Weiss discovered the formula that makes New Yesterday what it is, he created the phenomenon that sends time all loopy. But the doctors synthesized his formula. They combined his work on Lumino-Spectrominal-Entanglement with their medicines. And there you have it. Miracle drugs. At least, that's what they tell me."

"You don't believe them?"

"Changes aren't so easy. I'm a stubborn man. I'll admit it. What I need is a son. A reason not to pick up the whiskey bottle in the first place. The specialists are trying to fix my situation, but I doubt they'll manage it."

"Are they trying to retrograde a family for you?"

"My consultant will be in their office right now making phone calls, acting like a cross between a social worker and insurance broker. The nurses are the only ones administering medicine these days. It's a joke. But I'm not too worried. I've had a good life. What about you? You got kids?"

I shook my head. "Not that I know of."

"Good. Because if you did, they'd be worried sick."

"What do you mean?"

"No need to be coy. I've seen your face in the paper. They've still not caught you, then?"

A chill blasted down my spine. I reached for the curtain, poised to run.

"Wait," he said. "Don't go. Not yet. Let the cream do its work. I don't care if you've gone linear or not."

"Keep your voice down, Bill!"

"Ah, nobody's listening. Even if they were, what could they do? It isn't like any of the nurses would believe them. Probably just increase their medication."

Beyond the curtain, a voice floated. "Who are you talking to in there, Bill?"

A nurse. Her fingertips crept around the gap to pull the curtain back.

"Do you mind?" Bill shouted. "I'd like a little privacy."

She stopped. "Is everything okay?"

"Perfectly alright. But there are some things a gentleman must do alone."

"Oh. Alright. I'll be here when you're ready, okay?"

Nowhere to hide.

Nowhere to go.

She guarded the only exit. And she wasn't moving until she'd seen him.

Bill sat up. "Help me to my feet," he whispered.

I gave him an arm. My side roared as he lifted his weight onto me.

"When I pull the curtain, you slip behind it," he said, pointing to where it draped behind him.

He doddered forwards on his legs, grasping my arm, tugging the metal frame where his medicine-bag hung.

"Bill?" the nurse said.

"And take *them.*" He pointed to the bandage and the antiseptic cream. I pocketed both.

"Ready?" he whispered.

I nodded and released him, moved around the bed and stood at the opposite side of where the curtain hung. His shaking hand yanked at the drape, and he stepped forwards, falling into the nurse. As he pulled the curtain, I did the same.

"Bill! What are you doing out of bed?"

I closed it behind me so the drape concealed where I stood.

A new bed stood before me. The man lying in it slept. As did his visitor in the chair beside him.

"I was quite in the mood for a stroll with a nice young lady." Bill's voice drifted from beyond the curtain. "And I wanted to muster up the courage to ask you if you'd join me."

"I'm flattered, Bill. But you know you shouldn't be out of bed. It's so unlike you."

"The body's old, but the heart is young."

My legs withered beneath the fire in my side. *Just stay still.*

"Alright, Bill. You can lie back. That's it. Is that better?"

"Much."

*Don't move.*

"Okay. I'll be back again soon to check on you. Don't go wandering off, alright?"

"I'll behave," Bill said. "I promise."

The cart's wheels scuffed across the floor.

"Will you draw the curtain on your way out?"

"Sure, Bill."

The rungs grated over the rail. The old man coughed. Not very convincingly.

I stumbled back through the curtain and gripped onto his bed. My heart pounded. Muscles ached.

"How are you feeling?" he asked.

"How am *I* feeling? What about you?"

"What a pair, eh? You know, I think we just about got away with it. You can rest up now. There's no rush. The longer you remain still, the less it'll hurt."

"I need to go."

"Alright. But if you're thinking of running, you'll need to keep your strength up." He pushed the wheelie-tray with his food towards me.

"Don't you want it?"

"Have you tasted it? Trust me, if you eat it, you'll be doing me a favor."

"How about we share it?"

"No, I'm not having any."

"Now come on, Bill. What kind of host lets their guest eat alone?"

We split the tasteless mash and few chipolatas that might as well have been Pleistocene for all the flavor they had. Watery gravy turned the whole thing to mush. Once the plate was clear, I rubbed my hands on a baby-wipe from a packet kept open on his side-table.

"What's your next move?" Bill asked.

"Getting out of here for a start."

"I guess that means no more visits."

"Afraid not."

"Oh well. It was nice while it lasted."

"Thanks for all this, Bill. You're a good man." I stood. Pain shot through me, but it was duller than before. I forced my weight onto my side and could tolerate the bite. I reached for the curtain's edge. "One question I've got to ask." I turned back to face him. "Why'd you help me?"

His wrinkles faded as his smile widened. "I've been locked up in here for a week now. This is the most fun I've had the entire time. Besides, I'd do anything for a patient."

"You take care, Doc."

"Mind how you go."

I drew back the curtain and walked straight past the other beds to rejoin the corridor. A screen had been pulled in another room, but shadows on the perspex wall showed nurses surrounding a bed. From inside the curtained-off area, a machine spoke the bleep, bleep, bleep of that thin green line, rising and dropping with each thump of the heart — valleys and craters on a steady horizon.

I saw those lines. Heard the machine. Watched from where I leaned on the wall, tucked out of the nurses' way as they dashed through the corridor. And yet, I was somewhere else. Trapped inside another memory, sitting on a chair with those same blue curtains hanging behind me.

*Lottie laid on a bed.*

*They called it a bed. It was more like a metal skeleton, twisted into a frame. A paper-thin mattress warped below her. Wires fed into her arms. She was stirring, just waiting to come round.*

*"Lottie, darling. Can you hear me?" I whispered.*

*She nodded her head. "Where am I? What happened?" Bleep, bleep, bleep, the machine echoed in a steady rhythm.*

*"We're in the hospital darling. Don't worry. You're alright."*

*"Hospital?" Her eyes shot open, the depths of her pupils searching my own. Her hand rushed to her stomach, and she patted her flat torso. "The baby?"*

*She panicked, those same eyes gripped in fear as her face took on the strain of her surroundings. The beats of her heart on the monitor raced faster. Faster.*

*"Shhh, it's okay." My hands drew her closer to me, and she wrapped her fingers around my chest, tugging at the wires feeding into her arm. Her hair fell over my fingers, tickling the skin as tears doused her hospital gown. She pulled away, her hand gripping her stomach in pain where the bandages cushioned the stitches. "There'll be a scar, but it's alright. The doctors have already shown me how to change the dressing and keep it clean."*

*"Adam. It's not true, is it? This isn't real."*

*"It's not your fault. It's nobody's fault."*

*"Why? Why is this happening?" Her words barely contained syllables, coming out more like shrieks, but I*

understood them well enough. I'd been asking myself the same thing all morning.

"It's complicated. The doctors can explain it better than I can."

"I want to see him . . . want to see . . . my baby."

"We can say goodb . . ." My voice broke. Keep it together, Adam. ". . . say goodbye to him when you feel ready."

"No!"

"I'm so sorry, darling."

"Can we . . . is it . . . where's my . . .?"

"The important thing is that they saved you. They brought you back to me."

"Adam, it isn't . . . this can't be it . . . we can try . . . try again?"

"Darling. A hysterectomy was . . . it was the only way. Or else you both would've . . ." I couldn't say the words. "I'm so sorry, my love. But I couldn't face losing you both."

I squeezed her hand and closed my eyes. I couldn't bear to watch her in such anguish. Blocking out the pain she released in outcries between sharp breaths, my ears focussed on that mechanical, rhythmic bleep.

In the corridor outside the room, the same noise whined over and over. I stumbled back from the precipice of memory and bumped into another visitor.

"Watch it," they said.

They'd knocked my side, but I felt nothing. Numb, I staggered to a table where empty jugs had been left standing, waiting to be refilled with water for the patients. I grabbed a couple and disappeared into the toilet, running the faucet cold so the jugs whirled to the brim.

My head was anywhere but the bathroom. Flashes of our last conversation, our last argument, filled my mind. I heard her voice, replaying it over and over. "*Is our life not good enough for you anymore?*" she'd said.

"*It isn't like that, honey. I just—*"

"*You just what? Thought it was about time for a change? Do I really make you that unhappy?*"

It wasn't unhappiness. Being with her was the greatest joy I'd ever known. But burying our little boy, our precious Harvey, and knowing we could never have another — there was no consolation for that kind of hurt. Grief had arrived on our door, tainting even the happiest of lives, lacing even the most wonderful moments with misery. It was like a filter that washed everything gray. We weren't unhappy. But that didn't mean our lives weren't without a terrible pain we both wanted to forget.

"*Lottie. The whole reason I went to Anderson Whitman was . . . it was for you. For us.*"

"*For me? So it's my life you want to change, is it?*"

"*I just want to give you what you deserve. What you want.*"

"*And you think I can get that in New Yesterday? Don't you know me at all?*"

I just thought if we could get to the city, then maybe things would be different. Maybe we could undo those months, those years we'd spent trying to move on. We'd been frozen in time, stuck in that hospital, living as though we were existing in some 'what-if,' rather than our real lives that waited somewhere beyond us. Our lives were with Harvey, watching him grow, helping him learn, listening to him chattering senseless words while the TV played repeats of the cartoon he obsessed over. That was the life we were really living, somewhere else. But not here. Not now. And maybe New Yesterday could change that for us?

But then, when she'd looked into relocating, and called up her old school friends who'd moved to the city, she'd found Tammy, and now she was gone. Along with Harvey. Perhaps she'd found that life we always wanted, and they were both waiting for me to join them?

Water spilled down the side of the jug and poured on my trousers, pooling below my feet. I left the bathroom, retraced my way back through the corridor and clambered through the window. Back to the car park. The car door shut and I rested the water on the back seat. My eyes flashed to the cardboard box and the files inside, the laminate cover stained with streaks of dried blood.

Two files waited for me. The information from the planning board.

I'd stolen the records. Risked my life. Somehow survived.

*This had better be worth it.*

## TWENTY-TWO

'APPLICATION TO RELOCATE Gracy's store. Approved.' At least the title made sense. Why did they make planning jargon the most unnecessarily complex of the lot? Celia had been so good at this, at seeing through it. If she were here now, she'd have decoded it in seconds. My eyes re-read the same sentence three times and I was still no closer to understanding it.

I gulped water from a plastic jug as the bandage pinched at my side. Sunlight lengthened, dipping behind trees. The pattern of their leaves discolored the tarmac, speckled in a lattice across the ground even after the sun was gone. That was all I needed. The faintest clue of something left over from before, trapped inside this complicated script.

Land search results, economic impact studies, surveyances, architectural schematics and statements of intent were all laid out to bamboozle. Lists detailed a brief history of the store to support the application, comments from staff and customers alike. By the length of it, this wasn't the first time this Gracy's had moved.

The files splayed across my lap, but the car's interior was barely big enough to spread the pages out, let alone think. How was I meant to see anything cramped up like this?

I closed the file and picked up the next. 105 North Parkway. Another jumble of words that refused to unscramble.

I rubbed my eyes. What I needed was space. Space to move. Space to think. I couldn't do that stuck inside this car. But it wasn't like I had an office to go to. A boardroom with a large oval desk to spread these pages across. There was a reason we'd bought that oversized table at SSA, and it wasn't just because Jeff insisted it made us look successful.

My mind recalled the poster at The Phoenix Hotel, just around the corner from City Hall. Gabby's book launch. Part of me wished I could've been there. I'd have finished early, driven the Porsche back and been getting an earache over having chosen the wrong necktie. Gabby liked the green one, but I favored the blue. 'Help me into this dress.' I could almost hear her voice as I imagined pulling the zip up the soft arch of her back. She'd quiver and I'd kiss her shoulder. 'You'll do great,' I'd tell her, and she'd smile, before disappearing to the closet to grab the green tie, threatening not to go unless I slipped off that horrid blue thing and acceded to her better taste. Which I would.

What would Lottie have thought to that kind of life? The one I recalled so vividly with Gabrielle. How many black-tie events had we organized for the benefit of the AWG? Tonight would be no different. They'd be out in droves, sipping at champagne and admiring pictures of Mrs. Campbell's latest boat.

The thought struck me like a slap to the face. The group would be out in force if Sinclair's was sponsoring the book launch. All the best clients would have bought seats at one of those tables. They'd be dolling themselves up, getting ready to arrive. That included the crowd from Gracy's, John and Mrs. Campbell.

There'd be plenty of space on their luxury yacht, with them miles away, getting ready for the party. I pulled out of the hospital car park, half-filled jugs of water sloshing over the back seat. Away from the suburbs, I steered through the city to the harbor.

\*\*\*

Donned in sunglasses, I carried the cardboard box towards the harbormaster's shack. He stood guard over the many boats scattered across the bay. The top of Tammy's flowers poked over the box's lid, and I hid myself behind them. The wicker basket covered what else lay hidden beneath furry leaves and white lilies.

"Delivery for Mrs. Campbell," I said from behind my sunglasses.

He shot up from where he reclined, a lifetime's tales woven into his torn wool sweater. "I can take the package," he said. His face flecked with the sturdiness of stone, a living shanty.

"Fine by me. You'll have to sign for it though. And she wants the cabin cleaned, and these placed throughout the interior." He scowled at me, removing his cap and rubbing his balding head. I shrugged my shoulders. "You know what she's like. She takes such pride in it."

He ran his hand across his face. "You reckon you'll be long?"

"Hope not."

He craned his neck over the array of boats, shook his head, and blinked at the setting sun. "Alright. You know which one it is?"

"Yeah. It's the . . ." I scratched my head.

"*Grace of the Sea.*"

"That's the one."

"Pier Seven."

"Thanks."

His fingers reached below his desk and a buzz echoed from behind him. The gate's latch clicked open. I hauled the bouquet down cobbled steps to where a wooden jetty wound between boats like a maze.

Pier Seven was marked at the end of the quay. Planks groaned underfoot while the tide trickled between cracks, spurting up to wet the deck in salty pools. A crisp tang seasoned the air, blown from the crest of waves and caught in the breeze.

One after another, the boats grew bigger. Each sail competed with the last. I guess they call it show *boating* for a reason.

Finally, I reached the *Grace of the Sea*, a reference to Gracy's that Mrs. Campbell had probably decided was a tasteful enough way of disguising her wealthy connections, while at the same time, showing them off. Rising from the water like the white whale of Moby Dick, its oversized deck dwarfed the other boats. If owning a luxury yacht was her entry into a competition, Mrs. Campbell had already won by a mile.

A thick rope anchored the boat two feet from the decking. Planks of wood stacked on the pier, buckled in a vice. I lifted one and let it fall onto the sleek fiberglass shell of the floating mansion.

I balanced across the makeshift bridge to board a red-stained deck. A small staircase with gold handrails led to the cabins below, and a chunky padlock bolted the door shut.

I reached below the flowers to the evidence bag. Slowly, my fingers wrapped around the handgun. I gripped the metal cylinder of its barrel, glanced over my shoulders before I raised the gun above my head, and slammed the butt of its handle down on the padlock.

A clunk rattled through my arm. I peered over the steps, my eyes scouring the jetty. The fishermen on the harbor wall didn't turn. The man painting his yacht didn't look up. The harbormaster's feet remained propped on the desk, from the looks of his shadow through his shed's window. The clang must have been lost to the washing tide.

I turned back to the padlock and heaved a second time. Slices of grazed metal chipped away from the lock. Rust speckled beneath the silver stain, blistering the catch. The salty air had done its work.

The second blow had ripped a hole in the bag, and I pulled the gun from its protective film. Its touch was cold and clinical, insensitive to all that surrounded it. There was no malice in the gun itself. It was a tool. No different to a scalpel or a mallet. But this tool had been used to take Lottie away from me.

As I stood holding it, I expected to feel pain. Some shred of sorrow. Some memory to come flooding back. Yet, there was nothing beyond its cool steel. It held no secrets that had not already scarred me. It was dead to me. A single bead of sweat fell from my forehead and my fingers tightened around the barrel.

With the third blow, the bolt tore from the latch and the padlock buckled in two. I threw the handgun in the box, twisted the knob, and swung the door open.

A creak floated through the dark cabin. Shafts of light poured through portholes, and I reached for the switch. The soft haze of auburn bulbs flooded the room. A bar curved along the wall, framing the sweep of lavish green sofas. Plush fabric of three chesterfields surrounded a long, glass-topped coffee table.

I rested the flowers on the bar and emptied the folders across the coffee table.

*Somewhere big enough to think.*

I spread the pages and shuffled back to the door, tossing the padlock overboard, where it slopped into the water. Mrs. Campbell could afford another padlock. Besides, hadn't Gabby said that Mrs. Campbell invited us to see her new boat? I was simply taking her up on the invitation. What better place to dive into the planning applications for Gracy's than on the luxury yacht of the store's CEO?

The door clicked shut, muting the slosh of waves to a distant lull. From behind the bar, I grabbed a glass of water, and perched on the nearest sofa. I scanned the pages of the planning application.

*Let's try this again.*

Lines of text meshed together, forming patterns of code. Huge chunks could be discarded, but now that the pages were laid together, words sprang out as important. Words like 'necessary,' 'unalterable,' and 'only.' The person who'd written this application left no margin for maneuverability. It came across as desperate. Rushed.

Why else would it have been so sloppy, so insistent? And why hadn't I seen it before?

Even stranger were the risk analyses and cost benefits. The graphs showed no predicted upsurge in gains. Where was the incentive for the store to move without any profit to show for it? What made it so 'necessary'?

The lists of the store's previous addresses emerged from the background like a photograph developing in water. Jones and Castro Leather Goods, Saul Creswell Suits, and a Tommy Veducci Shoe Emporium. Snapshots of memories flashed over me.

*In my closet, I toyed over which shoes to wear to meet a client, before settling on the tan ones with tassels. Gabby shook her head and blurted out laughing.*

*"You're not wearing those, are you?" She snorted through her coffee.*

*"Why not? What's wrong with tassels?"*

*"It's just not very manly. Are you sure you want tassels to be your first impression?"*

*"These are Tommy Veducci tassels, thank you very much. If it's good enough for Tommy Veducci, it's good enough for—"*

Then another flash of light, like a photographer's bulb, transported me forwards. *A hollow knock tapped on the front door. Celia swept it open, stepping through.*

*"Mr. Swann? Are you home?"*

*"Come in, Celia. I'll be down in a minute."*

*A dark bag flopped over her arm. She grabbed the tip of the hangar, extended her hand, and the bag hung straight.*

*"Here, Mr. Swann. Fresh from the cleaners."*

"Thanks, Celia. Where would I be without my lucky suit?"

"What makes it lucky?"

"This is the suit I wore for my interview at SSA. Don't you remember?"

She shook her head.

"Have I never told you the story? My very first Saul Creswell suit. It was—"

Another flash.

I scrambled around the drawer of my desk. My hands dashed over trinkets tossed randomly inside. Where was it? It had to be here. It just had to be.

The phone blared. I sat up straight and heaved the receiver to my ear.

"Yes?"

"Am I speaking to a Mr. Swann?"

"That's me."

"Can you tell me your first name?"

"Adam. Who's this?"

"My name's Stuart and I work at the bakery on St Elmo's. A wallet's been left here, and it's got your ID, bank cards and stuff."

I exhaled. "Stuart. You're an absolute lifesaver. I've been going mad thinking it's lost. I'll have my assistant call to pick it up."

"Could you tell me what it looks like?"

"You mean the wallet or my assistant?"

"The wallet, Mr. Swann."

"It's brown leather. It's got a magnetic clasp and there are three slots on each side for cards."

"What make is it?"

"The make?"

*"Yeah."*

*"I think it's a Jones and Castro?"*

*"That's fine. So this assistant—"*

I was back aboard Mrs. Campbell's boat, staring down at the list of stores. It was like looking into the past. My old life in New Yesterday.

In quick breaths, I collapsed on the sofa.

Was it a coincidence that my clothes, shoes and wallet all came from the stores this Gracy's had replaced? *It has to be.* There wasn't another link between the stores.

Whoever had written this planning application was in a hurry. They'd written their desperation into the fabric of the text.

What if I was looking at this all wrong? Maybe it wasn't Gracy's that was important. What if the reason this store needed moving had nothing to do with Gracy's and everything to do with the stores it replaced?

Why move a store if there was no profit in doing so? At least, there was no profit to Gracy's. But was there profit in getting rid of those other stores? Of making them disappear? Of making *me* disappear?

I had items from each of them. I'd run the accounts on Gracy's at SSA.

The room cooled, blurring as my vision dimmed. My mind fought to suppress something. I paced across the lush carpet. My head shook, pulse raced. Turning back to the papers, I brushed the cardboard box and knocked it to the floor. The gun tumbled onto the carpet. Its silhouette nestled into the plush fibers where my footprints still lingered. It stared at me. Accusing. And then I saw it.

The bridge between the stores.

My hands covered my mouth.

*Could it have been me?* Was I responsible for writing the application? There was only one reason I'd want to have Gracy's moved. Only one excuse for the poorly disguised pleading in the papers. *What was I trying to cover up?*

My mind hurried back to that last fight with Lottie. It was fierce. I'd stepped away from the door and left. Hadn't I? What if . . .? *No. No, it was impossible. It couldn't have been me.*

I scooped the gun from the floor and staggered back to the papers, my eyes devouring the pages, looking for a reason, any reason, to prove it wasn't me. The signatures authorizing the documents were scrawled illegibly on behalf of the Anderson Whitman Group, acting for Gracy's Stores Inc. It wasn't my hand that had signed it.

There was nothing familiar about the page. It stirred no memory. I glanced down at the gun I held. If I'd pulled the trigger, then I'd have surely recalled doing so the instant I touched the gun. But gripping it now, I felt nothing. There was no inkling, no whisper, no ghost of the past summoned through my fingers. Besides, the gun was from New Yesterday, and the store it came from had moved before I'd ever set foot in the city.

*The store it came from.* 105 North Parkway. I had the documents to prove it.

Opening the files, I laid them over the Gracy's papers and scanned their contents. The same words screamed at me from the lines of text. 'Necessary,' 'unalterable,' and 'only.' The same person had written both applications. *The same person.* They'd moved Gracy's to cover their tracks. Removed the gun store. Why erase the store unless you needed to disguise the fact you'd bought a gun?

The person who wrote this had bought the gun.

I stopped. My head swam. I paced the room, trying to understand the words repeating through my brain.

*The person who wrote this had bought the gun.*

My wife's killer was the author of these pages. Tammy was right. How could I have been so blind?

*We're close, Lottie. I can feel it.*

But who in the Anderson Whitman Group could have wanted Lottie dead? Out of everyone who'd belonged to the AWG, I was the only one with any connection to her. And I couldn't have done it.

Why would someone like Mrs. Campbell risk their fortune and reputation over Lottie? Where was the sense in it? I remembered their faces as they lounged in the living room after one fundraiser or another, the wrinkles of their old smiles.

*Am I going mad? Is this what it feels like to grasp at straws? Seeing things that aren't there.*

I poured another drink as the sun's red ball vanished beyond the horizon, and the last trace of daylight dissipated across the water. Only the faint sprinkling of yellow bulbs warmed the cabin, casting shadows across the laminated pages.

The *laminated* pages. Every page was laminated. What if the answer was staring at me through the pages all along? What if the signatures weren't important, but the way they'd been bound was the key? Some secretary must have laced the paper to preserve the contents. Some secretary who worked for the Anderson Whitman Gro . . .

*No.*

She had her own laminating machine.

*It couldn't be.*

The list from her desk had led me to this Gracy's in the first place.

*I don't believe it.*

She'd even told me that she didn't remember why she came to New Yesterday.

*It isn't true.*

She had those pictures and the shoebox, and the card with Gilligan Kennedy's address, the sickly collector who kept the police report, and the history of Lottie's death.

*It couldn't be true.*

And now she'd fled New Yesterday.

Celia had seen countless documents pass over her desk. Copying and pasting sentences to splice a forgery together would have been easy enough for any secretary. All of them had the means to change whatever they wanted with a simple signature and laminating machine.

*But Celia? She wasn't capable of such a thing. Why bring me to her house? Why give me the photos?*

Proof. Where was the proof? There must be a record of who logged the applications with the AWG. The bite of my teeth stung my lips as I replayed it in my head. *Where was the proof?*

There was only one place it'd be. Now that it was dark, there might even be a chance.

At the far end of the room, I slid a door open to a bedroom. Behind the double bed, two panels parted to reveal a wardrobe. His and hers. One half for Mrs. Campbell, the other for John.

I stripped out of my clothes and grabbed one of John's black suits from the rail. We weren't so different in size. Snug around the paunch, but it'd do.

The problem was my face. How to disguise it so I could move freely without being recognized?

The tiny bathroom held a cabinet with bottles upon bottles of products, so that whatever the problem, there'd be a chemical solution.

Hair dye. Jet black. Fast acting.

Variants of fake-tan boasted 'retro-application for instant results.'

A few splurges later and my hair turned raven, my skin a sunbaked olive. John's bedside drawer gave up a pair of reading glasses to complete the transformation.

I flicked off the bedroom light, gathered the files back into the box, and slipped the gun into the deep pocket inside my new suit blazer. My coat fastened over a blue necktie and crisp shirt. I left the flowers for Mrs. Campbell and scrawled *'Sorry about the padlock'* on a napkin, sliding the wicker basket over the note. There was every chance things might have changed by the time she found it, but it was the least I could do.

Up the steps to the deck and along the planks, I strutted back over the jetty, carrying the files inside the box under my arm. In the darkness of night, the air was cold and the sound of waves droned louder somehow. The harbormaster's torch blinded me at the gate. When he dropped it, the absence of light was as piercing as the white beam.

"Who are you?" he asked.

"I just finished on the *Grace Of The Sea*."

"Oh, it's you. I didn't recognise you."

*Thank you, tuxedo.*

A buzz from his shed released the gate, and I stepped out of the harbor, tracing my way back to Celia's car.

Right now, straws were all I had to grasp hold of. If this haystack had a needle, I'd need more than straws.

At the head office of Anderson Whitman, I'd get the evidence, the proof which would either clear Celia of killing Lottie, or condemn her for it. They'd hold the records. They'd have the signature on file. The person who'd authorized moving the store. The name of my wife's killer.

## TWENTY-THREE

'WELCOME TO Anderson Whitman,' read the sign. My fingers brushed the gun in my pocket. *You know what you have to do.*

In the heart of Old Town, the rustic palace looked more like a museum than an estate agent's head office. But the AW logo emblazoned on railed gates and the billboard within the grounds boasted otherwise.

*You can't leave without that document.*

Gravel crunched as I marched the path to an archway where pillars supported a slab of rock. 1541 was chiseled into it.

*No matter what it takes.*

With the cardboard box in hand, I pushed the thick door. Marble lined the floor in diamond tiles. Sterile walls reflected a sharp glare, the light itself stabbing through John's reading glasses in pinpricks to the eye.

*Just stay calm and no one gets hurt.*

A lone guard reclined behind a desk, staring at a monitor, wolfing down a jumbo bag of cashews. The wisp of an almost-mustache framed his youthful, flabby jowl, the kind that college kids grow to look 'macho.' He couldn't have been much older, chewing in circles like a young goat.

My footsteps clacked over marble diamonds, echoing across the black and white tiles.

The security guard stirred, raised his eyes at me, and dropped the bag of cashews. His beige uniform's short sleeves pinched at tanned, chunky arms. A brown leather belt supported a set of handcuffs and a pistol holstered on his hip. He ran his thumb and forefinger over the fur of his mustache, before pulling out his earphones and rising to his feet.

Maybe it was the suit I was wearing, but he seemed in no hurry to interrogate me. I'd worked out answers to the questions I might face. Who am I? What am I doing here? Where was I going? But he just sniffed and stretched.

"Don't tell me," he said. "You forgot to close a window, right? No. No, it was a cupboard. You didn't lock it and you only just remembered. Am I close?"

"Something like that." I was only a few steps from the desk.

"You suits. You're all the same, y'know?"

"How's that?"

"You might look smart, but you sure are dumb sometimes."

"Guilty as charged."

"Rookie mistake. I seen 'em all. Okay. I'll buzz you in. Let me see your pass."

*You can do this.* I placed my box on the desk, reached for the inside pocket of my jacket, and drew the gun, pointing it straight at his grease-stained chest. His eyes widened and cheeks paled. Frozen stiff, the crook of his throat wobbled in a nervous gulp.

"What were you saying about rookie mistakes?" I said.

"Listen, man. Just cool it, okay?"

"I want you to take your gun with two fingers, nice and slow, and drop it on the floor."

"Sure. No problem, man. We're good, right?"

"We will be soon."

His hand moved a millimeter at a time towards his holster. At this pace, it'd take him five minutes to reach his gun. *What's he doing? More to the point, what am* I *doing?*

"Okay, you can move a little faster than that," I said.

"You sure? I don't wanna spook you."

"Are you trying to stall for time or something?"

"No, no, no. I'm not playin' no tricks. I just don't want you shootin' me because I moved too fast, y'know?"

"I'm not going to shoot you. Okay?"

"If you're not gonna shoot me, why would you point a gun at my face? It isn't cool, bro."

"Just get the gun and drop it, alright?"

"Yeah, yeah. No problemo. Everythin's chill, man. No worries." The gun clattered to the floor, and he kicked it away. It slid to the far side of the hall. "I know you didn't tell me to kick it, but I thought it might make you feel better."

"Where's your phone?"

"My phone? It's in my pocket. You need to make a call?"

"Same thing as with the gun. You know the drill."

He pinched his phone in two fingers and laid it on the desk as though it was a weapon. And he was right. The phone was far more dangerous than the gun he carried. At any moment, he could place a call and have me arrested before I'd even walked in here.

"Anythin' else you want me to do?" he said. "I can keep my pants on? Right?"

"You can take those handcuffs and fasten them around your wrist."

"Seriously?"

"Yeah."

"You ever been in handcuffs? They're uncomfortable, man."

"No whining. Just do it."

"You're not being very friendly, y'know. I got rid of the gun. I got rid of my phone. I'm glad you're lettin' me keep my pants, but how about cuttin' a guy a little slack, huh? You feelin' me?"

"In the handcuffs. *Now.*"

He shook his head. "Okay, okay. Mr. Grumpy, here. You sound like my old teacher. He did the best Arnold impression. We used to call him 'Kindergarten Cop.' You seen that movie? Pretty good, right?" From his waist, he scooped the cuffs and fastened one to his left wrist so it hung like a bangle.

"Stretch your hands out and don't move."

"You'd make a good Arnold with an attitude like that. You just need to work on the accent. And the muscles. Obviously."

I grabbed his arms and fixed the second loop around his other wrist. He winced as the strap clicked into place. "Where are the keys?" I asked.

"They're in the drawer." His eyes dropped to the desk.

"You don't carry them on you?"

"When do I ever use 'em? I sit here at night and watch videos. That's the gig, man. Excuse me if I'm not used to this. It's my first time gettin' held up. Unless you're countin' traffic. Oh, man! Did you just hear that? Write that bad boy down while it's still fresh."

"Okay. Settle down. I'm putting my gun away, alright?" I replaced the pistol in the lining of my jacket. Its weight pulled at my chest, and the cut on my side jabbed like a punch to the gut.

"They told us in trainin' not to struggle, y'know?" he said, half to himself. "They told us, 'Just let 'em get on with it, and once it's done, we'll fix it so it never happened.' Nice of 'em, isn't it?"

"How long have you been working for Anderson Whitman?" *Stupid question. How would he even know?*

"Since college. A buddy of mine set me up here. Pretty sweet, right? He actually wanted to swap shifts with me tonight to give me a night off. But I told him, 'Does Batman get a night off?' No chance. When he finds out about all this, he's gonna go crazy. You'd like him. He's a real nice dude. Doesn't go tyin' people in handcuffs. At least, I don't think so. This your first time lockin' somebody up?"

"The less you know about me, the safer you'll be."

"Ooh, mysterious. You're gonna tell me what it is you want, though? Right? Maybe I can help, and we can get this over with?"

I frowned. "You want to help?"

"Why not? You seem like a reasonable guy. I mean, you didn't shoot me, did you?"

"Not yet."

"Oh, snap. You got a sense of humor, dawg. We vibin', man. We vibin'. How about it? What's a guy dressed like you doin' holdin' up an estate agent? You need a mortgage or somethin'?"

"Don't you recognize me?"

His brown eyes squinted. I took off John's glasses and the proverbial penny dropped, along with his face. "No way! I don't believe it! You're the linear guy? Oh man, are the cops comin'? Am I gonna be on the news? Do I look okay? Have I got nuts in my teeth?"

"Keep your voice down."

"Sorry, bro. It's these cashews, they get stuck in there and then you look nasty. The cops have been lookin' for you for months. I thought you'd have grown a beard or somethin', to throw 'em off, y'know? Instead of just that little pepper on your chin. What is that? Like, 2 o'clock shadow?"

"They've only been chasing me since yesterday."

"For reals?"

"That's why I'm here."

"There're better places to hide, man."

"I'm not hiding. I need something to clear my name."

"What is it? You been set up? Framed? Who done it? Was it the butler? Mistress? Baby? Nah, man. It's never the baby. I got it. Someone killed your dog, right? That's when stuff starts goin' down."

"It's a long story, but I've done nothing wrong."

"Yeah, I hear ya. But doin' nothin' wrong, and gettin' set up, that's not the same thing, is it?" He tilted his head at me, his eyes filled with sass, like a schoolteacher dressing down a student who interrupted their lesson.

"Where does Anderson Whitman keep their records? Is there a vault or something?" I said.

"It's all below ground."

"Below?"

"Eight stories down, three streets wide."

"That's a lot of records."

"You're tellin' me! It's like a warren down there. You know what you're lookin' for?"

"How do I get underground?"

"My keycard. It's in the phone. Well, not *in* the phone. It's . . . look, it's just there."

I flipped the case that housed his phone open, and yanked the plastic card from the slit, pocketing the handset. "This it?"

"You got it, man."

"Good. Now, you want to be helpful? Where's the nearest storage closet?"

"Storage? What do you need to store?" He peered over the lip of the box, still resting on his desk, then looked back at me. I tilted my head and glowered at him. "Aw, no way, man! I'm not gettin' locked in no cupboard!"

"You're going to tell me where the nearest storage cupboard is, and then step inside, sit down, and not make a move."

"It's not *my* moves I'm worried about. What about you? What's *your* next move?"

"Get to the vault. Find the records I need. And get out of here as fast as I can so nobody gets hurt."

"That's the plan, huh?"

"That's the plan."

"How many records you after?"

"A couple. Maybe just the one."

"You got any idea how long it'll take you to find *one* file down there? How are you gonna make your way through the record rooms? Do you even know how the stuff's cataloged? What floor to start lookin' on?"

"I'm sure I'll figure it out."

"Yeah, yeah. Sure you will. Give it a few weeks, you'll get what you're lookin' for."

"What's your point, kid?"

"Listen, why don't you take me with you? It beats bein' stuck up here, and it definitely beats gettin' locked in a cupboard."

I glanced across the empty hall, to the gun he'd slid, propped in the corner at the far end of the room. "How do you know where to start?"

"I patrol the corridors every night. I'm like a ninja down there. A vault-master. Just call me 'sensei', bro. I know 'em like the back of my hand. Come on! Lemme come. I can help. I'm serious. What do you say?"

*How much time am I going to waste arguing with this kid?* "Alright. Lead the way."

"Yeah, yeah, yeah man. Let's go. Let's do this. I'm all over it. Follow me. Just let me grab one thing." He reached over the desk, and my hands darted back to the handle of my gun. His fingers closed around the bag of cashews. He straightened up, offering me the bag. "You want one?"

"Let's move." I grabbed the box and followed him across the reception room, swiping the keycard on a turnstile that led deeper into the palace.

In the new room, a decadent chandelier glistened over luxurious sofas. Our footsteps padded the lush carpet. Three doors were carved into the furthest wall. I swiped his card over the handle of the last one. A beep followed, and the latch clicked open. We stepped into a plain, white corridor. No windows. It stretched long and straight and ended in the silver panels of an elevator.

"Where are all the security cameras?" I asked.

"If we need 'em installed, we'll just retrofit 'em in. They look ugly, man. Not their style." He nodded at the walls.

Black-and-white photographs lined each side. One picture showed a manor house in Tudor style with a wooden lattice gracing the front, and on the frame beneath it, 'January' had been stenciled. Another photograph showed a building in an ultra-modern design, all lean curves and glass panels. 'February.' The third photograph was a dome, like the kind that appeared on the front of classic science-fiction paperbacks from the 1950s. 'March.' Each photograph was a unique building, from skyscrapers to cottages, one for every month of the year. My eyes fell on this month's photograph. An old palace, supported by pillars and large windows, and a slab above the door with the year 1541 chiseled into it.

If they changed the building every month, it's no wonder they kept their records below ground. Every time something altered up top, their inventory would always remain the same. It didn't shift like the city. It was constant. Stable. *At least something is.*

"You like the pictures?" the guard asked.

"Sure."

"I don't remember any of 'em. The changes, I mean. I don't know why they keep 'em up here."

"Probably to remind you of what they can do."

"Sounds about right. They like to keep us in line."

"I know what you mean."

"You do?"

"Oh yeah. I know all about the Anderson Whitman Group."

"Really? I always figured you'd be an outsider, y'know? That's maybe why the cops were tryin' so hard to track you down. What were you before? I mean, before you went linear?"

"What does it matter?"

"It matters to me. Why do you think I work here? I got a lifestyle package, and it ain't cheap. What do you reckon I pay Anderson Whitman for, huh?"

"Fresh cashews?" We reached the front of the elevator, and he pushed the button. The whir of the lift rumbled from below.

"I don't have a lifestyle package for the *changes.*" He nodded at the pictures on the wall. "I pay 'em every month to keep things from changin'. Anybody can come to this city and change their life in a couple of blinks. But you got no control over what stuff is different and what stays the same. One minute you're an actor. Then next you're a waitress and it's all gone, just like that. But with Anderson Whitman, you get security. They give you the life you want, and everythin' you need to *keep* livin' it. That's what I pay 'em for."

The doors pinged, sliding open, and we stepped inside the empty carriage.

"It's why I reckoned you had to be a randomer," he said. "Nobody goes linear with a package from Anderson Whitman. Out with the old, in with the new, y'know? But if they can't stop a person goin' linear, what am I payin' 'em for? It matters. See? Now what floor?"

"Not a clue," I said. "Isn't that what you're here for?"

"What records you want?"

I pulled a folder from the cardboard box and flicked through the file, showing him the planning applications.

"I need to find who approved these plans for the Anderson Whitman Group. Who proposed them, and who signed off on them."

"Buildin' plans? Floor seven." He pressed the button and the doors closed. "See? Beats puttin' me in a cupboard."

"I'm not so sure."

"Hey, watch it. Floor seven's big. You could get lost down there. Anyway, what do you want with some borin' plannin' records?"

"I think someone's been manipulating changes in the city."

"What you mean?"

"I mean faking plans to get rid of businesses."

"You mean, like, they forged those records and got some moolah?"

"Maybe."

"Ah yeah, man. That's more like it. Why you think they're fakes?"

Celia's face flashed across my mind. "Just a hunch."

"Okay. That's a good start, but it's not the whole story, is it?"

"What makes you say that?"

"Well, if you thought somethin' fishy was goin' on, why not just tell the big dogs, y'know? I reckon there's gotta be somethin' else. Must be pretty important, whatever it is."

"Oh, really?"

"It made you walk in here with a gun, didn't it? I didn't think a plannin' application could be that important. What are you expectin' to find in there?"

My head dropped. My whole body hushed. "The name of my wife's killer."

"Oh. Oh no." He looked like a waiter who just smashed a plate. "Oh, that's rough. I'm sorry, man."

"What are you sorry about?"

"Is that why you came to New Yesterday?"

"What do you mean?"

"With the changes, and all?"

"There are some things you can't change," I said. "Even here."

He lifted his cuffed hands to scratch his head. "Can I ask you a question? I mean, that's a question, right? But that's not it. What I wanna ask is, what's it like to go linear?" He looked at me with a childlike curiosity — the kind of innocent inquisitiveness that belongs to the young.

"It's like being everywhere and nowhere. Knowing everything you ever did, but none of it happened. Like you're living out every possible life you could ever have at once."

He nodded. "Yeah, man. But what's it *like*? Y'know? Is it pretty sweet, or is it a pain in the butt?"

I rolled my eyes. "Let's put it this way. Are we in a palace right now?"

"Duh! Of course we're in a palace. What does it look like to you? A dog kennel?"

"Okay. And if you believe the plaque outside, it was built in 1541, right?"

He frowned. "Are you feelin' okay?"

"In 1541, this place was nothing but woodland. A marsh or swamp or something. But all Anderson Whitman has to do is snap their fingers and all of that gets undone by mortar and stone. For hundreds of years, this palace has never and always existed. So you tell me. Which is real? The building or the woodland?"

He tapped his chin. "Well, we're in a buildin' now. So I say this is real."

"And next month, when the palace changes to a converted windmill built in the 1800s, this goes back to being woodland for three hundred years. What's real then?"

"I guess, the woodland."

I nodded. "Right. Which means we're standing in a building that doesn't exist."

He shook his head. "But it does. Because how could we stand in it if it doesn't exist?"

"Exactly. It does and it doesn't."

His shoes squeaked on the floor as he shuffled from left to right. "Are you tryin' to give me a headache or somethin'?"

"The fact is, one reality at a time is all we can handle. Otherwise, how do you know what's real and what isn't?"

"You tell me, man."

"When the knot of reality loosens, the world unravels. That's what it's like to go linear. You've got all these different histories playing out, and unless you can figure out what's real, it drives you crazy. I mean, how are you supposed to *not* be paranoid when you can't even trust your past?"

He sniffed, nodding. "You could've just said it was a pain in the butt. I can see why the cops are chasin' you."

"They think I'm dangerous. That I'm going insane."

"Well, you did threaten to shoot me."

I grimaced. "And if there was any other way to do this, I'd have taken it. But I'm not crazy. I know the truth. All I need is a name, just one name, and I can prove it."

"So what's real for you, bro?"

"My wife. And the person who took her from me. I realize that what I'm doing isn't exactly legal. But wouldn't you have done the same if it meant keeping hold of what's real?"

The lift stopped and its doors swept open. Twisting like the coils of a serpent, the subterranean passage wound in corners, always curving. Doors lined the hallway between shelves of binders stacked floor to ceiling. They'd coded each bookcase, the dizzying patterns irregular and confusing. A-F would be next to Y2-Y7, and 12075-13999 next to that. *How is anyone supposed to find anything in this mess? It's like they're* trying *to keep the past hidden.*

I'd seen those binders once before in the office of a salesman. Lifestyle packages that showed the options of a life, a house, a job. These shelves were the hard copies of people's lives. Disordered, chaotic, lost.

The guard led me past one door and another, deeper into the labyrinth. His shoes scuffed on the concrete floor, each step soaked up by the surrounding shelves. Strip lights on the ceiling swathed the corridor in an unrelenting grayish glare.

"How much further?" I asked.

"Almost there. Next on the left."

We stopped outside the door. On its front, a clouded glass panel revealed blurs in the room behind, indistinct and shadowy. Dark letters across the glass read 'BUILDING ARCHIVE.'

"What did I tell you?" He puffed out his chest.

My fingers squeezed around the door's handle. It didn't budge. I dropped the cardboard box and folders spilled onto the floor. I tried the handle with both hands, but it wouldn't turn an inch.

"Where's the key?"

He shrugged. "Beats me."

"*What*?"

"Hey, cool it. I got you this far, didn't I?"

"*Cool* it? My wife's killer is on the other side of that door, and you expect me to cool it?" My forehead strained, reddening as adrenaline flooded my veins. My chest drilled with a pneumatic pounding. Our faces were close, almost touching.

The smell of cashews on his breath clouded the air between us. His mustache-fur twitched as lines surrounded his squint. "You gotta get yourself together, man. Take a breath. Deep breaths. In and out. Okay?"

A buzz shot down my leg. I backed away and dragged his phone from my pocket. It shook in my hands, its screen flashing as the call came through.

"Who's JACKY D?"

He shot me that same look of a disgruntled schoolteacher. "Did you think there'd only be *one* security guard lookin' after a place like this?"

"There's more?" A shiver rippled from my spine to my fingertips. Cold sweat broke out on my face.

"Yeah, man. Jacky's probably found the gun in the reception by now. If I don't answer, game's over."

So that's why he slid the gun away. Leaving a crumb for his fellow security guard to follow. Why hadn't I picked it up? Pocketed it? Done anything except leave it there?

"You gonna answer or what?" he said.

My head rattled, same as the phone in my hand. "If I do, this all disappears."

"Same if you don't, bro. It was fun while it lasted. I really thought we were gonna get the file you wanted, man. Talk about bad timin'. Look, I'm sorry. You seem like a good guy."

I trained the gun on him. "Answer and tell him this is all a big mistake. Tell him you dropped your gun or something."

He took the phone from me. "You gonna shoot me if I don't? You don't seem like the shootin' type, man."

"Please." I held the gun at his head and he gripped the phone in his hand. "Please don't make me do this."

He stared at me with a cool deliberation that broke my gaze.

My arm buckled beneath the strain of that incessant ringing. "Who am I kidding? I couldn't shoot you."

"Didn't think you would."

"I'm sorry," I whispered.

"No need to apologize, man."

"I'm not apologizing to you. I'm talking to Lottie."

"Lottie?"

"My wife. I came all this way. Suffered all this pain. For what? I failed her. Again." I lifted my head to the ceiling. "It's over, Lottie. I'm so sorr—" but I couldn't speak any more, and my lips stiffened as I choked on the pain of losing her all over again.

The phone tolled like a bell. He stood watching me as though I was a wounded zoo animal.

*Just get it over with already.*

He swiped the screen and held it to his ear. "Yeah, Jacky D . . . s'up dog? . . . Yeah, I'm fine . . ." *With a word, those cuffs will change from his wrist onto mine. This corridor will fill with police. We'll forget all this.*

But he said nothing.

He just stared at me and frowned. ". . . No, I'm still here . .. Yeah, yeah, is that where I left it? . . . I know I shouldn't leave the desk but . . . You know how clumsy I am . . . Nah, man, just a false alarm . . . Say, you don't know where the key to Floor Seven is, do you? . . . Nah, I took a patrol and heard a noise and wanted to check it out . . . You'll retrofit it for me? Send it over, yeah? . . . Thanks bro, I might be tied up here for a while . . . Yeah, I left 'em in the drawer for you, a full box and dips and everythin' . . . Alright, peace out."

He hung up and reached into his pocket. A set of keys jangled in his hands, retrofitted by the other guard. He unlocked his cuffs, rubbed his wrists and offered me a tissue from the packet he carried in his other pocket.

"Wipe that snot from your face and let's find this killer, eh?" he said.

I stooped to gather the files back into the box. "Why are you helping me?"

He shrugged his shoulders. "I dunno, man. Maybe I wanna see who set you up. Maybe I'm thinkin' if this could happen to a guy like you, it could happen to me. And I don't want that. Besides, sounds like somethin' bad's goin' down, man, and I can't just let that slide, can I? And anyway, I've got my phone back, so I can always change my mind, right?" He smiled, his teeth littered with flecks of nut.

"Thanks. What's your name?"

"What does it matter?" He inserted the key.

"It matters," I said.

"You can call me Carlos. Like Santana. You know Santana?"

"Sure."

" 'Senorita full of sin . . .', you like that song? 'You don't need to let me in . . .', yeah, man. That's my jam. 'But I'll change the world for you if you tell me your name . . . Senorita, take it slow . . . it's a secre—'"

"Alright, Carlos. I'm Adam."

The latch snapped and the door swept open. Cabinets and bookcases lined the walls, just like the archive at the planning office, except twice as big. Reams of binders bunched tight on the shelves swamping the stuffy room.

"You know what you're after?" Carlos asked.

"I think so."

" 'Senorita, take it slow . . . it's a secret we both know . . . that sorry comes too late when there's someone to blaaame,* " he sung below his breath as his fingers mimed a face-melting solo on an invisible guitar. He bit his lip and nodded his head with his eyes shut, lost in music as he leaned against the wall, leaving me to wander among the dusty volumes of plans stacked on plans stacked on plans.

I hunted the records, picking out the address, district and time of construction from the pages I already had until I found the right shelf. The first binder came up short. The same with the next, and the next after that. At my feet, the pile of discarded binders grew until I finally leafed to a page that matched the plans I searched for. Side by side, the details were identical.

*This is the one.*

I flipped the page and there it was, taunting me in black ink. The killer's name and signature.

## TWENTY-FOUR

*"HELLO, YOU'VE REACHED Sinclair's. How may I help?" chimed the receptionist at the lavish counter. I skirted past them to Celia's desk. My fingers tightened around the files, still warm from the laminator.*

*"You look terrible, Adam. Is everything alright?" She brushed her hair behind her ear.*

*"Fine. I'm fine. It's just—" I glanced around the open office. Every head was buried in a monitor, fingers frantic across keyboards.*

*"What is it?" she whispered, leaning forwards.*

*I crouched beside her, cradling the files to my chest. "You know that thing I've been working on? Those records I was tracking down?"*

*"You found them?"*

*"Eventually. I've just finished laminating my notes. It's the same as Tammy's, Celia. The same."*

*"So what are you going to do?"*

*"I can't sit on this. It's too dangerous."*

*"Dangerous? How?"*

*"I'm sorry I dragged you into all this."*

*She placed her hand on my shoulder. "You couldn't do it on your own, Adam. I'm glad you told me."*

*Despite the risk, I was glad too. "Will you do something for me, Celia?"*

"Anything."

"Will you take this somewhere safe?" I pulled the police record from the bundle of files and passed it to her. "If something goes wrong, it might be all that's left."

She slipped the folder from my fingertips, and it was gone. The first time I'd been without it in all these months. "I know just the place. A collector across town. Gilligan Kennedy. He'll keep it safe enough."

"Can you take it now?"

"Right away?"

"It can't wait, Celia."

She drummed her fingers on her lips. "I guess I can clock off early without it looking too suspicious. You think it's that serious?"

"They might already be looking for it. I had to call in some big favors to get hold of those records. If word gets out—"

"Okay, Adam. I'll go." She locked her screen and stood, grabbed her coat and draped it over her arms, disguising the files with its long folds.

"How can I ever repay you for all this?" I asked.

She moved towards me and pressed her ruby lips against my cheek. Warm and soft, they lingered for a moment before she pulled away and tiptoed to the elevators.

"Wait a sec." I dashed around to the box I kept stashed beneath my desk and forced it into her hands. "This too. To go along with the other stuff."

"What's in here?" She shook the box and the gun thumped around its bottom.

"Do me a favor and don't look," I said.

*She shrugged and dropped the folders through a crack in the box's rim, slapping the lid shut tight. She stood frozen, as though something was holding her back, stopping her from moving. Her body tilted towards me. "I'm scared, Adam. Can't you at least tell me what's going on?"*

*"Not here."*

*"How about later? Isn't there somewhere we could go?"*

*My eyes scoured the office, but nobody was watching. "I know a place. A beach. It's private, only a short drive away. There's this old lighthouse."*

*"Shall I pick you up in, say, an hour?"*

*I nodded. Her eyes stayed on me, and with a half-smile she breathed deeply and lugged the box across the room. Swallowed by the ping of elevator doors, she disappeared.*

*Bodies blustered around the office, oblivious. Unaware of this moment. The few quiet seconds before the storm.*

*I should just call the cops. Leave it to them to figure out this mess. But not before I'd heard him beg for forgiveness. I hadn't come all this way to hand him over to the police without facing him.*

*A letter-opener slotted into my pocket. I'd spent so many hours sharpening it to a razor's edge, imagining what I'd do with it when I finally got the truth. How I'd carve out retribution for her. How killing him might mean she could . . .*

*No. I couldn't kill him. That's not me.*

*She wouldn't have wanted me to become that. Not for anything.*

*He sat in his office. Alone. Her murderer. Separated from me by the length of a corridor. So close. It'd be so simple to make him pay. Blood for blood. Life for life. Take from him what he took from me. Plunge the thin blade through his heart and rip it from his chest, watch him suffocate without it.*

*He'd broken my heart into pieces the moment he pulled the trigger. She deserved vengeance. He deserved . . .*

*Just cool it, Adam. If you lose it now, you lose everything.*

*Take a breath.*

*Celia had the files. They'd be safe, no matter what. I'd made the call to the paper. All that's left is to hear him admit it.*

*I only wanted to hear him admit it.*

*Just once.*

*What's that expression? Confession is good for the soul. It was good for police evidence too.*

*I took out my phone and hit the voice-recorder, stuffing it in my pocket.*

*It was time. With the remaining files under my arm, I marched the corridor to the office of the CEO.*

*My fist pounded the door where letters chiseled in gold leaf spelled 'Jeff Sinclair.'*

*"Come in." A faint voice carried through the wood.*

*I can do this.*

*At the end of his spacious office, the boss sat behind an imposing desk. His silver hair swept in a flourish. The knot of his Armani tie squeezed his neck. He reclined in his chair, rocking on its hinges as he sipped a glass of port.*

"Ah, Mr. Swann. More paperwork for me to go through?"

"Something like that, sir."

He waved his fingers in a motion that beckoned me towards him, and I pushed the door shut.

Keep it together.

"At least it'll give me something to do, eh?" His chair twisted to face me. Don't lose it.

"Busy day, Mr. Sinclair?" I inched closer, his silhouette growing with each step.

"You could say that. My decanter hasn't stopped since this morning." He nodded to the drink cabinet by the wall. His eyebrows raised and his mouth curled in a smug grin, wrinkling his smooth skin. "The privilege of middle age, I call it."

"Us lowly secretaries wouldn't know about that, Mr. Sinclair."

"I expect not." He drained the last drop of red.

I laid the folders in front of him, arraying them in the usual spread, like a hand of cards waiting to be turned. Maybe I should strangle it out of him?

Get a grip, Adam.

From his handkerchief pocket, he pulled his reading glasses and bridged them on the end of his nose. "Anything in here I should be worried about?" He skimmed the first page of the nearest file.

"That depends, Mr. Sinclair." I stood to one side, a single pace from the desk, my hands clasped together in front of me.

"On what?"

"On whether you think murder is something to worry about?"

*He stiffened. His hair bristled. The pinstripes of his suit sharpened. The only thing that moved was the second hand of his watch, and even that seemed to have slowed.*

*My chest collapsed. I'd been preparing for this moment. But now that it had arrived, all my careful plans were forgotten and what remained was the surge through my ribcage. Tightness cramped my breath. Blood hammered through my veins, pummeling me with each passing second. I rubbed my wedding ring.*

*His eyes lifted to mine. Ice met fire, and between us, the air melted, blurring everything but the pincer of his stare.*

*"I beg your pardon?" He raised a hand to his collar and loosened the choke of his tie.*

*"Murder, Mr. Sinclair. The murder these files prove you've committed."*

*"Is this some kind of joke?"*

*"Let me tell you a story, sir. It won't take long. It's about a girl called Tammy who opened a florist in New Yesterday. A small, unassuming place. Independent. You know the kind? She made a tidy profit. Nothing too splashy, but enough to get by.*

*"Then some corporate bigwig from the AWG saw her smallholding and thought, 'what's an independent store doing there when our clients could earn megabucks in that location?' and then, bam, just like that, they'd arranged for Tammy's profit to simply disappear. Swallowed up by changes. Retrograded out of existence. Before you could blink, she'd been forced out and a new Gracy's had popped up out of nowhere with years of backdated cash.*

*"And who banked the profit? The corporate bigwig whose idea it was. Sound familiar?"*

*His hands slammed his desk. He staggered to his drink cabinet, glass brimming with another port and he tossed his head back. "That's an interesting story, Mr. Swann. Where did you hear it?"*

*Just admit it. Say you did it! Say you swindled her! "I've heard all sorts of things working here, sir."*

*"You've got a great imagination. I'll give you that. But what you're talking about is illegal, Mr. Swann. You know the penalties. Why risk it?"*

*"Why risk anything? How much did you make from it? Enough to get away with it, I'll bet. And you did. The first time. How long was it before you tried again? A week? A month? A year? But the next time, it wasn't so small was it? When your clients found out about it, how much did they offer you to arrange a few years of prime space? Eventually, you'd have to be swapping stores left, right, and center to cover it up. Until Tammy got caught in the crossfire."*

*He dropped his glass, his eyes fixed on the folders waiting on his desk. "Bribery? Really? You think these building applications prove that, do you?"*

*"You know they do."*

*"Is that what I know? As far as I was aware, these kinds of swaps happen all the time in New Yesterday. Keeps things fluid."*

*"Fluid? Like your bank account?"*

*He whitened, his eyes manic. "You've seen my accounts?"*

*"You didn't recognize the copies in that last folder? They show all the payments siphoned off from each move. All the bribes paid for the best spots in town. It all matches. But I'm sure that's no surprise."*

*His hand squeezed his empty glass. Any tighter and it'd smash.* "Those records are private. How did you get copies?"

"Does it matter?"

"It's a crime to obtain data that doesn't belong to you."

"Is that a threat?"

"Just a fact, Mr. Swann. Where did you get them?"

"If you're looking for a chance to retrograde it, you won't find one. You remember what you told me when you hired me, Mr. Sinclair? 'The appearance of success is success. If you want it enough, you'll be seen to have it, and when that happens, you've already got it.' Turns out I was listening."

*He paced, his breathing clipped.* "Quite the student, aren't you? Well, you've told a nice little tale. Almost had me feeling sorry for your dear little florist. But what I'm confused about is how a handful of planning documents convict me of murder?"

"I think it's obvious."

"Obvious? Are you sure you're quite well, Adam?"

*Stop trying to hide how scared you are, old man.* "Oh, I'm in the best of health, sir."

"All the same, I think we should get you checked out. I'll call for a doctor." *He reached for the phone on his desk.*

"The story's not finished." *My hands balled into fists.* "Don't you want to hear how it ends?"

*He paused, rooted to the spot.* "I'm listening."

"You see, Tammy had friends. A man and a woman who wanted a baby, but hit a brick wall. So they thought about trying their chances in New Yesterday. See if it might change anything. The woman looked up her florist friend whose business reeled in a steady profit, only to find she'd been bankrupted months before, having never made so much as a nickel from her store. Tammy couldn't remember it any different. So the woman figured something shady was going on and started a petition online. Ring any bells, Mr. Sinclair?"

His eyes closed. His forehead creased. Sweat misted his face and he tugged at the collar of his shirt, desperate to loosen it.

"You couldn't let it get out, could you? What you'd done? You'd have been ruined. All those years of hard work, building the city, making it what it is — gone. Like it never happened. And with the petition taking off, with 'Transparent New Yesterday' becoming a movement, you had to act fast."

"That petition." He shook his head. "It started so small. I never thought it'd get so out of hand."

"Greater transparency would expose you. You'd have to show the world what you'd done, and there'd be nowhere to hide. No retrograde to make it better."

"I should've nipped it in the bud when I had the chance."

"You tried. Remember? You made an appointment to see the woman who started it."

"I—"

"You had to put a stop to it, one way or another."

His guard dropped, succumbing to the fear that gripped him as his eyes burst open. "No! It wasn't like that." He backed against the wall.

"You went to see her at her apartment and put a bullet in her."

"No, you don't understand. It was . . ."

*"You gunned her down in cold blood to keep her quiet."*

*". . . it was an accident . . ."*

*"To cover up your dirt."*

*". . . a mistake. I never meant to . . ."*

*"You squeezed the trigger and silenced her."*

*". . . hurt her. It all happened so fast . . ."*

*"For good."*

*". . . NO!" He raked his hair, pulling at his suit. His crazed eyes possessed the wildness of a madman. All the sharpness of his features, the crispness of his outfit, was undone by the disarray of his mind. "I offered her everything, but she wouldn't take it. She just stood there, her eyes red like she'd been crying. Those eyes. She kept shaking her head. I mean, what was I supposed to do? I tried pleading with her, negotiating. None of it worked. The gun was a threat. That was all. Just a threat to show her how serious it was. And those eyes. I didn't mean to. It was an accident. Understand?"*

*His words stirred a fire in my gut that burned through every pore. Every fiber of me yearned to grab his throat and tear him to pieces.*

*My fingers reached for my pocket. The letter-opener.*

*Don't lose it.*

*Accident or not, I had him on the record. Keep it together.*

*"She was my wife, Jeff."*

*"Your what?"*

*"You took her from me. And ever since, you've been swapping stores in the city to cover your tracks, just like you covered the rest of it. Getting rid of the store you bought the gun from might have seemed like a smart*

move, but it wasn't. It pointed straight to you. You're the only one that linked Tammy and that petition. The only one who could've covered it up. It wasn't the murder that gave you away. It was your retrogrades."

"No. No, Adam. I haven't been covering it up. Don't you see? I've been trying to undo it."

"Undo it? You think you can change this?"

"You've accused me of making deals to cover up a mistake? But you've got it wrong. I've been trying to erase what I did ever since that first moment of weakness. I was young, foolish. I thought I could get away with swapping one store for another and nobody would be the wiser. But it's not that simple. I've tried to change it for so long, and I'd almost cracked it. I was nearly there. And then she — your wife — oh, Adam, what have I done? Adam, I'm, I'm sorr—"

"Don't!"

"Don't what?"

"Don't tell me you're sorry like this is a parking ticket or some bad joke. You killed my wife!"

"What do you want me to say?"

"You put a gun to her head and you—" Don't lose it. Don't reach for your pocket.

"I did. And I'm sorry. You don't think I'd take it back if I could?"

"Maybe you can." I clasped the letter-opener.

Drop it.

Drop it now.

"What's that supposed to mean?" His eyebrows ruffled.

I paced towards him, blade in hand.

He squirmed and I . . . I liked it.

*"Adam. What are you doing? Talk to me!"*

*I grabbed him by the collar and pressed the tip against his throat.*

*"Adam, please! You don't want to do this!" His voice shook. His whole body trembled.*

*"You're not the only one whose tried undoing things, Jeff."*

*One flash of the wrist. It'd be so easy.*

*"Please, Adam—"*

*"I tried to get her back. Ever since I moved here. But every retrograde worked out the same. The fact is, her killer's still here. As long as her murderer's alive, she's not coming back."*

*Terror paled his features, made him frail. His legs jellified. "It doesn't," his voice was barely audible, "doesn't do you any good, if you just think about it. You don't want to do this."*

*"No? If I kill you, then her murderer is gone! It's you being alive that's keeping her from me. You didn't just kill her once. Every day you wake up is another day where you pulled the trigger, over and over again. I can't retrograde it any different unless you're gone. But with you dead, maybe I can get her back? Maybe I—" I pressed the blade firmer against his tender flesh. Just one lunge and it'd be over.*

*"No, Adam. You're wrong. If you kill me, you'll never get her back." His sweat dripped on the silver edge.*

*"You don't know what you're talking about!"*

*"Listen to me. You can wash away the past, but the stain on your conscience will never fade. Trust me. I know all about it. Even when the past is gone, the guilt is still there. Kill me, and you'll carry a part of me with you*

*always. You'll be the one condemning her to death. You can change your past, but you can't escape your conscience. You don't want to kill me. Face it, Adam. You need me."*

*"Shut up!"*

*"You know I'm right."*

*"I can end this!"*

*"It'll be the end of you as well."*

*I tightened my grip on his collar, teeth grit together as I snarled at his face. The last face she ever saw.*

*If I let him live, she's gone. If I kill him, he'll plague me forever, and I'll never be able to bring her back. How can he still be killing her, even when I have him by the throat?*

*"This doesn't have to be the end for you," he said. "For either of us. Let me help you."*

*"It's too late for that."*

*"Adam, I—"*

*"You have to pay for what you did! We all do, in the end."*

*"You think it's too late. But it's not. Not in this city."*

*"Face facts, Jeff. If she's gone, then it's because of you."*

*"You're hurting. You're in pain."*

*"You have no idea."*

*"What if I could fix it? Make you forget that pain?"*

*"Why should I trust you? You're nothing but a murderer."*

*"Slit my throat and what'll that make you? The same as me. Is that what you want?"*

*"I—"*

*"It's not too late. Drop the knife and let's talk."*

*Don't listen to him. Don't believe him. Even if he's right.*

"Come on." He reached for my hand and I let him ease it away. The letter-opener dropped to the floor. I released his collar and he straightened out his suit.

*She wouldn't have wanted blood on my hands. Even if it meant bringing her back.*

*Just breathe.*

*I still have the recording. The files are safe. He's going down for this, whatever happens.*

"You blame me for taking her away from you," he said. "I get that. But it's not me who's keeping her that way."

"Are you saying I'm wrong to keep her memory alive?"

"And all the pain that goes with it. Think about it. Get rid of that ring you wear around your finger and how long do you expect you'd remember her? In New Yesterday? You wouldn't last the night. How long have you been in the city? A few months? Have you forgotten what she looked like yet? What color was her hair? Her eyes? Those eyes. Have any of those details started to slip away from you? What was her name? You haven't said it once. Can you even remember?"

"I . . . of course I—"

"You're holding onto her. Just let her go, and you can have anything you want. Anything. I know what I need to do now to make things right. To make all this legitimate. What I need is a partner. I can't undo my financial blunders without one. You could be that man, Adam. Forget this secretary nonsense. I'm talking about partners."

*You and me. I can take care of you. Just say yes and you'll never feel pain again."*

*"You think I want to forget her?"*

*"Give me that wedding ring. Your wallet. Your clothes. If you still remember her, you can have them back. If not, you'll have made the best decision of your life."*

*"No. I won't let her go."*

*"My boy, you could have so much more."*

*"You expect me to give her up? You're crazy."*

*"What's crazy is walking away from all this, for the sake of a woman you can't even remember."*

*"You don't get it, do you? There's no way out of this. I wasn't just twiddling my thumbs while I copied those files. I've already called the papers. Anonymous tip-off. There'll be reporters coming soon. Maybe not today. Maybe not tomorrow. Could be weeks. Could be months. But they're coming. Then what are you going to do?"*

*His eyes darted left and right, like snared prey. "There's always a way out. Just give me the ring and this all goes away. By the time they get here, there'll be nothing to report."*

*"Can you hear yourself right now?"*

*"Adam, don't do this. Think about it, man. You're about to make the biggest mistake of your life. Don't be a fool."*

*"Goodbye, Jeff. I'll see you in court." I clutched my phone, turned my back, and stepped towards the door.*

*"Who're you gonna call? The police? You think it's that simple? Think you can just walk out of here?"*

*Before I reached the door, it swung open and Bulldog walked in. "Mr. Sinclair, sir, I've got those—"*

"Stop him!" Jeff yelled.

The man grabbed hold of my arms, bulldozing me back into the room.

"Out of my way, Bulldog!" I warned.

"You heard me! He isn't to leave this room." Jeff gathered the files.

I charged at Bulldog, but my malnourished body stood no chance against his broad shoulders. All that weight I'd lost since she'd gone. It betrayed me now.

Jeff closed the door while Bulldog pinned me back. I cut off the recording and dialed the police. All I'd need is a couple of seconds to call it in and we'd be at the station.

"Get that phone!"

Bulldog lunged at me. I pushed back. His ironlike fingers wrapped around my wrist and he grappled it from my hand before the line connected.

"Give it here." Jeff stood with his palm outstretched.

I threw myself at Jeff, releasing all the rage I'd carried with me these past months. But my blows struck air as Bulldog forced himself around me.

"Hold him!"

Like chains, Bulldog's paws gripped me. He stood at my back, looping his muscular arms around my shoulders. He shackled me in his hold, and forced me rigid.

Jeff dropped the phone, smashing his heel through the screen. It cracked to pieces, destroying the recording with it. He stepped towards me and reached for the ring.

"No!" I writhed against the arms that pinned me, but could do nothing to stop it.

"You'll thank me for this one day, partner." Jeff slipped the ring from my finger and it seeped out of me —

*the sound of her laugh, the perfection of her face, the scent of her perfume. Years faded, like twilight.*

*I couldn't let her fade away.*

*I couldn't let him strip her from me.*

*Unleashing a scream, I channeled all my strength and thrust my head backward. Bulldog's nose erupted over my scalp and his grip weakened. I slipped an elbow free and rammed it into his gut. His other hand still clenched around my good arm, and I bit down on his fingers. He cried out, releasing me.*

*I spun, ready to pounce on Jeff, but the shimmer of a decanter filled my vision as it came down on me.*

*Glass smashed across my skull, showering me in tiny cuts, and the cold liquid trickled down the back of my head, wetting my hair.*

*On one side of my face, the fuzz of carpet brushed against my cheek. A faint voice drifted to my ear in waves, as though I was underwater. "Bulldog, I want you to get rid of these files." Footsteps thudded past me, the tremors of an earthquake. I tried to move, but I couldn't. "Hello? Is that the office of Anderson Whitman? . . . Mike, I need a favor . . ."*

*I felt for my wedding ring, but flesh was all my fingers met. It was gone, and so was I, slipping away as darkness sprawled its tendrils over me.*

\*\*\*

I dropped the binder where Jeff's signature scrawled across the page, and it clattered to the floor with the rest. My spine jarred against the shelves behind me. The memory clawed at my head with stinging talons, raw as an open wound.

I ripped the signature sheet away from the binder and shoved it inside Lottie's police file. The missing piece. All I needed to prove the identity of her killer. The folder tucked into my belt. I picked up the box and straightened my back, sliding around the bookcase towards Carlos.

"*Sorry comes too late when there's someone to blaaame . . . Senorita . . . sweet Latina . . . wanna free ya . . .*" Carlos' voice bellowed the lyrics as his hips shook.

"Ahem," I said, clearing my throat.

His eyes opened, breaking Santana's spell, and he grinned. "Hey, bro. You find what you were lookin' for?"

"I know who did it. And I know what I've got to do."

"Hey, that's great, man." He fumbled at the screen of his phone.

"What are you doing?"

"Callin' the cops."

"The *cops*?"

"Yeah, you said you found the dude who killed your wife. So now we call the cops and bring in the big guns."

"The cops are the ones trying to take me in."

"Yeah, but it'll be different now, right?"

As if the police would be interested in anything I said. I'd gone linear. I might as well have been wearing a straight-jacket as far as they were concerned. All this evidence would disappear, along with the rest of me. Along with Jeff. Again.

My head swelled, veins throbbed as my eyes scoped the room. His keys hung on the outside of the door, still protruding from the lock. It was the only way out.

Carlos' smile waned and his expression became serious. His fingers smoothed out the tuft of his mustache. "Look, this is a crime. You gotta call the police."

"But—"

"You wanted my help? That's the deal, bro."

Our eyes locked. There'd be no stalling him. No talking him out of it. What else could I do? "You're right, of course you're right." My chin dropped. "At least, let me be the one who calls it in?" My palm stretched towards him, and my eyes pleaded with his.

"Okay. I guess that's fair." He pushed the phone into my hand, its weight like lead.

"Thanks." My thumb trembled over the screen, hovering above the green 'call' icon.

"Well, what are you waiting for?" He tilted his head back and scooped a handful of cashews into his mouth.

I rammed my forearm into him and sent him staggering against the wall. My side roared as I bounded into the corridor. He gained his feet and thrust forwards but I slammed the door, his hands just prints on the window as my wrist flicked at the keys, and the latch clasped shut.

"What are you doin', man?" his muffled voice floated through the door.

"I'm sorry, Carlos. Really, I am. But there's something I've got to do, and I can't have the police messing it up. Understand?"

"Listen, man. Let me out of here, okay? You said you wouldn't lock me in a cupboard!"

"You'll be alright. I'll come back for you."

"Hey, *hey!*"

The handle shivered as he forced it over and over. His fists pounded on the clouded glass, but there was no risk of it breaking, reinforced solid as steel. The keys slipped out of the lock and into my pocket, along with his phone, and his voice trailed into the distance as I limped back to the elevator, ignoring the agony burning beneath the bandage.

His pass-card swiped over the scanner, and the lift vomited me into the straight, windowless corridor. I passed the photographs of Anderson Whitman's HQ and slunk through the soft fabrics of the reception room to the marble-tiled lobby.

Behind the desk, an older security guard twisted in his chair. Carlos' gun was on the desk, beside the monitor. *This must be Jacky D.*

I nodded towards him, and he raised his hand in a wave. His face screwed up as he tried to place my own.

"Forgot to lock a drawer." I rolled my eyes. "Rookie mistake."

"Happens to the best of us. Have a good night, sir."

Into the darkness, an icy breeze rushed through my suit, fluttering the pages of the folder pressed into my trousers, hidden by the jacket which blustered in a howl of wind. Through the iron gates and along the wall I hurried. The windows of Anderson Whitman's HQ watched me leave, its eyes fixed on my every step until I passed beyond its gaze.

The car door closed at my side, and I rubbed my hands together. From my pocket, I grabbed the phone, tapped in a random code, and it unlocked at my first attempt. *So much for cybersecurity.* Passwords changed with whoever used the device, unless someone had bought the AW upgrade. And who wanted to fork out for upgraded security when all a person needed to do was report something stolen and a replacement would appear instantaneously, as though it had never been out of their hands?

I tapped the internet search app. What was the name of that paper? The one that had phoned for Gabrielle. The Daily . . . it was The Daily . . . I typed in 'The Daily' and the search engine filled in the rest. 'Post.' *Duh.*

I waited three rings before someone answered. "I need the editor who was trying to speak with Gabrielle Laurent." A few beeps as the call transferred.

"Who is this? What do you want?"

"Are you the editor looking for Gabrielle Laurent?"

"You didn't answer my question. Who are you and what do you want?"

"We spoke before. You were trying to reach her."

"What of it?"

"Well, I know where she'll be tonight."

"You got a number I can speak to her on?"

"Yeah, but first, I want you to do something for me."

"Oh, I see. Scratch my back, I scratch yours. Is that it? Go on. Hit me with it. What are you expecting me to do?"

"Just listen. That's all."

"Listen? Who do you think this is? The Samaritans? I haven't got all night to spend listening to random strangers offload. Find yourself a priest if you need to talk. Unless you've got something to say, that is?"

"I've got plenty to say. Five minutes, that's all I need, and then you'll have Gabrielle Laurent and a whole lot more."

"Clock's ticking."

Ten minutes later, the line rang dead. Gabrielle's editor had his address. The hotel where she'd be launching her book, where the elite of Anderson Whitman gathered to indulge in a night of champagne, where Sinclair's clients nested in decadence, feasting on revelry, bathing in the pleasures of their wealth. He'd be basking at his table, surrounded by his accomplishments, the ringleader of luxury, the one behind this whole thing from the start. The man who'd pulled the trigger and sent my Lottie to oblivion.

Gabby's editor had been right about one thing. The clock was ticking. It wouldn't be long before Jacky D found Carlos locked on the seventh floor. If this had any chance of working, I'd need all the help I could muster.

I opened a webpage on the screen. Searched for Lottie's petition. Logged in.

'Protest tonight. AWG gathered in one place. Time to act. #TNY.'

Within a few seconds, my message had been re-sent a dozen times.

Replies tumbled in.

'When and where?'

I typed the address and pocketed the phone.

No time to waste.

Tires squealed in the direction of The Phoenix Hotel. The place where I'd reunite with my friend and partner. My mentor.

The murderer of my wife.

## TWENTY-FIVE

THE PHOENIX HOTEL

MIDNIGHT TONIGHT — BOOK RELEASE

'REMEMBERING GUINEVERE'

SPECIAL APPEARANCE BY

GABRIELLE LAURENT

DOORS OPEN 10:00PM

THE POSTER GLEAMED in the hotel window. My watch's hands spun towards the clap of midnight. Beautiful people paraded outside the entrance in their best floor-length gowns or pressed tuxedos, blowing cigarette smoke to cloud the frigid night air.

*Head down.*

The lobby hummed with activity. The buzz of Gabby's book release charged the room with electricity. Guests compared swag-bags, grouped in a 'who's who' of the AWG to toot each other's champagne flutes.

*No eye contact.*

Across the lobby, two banks of elevator doors were chiseled into the wall. Beside them, a poster propped on an A-frame showed pictures of a high-ceilinged banquet hall lit in soft amber. 'Special Event — Invitation Only,

Floor 35,' read the advert, beside another mockup of the book.

At the rear desk, a lone receptionist held a telephone to her ear. Above her, a huge mosaic of a phoenix rose to fill the back wall.

The elevator whirred through the floors as the receptionist's voice tumbled over the lobby's din. "It doesn't make a difference what paper you're from, Miss Laurent is not to be disturbed." She rolled her eyes. "We've gone through this already, sir, the best I can do . . . the *best* I can do is to—"

*One angry newspaper editor keeping the staff busy, check and double check.*

I pressed for floor 35. Up through the procession of floors, a chime emptied me onto a lush red carpet, spread across the narrow hallway. Beyond a curtain, music played below the rustle of conversation. Hushed voices melded into a single murmur, broken only by a laugh or cough that rose above the constant hum of the crowd. But my heartbeat thrummed over the voices, swelling as blood pulsed through my ears.

A few steps from where the curtain draped, a security guard stood rigid. His bulk filled the space, and his shaved head matched the grizzle of his face. An earpiece ran into his jacket, misshapen by the bulge of his muscles tearing at the seams.

My eyes lowered to the floor as I ambled towards the curtains. I pushed the glasses up the bridge of my nose. Files slapped through my shirt, tucked into my belt, concealed down my back by the fall of my suit. His hand pressed against my chest, stopping me dead.

"Invitation, please," he said.

"I'm sorry. I don't have one."

"Then I can't let you through, sir."

"Look, all I need is a minute to speak with a gentleman inside."

"I can't do it, sir. Invitation only, I'm afraid."

"You don't understand. I have to get in."

"Sorry, but if you're not on the guest list, there's nothing I can do." The air blew in gusts from beyond the curtain, slapping me in the face like a schoolboy's taunt. *I'm never getting through this human pit-bull.*

"You sure there's *nothing* you can do?" I raised my eyebrows as if they were dollar signs.

"'Fraid not, sir. Say, don't I know you from somewhere?" He screwed up his face.

*Run. Now. But where? The elevator? The bathrooms? Sure, they'll never find you in there.* I checked my watch. "You know what? It's no problem. Is there somewhere I can wait until the event is over?"

"You can wait anywhere, sir. I just can't let you through the curtain."

"Thanks."

I paced the hallway. The same beautiful people who'd braved the night for a cigarette passed by me, sauntering from the lifts through the curtain with a simple flash of their pass.

I swiped the phone.

No new messages on the petition site.

Along the wall, pictures of previous events played on screens, hung in frames. Several bands took the stage, one after the next, interspersed with tables set out at different angles, like the solution to a geometric puzzle.

*What if they couldn't get into the ballroom?*

Closeups of the menu. Guests caught laughing, some harder than others.

*What if they got blocked by the brick wall of a security guard?*

Every picture told the same story. Rich people in suits and dresses, celebrating the same party over and over, stuck on repeat.

*What if they decided to do something more than just a protest?*

The security guard's walkie erupted in a tirade of garbled screams. He disappeared through the drape and I rushed to follow him.

Bodies stampeded the room. They thrashed in the carnage, mauling each other to get away from the handful of people in the center who aimed guns over the crowd. One held a banner. #TNY. A megaphone blared their chant.

"Transparency in NYC, let us see our history. Transparency in . . ."

Security guards charged the frenzied mass. It was a far cry from the pictures in the hallway.

Spotlights pierced the stage where Gabrielle stood with a copy of her book. Speckled in reflective diamantes, she wore more glitz than a disco ball. She searched the crowd, looking for someone. For him.

I followed her eyes and saw where he'd been swept along in the mayhem.

Against the tide, I barged through the mob, crashed against the surging waves, battered by shrieks and wails. Disarray reigned as king.

Tugging, pushing, heaving through the barricade of suits and gowns, I approached where he stood. His silver hair and olive skin, an all too familiar silhouette. His aftershave was so strong, it stabbed at my eyes, reeking of an artificial musk which hid everything beneath it.

I lodged the gun into his spine.

"The emergency exit. Now!"

Jeff craned his neck to face me, but I rammed the gun deeper into his back. Together, we slammed through the crowd and emerged beyond the chaos. He pushed the bar on the emergency exit and I followed him into the stairwell.

Everything stilled. Silence.

"Friends of yours?" Jeff asked, nodding beyond the door.

"The service elevator. Move!"

"Alright, alright. Don't get jumpy. I wouldn't want you doing something you'd regret."

"You would know."

His mouth opened in response, but I raised the barrel to his head and it stopped him short. Past the staircase, I marched him across the landing and called the lift. His feet scuffed over the concrete as I shoved him inside and the doors closed us in.

G.

The cart rumbled, descending.

"Empty your pockets, Jeff."

He stiffened. "How do you know my name?"

"Just do it."

He took out his phone and dropped it. I kicked it across the floor. Same with his wallet and keys.

"Who are you?" he asked.

"You don't know? We go way back, you and me."

He peered at my reflection in the mirrored panel on the wall. I pocketed my glasses and his eyes brimmed white.

"I suppose I should be excited," he said. "It's not every day you get to meet a celebrity. Not that going linear is the kind of fame anyone wants. How long have you been on the run now? Three months, is it?"

"Long enough."

"I guess you've been in worse scrapes than this. With the police at your back, and no way out. Shouldn't be long before they arrive to break up that little soirée your people threw."

"They aren't my people."

"No matter. The place will be swarming with cops before long, if it isn't already. You'd have done better taking me to the roof. Personally, I'm fascinated to see how you'll get out of this one."

"It's not me you should be worried about, Jeff."

"You think you can threaten me just because you're pointing a gun at my back? You don't realize who you're dealing with. This could be the single greatest opportunity you've ever had to make something of yourself, and you'll miss it if you're not careful." Classic Jeff. The more scared he got, the smoother he talked.

"Are you offering me a way out, old man?"

"Why not? I like your initiative. That instinct's priceless in business. And I need a partner."

"You never learn, do you?"

"I never learn what, exactly?"

"We're already partners. As a point of fact, we're good friends."

"You got any other jokes?"

"I'm being serious. That's why it hurt so much, when I found out what you did."

"When you found out?"

"I know everything, Jeff."

The doors opened. A corridor ran in both directions. I pushed him one way, towards a door with a small circular window cut into it. I pinned him against the wall and peered through the glass.

The lobby crawled with police. Tailored gowns clumped together in groups, all supervised by officers in full SWAT gear. It was a savannah patrolled by too many predators to cross without being devoured.

"Back the other way. Move."

"See? What did I tell you?"

"And what did I just tell *you*?" I shunted the pistol into his ribs and he scurried down the hall.

The door at its far end opened onto an alleyway. Rotting fish bones festered in trash cans, spitting their putrid tang across the dark. The night bit at my skin, slowing my movements.

I trained the gun on his face as he skulked towards the shadows of a fire escape.

"What did you mean, you know everything?" he said.

"Don't be so coy, Jeff. Embezzlement's a serious business."

"Are you — how did you — Listen. All this can be straightened out."

"Let me guess. You're sorry you did it and you need a partner to make things legitimate?"

"You catch on fast. What do you say? Are you in?"

"I was in once before. You forced me in. Remember?"

He creased his brow. "I've never seen you before today. Except on the news."

"Yeah. Thanks for that."

"What are you thanking me for?"

"You seriously don't know who I am, do you?"

He shook his head. "Sorry."

"What can I say to jog your memory? Would a glass of port help you figure it out?"

"Now you're talking. Look. Whatever it is, it's been retrograded. You can't blame me for that. Retrogrades are a tricky business to get right. If something's slipped my mind, it's not because I didn't try. Okay?"

"*Slipped your mind?* Are you for real right now?"

"I could ask you the same thing."

We stood facing off, both clueless. He had no idea what he'd done to me. To her. And how was I supposed to know whether to pull the trigger or keep talking?

"Okay, here's how this is gonna go," I said. "I'll tell you everything you're going to admit to. And then we'll take a trip downtown. Understand?"

"But—"

"I said, do you understand?" I rushed towards him, both hands on the gun.

"Okay, I get it. Boy, they were right about going linear. It makes you crazy." His skittish eyes roved around the alley. Steam vented to coat the air in a thin veil.

"It's all in here." I pulled the file from my trousers and waved it.

His face glued to the folder. "What's that?" he said, sweat streaking down his forehead.

"Proof, Jeff. Of everything you did. Sure, there are a few gaps, like the clauses you got Anderson Whitman to put into my lifestyle package."

"What clauses?"

"To get rid of me if I ever found out."

"What are you talking about?"

"You remember? In your office. You'd just smashed your decanter over my head and you rang to call in some favors. What did you use? Bribery legislation? Erase me if I came across the stuff you stole? If I ever touched anything to remind me of what you did? It must have cost you a small fortune."

I stepped closer to him.

He backed against the bricks. "You've got the wrong guy, pal."

"And then getting rid of the goods. Pawning it off under my nose and using Gracy's to do it. Swapping stores so your 'deposits' would vanish with them. Was that always part of your plan? Have me lose everything while Mrs. Campbell gets a brand new boat?"

Closer.

"Is this bringing any memories back, Jeff?"

"How d'you know about the boat?"

"How many times have you done this before? Was it just me, or were there others? How many peoples' lives have you taken by one of your deals?" Houdini's face flashed across my mind, raving about the store someone had swindled him out of.

And then it hit me.

The gun store. 105 North Parkway.

When I first got to the city, I'd tracked the owner and showed them the police report, even gave them the document to prove the store had disappeared. Houdini. He didn't have a clue. Not back then. It must've taken some other memory to snap him into going linear, and send him looking for me.

"I never hurt anybody, you hear?" Jeff insisted.

"You took her from me once. And then you took her from me all over again."

Closer.

He arched back, but there was nowhere for him to go. "Took who?"

"I found the ring, Jeff. The day before the mall went up. And you'd have gotten away with that too. You'd have erased it, along with the jewelers where you palmed it." I pressed the folder into his chest. "The rest is in there."

He flicked open the first page. Light from a second-story window poured down, glistened across the laminated sheets. "What is this?"

"It's everything I need to put you away. It proves you murdered her, and you tried to cover it. All because she'd figured out your little scam and you needed to shut her up."

"Look. I might have made a couple of bad decisions over some recent deals, but that's all. Murder? I'd never do something so stupid."

"A couple of bad decisions? Is that what you call it? You *killed* my wife."

"Your wife? Listen, what you need is some help."

"I've got all the help I need in this folder."

"Whatever you're holding onto, it's not worth it."

"Whose gun is this, Jeff?" I shoved it between his eyes. They flashed to the barrel, staring it down.

He shook his head.

I did the same. "You want to know where I got it? I picked it up in my apartment. Left behind by the man who killed Lottie in cold blood. Take a good long look. Is nothing coming back to you?"

"I told you. I'd never do something like that."

"No memories of pulling the trigger?"

"I've never seen that gun in my life."

"Sure. You keep telling yourself that."

"All I did was hedge a few bets. I didn't know anybody else was even aware of it until you pointed that gun in my face." He said it with such confidence I could have believed him. *Just because he doesn't remember it, that doesn't make him innocent.*

"If you don't believe me, then take a look."

He turned the pages, shaking his head as his eyes flicked left to right, scanning the contents. When he reached the end, he closed the file and laughed.

"What's so funny, Jeff?"

"You think this proves anything? Oh, my dear boy, what you need is a stiff drink. This proves nothing. It's just some old police report anybody could have mocked up. Those planning records, by tomorrow they'll be replaced by new ones. You've got nothing about the moves we're making on the promenade. What you've got is a lovely little fantasy, but that's all it is. A fantasy. Do you think a few planning applications and a photograph of some dead woman prove anything?"

"But, you told me, Jeff. You told me you killed her. You looked me straight in the eye and said it was an accident. And when the police arrive, you'll tell them."

Behind us, the door slammed open. I spun, the gun still pressed against his forehead.

In the doorway, a figure stood glittering in diamantes.

"*Jeff!*" she screamed. Her feet carried her towards us, but I raised a palm and she froze to the spot.

"Gabby, what are you doing here?" I said.

"I was looking for — I used the 'find a phone' — but . . ." She saw the gun and gasped.

"You shouldn't be here."

Her hands covered her mouth. "What's going on?"

"Why don't you tell her, Jeff?"

"Gabrielle, my darling. There's no need to panic."

"Are you alright, mon amour?"

"Tell her, Jeff. Tell her the truth."

"What is he talking about?" she asked.

"It's nothing, my darling. The man's crazy," he said.

"Admit it! Tell her what you did."

"Stop this," she said. "Please."

My hand shook. The gun's weight grew heavier and heavier, like an anchor at the end of my arm. "*Enough!*"

Silence.

I backed away from him and cleared a path between them. "Give her the file, Jeff."

She paced towards him. "Mon amour?"

"Gabby, you see that file he's holding?" I nodded at the police report he gripped in his thumbs. "It's all in there."

Her eyes fell to the folder. "What is?"

"The reason we're here."

Jeff dipped his head and scowled. "Don't listen to him, darling. He's delusional."

"Your fiancé's a killer, Gabby."

"It's all lies," he spat.

"Give her the folder!"

As she reached him, he pulled her close. He cradled her in his chest. She shivered, and he rubbed his hand across her bare arm.

She looked down at the file. "Let's just do as he says." Jeff didn't move.

"I won't say it again," I said.

Her hand slipped to the folder and she tugged it, but he wouldn't let go. "Mon amour?"

He stared at me with callous eyes, releasing the file, and she clasped it to her chest. *Just open it, Gabrielle.* But she couldn't. In one swift motion, he'd grabbed her wrist and yanked her in front of him.

He spun her so she faced me, shielding himself from a clear line of sight. His arms wrapped around her shoulders and his hands gripped tight to her neck. As I stepped towards them, his fingers squeezed.

"Drop the gun," he said.

"Are you threatening me, old man?"

"Not you, no." His eyes flashed at Gabrielle, then glared back at me, wide and manic.

"Jeff, you're choking me." She raised a hand to pull his arms from her throat. Her lips parted and she gasped for air.

"Don't worry, darling. You won't remember any of this, as long as our friend here does as he's told."

"Jeff, I can't—" She lurched forwards in a spasm. Her head rocked side to side.

"Drop it," he said. "Now!"

My mind flooded with the sight of Lottie laid out on the floor of our apartment in her jade green blouse, her body floating on a reservoir of blood. In front of me, history was repeating itself. *What choice do I have? He isn't going to stop. Not until Gabby drops dead.*

I let the gun slip from my hand. It clattered on the concrete at my feet.

"Now, back away. Nice and slow."

I shuffled back.

Jeff released Gabrielle and knelt for the gun. He lifted it and the black abyss of its barrel fixed on my chest.

He shuddered. His face twitched. His eyes darted everywhere at once. His jaw slackened and he shook his head, pupils dilated sharp, and his stomach jolted him forwards in a violent wretch. He stood upright and screamed. His free hand gripped his head. "No. No, it was an accident."

"Not the first time you've held that gun, is it, Jeff?" My thumb reached for my wedding ring.

"Stay back!" he yelled.

I stepped towards him. "Bring back any memories?"

"It wasn't my fault!"

Gabrielle rubbed her neck, staring in terror as she witnessed the truth grip his mind, revealing the monster within him. "I don't . . . what *are* you?" she whispered.

She glanced down at the police report and opened a page. Beneath the laminate, jagged black and white shapes showed Lottie's body from different angles. She flicked through them, one at a time. Her eyes lifted in shock. She stared at Jeff and touched her neck again.

"I can fix this. I can, I can fix it," he said. "Your purse. Gabrielle. Give it to me. *Now!*"

She threw it at his feet.

He emptied it and snatched her phone, hammering the screen. "There. Our carriage awaits us, darling."

At the end of the alley, a limo pulled up.

"I'm not going anywhere with you," she said.

"I'm afraid you don't have a choice, my dear." He turned the gun from my chest to hers.

I leapt between them, but he shoved me back.

"Move, and she dies," he said. "Understand?"

"I can't let you do this, Jeff."

He wrenched the files from her and tucked them in his belt. "I'm not messing around. Unlike you, I can actually pull the trigger." He tugged her wrist and dragged her down the alley towards the limo. "The police will be fascinated to know where they can find the man they've been chasing all this time."

He whispered to her and she tensed, but followed him to the open door of the black limousine. She climbed in, as did he, and he lifted the phone to his ear, smiling at me. The door closed and the car pulled away.

I turned and sprinted deeper into the alley.

Sirens bounced off the walls behind me. Gaining on me.

Around the corner, a metal wire fence barred the way.

I scaled it, knees thudded on the other side. The impact jarred at my ribs. The bandage ripped away.

Feet pounded.

An exit brought me onto the street. One block from Celia's car.

I climbed in.

Tires screeched as I plunged through the gears. Streets rushed past me in silver blurs.

*Where will he be going?* Somewhere he can retrograde things. *Anderson Whitman?* No, too many witnesses.

My eyes scoured the traffic that chugged through the city.

*Sinclair's.* It's halfway across town, but it's quiet. He'd have everything he needed.

*It has to be Sinclair's.*

There.

A black limousine dawdled below the streetlamps.

My foot stamped the pedal, and the engine screamed.

I cut in behind the limo and gripped the wheel tight.

*Can't let him reach the office.*

Revving forwards, the car surged. Headlights smashed into the bumper. A clap of lightning above the engine's thunder.

The seat jarred into my back, pushing on my side where the bandage had torn. Heat rushed from the wound as the balm rubbed away.

The limo swerved, shunted out of control before the brakes straightened it, and I smashed into it again.

In the rear window, Jeff's face appeared. Wild.

His silhouette clambered through the limo towards the driver. Gabrielle's blonde hair flashed across the glass as the vehicle careened from one side to another.

I shunted it a third time. The driver's door opened and a body tumbled, rolling down the highway. A man wearing driver's gloves.

The limo pulled away, gaining speed.

Behind us, auburn streetlamps melded with the flashes of police lights.

With Jeff at the wheel, the limo blitzed through traffic. A battering ram, breaking through everything in its path. Metal scraped as he plowed the gap between rows of cars queued at traffic lights, knocking them out of his way, dominoes falling.

Debris littered the tarmac as I followed in the wake of his destruction. Lights turned red ahead and everything slowed. He swept an arc off the road and mounted the curb.

Pedestrians hurled themselves into the road as he roared onward.

My seat lurched over the concrete curbstones, horn blaring.

Lines of traffic streamed from left to right across the intersection. He sped towards the oncoming cars.

Brakes squealed. Steam scorched off tires as the line of cars buckled. A truck skidded, but too late. It hurtled at the limo, collision inevitable.

The fury of burnt rubber stung the back of my throat.

The truck's titanic chassis streaked ahead.

Jeff plowed on.

Their course was set.

Inches apart.

Barrelling towards each other.

And then the line of traffic vanished.

Streaks of burnt rubber disappeared. The char of its smell dissipated. Across the intersection, police had set up a cordon, blocking the traffic from ever crossing. Retrograded to safety.

Ahead, a stack of cars which queued at traffic lights dissolved, like they'd never been there.

The road emptied.

All exits blocked.

Sirens blasted from behind.

In front, a squad of police cars barricaded the street. Officers aimed their guns at us. No way through.

Jeff motored on, gaining speed, unswerving.

The cops stood fast as the limo sped faster.

Faster.

And then the limo vanished too.

I grabbed the phone but there'd be no time to retrograde a different route before I collided with them.

One crossroad between me and the blockade.

Tailed by cops, I charged at the barrier. My foot slammed the brake, turning the wrong way down the crossroad.

Headlights stared me down as I raced towards cars head-on.

They disappeared, one by one. A constantly changing tapestry that I tore through.

Shadows of police cars replaced ordinary vehicles, crowding me in.

I connected the phone to the car's SatNav.

The net of cops tightened around me.

Retro-Routes app loaded.

Sirens everywhere.

Three routes available.

Surrounded.

I selected one and hit the brakes.

In an instant, the street changed. Traffic bumbled along. Serene. Safe. I'd been nowhere near the mayhem downtown.

I turned off the main road and skirted around the Sinclair's building. No sign of a limo.

*What if I'd been wrong? What if this wasn't where he was taking her?*

And then a long black shadow pulled around the corner towards the off-ramp to the parking garage.

I charged ahead. Rage rammed my foot to the floor. Jeff's face filled the window as I steamrolled into the side of the limo and sent us spinning into oblivion.

## TWENTY-SIX

WARM LIQUID DRIPPED into my eye. Thick. Gloopy.

*Where else am I bleeding?*

My lungs pleaded for air. It stabbed my chest as oxygen flooded in.

I lifted my head from the airbag and collapsed onto the tarmac.

A trail of shattered glass and twisted metal led to a mangled mess of cars. The front end of the limo crumpled to nothing.

I forced myself to stand, staggered towards it, flung the rear door open. Gabrielle stretched out dazed. Eyes closed.

"Talk to me, Gabrielle." I reached in and checked her pulse. Still breathing. She bled from a gash across her waist. "Can you hear me?"

Nothing.

I grabbed the cream from my pocket and smothered it over the tear. The touch of her skin was so familiar.

She stirred. "Who? Where am I?"

"You're alright. It'll be alright. Wait here, okay?"

She nodded.

"You'd best keep this." I pressed the antiseptic tube into her hand. "It'll help with your injuries."

"Merci."

"And here." I left my phone with her and scoured the aftermath of the crash. "Call the police."

No sign of Jeff. A familiar ping drifted from the garage below. The elevator.

My feet dragged to the parking lot as though concrete filled my shoes. Drops of Jeff's blood spattered towards the lift, and I stumbled after them. Above the doors, a plaque showed numbers counting up. They stopped on 27.

A few moments later, I ascended inside the metal cage.

My body was a volcano, every muscle hot as lava, the pressure building on my head, ready to erupt and overwhelm me. Steel shone blue in the lift, dulling as my vision faded, black invading my surroundings, pushing in on me.

*Keep it together, Adam.*

The doors opened. Letters blurred above the reception desk. *NC . . . I . . .*

I squinted.

*SINCLAIR'S.*

I stalked the droplets of blood across the carpet to the boardroom.

Every step stoked the fire of my molten bones.

The wall steadied me as I fought my way through the open door.

On the oval table, papers from Lottie's file sprawled out. Blood soaked the pages as Jeff spread his hands across the desk. His silhouette looked broken against the glimmering lights of the city through the windows at his back.

His eyes flashed at me.

"Hold it!" The gun rose, his hand shivering as he held it in my direction. He gripped his stomach.

"It's over, Jeff. There's no way out of this."

A sadistic smile slithered across his face. "You think you've got me trapped, don't you? But there's always a way out. Didn't I teach you that when we were partners?"

"Appearances. That's what you taught me. The mark of success. You're bluffing. You're scared."

"Scared of what?"

"Of losing. Scared of what's in that file."

His head dropped to the police report. "What you've got here, it's useless. Look at this. Look at the date." He grabbed the black-and-white of Lottie's body, the pool of blood beneath her corpse relegated to an inky splodge on our apartment floor. "You see the date? That was the week I proposed to Gabrielle. How do you explain that?"

"Until a few days ago, Gabrielle was with me."

"Do you really think anyone will believe that?"

"You stole my life, Jeff. Twice over. And there's nothing you can do about it, is there? Face it. If there was a way of retrograding all this, you'd have done it already. No matter how many times you've changed things, you've always been a thief. And you'll always be a thief. Some scars are so deep, they never fade. It's no wonder you're afraid."

He snarled at me. His hands thrust across the table, sweeping the pages away. He stared at the blank top, his chest heaving.

I staggered forward. "That's what you do to the past, Jeff. You wipe it away and what are you left with?" I nodded at the empty table. "Nothing."

"What would you have me do? You want me to live with my mistakes?"

"You've never faced the past. Never."

"Why should I? In New Yesterday, of all places, you have the audacity to lecture me on the past? Who do you think you are? Huh? You think you've got everything all wrapped up, but you don't know the half."

"I know enough."

"Rubbish. There's nothing in that file about what's really going on. About the expansion on the promenade. All those deals, and for Anderson Whitman too. You think it's my fault, but all I do is shake hands and sign. I'm in the clear. As far as the police are concerned, there's only one of us in the wrong, and it isn't me."

My legs tottered. I gripped hold of the table's rim. *Focus.* "The promenade? You've been at it again, haven't you? You're a fool, Jeff."

"That's rich, coming from you."

"Two days you've been without me, and already you've slipped back into your old ways. You've learned nothing. But how could you have learned anything? You didn't remember any of it, did you? You've got no regret. No remorse. So how can you learn?"

"Right now, my only regret is letting you live." He stepped towards me, the gun fixed between my eyes.

"You just keep on making the same mistakes again and again. You're stuck on a loop, Jeff. Can't you hear yourself?"

"I can hear myself just fine. The question is, can you? You're right. I can't undo this. Not by myself. We need each other, you and I." He stopped, shuffled to his drink cabinet and winced as he poured two glasses of port. "Do you understand what it is I can give you? Do you know what you're missing, Adam?" He downed one glass and limped towards me with the other, resting it on the oval

337

top. "My offer's still on the table. Partners. What do you say?"

"You made me that same offer a long time ago, and I tried to walk away. I'm not walking away now. But neither are you. You'll have to live with what you've done. It's the only way you'll learn."

"You think I need a long list of regrets? Is that what you want?"

"We all do. You need the past. How else do you expect to have a future? You keep spinning around and around. Living the present like it's your only tomorrow. Going nowhere. You want to live on a carousel? Lottie deserves justice, whether you remember it or not. You can't outrun the past, Jeff. Not anymore."

"What is it you *want?*" he yelled. "You want Gabrielle? Then take her. You want your old life? It's yours. You can still walk out of this on top. Think about it. If you refuse to give me what I need, where can you go? Forget the past. Think about your future."

"You put a bullet through my future when you shot my wife. If you're going to pull that trigger, get it over with."

His eyes flashed alert and wild. But there was no way out. For either of us.

My hand shook. Darkness clouded the boardroom.

He cocked the pistol.

*What are you waiting for?*

Shapes emerged in the black void. They crept over me. *I saw Lottie. Her smile. Her jade green blouse. The decanter smashing over me. A lighthouse by the sea.*

Blood spewed out of my mouth, drowning the vision. The impact of the crash had caught me at last, and I gripped my stomach. I collapsed onto the table, my hands knocking the port to meld with the pool of blood.

Jeff's finger wrapped around the trigger.

*Just one squeeze.*

He shuddered beneath the barrel.

Helpless.

"I can fix this!" he yelled.

"No. You can't."

"You can have a new life, Adam. Just say the word."

"This . . ." I pointed at the papers strewn across the floor, ". . . this is your life, Jeff."

"It doesn't have to be. There's always a way out."

"Not from this. How does it feel? To remember what you did?"

He cradled his head. "Get it out! I want it out of my head!" He stumbled back, turned and faced the window. His hand reached for the glass pane, propping himself upright as he clutched his stomach and surveyed the city. "Look at it, Adam. Just look at it! Don't you see? Look how beautiful it is! *I* did that. I *built* this city. Made it what it is. Without me, it's nothing. You sure you want that on your conscience?"

Blood choked me as I gasped for air. "You. Someone else. What difference does it make, Jeff? We live in a city of constant change, and yet, it never changes. It just keeps going round and round. You can't escape."

He looked down to the street. "How did they . . .? What did you do?"

My legs gave out. I fell from the table and dropped to the floor.

"The police have surrounded the building," Jeff said, his voice manic.

*Gabby.* Any minute now, they'd batter down those doors.

I prayed for the darkness to envelop me again.

*Show me Lottie one more time.*

"There's always a way out," Jeff said. "There's always a way out."

Black shapes crowded out the boardroom. Blotches swam from the darkness, replacing the speckled glow of bulbs overhead with empty talons of ink.

From behind me, footsteps ruffled, beating on the carpet like a drum.

A gunshot tore through the air, followed by a downpour of shattering glass.

Gabrielle's perfume washed over me. A gentle hand pressed against my forehead. The faint echo of voices drifted. So many voices I didn't recognize.

"Step away from the ledge. Sir, you don't want to do this."

Then the darkness swallowed me, and I was gone.

## TWENTY-SEVEN

STROBES OF COLOR FUSED into shapes.

*Where am I?*

Air billowed over my face. A tick, tick, tick sharpened as shadows passed across my vision.

*The boardroom? No.*

Details broke through the haze. A cord. A tile. An ivory ceiling fan whirled overhead, blowing crisp air towards me. Soft blankets tucked around my torso.

"Can you hear me, Mr. Swann?" A girlish frame in a pale blue gown hovered beside me. Her hand squeezed mine. The warmth of her skin thawed the chill of my arm where the fan had been blowing.

"Where?" My voice crackled like a busted speaker.

"It's alright. Take your time. You're safe now."

"Where am I?"

"The doctors patched you up real good. Shouldn't be long before you can go home."

"Wait. What did you call me?" My numb tongue slid around as if it was skating on ice, slurring the words.

"Say that one more time for me, Mr. Swann."

"You know my name?"

"It'll take a while for the anesthetic to wear off. But after that, you'll be good as new."

A jab twitched my skin. My eyes rolled to the IV. A thin tube meandered to the bag suspended above my head, dispensing fluid in slow drips. The gown itched at my chest and I pushed myself upright.

"Woah, Mr. Swann. Take it steady." The nurse gripped my forearms and pressed me back into the cushions. "You've got to rest. The doctor was very insistent when he prescribed you this. Your injuries will be gone by lunch, but only if you lie still. Okay?"

"What happened?"

"You were in an accident. Nasty collision, you're lucky to be alive."

"I know that. But what happened?"

"You just lie still, alright? Nice deep breaths."

On the side-table, a buzz rattled the screen of a phone. I lifted my arm to reach across for it.

"What did I just say about staying still?" she said.

"Alright. Will you answer it for me?"

She nodded. "Hello? . . . Yes, he's just coming round now . . . Just a minute." She dropped the screen to her chest and looked at me. "It's someone from your office. They want to know whether they should send a driver for you later?"

"Pass me the phone."

"He wants to talk to you. He's still coming round, so be gentle, okay?" She held it in front of me and put it on speaker.

"Who is this?"

"It's good to hear your voice, sir. How are you feeling?" a man said in an unfamiliar, whiny tone.

"I'm fine. I think. Where are you calling from?"

"The nurse said you were just coming round."

"Who are you?"

"It's me, sir. Dan."

"Dan?"

"Your assistant. At Swann's Accounts."

"Swann's?"

"Wow, that guy really did a number on you, didn't he?"

"Dan. What's going on? The nurse won't tell me anything."

"As far as I know, you were in a car crash on your way to the office, and then some nut-job tried to mug you and took a walk off the building. Went linear, so the cops say. You were just in the wrong place, wrong time, I guess. But I can schedule an appointment with Anderson Whitman and we can fix that later, can't we? The important thing is getting you back."

"He's dead?"

"Who?"

"The man who tried to mug me."

"As a dodo. I just got off the phone with the detective. They're burying him later."

"Where?"

"I'm not sure. Didn't think to ask."

"Can you find out for me?"

"No problem. You want me to send a driver?"

"And a suit."

"Is there anything else you need?"

"No. No, I don't think so. Thanks." I nodded at the nurse and she replaced the phone on the table. My fingers traced the wound on my side, but the skin was smooth and unbroken. If they could fix me up by lunch, how much of a problem was a cut?

She smiled. "All sorted?"

"What time did you say I could get out of here?"

\*\*\*

Gray light tinted the air. Bunched in tight bouquets, flowers doused the open casket's top in tangy perfume.

Mauve curtains surrounded the walnut coffin on three sides, hiding the furnace beyond. Draped with dust, the fabric faded with flecks of silver ash.

Behind the pulpit, a white collared priest conveyed the service like a surgeon. Clinical and sterile. Cold as the crematorium. Empty as the surrounding pews. He trailed off more than once, groping for words to fill the gaps. A dot-to-dot sermon he'd lost the thread of.

"Feel free to take a moment to pay your last respects," he said, stepping from his perch.

I pulled myself up, collecting papers bound in twine from the cardboard box at my shoes.

A woman's footsteps clacked ahead of me, trickling like rain in the somber quiet. Her steep heels lifted her above the casket. Her black dress stopped just above the knee, and her hair fell around bare shoulders. "I guess we'll never get to finish that interview," she said in a French lilt. Lace gloves clasped around a notepad as her pen scurried across it. The brush of her pen-strokes whispered as she glanced between body and page.

I waited behind her.

At her side, a bald man stood massaging his pink scalp. If he'd had hair, his chubby fingers would've cloyed it out. It wasn't grief that kept him fidgety, just impatience.

Across the aisle, one other man made up the entire audience. He sat motionless, overlooking proceedings. His Armani pinstripes creased as he reclined. *The salesman from Anderson Whitman.* His hawk eyes scanned the cavernous room, and he nodded at me with a sickly smile.

The bald man tapped Gabrielle on the shoulder.

"Come on, Gabby. That's plenty for the article." I knew that voice. The editor.

She stepped away from the casket, slipping back to her seat in front of the pulpit.

I shuffled forward. The coffin's lip grazed my knuckles as I leaned in and stared at the body. His eyes were closed. His face serene. Silver strands reflected the light across his scalp. Without his youthful smile, wrinkles pinched at his eyes and lips to make him old. He looked the same way he did after he'd sipped one too many ports and dozed off in the boardroom. The suit clung to him, puffing out his arms folded across his chest.

Above his head, a golden plaque shimmered with his name etched in gilt letters. Laid to rest in the city's biggest crematorium with his name in gold. What did he used to say about ostentation? The mark of success? Too bad nobody was around to see it. The only thing his success had led him to was three hundred empty seats.

I cradled the police report. Papers stuffed the folder, riddled with notes. It bulged with every shred of evidence that had brought me here. Brought him here. A better testament to the man than the priest could ever give. I lifted the file into the casket and nestled it under his heavy arm.

"This belongs to you," I whispered. Then I turned and walked back to my seat.

*It's over.*

*It's finally over.*

The salesman didn't even bother standing.

The priest took to the podium once more. "We bid farewell to Jeff Sinclair. May God have mercy on his soul."

The vicar's fingers grasped for a switch on his pedestal and the curtains closed, blocking the coffin from view. Its lid thudded. Gears clunked, dragging it back automatically to the incinerator.

I picked up the cardboard box and followed Gabrielle and the man who babysat her. The salesman led us out of the room. The priest hovered at my back.

Through double doors, we emerged into a picturesque garden. Trimmed hedges lined a maze of blooming flowers. Our feet crunched over gravel to a gazebo where a buffet of hot drinks awaited us. We took turns pouring coffee into styrofoam cups, admiring the rockeries. The char of smoke drifted across the air.

"Thank you for the service," the salesman said to the priest. "It went very smoothly."

"How did you know him?" the priest asked.

"Client of ours." The salesman looked at Gabrielle, the bald man, and me, as if the priest had asked his question to each of us, and now it was our turn.

"He was the subject of a story for my paper. My editor wanted me to cover the funeral," Gabrielle said.

"Guilty as charged," the bald man barked in his irate blustering manner.

"What paper do you work for?" the salesman asked Gabrielle.

"Daily Post."

The editor cut in. "Best journalist I've ever had."

"Interesting." The salesman sipped his coffee. "Does she always need supervising?"

"Jealous?"

The salesman flashed a grin.

"And what about you?" The vicar interrupted, turning all eyes towards me. "How did you know the deceased?" The deceased? Less than five minutes and his name was already forgotten. By now, his gold plaque had melted, licked by flame to erase all trace of its engraving, as if no marks had ever tarnished the lump of precious metal. *Come to think of it, what was the man's name?*

"Old colleague of mine," I said.

A pause fell between us and we nodded together.

The editor broke the awkwardness. "Thanks for the drink. Time for us to go. I'll fetch the car, Gabby. Besides, I could do with a smoke."

"Smoking at a cremation?" The salesman winked. "That's a bit in poor taste, don't you think? What do you say, vicar?"

The editor's head flared a deep maroon as he muttered below his breath and stomped off, sending shards of gravel flying beneath his clumsy waddle.

The salesman turned back to Gabrielle, his teeth flashed in a crescent, white as the moon. "Daily Post? It's a good paper. You happy there?"

"Why do you ask?"

"I hope I'm not speaking out of turn, but before you leave the city, it'd be worth you popping to an Anderson

Whitman. A writer like you could have quite a life in a place like this, without that oaf looking over your shoulder."

"In New Yesterday?"

"Think about it."

A car pulled up across the other side of the garden, beeping its horn. She finished her coffee and handed the empty cup to the priest, glancing at each of us.

"Au revoir." She glided across the gardens and climbed into the passenger door. In a trail of exhaust fumes, she was gone.

"Well, if you'll excuse me, gentlemen, I must get back. The next funeral is due to start any minute now."

"Thanks again, vicar."

The priest disappeared through the double doors.

"Another coffee?" The salesman stole a second cup for himself and offered me the same. The bitter stench of black liquid mingled with the scent of smoke, masking death with caffeine.

"Better not," I said.

"Suit yourself. You know, I really didn't expect to see you here."

"You know who I am?"

"Of course, Mr. Swann. Who do you think the police called to clear up all this mess? Who do you suppose arranged your hospital treatment?"

"That was you?"

"On behalf of the company, can I just say how sorry we are about what happened?"

"Sorry? You've got some nerve."

"We've restored your lifestyle package. No charge to your account. Had to retrograde your journalist friend though. Shame, really. Her books were rather good. How are you doing after what's happened?"

"My injuries feel fine, if that's what you mean."

"Glad to hear it. Everything at Swann's Accounts working out for you?"

"Are you expecting me to thank you, or something?"

"It was the least we could do after the mixup. But nothing's set in stone. We've got an appointment booked with you some time next week, I think. If there's something else you'd rather be doing, now that a certain somebody is out of the picture, you only have to ask." *A certain someone. Is he talking about the dead man?*

"That's very charitable of you."

He slurped the last of his coffee and wiped his lips. "What's in the box?"

I shrugged. "Oh, it's nothing."

"Nothing? It doesn't seem like nothing, especially if it's brought you here. What you really mean is that it's none of my business. Am I right?"

"If you say so."

"We were very careful to arrange the retrograde so you got everything back. Police report, gun and bullets included. Pulled some strings with the detectives to make sure of it."

"Why are you telling me this?"

He smiled. "Bit of advice. Whatever it is you're carrying round in there, I'd get rid of it. Wouldn't want anything holding you back from what's yours."

"Holding me back? Is that supposed to be a threat?"

He straightened his tie and checked his watch. "You still don't get it, do you?"

I stared slack-jawed at him, and he rubbed his forehead.

"Alright," he said. "Let me give you an example. Let's say I put a million dollars in your bank account. How did you get it?"

"You put it there."

"In this timeline. Sure. But somewhere else, in a different timeline, in some parallel dimension or whatever you want to call it, you could've robbed a bank. You could've won the lottery. Maybe you sold a hit record, or you're a movie star, or you inherited it from a rich uncle. All those scenarios are playing out somewhere. What we do is grab hold of the one you want and bring it here. Bring it to the city, thanks to Dr. Weiss and his formulas. But take that million dollars away and none of it exists. Remove the effect, and you get rid of the cause."

"What's that got to do with me?"

"Don't you get it, Mr. Swann? The only limits are the ones you set for yourself. All that matters is what you keep in the palm of your hand right here, right now. The sole thing that's holding you back are those same things you refuse to drop."

"Are you saying I should forget about all this?"

"I'm saying that the possibilities are endless. But only if you allow them to be. Life is built by what a person let's go of as much as by what they hold on to. What you choose to forget is just as important as what you carry with you. In little cardboard boxes."

My eyes fixed on the box.

"Take my advice," he said. "Let it go. You'll find things could be quite different."

"Thanks for the advice."

"Anytime." He spun on his heels and paced forwards before he stopped himself and turned back. "And I really do mean what I said. All you have to do is ask and you could have anything you want. Do anything you want. Be anything you want. We're eager to put this episode behind us. But isn't that what this place is all about? Just think about it and let me know."

He passed me a business card from his jacket pocket, its laminate surface glaring in the pale light.

I pocketed the card. "No limits?"

"No limits."

"I can escape all this, if I want to?"

He shrugged. "So many people come here with the notion they can escape their past. But there's no escaping it. Not really. Not even here. Moving on from it — that's how you reconcile things. That's how you make peace with the past. If you can find a way to move on, all of those limits just fade away. And then, who knows what life you could find for yourself?"

"I'll think about it."

"I hope you do. See you around, Mr. Swann." He strutted off in the opposite direction to where my driver parked.

I shook my head, picked up my box, and walked over to the waiting Cadillac.

"Home, sir?"

"Home?"

"Or is there somewhere else you'd like to go?" The chauffeur's eyes bounced from the rearview mirror at me.

I fumbled at the wedding ring as I peered into the box cradled in my lap. Inside, the shadow of a handgun and the bullet that killed Lottie stared back at me.

"Do you know the lighthouse outside of town?" I asked.

"Yes, sir."

"You can drop me near there."

"Right away, sir."

Tires thrummed across the concrete, swaying the car over lulls and bumps as the city streaked past the windows. The drum pounded its familiar rhythm, muffled through the glass. That hiss of life, beep of horns, stamping feet, the cries and shouts of a thousand voices all mingled like music, a cadence repeated in a ceaseless loop without beginning or end. I cracked the window and the beat intensified, clearer in the air, sharp beneath the wind which shushed the music like the static of a car radio.

Above the streets, towers of steel looked down on everything, spectators to the race that carried on below. Gamblers, all of them, betting on the slightest alteration, growing taller in their winnings and just as likely in the next moment to fall.

The casino of the city sped by in a silver daze, but all its strands seeped into a single shape, the silhouette of change. A roulette wheel that never stopped. Forever spinning.

The engine revved away from the bypass down a slope to the coast. Amusement arcades lined the seafront. The penny slots swept back and forth. Mechanical arms pushed bronze coins to teeter on the brink, before the pennies disappeared, falling over the edge and into young hands, only to be fed in through the slot once again. A cycle as certain as the waves. *How many times did those same pennies cascade through the machine, over and over?*

The chauffeur steered us from the cobbles of the promenade where notices were posted of a brand new marina, coming soon. A complete redevelopment, due to have been finished twelve years ago. The Anderson Whitman logo plastered the billboards. As a footnote, the Swann's Accounts symbol was printed with the assurance that all existing independent stores were guaranteed a space in the marina complex. Every single one. *I'd gotten Bulldog to check it twice. Tammy would have a prime spot. They all would, so long as I was in charge.*

A narrow track stretched in straight lines to the white spire of the lighthouse.

From the box, I removed the gun and bullet. The cold metal scraped frigid on my skin. The barrel's sharp edge clawed at my fingers. Black as storm-clouds, it darkened the cabin. The bullet rolled around my palm.

"Here's fine," I said. The car slowed to a stop. I unclipped the buckle and opened the door. "Thanks."

"Good day, sir."

The door swooped shut. Discarded behind the passenger seat, the empty box was now just a box. The laminate Gilligan Kennedy had wrapped it in was ripped away. I peered through the glass and watched 'Lottie' dissolve from across its side, and in its place, 'Attic' was scrolled in red sharpie.

The car reversed down the track, fading into the distance as I rounded the far side of the lighthouse. Steps carved into the rock-face led to a sandy cove. Ocean spray puddled in the delves of charcoal rocks. Thick sludges of moss carpeted clumps of stony outcrops. The constant whisper of waves deadened the wind's howl. It blew in spurts and stung my cheeks red.

Wet sand rippled in curving lines, mimicking the ocean. My feet sank as I waded into the sea. White foam rinsed the gun in fine droplets, beads of salt to cleanse the stains of its past.

My eyes scoured the bridge where sea met sky, where cloud merged with the gray surface of an endless deep, the curtains pulled shut to hide unfathomable reaches.

I held all that was left of Lottie. All that remained. The shooter was gone. The evidence taken with him, whoever he was. Gone from the city, he may as well never have been here at all. In my hand was the weapon which tied her to the present.

I twisted my neck and gazed to the glass perch at the lighthouse's tip. Her scent filled my nose as I remembered proposing to her. My ears hummed with the sound of her voice. She was gone, but still with me, so long as I held that gun.

I squeezed it to my chest.

"Lottie," I cried into the wind. "Lottie, I'm sorry. I'm so sorry." From my jacket pocket, I drew the card the salesman had given me, and pressed it into my left palm. The gun and bullet filled my right. I stared at them.

In my left, I held the future. Change, whatever change might be. Whatever hope belonged to change. And in my right, I held the past. My Lottie. My whole world torn away from me, and the wound left open in my heart. My stomach tightened as my eyes passed from left to right.

The longer I nursed the hurt of losing her, the harder it would be to let go of the pain. I'd trap myself in her memory. And the last thing she'd have wanted was to make me a prisoner. She was gone. There'd be no changing that, not while I was trying to keep her with me.

*But how can I move on? How can I allow myself to risk forgetting all that she was, all over again?*

Guilt stabbed my stomach. "Lottie, can you ever forgive me?" I whispered. But no one was listening.

*You can't hear me, can you Lottie? The past is gone. It's vanished like steam on a window. What kind of future could I hope for by choosing to live in a dead past? To circle around like a vulture, picking at my own carcass? Better to move beyond the past than to have to face it over and over.*

"Forgive me, my love."

I braced my feet in the sand as waves sloshed against me. We'd caged each other. She was bound, jailed inside my memories of her, and those same half-remembered moments kept me chained to her. Those cherished recollections had buried us together. The only way to free her was to let her go. *What is the past for, except to put behind us?*

"I did everything I could to make it right. But I can't undo what happened."

I'd sewn the seeds of change so many times, but it had never borne fruit. Not while he'd been here. Not while I carried this pistol with me.

But now he was gone. And I had to let the past go with him.

*That's the only way to make peace.* It's what the salesman had said about moving on, and maybe he was right? Maybe the past only stops haunting a person when they let it. When they learn to grow beyond it.

Could it really be that simple? Could moving past my hurt be the missing piece, and restore what I once lost?

From deep inside, a silent voice screamed at me to stop. My hand tightened around the gun. 'Don't do it,' my nerves shouted. My stomach heaved. I glanced across the empty beach.

"I shouldn't have left you alone. I shouldn't have gone. I was wrong."

Regret pulled at me with strings as though I was a puppet, tugging me back, urging me not to.

I closed my eyes.

"Goodbye, Lottie." A tear fell from my cheeks.

"I love you."

I hurled my arm in one sweeping arc. My fingers loosed the gun and it pitched along with the bullet into the depths of the sea.

The last trace of Lottie's death devoured forever. Her murderer was gone. The police report, the weapon, everything connected to her death, destroyed, as if it had never happened. *I'd rolled the dice in the city of change. Spun the wheel on the future. Now to see where it lands.*

My vision faltered. A throb pulsed up my spine to split my head in two.

"Adam! What are you doing?"

*That voice. It couldn't be.*

"You'll ruin your suit. If you want to swim, at least take your jacket off!"

I turned.

My mind shook off the nightmare. *Her lifeless body. Our apartment teeming with cops. A handgun in an evidence pouch. Two glasses of port. Cars smashed together. The boardroom. A funeral parlor.* I raised my eyes as if I was waking from a dream.

Before me, she stood with her arms crossed, her hair blowing in the wind.

I dragged myself towards dry land, the waves breaking as years crashed over me and vanished.

"Lottie!" I cried, bounding to her.

My hands cupped her face and I stared into those perfect eyes. This was no apparition. The past was gone and she was here.

"You look like you've seen a ghost," she said.

My lips sought hers. Warmth flooded from her touch. Her taste had never been so sweet.

We stood for an age, our lips locked together.

*Never end. Never let this moment pass.*

She pushed me off, laughing. "What's got into you, Adam?"

The last ache pulsing around my temples faded. "I love you, my darling. I just . . . I can't believe you're here."

"Where else would I be?"

"I don't know. In the water, I caught a glimpse of what things might be without you. It was the strangest thing."

"What's this?" She picked up the business card from where I'd dropped it in the sand. "Anderson Whitman?"

"Just something for work. They owe me a favor, that's all."

"Are you going to call it in?"

"Later, honey."

"Do you know what you'll ask for?"

I ran my hand across her cheek as the wind glazed her eyes. "Yeah. Yeah, I think so."

She pulled me towards her and spun me so her slender arms wrapped around me, pressing her bump to my back. "Time to go," she whispered in my ear.

"Are you gonna tell him, or am I?"

"You tell him. It's your turn."

The gale tossed her hair around her face and I combed it back behind her ears, revealing her pleading smile. "It's always my turn, isn't it, darling?"

"That's why I married you."

"Harvey!" I called down the beach. "Harvey!"

He never tired of throwing rocks into the sea.

"Come on. It's time to go."

He stayed where he was, cemented to the spot.

"You'll have to go get him," she said.

"Yeah. Amazing how selective a five-year-old's hearing can be."

My legs carried me away from Lottie, towards our boy. He spotted me in the corner of his eye and turned in the opposite direction, squealing giggles, delighted by the chase. His trailing feet kicked sand over my suit, and I swept him into my arms.

"Gotcha!" I lifted him to my face and kissed his forehead.

"You silly, Dada." Harvey laughed, rubbing his nose on his sleeve.

I set him down and closed his tiny fingers in my fist, leading him in small steps back to where Lottie stood, her shawl blowing in the breeze. The silhouette of her bump swelled round and fat. *Is it really just two months until the baby comes? Where has that time gone?*

Lottie took Harvey's other hand and we swung him across the cove. Back up the steps to where we'd parked the car.

"You know," she waved the business card in front of me, "we could use this to get something for the baby?"

"I already know what I'm using it for. The appointment's not 'til next week. So you've got plenty of time to talk me out of it."

"But you could always call them. Push it forward. I'm sure they won't mind."

"We'll see."

Harvey shook himself free and rushed to the car. He clambered in, sprawled over the back with his legs stuck out of the door. She buckled him into his car-seat while I climbed behind the wheel.

She slid into the passenger seat, reached across and squeezed my hand, pressing the card into my palm.

"So are you going to leave me hanging or tell me what you've decided?"

"What's with all the questions?"

"It's not every day that Anderson Whitman owes you a favor. You could ask for anything. Literally, anything. So I'm intrigued to know what you want."

"This," I said.

"What does that mean?"

I took her hand in mine. "I'm going to ask them for this. You. Me. Harvey. The baby. I don't want it to change. Ever."

She leaned over and kissed me, the heat of her lips as constant as the waves. *Where would I be without her?*

My wrist flicked the car into gear, and I reversed away from the lighthouse, spun us round and set out for home.

Just like every day since we'd moved to New Yesterday, as far as I could recall.

## Acknowledgments

First up, I want to thank you. Yes, YOU! A lot of people say it's up to an author to breathe life into their words. But I don't think that's the whole truth. It's the reader who brings words to life in their willingness to imagine. So thank you for lending me your imagination for a little while, and for letting my story live. It's the greatest gift a writer could receive, and I'm truly grateful for your time. I hope you felt it was worth it!

Secondly, there are a number of people whose contribution and support to *New Yesterday* has been amazing, and this next part is for them. (Warning: it might get a bit waffly, but I've got a lot of people to be grateful for, so that's hardly my fault, is it?)

Almost everything enjoyable about *New Yesterday* is a direct consequence of the fact my CP critiques like a ninja. So, Elise, thank you for your sage counsel, and for your patience, care, and belief. You're so generous for granting me such liberal use of your brain. TCH4L.

My beta readers have been so kind. They saw the book in its infancy, and were instrumental in helping me shape it into what it is today. In the early days, I want to especially thank Lisa, Anthony, Matt Ward, and KD Karnik. You gave me feedback that hasn't just helped with *New Yesterday*, but will improve all the books I write.

Among my beta heroes is Dawn Ross, a fantastic author of the *Starfire Dragons* series. She's supported me so much, and she made me feel like a real writer long before I got into print.

Mark Everglade, cyberpunk author of *Hemispheres*, helped me to refine the details, and he pointed me in the right direction with how to get *New Yesterday* off the ground.

Davene Le Grange has always championed my stories, and her confidence in my writing is beyond amazing. The way she helped me clean up the later edits with such precision was more than I could ever have hoped for.

But most of all, EL Strife has been my anchor. I can't thank her enough. She's written so many amazing books that blend sci-fi action with heart-stirring feels. Her skill to create a story that's both contemplative and thrilling is awesome, and she's been so accommodating in the way she's lent me those skills. She's my Master Yoda. Thank you, Elysia. (Check out her website for loads of great sci-fi, by the way.)

Thanks go to Erika for editing a portion of the story, and to Nadine for her eagle-eyed proof reading skills.

To my Twitter family, particularly the people who've shown an interest in the book, thank you. You don't know how much it means to me that there's a community of authors looking out for one another which I get to be a part of, and I'm so glad to have found such wonderful people to bounce ideas around with. You invigorate my confidence, and you're all awesome. And there are some of you (you know who you are) who have made this journey an absolute blast.

To all the literary agents who rejected my queries, thank you. You were never too busy to consider my work. Your personal feedback along with the abundance of kind comments in your rejection emails encouraged me no end. I know it seems a bit daft to be thanking you for not taking me on as a client, but you're part of this book's history, and I'm glad you got to consider it, so thanks.

I couldn't have asked for finer friends who volunteered to read *New Yesterday*, and who gave me the boost I needed. Maredudd, Rochelle, Jess, Jamie — thank you. A special thanks goes to Richard. His clarity and vision are immense, and he's always had my back from day one. Without him, I don't think this would've happened.

My wife has been so patient and understanding, always willing to listen to my tirade of nonsense as I figured this out. She's my muse, my inspiration, my heart, and my greatest adventure. I'll always be her number one fan. Also, if she wants to be the one who reads this little adventure to our son one day, I won't mind a bit.

And that's about it. I've probably missed people, and if I have, then I'm sorry. There'll be people who will help me in my future, and I'll wish I could've included them in these pages, so to all my future helpers, thank you in advance. If I could retrograde you into this list, I would.

Although my name is on the cover, this book is a city in itself, built from the input of those who passed through and left their mark, and it's all the better for it. When I think back on this novel's journey, from its concept to the finished page, I can honestly say that, if I were living in New Yesterday, I wouldn't change a thing.

To everyone who leaves a review of this book, whether good or bad, thank you. For indie authors, reviews are like oxygen. They keep us alive.

And lastly, if Keanu Reeves ever reads this, and decides he wants to make a movie out of it, then thank you Keanu, and I accept.

## TIME'S ELLIPSE

No solution saves everyone. Only one keeps us human.

The hope of a dying Earth rests on a crew of astronauts. Their mission: find a new home. But when they touch down on a distant planet, a time-bending anomaly traps them in a situation that no one could've predicted, causing them to question the nature of humanity, the snare of destiny, and the shape of time itself.

Time's Ellipse spans generations, orbiting the lives of the scientists and astronauts involved in this historic mission as they discover that escaping the planet is simpler than evading its legacy.

# TIME'S ELLIPSE

## DOCTOR ROLANDS

### I

April 2047

Time stopped in the bunker. Bodies crammed into the tight space, pressing against me, but not as much as the darkness which seeped into everything, stilling the seconds while the storm raged above.

Hurricanes unleashed a throaty growl, overwhelming the sound-proof shielding in the ceiling. Hail blasted the roof louder than machine gun fire. Or it could've been swarming sand clouds. Either way, maintenance would need to replace the panelling. Again. Too many dents. There were always too many dents.

I crossed my fingers that the antenna which connected us to Wifi didn't snap, if a lightning blast hadn't already melted it. Without Wifi, we were alone with our thoughts. Which is the last place I wanted to be.

"So here's a question that should help us pass the time," I said to no one in particular, raising my voice above the storm's shriek. "Are we moving through time, or is time moving through us?"

"Another conundrum, Doctor? Really?" The voice came from among the huddle. Hard to tell exactly which of the sharp-suited business execs had finally lost their patience. "Haven't we spent enough time playing games when we should be talking about the launch?"

"We spent two hours in that conference room before the storm hit," I continued, ignoring him. "And time felt like it zipped by. But down here, the past two hours have felt like a million eternities. Isn't that strange? It's like time is speeding up and slowing down just for us."

"I'm sure you've got a theory for it, Doctor. But I've got a theory of my own. I think the reason you insist on raising these hypotheticals has nothing to do with keeping us occupied, and everything to do with avoiding the real issue. It's time for you to make a decision."

Grumbles of agreement could roughly be translated as *we wouldn't even be in here if you hadn't already kept us waiting.* They were right. It was my fault we were down here. My fault we'd delayed. But it was also my fault we even had a decision to make in the first place. 'The Great Doctor Emily Rolands.' If I'd never opened my mouth, and had kept my theories to myself, I wouldn't be standing where I am today. And neither would the rest of them. Maybe some of them would have preferred that. But maybes weren't going to save us. They were no use to anyone.

"How can any of us sanction the launch?" I asked. "Knowing what we know — there has to be another way."

Another voice from the dark. "Speaking frankly, how can we *not* sanction it, Doctor? Would any of us be here if it wasn't necessary?"

I shook my head. "Those are six people you're asking me to condemn to an early grave. Do any of you want that on your conscience?"

"Emily. Just listen for a moment. Really listen." Everything stilled in the bunker as the thudding on the roof grew louder. Louder.

"I'm listening," I said.

"We're only hearing that storm now, but you heard it first, didn't you? You heard every storm before it arrived. Before any of us. You predicted all of this. The tornadoes, tsunamis, the sun boiling us in our filth. Isn't that why you started Orbicon in the first place? And it's exactly *because* you listened all those years ago that we even have a chance. Just listen one more time. Can't you hear it? The world is condemned already. What are six more lives?"

I could've corrected them — told them I founded Orbicon all those years ago because I was too young to know the difference between a good idea and a bad one. Too young to resist being carried away by the lure of hubris. But what good was nitpicking over details when these sharks were right anyway? The planet had died long before any of us figured it out. Even me.

"I know you want to make this into an equation," I said. "Normally, I would too. Math is simple. Beautiful. It's the foundation of logic and you can use that logic to make yourself feel like you've done the right thing. Or convince yourself that this is a binary choice. Wrong or right. Live or die. But we're not talking about pitting billions of lives against six. We're talking about asking six people to come forward on a hunch. To send them to their deaths for the hope of maybe saving what's left of the rest of us. Maybe. The only guarantee for you to rationalise with logic is that six people are going to die. And *that's* what you're asking me to sanction."

"We're all guaranteed to die, Doctor. But it would be nice to have a choice about the how and when, don't you think?"

Was that a real question or just a sales technique? I couldn't tell anymore. I used to be able to know the difference.

A panel rippled under the force of the tornado. Everyone held their breath. But after a few seconds, it settled. The panel didn't buckle. Not yet.

That was too close.

How did we get to here? I remembered the first time I'd sat in front of these same businessmen, each of them wearing inhumanly pristine smiles to match their neckties. I could always spot the difference between a SpaceGen money-man and a scientist by their smile alone.

Back then, the execs were excited about the fortune my theories could gain for the company. AKA, for them. Every conversation ended in how the 'orbital constant' would make us all rich. How 'gravitational wave propulsion' would revolutionise our industry. Now, the lights were off. The smiles gone. And they were the ones lecturing me on the ethics of survival.

I knew what Chrissie would say if she was still here. She'd say *look how far we've come. Look how far your theories have taken us.* Yeah. How far backwards.

Poor Chrissie. She was so bright-eyed. So hopeful. How many of these businessmen and women — so concerned about preserving life — even remembered her? Could they describe the colour of her curls? Her eyes? The way the tsunami took her? What did they know about life?

"There has to be another way," I said.

"How many times have we been over this, Emily? We can't send machines, can we?"

"No. Asking machines to do the job would be like trying to program an AI to interpret how to love, or how to be angry. To a robot, a second is a second, just like gravity is gravity. We need to send people who understand more than just the mechanics of the situation. We need to send people who can understand the implications. Machines aren't an option."

"So that means sending humans to Trappist-1E. You can't get around it, Doctor."

I shrugged. "Or we could focus on Mars."

"After what happened with the lander? You know the only way we're getting to Mars is by going through Trappist."

I hated admitting that he was right. It used to be that Mars was the obvious solution. If we made a refuge off-world, it didn't matter if the planet died. There'd be somewhere we could hide. Somewhere to hunker down, to colonise. But figuring out how to land a spacecraft in the paper-thin gravity of Mars was like trying to slow down a bullet before it killed you.

It was no wonder the lander failed. No wonder the public turned on SpaceGen and NASA — accused them of wasting too many resources when the problem was at home. No wonder 'space' became a dirty word. And it didn't help when temperatures started rising and people stopped going outside. A whole generation of insiders — to them, space wasn't just dirty, it was a monster. The outside was a killer. If Chrissie hadn't persuaded so many celebrities to take a trip to Orbicon's Space Collider back in the day, there wouldn't be a space program right now.

We wouldn't be here in this bunker with at least an option on the table. We'd all just be in here wondering how much longer the toilet would keep flushing.

Too many dents. It was the same with the planet. There was no fixing it. We needed a new one. And that meant leaving.

"Doctor Rolands." Another voice in the dark. "I was looking over your proposal from years ago, when you argued that the Trappist system is our best shot at testing OCT. Has anything changed?"

Yeah. I grew up. "Nothing has changed. It's still the best site to confirm Orbital Constant Theory."

"So what's the problem in sanctioning a flight there? There's a cost to every experiment — didn't you say that once?"

"Yes, but—"

"Well, then. If the cost of keeping humanity alive is six volunteers, isn't that a price that's worth paying?"

Trappist-1E — it sounded ridiculous that an exoplanet I'd learned about on a YouTube video thirty years ago could potentially save humanity. Landing there wouldn't be a problem. The atmosphere was Earth-like enough to support life. And if my Orbital Constant Theory was proved right, it would change everything. Give us another shot at Mars. Or somewhere else. Somewhere we hadn't found yet. The solution to every problem was already out there, just waiting to be discovered. This was no different.

I hated admitting all of this. I hated that to save the world, we had to change its mind. We had to make space palatable again. This wasn't what scientists were supposed to do with their lives. We weren't a clergy. We weren't meant to shepherd the masses. How did we ever stray so far?

"Alright," I huffed. "Trappist-1E is a potential stepping stone. I'll agree on that. But you all know what happens when they land there. You all know that Trappist isn't the solution."

"But it's a start."

"We can make a start from here. Why do we have to send anyone? Telescopes could still present us with the answer. We might be able to find somewhere eventually. Another planet. Just look at everything we've discovered in the skies over the last century, all while keeping our feet on the ground."

"We don't have another century, Emily. It's time. There aren't any other options. Now what's it going to be? You know we can't sustain the Space Collider forever with our budgets. Look. If you approve the launch date, there are still a few months until then. We'll still need to do the recruiting and the training of the six who'll actually fly there. What if you said yes today, and then kept searching in the meantime? We can abort if you find another habitable world. But this sets the ball in motion. It keeps us alive a little while longer. And isn't that the whole point of Orbicon?"

Nobody could have heard me sigh above the gail that threatened to rip the bunker apart, and us with it. Pressure pushed against my chest like a pneumatic drill, and yet, I barely felt it.

"What good is saving humanity," I said, "if it means sacrificing people to do it? We'd be giving up everything that makes us human. And you want me to say yes, like it's the obvious solution. But there's no solution which keeps us human. Only one that keeps us alive." I stifled a sob and rubbed my eyes, grateful that the lights were off.

"Mom." Henry's voice echoed beside me. "It's okay. It's going to be okay. You don't have to choose who lives and who dies. I can handle the recruitment. It's enough that *someone* lives, right?"

Henry was never meant to be a part of this. Never meant to be sweeping up my mess. He was supposed to be like Halley. She wanted nothing to do with Orbicon, and I was proud of her for that. But now, my little boy was telling me he'd handle it. That he'd take responsibility for the lives I would destroy.

Oh, Henry. Why couldn't you have wasted your life playing video games?

And in this bunker. Of all places. The same bunker where Halley had drawn the O on her dusty bunk which had become the Orbicon symbol ever since. The same bunker where Henry had begged me to allow him to enroll in the company. Where Chrissie and I would talk long into the nights about how we'd get our next funding from the bigwigs at SpaceGen who'd say yes to anything if she asked them in her little red dress. Where the designs for the space collider had been approved. Where the wind had ripped the outer door open and Chrissie had been the one to seal it. Where the tornado had taken the shielding, and then it took her too. And now it was taking my little boy. Making him an accomplice to my crime.

This same bunker. In the darkness of this tomb. The same darkness that still consumed us after all these years. Of course it was here where the fate of our species was being decided by a few business execs in stuffy shirts. And me. Where else would it be?

Henry. I wish I could've saved you from what we were all about to become. But what other choice did we have?

"Fine." I whimpered the word, hoping nobody would hear it above the storm. Hoping that I could still take it back.

"Is that a yes?" More voices from the dark. They didn't wait for an answer. They knew.

"You've made the right decision, Mom." Henry squeezed my arm. The same way he used to when he didn't want to go to bed, and he thought a cuddle would keep him up a few more minutes. Now, he was about to choose who Orbicon would launch thirty-nine-light-years into space using gravitational wave propulsion, to the most distant grave in the universe. I'd just killed six people. And worse, I'd given my boy the job of choosing the victims in this little quest to save the world.

And all I could hear was Chrissie's voice. *Look at how far we've come.*

## II

August 2047

Backstage at the auditorium, reinforced walls deadened the sound from beyond. I wished they'd do the same for my nerves.

I checked my phone for the thousandth time. Not looking at anything besides the wallpaper of my screen. But it was enough to remind me that I should've prepared more.

*'Just make sure you're offline by 11.'* My last message to Halley. She should have been here instead of gallivanting online. Why did I agree to do this?

My earpiece received an announcement from the auditorium's microphone. Henry's voice filtered through static.

"May I introduce the head and founder of Orbicon — Dr. Emily Rolands."

That was my cue.

A spattering of applause rippled through the conference hall as I entered and edged up to the podium. Empty seats jeered at me, broken up by fourteen young faces. There was Henry, his assistant — I forget her name — and the twelve astronauts that made up the primary crew and the backup team.

I locked eyes with the captain of the primaries. He was a strong, handsome man of about twenty five, with dark hair and brown eyes. A dead man who seemed invincible.

I smiled at him. I didn't know why. And then my eyes passed to the woman next to him. Deliberately. I'd already decided that I wasn't going to begin until I'd looked every single one of them in the eye. They deserved that much.

The woman had beautiful skin, a lovely figure and a broad smile. The pilot.

Beside her, a shy-looking pale girl shivered, probably the youngest of the bunch — blonde, pony-tailed, with blue eyes. Must be the Doctor.

A curvy redhead who reminded me of Chrissie sat forward intently, focused, intelligent and alert. The Biologist. I liked her. A pit gnawed at my stomach, groaning open as I began sinking into it. But I closed my eyes, exhaled and moved on to the row in front of them.

The other two men who made up the last of the primary crew sat side by side. One was similar to the captain — strong, muscular. He was from Asia, what little of it was left after the floods. The Astrophysicist.

Next to him was a thin, frail, bearded man of about thirty, sat with his arms folded, frowning. He stood out like a sore thumb — the only one who seemed disinterested in being here. He yawned. Of all the astronauts, he was the one who looked most like a scientist. His scruffy hair gave him away. The Mathematician.

I'd stopped thinking about them as people after Henry had brought them on board, and more as jobs. Pilot. Biologist. That sort of thing. But now I'd laid eyes on them, their faces were inescapable. This was the crew I'd be sentencing to death with a pat on the back.

The backup crew were a similar mix, but this speech wasn't for them. It was for the ones launching in less than three months.

"Good afternoon," I said. "I'd like to thank you for being here today. As you know, I'm Dr. Emily Rolands, Chief of Orbicon. It's been my mandate for the past thirty years to achieve interstellar travel, and after decades of hard work, because of the diligence of thousands, it's my pleasure to be addressing you, the first humans that will reap the fruits of all that we've achieved. Make no mistake that your mission is historic by its nature. Succeed or fail, in three months time you will make history. Millions will applaud your bravery and sacrifice in choosing this mission, but I would like to be the first."

I stopped talking and clapped. They all joined in. So far, so good.

"The sacrifice you make in this historic venture requires courage. It's your courage that will be remembered, along with your names, for all time. There are many hazards — many unknowns — but I'm not here to brief you on the 'what-ifs'. What I'm here to talk to you about are the risks we *know* this mission will hold. The purpose of your voyage is to prove *Rolands' theory of the orbital constant.* I'm sure you all know it very well, but let me remind you of what it means."

I paused, sipping the water left for me behind the podium, my hands shaking.

*Pull yourself together, Emily. It's just a speech.*

"As you know, time is linked to gravity. And gravity is linked to orbit. That means the way we interact with time is connected to our orbit of the sun. One orbit equals one year, whether you're on Earth, or Mars, or anywhere else orbiting a star. Simple, yes?"

I mean, it was a lot more complicated. There's a reason the equations had earned me enough to set up this company. But this was as simple as it needed to be for these astronauts.

One orbit equaled one year. I wondered if they believed it. If that factored into why they'd accepted the mission. Or whether they'd even made the link until they were sitting here listening to me dance around the one thing I knew I had to say, but didn't want to.

"Initially, when I first set up Orbicon, it was with the idea that we could prove 'orbital locking' was more than just a theory, but a fact. Our information could then aid the Mars Project, which SpaceGen has tirelessly

12

developed these past years. Each day, we hear they're getting closer to cracking the problem of landing a shuttle on Mars."

I coughed. How long had they been saying that?

"But if we could prove Orbital Constant Theory, then we'd know for sure that landing on Mars would extend the lifespan of the human race. It would give us much needed hope. If time is fixed to orbit, then a year on Mars would be almost twice as long as a year on Earth. Mars takes 687 days to orbit the sun. Humans would experience those 687 days as one year. Every year of your life would effectively double. Imagine experiencing all that extra time, and devoting it to research and study — the things we would learn. Imagine expanding our life expectancy overnight. Imagine the world's greatest minds having twice as long to invent and discover. Isn't that a reason for hope?"

If hope had any meaning anymore. I'd parroted these lines so many times over the years, they were just words now. Just sounds that came out of my mouth. But it was what had brought me to this podium — the promise of Orbicon. The promise of hope.

"The situation today is more bleak and urgent than we could have anticipated when we first set out on this grand scheme. If we can't land on Mars, then our only hope is interstellar travel. It's the key to our future. For that reason, Orbicon has become synonymous with hope. Which is why my lecture today is such unfamiliar territory to me. I've made so many speeches about building a better future, that it seems odd to brief you on what is the very opposite — the very sobering reality of your mission."

Faces in the audience twisted, contorting into grimaces as eyes searched for the meaning in my words — as any good explorer's would. All except for the thin, disgruntled man, who appeared unmoved and sat stiffly with his arms folded. I swallowed hard, trying to remember what I was here to say.

"We've been determined to reach Trappist-1 since Orbicon was founded. But since the space collider was completed last year, we've delayed the launch for as long as possible. We invested in telescopes to try and find some other, more promising destination to send you, rather than Trappist-1E, the fourth planet in the Trappist-1 system. But we've found nothing, and we can delay no longer. The future is at stake, and we must act now, or face the consequences of inaction."

Another gulp of water. I shook my head.

"The reason we've delayed in sending you to Trappist-1E until now, is because of the implications of what 'Rolands theory of the orbital constant' would mean for you when you arrive on the planet. You see, if time and orbit are linked in the way that I've predicted, you will age one year for every orbit that Trappist-1E makes of its sun. Could we put the projection up on the screen, please?"

Behind me, the wall lit up with the graphic showing the Trappist-1 system and the exoplanets' rate of orbit around their sun. Little circles dashed around the large red sphere in the centre.

"Here, you can see the rate at which the planets of the Trappist-1 system orbit their red sun. Trappist-1E is the planet with your best chance of survival. It's perfectly placed in the goldilocks zone, and by all known tests, will be habitable to sustain human life. But for how long? That is the question I am here to answer for you today. That is what this graphic shows, and what I must prepare you for."

Their eyes fixed on the image of the planets, widening as they intuited my meaning. They stared back at me in disbelief and horror, even disgust. I glanced down at the podium. There were no notes, but I couldn't meet their judgmental eyes.

"One orbit of Trappist-1E is the equivalent of six Earth days. Owing to the principle of orbital locking, even if you arrive safely on Trappist-1E with no complications, your life expectancy of thirty years translates on Trappist-1E into thirty orbits."

"What are you trying to say?" the sprightly redhead interrupted, shouting from her seat, aghast.

"I'm saying that your total life expectancy, according to our projections, is—"

"180 days. Call it six months", the unkempt man with folded arms called out. I was grateful for his interruption. I hadn't wanted to say it out loud.

"Are you asking us to sacrifice thirty years of life on Earth for six months of life on Trappist-1E?" the redhead continued, shocked at what the implication of their mission would mean.

I glanced back up and met her eyes. I was just a kid when I'd blurted out Trappist-1 as the future of Orbicon all those decades ago, more interested in proving myself right than I was in things like responsibility and consequences. Accountability is something learned with age. Had I known then that I'd wind up facing this group of twelve people, six of whom I'd be asking to give up their chance of growing old, I'd like to think I'd have at least hesitated a little.

"Yes, it would mean trading thirty years for six months," I said. "Thirty years on Earth, for six months on a new planet, untouched, unexplored, holding the answers to questions we don't even know to ask. You'd be the first people to travel to another part of the galaxy. You'd be the first people to land on another world. You'd be the first people to extend the reach of the human race. You'd be trading your own future here on Earth for the future of everyone else stuck here on Earth. It's a one way trip. You've known that from the start. But what a way to go."

Silence settled in the room. The prospect of everything this mission entailed settled with it. A hopeless glaze of acceptance washed over their eyes. As it did, part of me wanted them to fight it. I wanted them to resist. To make it harder than it was. It was my choice to send them away. It shouldn't have been this easy.

"How can we agree to such a thing?" the redhead said, the last of them to let go of the horror of what I'd asked them to do.

"How can we not?" the bearded man with folded arms replied.

"It's alright for you," she blurted out quickly, and instantly regretted her words. Her eyes filled with guilt, dousing her fire, before she too glassed over, just like the rest of them.

And then it was over. I didn't say anything more. I just left the podium, walking away, letting the graphic play out and the exoplanets of the Trappist-1 system spin and spin, as my own head spun.

I rushed through the offices as fast as I could, up to my room, and banged on Halley's door. She opened and let me in, annoyed that her connection online had been interrupted.

I didn't say anything, but held her in my arms, dowsing her top in my tears.

What had I done?

### III

November 2047

Was it really a week ago that the shuttle docked at the space collider? The night of the launch had come round so fast. What was I thinking — letting Henry talk me into appearing on all the late night shows, being interviewed over and over about the very thing I wanted to avoid. But at least I wasn't there — Mission Control — having to look at the faces of the crew on the Icarus 1.

That night, lounging on the family couch, I watched the show — the interview we'd recorded earlier in the afternoon. From the other side of his desk, some young, interesting comedian scrutinised my every move. Lights blared down on me and an audience applauded everything I said. Even watching it now made me uncomfortable. Henry had insisted on tagging along. He was a good kid, and I was grateful for having him with me. He sat next to me on the couch, both on the screen and in the living room as we watched it play out.

"So, Dr. Rolands, how does it feel to be the most famous scientific mind alive today?" the host asked.

"I didn't think I was that famous," Henry said. "Oh, you were talking to my Mom. Sorry, my mistake." He was always good at talking — just like his Dad.

"I don't feel famous," I said, "so I guess it's much the same as anyone in the audience feels."

"Brilliant, and modest. Will you marry me?" the comedian joked. The spectators laughed, and I smiled, trying to see the compliment in it.

"I think your wife might have something to say about that," Henry said quickly, protectively.

The host turned to the screen. "Honey, I love you." More applause. Then he swivelled his chair back to me. "But seriously, Dr. Rolands, you've pioneered this project from day one at Orbicon. The whole reason we're launching later this evening is because of you. It's your greatest achievement." More like my greatest folly. "Time magazine listed you in the top five most influential minds in the whole of scientific history. You've got to be feeling pretty smart, right?"

"Smarts have little to do with it. Physics isn't just about brains. It's about discovery. You think of names like Newton, Einstein, Hawking. They're only famous because of what they *found*. Scientists are just like archaeologists, only we don't dig up the past, we dig up the future. Every scientist has the potential to strike gold. I'm just one of the lucky ones."

"Yeah, but for years you were the only one digging. I mean, it's not like there are hundreds of companies like Orbicon out there. I mean, just look at the space collider. Who else besides you could've built a hadron collider in space?"

I shrugged. "In the past, landmarks in space travel involved competition. Landing on the moon, for example. When I started in this business, I was told it moved fast. That I was entering a space race. But if what we were doing was a race, then Orbicon was the only one running it. The advantage of not having to compete with anyone is that I've had the privilege of working with the finest minds this planet has to offer. All the talent came to us. They're the ones with the real smarts. The launch tonight is not my success, it's theirs. Or should I say, it's *ours*."

I'd rehearsed that line especially for the program. Henry sat back and nodded. The crowd applauded. But listening to my voice as I said the words onscreen made me wince.

"Okay, so let's talk about the launch," the host said. "What exactly is the mission for these astronauts?"

"The mission is to land on Trappist-1E, which is an exoplanet roughly 39.6 light years from Earth."

"Exoplanet?"

"That's a term which describes a planet outside our solar system."

"Gotcha. I almost forgot I was talking to a scientist. Sounds like a long way."

"They'll cross that distance in a matter of moments, propelled by the gravitational waves we'll generate with the space collider. Then the real work begins. The crew will land on the planet and set up their camp, arranging telescopes on the surface. They'll point them in every direction, and communicate the results back to us."

"Why's that important?"

"It sounds crazy, because a lot of people think of space as this big, vast, open expanse. But in reality, space is full of little corners and pockets we just can't see around. If we're going to find a future home, we need to see the whole picture. And that's what this mission will mean. We'll be able to effectively map out all those nooks and crannies, like casting a torch into the universe. Who knows what we'll find?"

"Probably a Starbucks," Henry answered, and everyone laughed again.

"There's one on every corner on this planet, so why would it be any different in space?" The host continued the joke. I didn't care much for coffee. "We all found out about this mission just recently, but you've been living with this for the past thirty years. How do you get your head around that? Around the *gravity* of it all?"

And there it was — the same joke about gravity everybody had made for the past three decades. "The answer is there's simply no other choice. It's why six brave men and women are sitting tonight in the cockpit of that shuttle, ready to sacrifice everything. If there was any other way, we'd have found it by now." I said the words, hoping they'd bring me some comfort, hoping I'd eventually believe them. 'No other choice' was a platitude of the guilt-ridden. Wasn't there always a choice? Mine had been to send six people in a shuttlecraft to an early grave. Why? Because I had 'no other choice.'

"I understand that you first got your idea from a late-night chat show. So, universe, on behalf of late night chat show hosts, can I just say, you're welcome. How did that come abo—"

I clicked the remote and switched the TV off. Both Henry and Halley blurted out protestations.

"Come on, Mom. I was just about to get the biggest laugh of the night," Henry said.

"Why are you turning it off?" Halley asked.

I couldn't watch any more. The longer it stayed on, the more I was reminded of the thing I was trying to forget. "Let's see what else is on."

"There's nothing else on. Only broadcasts of the launch. That late night show is the last thing which doesn't have anything to do with Icarus 1, and I didn't think you wanted to watch the launch?" Halley said.

"You're right. Let's not watch anything, eh? Let's talk for a bit."

"Talk about what?"

"Anything. Something. Nothing. Pick one." The phone rang. 'Hank Carter' flashed across the screen. "I've got to take this," I said, and left the room. The TV went straight back on behind me, and I closed the kitchen door to block out the noise. "Hello?"

"May I speak with Emily Rolands?"

"Quit playing around, Hank."

"Congratulations, my dear. You've done it. How do you feel?" His voice was as smooth as ever.

"Honestly? I can't stand it. I wish it was me in that shuttle, and not those poor kids."

"You don't mean that. Not really. Once it's over, you'll start feeling better. Our boy looks good on TV, doesn't he?"

"Yeah, he does."

"So do you."

"Don't start, Hank. Not tonight."

"As you wish. I just wanted to say congratulations. Feel happy, Em. You did it. I'll give you a ring tomorrow. Ciao."

He hung up, and I was left alone, the noise of the TV from the other room muffled as it drifted through the door. My phone buzzed on the table — alerts from HQ updating me on how the launch was going. It vibrated every few minutes, then every few seconds. I turned it off, poured a glass of wine and sat there in the dark, propped on the bar stool, sipping red, swallowing guilt.

Then, through the window, a flash of light scorched a path through the sky, and a fantastic shot of black ripped across the stars. Starlight faded for an instant before returning, the briefest interruption to its shimmering meadow.

So long, Icarus 1.

Down went another glass of red.

I always knew that discovery would take me somewhere, that I'd soar on the wings of the secrets I'd uncover. And it had. My discovery had taken me to where I was today — alone, at the bottom of a wine bottle.

*Look at how far we've come.*

Look at how far we were going. Thirty-nine-light-years, riding the crest of a gravitational wave, all so we could roll the dice. All so that one day in the future, a comedian will get to tell a joke about it and the whole planet will laugh.

"Are we moving through time, or is time moving through us?" I asked out loud to no-one. And then I reached for another bottle of wine.

Next stop, Trappist1-E . . .

Printed in Great Britain
by Amazon